AM… …CS

1. Otto Penz… …GE DETECTIVE STORIES
2. Fredric Brown: THE FABULOUS CLIPJOINT
3. Vincent Starrett: MURDER ON "B" DECK
4. Otto Penzler, ed.: GOLDEN AGE LOCKED ROOM MYSTERIES
5. C. Daly King: OBELISTS EN ROUTE
6. Nancy Rutledge: BLOOD ON THE CAT
7. Otto Penzler, ed.: GOLDEN AGE BIBLIOMYSTERIES
8. C. Daly King: OBELISTS AT SEA
9. Phoebe Atwood Taylor: THE CAPE COD MYSTERY
10. Otto Penzler, ed.: GOLDEN AGE WHODUNITS
11. Nancy Barr Mavity: THE TULE MARSH MURDER
12. Roger Scarlett: CAT'S PAW
13. Otto Penzler, ed.: GOLDEN AGE CHRISTMAS MYSTERIES

www.penguin.co.uk

A NOTE FROM THE PUBLISHER

The stories in this book were written from the 1930s to the 1940s and contain language or depictions that some readers may find outdated or offensive today. Our general approach is to leave the story as the author wrote it. We are not endorsing its language or depictions; we are recognizing that the story has literary or historical value. We encourage readers to consider the work critically and in its historical and social context.

GOLDEN AGE BIBLIOMYSTERIES

OTTO
PENZLER,
EDITOR

AMERICAN
MYSTERY
CLASSICS

PENGUIN BOOKS

TRANSWORLD PUBLISHERS

UK | USA | Canada | Ireland | Australia
India | New Zealand | South Africa

Transworld is part of the Penguin Random House group of companies whose addresses can be found at global.penguinrandomhouse.com.

Penguin Random House UK, One Embassy Gardens, 8 Viaduct Gardens, London SW11 7BW

penguin.co.uk

Published in the United States in 2023 by Penzler Publishers, 58 Warren Street, New York, NY 10007

First published in Great Britain in 2026 by Penguin Books an imprint of Transworld Publishers

001

Printed and bound in Great Britain by Clays Ltd, Elcograf S.p.A.

The authorized representative in the EEA is Penguin Random House Ireland, Morrison Chambers, 32 Nassau Street, Dublin D02 YH68.

A CIP catalogue record for this book is available from the British Library

ISBN
9781804999455

Penguin Random House is committed to a sustainable future for our business, our readers and our planet. This book is made from Forest Stewardship Council® certified paper.

FSC www.fsc.org MIX Paper FSC® C018179

GOLDEN AGE BIBLIOMYSTERIES

CONTENTS

INTRODUCTION

If you like mysteries, and if you like books, what could be better than mysteries featuring the world of books? These wonderful tales have come to be called bibliomysteries. If you go to the dictionary (as a traditionalist) or hit your computer spellcheck, you will discover that there is no listing for this word, and if you type it onto a Word document it will appear with a squiggly red line underneath it, indicating that you have misspelled or entered a non-existent word.

Nonetheless, bibliophiles who also are mystery fiction aficionados certainly know what the word means, however abstruse or esoteric it may seem to those poor, deprived souls who do not share those pleasures.

As a "book person" my entire life, and a mystery fan for more than a half-century, I've had a special warm spot in my heart for books about books ever since I read Christopher Morley's *The Haunted Bookshop* when I was a teenager.

Admittedly, "the world of books" is a somewhat vague definition of bibliomystery because it overs a lot of geography and is not nearly as specific as some readers might wish it to be.

Defining bibliomysteries is somewhat subjective. It's pretty clearly in the sub-genre if the crime involves rare books, or if a book or books are the primary macguffin (another word not in the dictionary or accepted by spell-check). If much of the action is set in a bookshop or a library, it is a bibliomystery, just as it is if a major character is a bookseller or librarian. A collector of rare books counts, and often a scholar or academic working with rare books, manuscripts, or archives may be included. Publishers? Yes, if their jobs are integral to the plot. Authors? Tricky. If they just happen to write books (and it is amazing to note the number of fictional mystery writers who stumble onto corpses) and get involved in a mystery, it is a borderline call. If the nature of their work brings them into a mystery, or their books are a vital clue in the solution, they probably make the cut.

In compiling this anthology, I made a lot of judgment calls, perhaps edging closer to inclusion than exclusion, although I've read and rejected many stories that some would have included. As a simple example, I can point to the Mr. and Mrs. North series by Frances and Richard Lockridge. Jerry North is a publisher and so it might have been justifiable to include a story but his job did not include anything seriously bookish in the North short stories.

I'd have expected more bibliomystery short stories to have been written in the Golden Age of detective stories, the 1920s, 1930s, and 1940s, but it seems most authors became so fond of the bookish environment that they used it for novels. If you like reading books about books with an element of murder, permit me to recommend some bibliomystery novels that I am confident you will enjoy as much as I did; this is not a complete list and, in truth, a handful of these titles are not my all-time favorites (hello, Harry Stephen Keeler). Alas, some titles are out of print but most can be hunted down in used copies or e-books.

"Anonymous" *The Smiling Corpse*, 1935

Bristow, Gwen, & Bruce Manning, *The Gutenberg Murders*, 1931

Chandler, Raymond, *The Big Sleep*, 1939

Clason, Clyde B., *The Man from Tibet*, 1938

Daly, Elizabeth, *Murders in Volume 2*, 1941

de la Torre, Lillian, *Dr. Sam: Johnson, Detector*, 1946

Evans, John (Howard Browne), *Halo for Satan*, 1948

Fearing, Kenneth, *The Big Clock*, 1946

Fuller, Timothy, *Three Thirds of a Ghost*, 1941

Gruber, Frank, *The Buffalo Box*, 1942

Johnson, W. Bolingbroke (Morris Gilbert Bishop), *The Widening Stain*, 1942

Keeler, Harry Stephen, *The Sharkskin Book*, 1941

Lockridge, Frances & Richard, *Murder within Murder*, 1946

Morley, Christopher, *The Haunted Bookshop*, 1919

Page, Marco (Harry Kurnitz), *Fast Company* (1938)

Ross, Barnaby (Ellery Queen), *Drury Lane's Last Case*, 1933

Targ, William, & Lewis Herman, *The Case of Mr. Cassidy*, 1939

Taylor, Phoebe Atwood, *Going, Going, Gone*, 1943

Tilton, Alice (Phoebe Atwood Taylor), *Beginning with a Bash* (1937)

Wells, Carolyn, *Murder in the Bookshop*, 1936

Weston, Garnett, *The Hidden Portal*, 1946

—Otto Penzler
New York,
October 2022

THE JORGENSON PLATES

Frederick Irving Anderson

Frederick Irving Anderson (1877-1947), the creator of Sophie Lang, the charming and creative jewel thief, has been largely forgotten by modern readers, having produced only three books of mystery and crime during his lifetime; many additional stories were published only in magazines, mainly *The Saturday Evening Post*, some being collected in only one recent book,

Perhaps his best-known character is the delightful young woman who appeared in a single volume, *The Notorious Sophie Lang*, a thief of such daring and unmatched success that she is often regarded as a legend who doesn't actually exist. Much of her fame derives from a series of 1930s Paramount films recounting her adventures. She was portrayed by Gertrude Michael in all three.

In *The Notorious Sophie Lang* (1934), the police use a French thief to capture her, but they fall in love and escape. In *The Return of Sophie Lang* (1936), which also starred Ray Milland, the reformed adventuress is on an ocean liner with her elderly benefactress when she recognizes a "distinguished" fellow passenger; he is actually a jewel thief planning to involve Sophie in the disappearance of a diamond on which he has set his sights. The final film, *Sophie Lang Goes West* (1937), recounts Lang's predicament when she evades the police by boarding a train to California. It is not long before she becomes involved with fellow travelers, including a brash but charming Hollywood press agent and a desperate sultan who hopes the valuable gem he is carrying will be stolen. Curiously, although the films had some success, the only volume of Sophie's adventures was never published in America.

Anderson's other mystery collections were *Adventures of the Infallible Godahl* (1914) and *The Book of Murder* (1930), selected by Ellery Queen as one of the 106 greatest collections of mystery stories ever published. Deputy Parr, who is outwitted by Godahl in one book and Sophie Lang in another, again has his hands full with assorted crooks in his third collection. The posthumous *The Purple Flame and Other Stories* (2016) contains assorted non-series stories.

"The Jorgenson Plates" was first published in the November 11, 1922, issue of *The Saturday Evening Post*; it was first collected in *The Notorious Sophie Lang* (London, Heinemann, 1925).

The Jorgenson Plates

Frederick Irving Anderson

A FROSTY young moon coming up over the hemlock spires along the lake shore discovered a large man in an open fur coat working himself to a high pitch of frenzy over a pair of iron gates set in a patented thief-proof fence that extended to infinity in either direction.

The man was out of gas, and he said so to high heaven in a cultivated voice that shook under his emotion as the iron gates shook under his futile hands. His car stood hard by, an edging of polished nickel indicating its looming inanimate bulk. Saint Christopher, who from his high seat overlooks blowouts and empty gas tanks, had set him down tantalizingly at the sealed portals of one of those vast estates whose seigneurs indicate to the world the extent of their wealth by the extent of their fence line.

After a half hour's interview with that pair of gates his gorilla-like persistence came to an end, and he sat down on a white-washed boulder, holding his head disconsolately in his hands. From this reverie he was roused by a woman's voice, wailing thinly from the car: "Oh, Llewellyn! Why did we ever come out to these dreadful provinces!"

Llewellyn explained that they had crossed the line, were no longer in the provinces, were in the States, which area is, as everyone knows, highly civilized; but the lady, binding her head in robes, from the depths of the car predicted a raid of Comanches, Apaches, or Iroquois before the night was older.

Llewellyn was back at the gate, which he now examined methodically. He was not a walking man, else he might have deserted his wife and adventured down the road. The gate seemed the best bet, and he was hallooing loudly when he became aware of company. A diminutive person in peaked cap, stock, and putties, a paddock boy, evidently imported in bond, had come up beside him noiselessly. Llewellyn recognized the breed, common enough in country lanes back home.

"I'm out of petrol, boy!" he said.

"You ain't expectin' to git it of 'im?"

"And why not? Shan't he have it?"

"'Im"—in rising falsetto—"'ave it? Lor'! 'E owns it—hall of it!"

"Here's a quid, boy. Run down the road to the first garage."

The paddock boy turned his back on the glittering bribe; he eyed with awful malevolence the stalled car. It was in the ditch; that was where it belonged, said he; it had run 'im and 'is 'orses hoff the road, said he; and hit could bloody well sty, for all of 'im, said he. If it 'ad been a 'orse, now; and if it 'ad been a scuttle of hoats as was wanted, or a rub of liniment, or a surcingle, said he—but a gas wagon—no, sir, not for all the quids in the bloomin' land! said he. And he walked off, nor could any entreaties induce him to return.

"I order you! I command! I'll have you given in charge!"

"'Aw, go push the bloomin' bell!" sneered the boy over his shoulder.

Llewellyn sprang to the gate; he found the bell, which he had overlooked in his precipitancy. He leaned against it. He primed his ears. He envisioned a great manorial castle behind the trees, a servants' hall suddenly alive with his summons. He waited and waited and waited. He prodded the button with rising choler. He had heard of estates in America a mile to the front gate; possibly this was such a principality.

Then, as if a curtain had suddenly lifted, a gentleman, with two stag hounds on leash, seeming to have been projected from the gloaming, stood on the inside, making a Gainsborough picture in the crisp moonlight.

"Sorry! Devilish awkward! I'm needing petrol! A drop to carry me to the next stores! I didn't know, but—"

Llewellyn ceased speaking, to gape, first in wonder, then

in rage. For the gentleman, with the two silent stag hounds, reached up on a pole and turned a switch, saying coldly as he turned away, "Don't worry that button, please. I've disconnected it."

A streak of moonlight momentarily illuminated the gentleman's profile. Llewellyn, in the very act of shrieking "Damned American bounder!" found himself unaccountably crying after the retreating figure, "I say! You speak Greek, don't you?"

The night-walking gentleman turned.

"Well? What of it?"

"But you do speak Greek! Is it not a fact?" babbled Llewellyn, racking his memory. Where had he seen that face? What put that idiotic question into his mind? "Tell me!" he cried in desperation, for his haughty quarry was escaping. "You are fluent in both the modern and ancient tongues—Is it not a fact?"

"If it is any solace to you at this hour of night," said the disappearing gentleman, "I am; it is." And he was gone.

"Capri—Brindisi—Scutari—"

Llewellyn dived into the far-off Levant for that face, that supercilious intonation, that chill voice that spoke Greek. Then it came, like a thunderclap.

"Mullet!" he shrieked ecstatically. "Mullet! You old fish! Don't you know me, Mully? It's Sissy! Sissy! Sissingham! At Scutari, four years ago." He listened. Silence. "You did me an inestimable, an unforgettable service at that time, sir," he pleaded to the night. "It's Sissy; Sissy." His voice trailed. He played his last card: "Lord Blunes' brother!"

That should fetch him, an American. It did.

Mullet—for it was Mullet, none other—came back and turned on the light illuminating the gate; and in its rays he examined the eager face pressed between the bars. Plainly he was suspicious. Passers-by trumped up the most outrageous excuses to get a look inside here, especially at night.

"You have the better of me," was his final verdict.

"What a scoundrel, to abandon us like this!" came the agonized voice of Mrs. Sissingham from the depths of the car.

"A lady with you? I'll send a man with some gas," said Mullet hurriedly; and again he faded out in the night.

"Is he a rich American?" asked Mrs. Sissingham.

"Rich as cheese! Owns all this fence! As I recollect, he is the Baron of Connecticut or Montana, or something. I say!" Sissy felt an idea dawning. "I might manage to have him put us up for the night!"

They eyed each other meditatively. He crawled under the car, and by the light of a pocket torch and by sheer good luck he dislocated something vital. When the petrol arrived, it was brought, as good luck would have it, not by a flunky, but by Mullet himself, in a small car.

"I came back to make my apologies in person," he said with a curious stiffness. "I recollect you now perfectly. We were able to put you through the Turkish lines, or some such thing, were we not, Sissingham?"

"My word! You were able to put the Turkish Empire at our disposal! You and Lingard!" cried Sissy volubly.

"Wonderful fellow that, Lingard. Mastodonic! Dynamic! Volcanic! Typifies your titanic country! Blunes said to me, when we were packing to come out here, 'Sissy,' said old Bluenose, 'Sissy, my boy, when you make the States, just run up on dear old Mullet! Tell him for me—' Oh, I say!" exclaimed Llewellyn, breaking off in the middle of the message he was about to deliver in person for his august brother. "The blamed stuff is leaking out in the drain! Now what's to be done?"

Mullet had quite finished pouring in the gas, unconscious of the fact that it ran out as fast as it ran in. The greedy sand of the lake-shore road had drunk it all up.

"Now we are in for it!" moaned Sissy disconsolately.

They must have a mechanic, or at least a machine shop, before they could stir. It was midnight! It was cold! It was miles from anywhere. He shivered, locked his fur coat about him. It was plainly an impasse. Sissy was just beginning, with ponderous volubility, to thank Mullet for the service which had been so unhappily ineffectual, when a half-smothered sob from the interior of the car brought affairs to a crisis. Mrs. Sissingham, visioning the savages that would probably devour her during a night in the open, was voicing her anguish. Mullet, who had been drumming nervously on the fender, seemed to be brought to sudden decision.

"You'll find my hospitality a bit thin at this time of year," he said awkwardly, "but such as it is, I proffer it you. Perhaps Mrs. Sissingham would overlook any lacks."

"Present your friend, Sissingham!" cried the lady, putting out her hand. "Mr. Mullet, I am overcome. We should be most happy, most happy, I assure you!"

Mullet made fast a towrope and drew their majestic equipage along behind him, while the triumphant Sissy held the wheel. The swept-and-dusted drive led among stately old trees; they knew they were at last nearing the house when they came upon a phalanx of tall poplars standing at attention against the moon. The palace itself lay fantastic in the mystic lights, its rambling roofs and marble copings gleaming; its windows deep and mysterious; about it was a shaven park, with gardens winter-locked and fountains dry. They stood in a vaulted hall, thrilling, while Mullet patiently tugged at a silken bell cord. A sleepy man finally appeared to carry up their boxes. Mullet himself conducted them to their apartment in what was apparently designed as a Tudor wing. He apologized for the slackness of the servants. They had not expected their master and mistress up here so late in the fall.

"Really, they are quite peeved that we should walk into our own house out of season," he said.

"Out of season?" put in the lady. "You have an establishment for each season then?"

Mullet modestly admitted to six establishments.

"That is," he amended, "in this country. There is, besides, the villa at Biarritz; and a chalet at Chamonix." He reckoned mentally. "Eight, isn't it? Seems to me there should be nine. There must be another knocking about somewheres. I have it! There is an island, in the Leewards."

"Imagine!" gasped Mrs. Sissingham. "Having so many establishments, I suppose one does grow forgetful. You keep them open the year around, sir?"

"Oh, yes; one never knows. Now, only yesterday my wife had the whim to come up here to the Box for a nip of mountain air. That accounts for the happy accident of our being here to receive you." And a smile drifted across the chilly countenance of the host.

"Oh! This is your shooting box!" exclaimed Mrs. Sissingham, emerging from her great tweed motor coat as a well-corseted matron of, say, forty kind summers. She patted her hands in raptures, smiling on her pompous husband. With a glance around at the massive funereal apartment in which they stood she gushed, "Oh, you wonderful, wonderful Americans!"

As the mahogany door closed behind Mullet, Mrs. Sissingham watched it for several seconds askance; then she threw her arms about her husband's neck and kissed him.

"You're a clever man, Llewellyn," she whispered. "However did you manage it?" She turned on the door. "How child-like he is! He doesn't seem quite sure of himself. Is he so very recent? Do you imagine it is our distinguished family connections that rather strike him dumb?"

A tray of refreshments arrived from their host, with the word that as Mrs. Mullet had retired she would greet them in the morning.

Sissy, warm within and without, and happily convinced of his diplomacy, explained that the wonder was not so much that these Americans possessed drawing rooms, as that they knew how to enter them at all, even on all fours. They had come up so recently from nothing.

"He is what is known out here, I believe, as a self-made man," he said. "And a self-made man, my dear, is usually rather proud of his maker. Haw! Clever! What!"

A tardy maid tapped for admittance; she was a pert little thing, with a widow's peak, and a bird-like toss of the head; and she curtsied and said prettily, "M'sieu! M'dame!" She carried madame off to unhook her, and to undo the boxes; as she shook out Mrs. Sissingham's things and hung them in a *garderobe* as capacious as a box stall, she delivered in bewildering syntax *les compliments* from her meestress, who begged that madame would find herself *chez elle*. The astounded Englishwoman found herself inducted into a peignoir and mules, and submitted her tresses to the deft fingers of an expert; the girl was a marvel! So at least she thought until the maid, in the act of suspending madame's ponderous motor coat on a hanger, let the thing drop, which it did with a startling metallic thump as if it were loaded. Upon which the lady, recovering the coat, curtly dismissed the girl for the night; and throwing it across her arm she went in to her lord and master, who was already sighing contentedly between sheets on his luxurious couch.

"I have been carrying it now for two months," she said, tucking the tweed coat in beside him as if it were a babe that required warmth. "It is getting heavy," she added with a weary sigh.

"On your conscience?" ironically inquired Sissy.

"My dear, tell me, are there any more customs ordeals to go through with?"

"No; we passed the last at that little place they called Alburg. I must say you behaved beautifully."

"Tomorrow morning I shall rip them out," said Mrs. Sissingham absently. She kicked off her slippers. "I'm going to stay here with you, Sissy!" And she crawled in beside her motor coat. "Box!" she tittered. "Imagine! Calling this monstrosity a box! I'm keen to see the thing by daylight. I counted four different periods in the architecture of the hall."

Dawn was pinking the drawn shades when Sissy said in his habitual subdued tone, "My dear, are you there?"

She was.

"He would pay a thumping price for them."

"Yes," said his wife, with the instant agreement of a parallel thought. "What is his wife like?" she whispered after a moment of cogitating silence.

"I haven't had the honor really," admitted Sissy.

Mrs. Sissingham put her lips to his ear.

"I might contrive to let her catch me in the act—ripping the seams—taking them out," she whispered. "Then I could break down—and confess."

"You are the deep one!" Sissy rearranged his pillow under his cherubic cheek. "Now I believe I can fetch a bit of sleep, what?"

It was ten o'clock when a maid—not the one of last midnight—entered and rolled up the shades; she touched off the fire, and departed, leaving the tantalizing aroma of coffee in her wake.

Fortunately—because Mrs. Sissingham craved a little time to strike the Mullets stone blind with her gentility before she opened with her big guns—Sissy had done a more thorough job of rendering his car *hors de combat* than he had realized in the first flush of achievement. It was one of those cars that are first laid down on the drafting not as a series but as an individual. Each part had a name and a number, and, it seemed, an odd screw thread. It would be necessary to send out to have several small items fabricated. A village mechanic, noting down the identifying marks, started a telegram moving from one regional director of replacement of parts to another; until finally word came in that the damage would be repaired by special express arriving Monday on No. 36. To complicate matters, there were no household chauffeurs at the Box, Mullet explaining ruefully that in coming up here for a nip of air he had left his trained troupe behind, to be free for a few days from their arrogance and temperamental vaporings. Servants, lower and upper, were his sore point. In this country, he admitted, the serving class regarded their menial status as a way station on the way up; democracy held out so much promise to them.

To which Sissy replied, "At home, now, we do not permit

them to fall into that error of mind." Reverting to his own predicament, Sissy said weightily: "It is pretty of you to put such a good face on our piling up on you in this way. As if you hadn't put me and dear old Bluenose everlastingly in your debt, for Scutari! You and your friend Lingard. Wonderful man, that! Human locomotive, I say, by Jove! I must run him down while I'm out here."

"My wife is enchanted to receive you," admitted the simple Mullet. "There is one thing about which I wish to speak to you," added he shyly; and he took his august guest by the arm and led him out of earshot of the house. "Below stairs the rumor is rife that we entertain a great lord and his lady. I suspect it is that romantic French maid who is responsible. She has laid it on a bit thick, I fear, Sissy. Rather an awkward misapprehension to correct! And it would so disappoint the simple souls to disabuse them! Eh, Sissy? Now they are puffed up with importance, with a lord and a lady to serve. It reconciles them entirely to our breaking in on them here, out of season. If you could let it go by default, Sissy, dear fellow! You understand, don't you?"

"My word!" Sissy stared at his host through the lower hemispheres of his bifocals, the while he drew out his long mustaches. Raising a finger he said confidentially, "Fact is—we don't speak of this outside the family—my wife, you know, she is the Lady Mary of her line! She can carry the three leopards, argent, and the ceinture d'or of the Dalvarys, if she so elects. Male line extinguished, blown out—and a very good job, too, I might add. We are very tender about it—we haven't the means to keep it up. But some of the county families at home who are sticklers for form give her the precedence over me! Haw! Fancy!"

As they re-entered the palace they ran into the housekeeper, who was making haste to efface herself when Mullet called her back.

"Mrs. Bright," he said, "at home, in England, the Lady Mary takes precedence over her husband. It is a phenomenon arising from an age-old custom among the nobility, into which we will not inquire. But I think it would be well should you caution the household to remember this distinction. And, by the way, see that the covers at dinner are properly laid."

Sissy, hearing himself thus demoted, bowed gravely in assent. Women fed on these little distinctions; why should he say them nay?

His wife and her hostess remained behind the curtain during the afternoon; Mullet had some letters to post, and Sissy had the run of the grounds. There were horses that needed exercising; dogs that needed hunting; there were whole panels of guns itching to be triggered. It was obvious to Sissy, who keeps fit even at ponderous fifty, that his host was not a sporting gentleman, for all his livestock and paraphernalia. Mullet was as soft as a houseman; doubtless he maintained the Box in its astonishing completeness not for himself but for such random guests as evinced sporting proclivities. Everywhere he poked his inquiring Norman beak Sissy was met by obsequious grooms who mi-ludded him with such evident relish that Sissy, not without a sense of humanity, felt positively philanthropic.

While he dressed for dinner he caught sight of the smart swing of the French maid who had set in motion the news of their supreme eminence in the servants' hall. She was putting finishing touches on the Lady Mary. There was no time to get a report of progress before they went down.

Whatever crudities Mullet may have permitted to stick to his coarse hide in his ascent to riches, considered Sissy as he craftily examined the scene in the drawing room, Mrs. Mullet certainly lacked nothing in breeding. As the ceremony of the first dinner wore on to a close the astute Sissy became convinced that this American millionaire had picked a wife with the same care and circumspection that he had caused to be exercised in the stocking of his stables and kennel. Sissingham was not impervious to female charms, and when they finally rose there was a glow in his veins which may have come from the excellent port, but certainly owed much to the exotic pleasure of watching the play of the lady's head and shoulders, and drinking in the flute-like notes of her voice as she assured him less by words than by manner that she was not insensible to the honor of their presence. He told himself she would have graced any board, no matter how exalted. His wonder grew at her astonishing familiarity with so many of the people at home. At home one who was anybody was expected to know everybody; but surely such a social eminence was a rarity out here. He had a curious sense of having seen her before; possibly at some great house.

It was not until midnight, when his wife had dismissed the French maid and again begged permission to join her august consort in his regal bed—with her great motor coat for company—that the Sissinghams had a chance to exchange confidences.

"Such clothes!" gushed she, making a bull's-eye of the exclamation point in Sissy's ear. "But she wore no jewels. Why?"

"I imagine, possibly," rumbled Sissy hollowly, "from a sense of delicacy. She is a most extr'ord'nary woman. I've been impressing Mullet with a sense of our poverty. Doubtless she took pity on us, my dear—and our lack of adornment!" He kicked his wife's tweed motor coat, and chuckled. "But where have I seen her before?"

"Or somebody that looks like her?"

"Yes; or somebody that looks like her!" agreed he.

"Guess!" invited Mrs. Sissy mysteriously. But Sissy was not good at guessing. "I have the most amazing tale to unfold!" She let this sink in, for piquancy; then she breathed, "I have an ally! Under this very roof!"

"Gently, gently."

"Have you noticed my maid?"

"How often must I tell you, my dear, that I never notice servants? I simply don't see them, that is all."

"Make a point of noting this one. It will amply repay you." And she murmured, "Most astonishing likeness—of her mistress—Mrs. Mullet!"

Sissy's head emerged from the depths of his pillow.

"My word! Then I must have noted the creature subconsciously."

"You are apt to do that, Sissy," accused his wife easily. "It is a most astonishing tale!" whispered she, returning to her morsel again. "I surprised it—I forced it out of the poor creature."

"The maid?"

"She is a natural sister, my dear! Some rascally Frenchman for a parent! Mrs. Mullet gives her a home here, but never recognizes her. Think of it! Of course the poor child is miserable. Sissy," said Mrs. Sissy in a still lower tone, "I am petting her! I gave her a sovereign!"

"Ah, you're the clever one!" said Sissy, sleepy now. "Go easy on the l.s.d., my dear!" was his injunction as he gave himself up to slumber. With a rebound from a possible nightmare Sissy muttered, "Make the transaction in cash dollars, not guineas, my love. These bounders have the exchange against us yet, by Jove!"

Sunday evening, with thin snow outside, Sissy was passing from the billiard room to the library to replace a volume of Pepys with which he had been drowsily wasting time. Passing the open door of Mrs. Sissingham's sitting room he caught sight of his hostess and his wife. It was a pretty scene, tenderly feminine. The tea things lay neglected; the lighting was from a high window, a soft luminous haze reflected from the snow-strewn sky. His wife was sunk in a great chair. She had been weeping, for she was blowing her nose, an indulgence she never permitted herself without the excuse of tears. Beside her on her knees was the lovely Mrs. Mullet, babying her with infinite gentleness. Some protective feminine sense must have warned the comforter of the eavesdropping of an unwanted male, for Mrs. Mullet turned, and catching sight of the bland countenance of old Sissy, peering in and tugging at his long mustaches, she moved her lips warningly, saying as distinctly by pantomime as if she had shouted it, "Go away!"

Sissy moved off softly on slippered feet. He muttered, "Wonderful woman! Wonderful! Her price is above rubies!"

No. 36, on which the replacement parts for Sissy's pedigreed car were to arrive, was an accommodation train of disreputable habit, making connection with the Montreal express at six, at Tupper Lake Junction. There was seldom much to connect with; but this morning the northbound express dropped superciliously, without stopping, a private car, a thing all mahogany, plate glass with drawn blinds, and polished brass. The nobs inside still slept when the indignant accommodation backed down the line and retrieved the chariot and hooked it on behind the caboose. Eight miles north at a private siding the glittering car was uncoupled; the accommodation conductor personally superintended the operation, which was conducted on tiptoe so as not to break the slumber of the fortunates within. A few early rustics gathered and stood guard at a respectful distance, occasionally visiting among themselves. At eight the galley stove showed signs of life; a Nubian slave, in white coat and gold-filled teeth, regarded the patient railbirds informally as he raised the blinds. Shortly the assemblage was rewarded by the sight of a large yawning man in a Turkish bath robe being fed off polished plate. A brief interval elapsing, the large man emerged and hopped to the ground from the brass embrasure at one end. He was now accoutered in the rough fashionable attire in which the natives of this section, deep-woods guides and trappers, were accustomed to find their sports, as, without disrespect, they styled their city clients.

The large man nodded a good morning at the line, and gripping his stout stick firmly in a big fist he started down the road at a brisk stride.

"He's a good fellow!" admitted one of the spectators approvingly.

"Sure! Who wouldn't be?" commented a second.

They watched him disappear around a bend of the road. The large man trudged on in the crisp morning till he came to the shores of a beautiful woods lake. The gates of the Box, at which Sissy had beaten with such startling success four nights gone by, stood ajar, an unwonted occurrence, at which the large man paused to consider. The gates were open because, but a half hour before, the village mechanic had arrived with the spare parts for Sissy's car.

Sissy was up betimes. Now that his affairs had taken this sudden turn for the better, he was anxious to repair the damage and be off. He was considering the size of the gratuities he must leave among the servants, among whom he had moved and spread sunshine for the past four days. The curtains in the family wing were still drawn. Sissy was attracted to the garage by the tinkle of tools; and unbending a bit he gave the mechanics a good morning and complimented them on their skill. Wearying at length of their talk, which had mostly to do with odd threads, evidently regarded as something unethical, Sissy strolled out across the park to the main drive, down which he moved absently, ruminating on the blessedness of coincidence, the undying quality of the Greek tongue, and the virtues of his wife, who had managed the whole affair in the guise of a great misfortune, from which the tenderhearted Mrs. Mullet had insisted on rescuing her.

The large man in sports costume, gripping his stick with determination, was coming up the drive. At sound of footsteps, and at sight of an intruder in these precincts where he himself had been forced to use so much diplomacy to gain entrance, Sissy paused, took a mustache in one hand, and raised his head to examine this person through the lower hemispheres of his bifocals. The other came on.

"My word!"

Sissy stared, dumb-struck, for the moment.

"A moment!" cried he. "Don't speak! I'll have it! I know you! Capri—Brindisi—Scu—" Then: "Lingard! The dynamic—the mastodonic—the volcanic! I say! What the devil are you doing here?"

Lingard came on, scowling, and gripping his stick ever more tightly in his bruiser's fist.

It was Stephen Lingard, the great mogul. He paused, nose to nose with the beaming British object.

"What the devil are you doing here?" he demanded. "Who are you anyway?"

"It's Sissy! Sissingham! Lord Blunes' brother! You haven't forgotten? You did us an unforgettable—an inestimable service—at Scutari—four years ago. My dear fellow, you placed the Turkish Army—no, by Jove, it was the Turkish Empire—at our disposal! You and your friend Mullet! Wonderful scholar, there! So polished, so clever, so learned in classic lore! It was his fluency in Greek, if you recollect—"

"Yes, yes, yes. But what are you doing here?" insisted Lingard, easing a little.

"My boy, this is old Mully's place! Imagine! Most amazing coincidence! We'll speak of it later! Isn't this magnificent?" demanded the blooming Sissy, encompassing the park with a sweep of his hand. "You know I suspected Mully was as rich as cheese! He had the air, the flair, the *haut ton*! But really, I was ill-prepared for this splendor! We've been spending the weekend with them! We broke down at the gate. I say, you didn't break down at the gate, did you? That would be jolly, now, what! I say," said Sissy confidentially, "what a marvelous woman is Mrs. Mullet! I—I—I—" Sissy was utterly incapable of expressing himself adequately.

"At Scutari—four years ago," repeated Lingard. "I recollect very well, now. So our friend Mullet has been entertaining you here, has he?"

Lingard was smiling, a rare thing with Sinful Stephen. They fell into step. At the entrance to the terrace Sissy pointed out his host, Mullet, emerging, still a bit stiff with the early morning.

"Sissy," said Lingard, drawing back, "I want to surprise dear old Mully. Take a walk—like a good fellow—will you?"

"Haw! Quite! He'll be stricken pink, I vow!" ejaculated the obliging Sissy, and he turned and made off on his morning constitutional.

He was nearing the gate when a limousine turned in, and came to a stop at sight of him. Recognizing one of two men in the car, Sissingham momentarily lost his *sangfroid*; but he immediately recovered it.

"My word! Arbuthnot! This gate is fairly hinged on coincidence!"

"Step inside, Sissy," said Arbuthnot curtly, throwing open the door.

Sissy obeyed. He sat down, tugging at a mustache, waiting to be addressed. His face was perfectly blank.

"I did you the injustice," said Arbuthnot slowly, "of suspecting you, too, in this last affair. Your departure and your silence certainly had all the aspects of flight."

He paused. Sissy stared at him woodenly.

"We traced you through the customs at Alburg. Then we lost you. Then I was sure. But when we found you had telegraphed your motor number all over the States, looking for a replacement, I knew you were all right. Nobody but a fool would do that, Sissy. I apologize."

Sissy continued to stare, blinking. There was a question on his lips; he seemed to lack courage to ask it.

Arbuthnot nodded.

"Yes, it's happened again, Sissy," he said. "This time it is His Grace's emeralds. Tiara, stomacher, dog collar. Complete. Famous old settings—must have weighed a ton! She was seen, in the act, by one of the servants, who feared to speak."

Sissingham, with a groan, buried his face in his hands; when he raised his head again his eyes were red as from weeping.

"The hereditary taint!" he moaned tragically. "That fall from the horse accentuated it! She's never been right since. And I brought her out here for peace and quiet. Oh, sir, what is to be done? Oh, my poor stricken flower!"

"As usual," said Arbuthnot, keeping his steely eyes upon him, "nothing is to be done. His Grace so directs. This gentleman, Sissy, is Mr. Parr, deputy commissioner in charge of the detective bureau of New York."

A pallid line showed itself about Sissy's lips. Through an awful moment His Grace's man of business, and Mr. Parr the great manhunter, regarded each other in silence. In that instant Sissy seemed to catch the clank of chains.

But Arbuthnot was talking again; he was saying: "The commissioner has consented to act with me in his private capacity, not as an officer of the law. It was through him we traced your motor."

The revelation that his beloved wife had again been overtaken by a seizure of the intermittent kleptomania that had marred her career seemed to weigh poor Sissy to the dust. Fortunately it had always been, as in the present case, the strongbox of a relative against which her moral lesion was directed, so they had always been able to prevent a public scandal. Now what worried Sissy most was that Mr. Mullet, a very distinguished American, upon whose hospitality they had been thrown by a remarkable coincidence, should be embarrassed by the disclosure.

"Mullet?" said Parr. "I thought this was Steve Lingard's Folly."

"Oh, you are mistaken," interposed Sissingham. "It is one of Mr. Mullet's many homes. He has eight, I think. No—or is it nine? I forget. By a curious coincidence Mr. Lingard happens to be here—just arrived! To witness my poor beloved's degradation! What a horror! What a horror!"

It was Lingard who met them at the head of the drive. He explained that Mullet had been called off by a peremptory telegram; Lingard said Mullet had left him to do the honors.

"Why, hello, Parr! What brings you here?" cried Lingard, as the manhunter hove in sight. Parr passed his arm through Lingard's and drew him to one side.

"My particular job at present," said Parr, "is to draw the wool over your eyes, while our British delegation is holding a family conference. But first, who is Mullet?"

Lingard looked back to see if they were observed. Then with a laugh of pure joy he said, "Mullet? He's my manservant. I left him in charge here last week when I ran to town." Indicating the retreating group: "Do you see that blooming jackass over there? Well, four years ago, in the Mediterranean, he pestered the life out of me. He and his fool brother, Lord Blunes, who is another, once removed. To get rid of them I turned them over to Mullet, introduced Mullet as a gentleman!" Lingard's mirth momentarily overcame him. "They swallowed Mullet whole—took him for a nob! He happens to speak Greek, and with my help he put them through the lines into Scutari. Well," went on Sinful Stephen, recovering himself, "our friend the British ass had to break down at my gate the other night. Poor Mully couldn't resist the temptation of resuming the role of gentleman and inviting him in! Oh, I gather Mully's been laying it on thick! Told the housekeeper it was by my orders; spread the news that Sissy was a duke or something!"

They strolled on, while Parr detailed the latest dereliction of the distinguished kleptomaniac.

"They say it is a hereditary taint," said the manhunter. "I suspect it is a gift! I wouldn't be surprised to find that she and that bally ass of a husband of hers have been making a good thing out of their titled relatives for some time past. However, not a word, Steve. I am deputized to keep you ignorant, until my lady gives up the emeralds. What have you done with Mullet, Steve?"

"I'm holding him incommunicado in his quarters. He couldn't face them now, of course." Lingard went off in another roar of laughter at the mental picture of poor Mully striking an attitude before the British aristocracy, with all this borrowed scenery.

They were in the kennels when a housemaid brought word that Mr. Arbuthnot waited for them in the main hall. The inquisition had progressed to an impasse when they reached the room where Sissingham, his wife and His Grace's man of affairs were in conference. Sissy still preserved his role of being utterly crushed by this latest cruel stroke of fate. His wife, on the other hand, presented the guileless and untroubled countenance of a child.

"In the absence of Mr. Mullet," said Arbuthnot, "we will have to ask your aid, Mr. Lingard." He spoke in a low anxious tone. "It's pitiful. She admits it, smiling. She doesn't realize, of course. Look at her! Her face is as smooth as a baby's. A terrible affliction, sir!"

"Of course I am at your service in any way, Mr. Arbuthnot."

"Here's the rub—she has sold the emeralds—to—ah—to Mrs. Mullet," explained the embarrassed man of business. "You understand how unwilling I am to involve the American lady. But—ah—Mrs. Mullet must be seen, must be interviewed. Yet apparently Mrs. Mullet cannot be found! The servants are very strange—"

"Mrs. Mullet?" ejaculated Lingard. "Why, there isn't any—"

At this juncture Parr, whose sixth sense had suddenly begun

to bristle, stepped on Stephen Lingard's toe, and in apologizing managed to catch the eye of that gentleman. Lingard rearranged his words: "Why, there isn't any reason why Mrs. Mullet should object to being seen."

"I have the money here," explained Arbuthnot. "Mrs. Sissingham surrendered it without hesitation. I have no doubt when the situation is explained to Mrs. Mullet—as it must be, now, sad to say!—everything will be smoothed over satisfactorily. But where is she? The housekeeper says that she had been called to the village hastily, drove away in her own car just before we arrived. I swear," he added, lowering his voice, "a thunderclap seems to have shattered the economy of this household. I can't make head or tail of it. Excuse me, sir, but it is a very delicate situation for me to handle."

He unceremoniously thrust the bundle of banknotes, bound together by a paper band, into Lingard's hand, with a gesture as if, by that one act, he were ridding himself of the whole responsibility. Lingard awkwardly regarded the bundle of cold cash the titled kleptomaniac had so blithely surrendered on being caught. One of the notes caught his eye. He dragged it out.

He rushed to the window with it, and after an instant's examination he exploded, "Jumping Jehoshaphat! The old Jorgensen plates!"

Parr, who had discreetly wandered off, reached Lingard's side in one bound. One look at those counterfeit banknotes was enough.

"Sophie Lang!" he roared. "So she's finally peddled them!"

He pounded the aghast Arbuthnot.

"She's gone, you say? An hour ago? Where? Which way?" He snarled like a thwarted animal.

Sissy, glassy-eyed in astonishment, supporting the now terrified Mrs. Sissy on his arm, started forward. Parr seized the telephone, banged it violently, and tossed it aside. The telephone wires were cut. Of course! Count on Sophie! The realization that, coming up here to do his friend Arbuthnot a little friendly service, he had missed the notorious Sophie Lang by an hour, seemed for the moment to unhinge Parr's mind. Servants were sent scurrying in all directions. It was Sissy who brought the situation back to normal.

"I say," implored Sissy, tugging at a mustache, "won't you please elucidate?"

"Elucidate?" bawled Parr. "Why, you bally ass, you've been entertained by the slickest crook in two hemispheres the last four days! She's off with your emeralds. Call your housekeeper, Lingard!" he snarled.

Mrs. Bright was had in, from the other side of the door, where she had been kneeling.

"Who was this woman who has been playing hostess here?" demanded Parr. "Where did she come from?"

Brighty, pointedly making her replies to Lingard, explained that it was the new lady's maid, straight from Paris, who had come to Mrs. Lingard with such good letters, only last week.

"Call Mullet!" angrily commanded Lingard. The valet was produced, Sissy and his wife turning to wood at the sight.

"Deputy Parr, of the New York police, Mullet!" cried Lingard.

"Now, Mullet, we want a clean breast of it," howled Parr. "The whole story this time! Who was this woman, this 'wife' of yours, who so charmingly assisted in entertaining your titled guests?" And Parr bowed ironically to the staring pair.

Mullet, with much difficulty because of the obvious shock to the aristocratic sensibilities of his recent guests, and entirely ignorant of the unlooked-for denouement, charged the whole matter to the devilish ingenuity of the new French maid. It was she who had inspired the affair from the very beginning. It was she who had persuaded Mullet to accept the exalted position with which Sissy had credited him, and to tender the motor refugees the hospitality which befitted their rank. The need of a fitting hostess suggested her position as his wife. She had helped herself to Mrs. Lingard's clothes. She had kept the troublesome servants in order, even good Mrs. Bright—who here interrupted to remind Mr. Lingard that she had always been instructed to obey Mullet as if he were Mr. Lingard himself. Furthermore, continued Mullet, to display her versatility the *cidevant* Mrs. Mullet had contrived to act as maid to the Lady Mary, without detection, making quick changes between roles. Here the Lady Mary subsided, weeping, on her husband's shoulder.

The complication of the emeralds and the counterfeit banknotes appalled poor Mullet. Up to the moment of his master Lingard's unlooked-for arrival on the scene the valet had seen it only as the kindness of a particularly versatile lady's maid in bridging over what to him, without her wonderful management, would have been a particularly mortifying predicament.

"Even a gentleman's gentleman," said Mullet, "has his own feelings, sir."

"Out here," put in Sissy, who during the last moments had regained something of his ponderous effrontery, "one finds it so very, very difficult to distinguish between the gentleman and his gentleman."

Parr sprang into the first motor car for the railway junction. But why this haste? he asked himself ironically as he sped along. Sophie, with her emeralds, had the whole North Woods to play in.

THE ALDINE FOLIO MURDERS
Lawrence G. Blochman

Lawrence G(oldtree) Blochman (1900-1975) was born, educated, and began his writing career in California, earning a certificate in forensic pathology. He was a reporter for San Diego newspapers before becoming a journalist in Tokyo, Hong Kong, Shanghai, and Calcutta, and then moving to Paris, where he met and married Marguerite Mailliard, in 1926. During World War II he served in the US Office of War Information. He eventually moved to New York and was elected the fourth president of the Mystery Writers of America in 1948-1949.

Blochman wrote more than fifty books and hundreds of short stories. His early novels and short stories were mainly adventures set in India and other countries in the Far East; his first mysteries featured Inspector Leonidas Prike in *Bombay Mail* (1934), *Bengal Fire* (1937), and *Red Snow at Darjeeling* (1938). A later novel, *Recipe for Homicide* (1952), and two collections of short stories, *Diagnosis: Homicide* (1950) and *Clues for Dr. Coffee* (1964), featured Dr. Daniel Webster Coffee, the former being selected for *Queen's Quorum* as one of the 106 greatest detective story volumes of all time.

Coffee is the chief pathologist at Pasteur Hospital in the fictional midwestern city of Northbank. He is assisted by an imperturbable Hindu man, Dr. Motilal Mookerji, and by Max Ritter, "the tallest, skinniest, and homeliest lieutenant of detectives on the Northbank police department" (but not the most gullible). Coffee carries out his criminal investigative work in the hospital's laboratory. The tales of the brilliant doctor/detective appeared regularly in *Collier's* for ten years before the best were collected in book form.

Unlike most of Blochman's fiction, which featured fast-moving action, exotic locales, and romance, "The Aldine Folio Murders" is a tale of pure detection, featuring Paul Mordant, "the one-man Fine Arts Department" of the French police.

"The Aldine Folio Murders" was originally published in the fall 1940 issue of *The Dolphin* (volume four, number one), published by the Limited Editions Club; this is the first time it has been published in book form.

The Aldine Folio Murders

By Lawrence G. Blochman

You MAY not remember the Café Grolier. It belonged to a Paris of another day—ten thousand years ago, it seems—before the steel monsters clanked obscenely down the Champs-Élysées, and the heavy boots of Heinrich Himmler's Gestapo began tramping upon the souls of men who such a short time before thought there was importance in first editions and the bouquet of an old burgundy. The Café Grolier was in a side street not far from the Hôtel Drouot and was frequented by bookmen and art dealers on their way to and from sales at that noted *salle des ventes*. The proprietor was as proud of his clientele as he was of his cellar and his succulent Tournedos. To prove it, he miraculously wangled an appropriate telephone number: Gutenberg 14-56.

One crisp afternoon before the end of our world, I was sitting at a sidewalk table of the Café Grolier, scanning the catalogue of a library to be dispersed, sipping a Pernod, and reveling in the aroma of roasting chestnuts that used to herald the advance of autumn in Paris. A friendly hand tapped me on the shoulder and a hearty voice exclaimed: "*Tiens*! My old pal Bender."

"Inspector! Please sit down and join me."

I was genuinely pleased to see Inspector Paul Mordant of the Sûreté. I could usually count on running into him while in Paris, as he was something of a one-man Fine Arts Department of the French police. Museum thefts, crimes of bibliomania, art forgeries, and skulduggery in the auction room constituting his peculiar province, we frequented the same *milieu*. He was a tall, distinguished, well-dressed, gray-haired man. He delighted in pronouncing my name in the French manner. Bender *à la française*, he said, had a lusty, virile sound.

"Just arrive from New York, Bender?" the Inspector asked, as he rested his elbows on the table.

"No, I've been in London," I told him, "bidding on a collection of incunabula."

"And you crossed the Channel to bid on the Marsouin library, no doubt?"

"As a matter of fact, there are a few Marsouin items I might bid on," I admitted. "But what really brought me over was a cable from New York asking me to run up to the provinces to buy an Aldine folio."

Inspector Mordant nodded. "*Hypnerotomachia Poliphili*," he said, "Château de Beaumur."

When I asked him if he knew René François, who was selling the collection, he shook his head.

"I knew his uncle quite well," he said. "Young François just happened to inherit the library and is trying to turn it into money as quickly as possible. He doesn't know a quarto from a hole in the ground. You might be able to pick up a bargain."

"I'd thought of going to Beaumur the day before the sale opens," I said. "If the Aldine folio is in good condition, New York has authorized me to offer half a million francs for it."

As a matter of fact, the cable said $15,000, which was even more, but the half million sounded better. I hoped young François would be impressed, too.

"How are things in London?" the Inspector asked, as he sipped the Picon Citron the waiter brought.

I told him that London was quiet.

"You didn't run into Emil Daur at Sotheby's or thereabouts, did you?"

"Don't know the gentleman. Should I?"

"Perhaps not. He's the bald-headed museum thief who stole the Franz Hals from the Munich Galleries in 1926. He's only recently turned his talents from *objets d'art* to rare books, because they're more easily disposed of. He was in jail in Bucharest last year, but I hear he's out again. He always gravitates to Paris or London when he's at large."

"I'm afraid I haven't had the pleasure."

Inspector Mordant finished his drink, clinked some brass coins to the table top, and arose.

"Come and see me when you come back to Paris," he said. "And good luck on the Aldine folio."

* * * *

I went to Beaumur next day. The village was about five hours from Paris, in the rolling green hills of Burgundy. The château itself was a large pile of no particular beauty, with a postern of a different style of architecture from the main gateway, and a tower that had been added at still another period. It was not even sufficiently distinguished to have been restored by Viollet-le-Duc, although it was famous in the countryside because part of it, at least, dated back to the tenth century.

The new chatelain, René François, greeted me cordially and insisted that I stay at the château instead of at the village inn.

"If you don't mind the fact that we have forty-five rooms here and one bath," he said with a smile. "My late uncle refused to defile his precious château with anything as modern as plumbing or electricity."

I was easily persuaded, as I liked young François on sight. He was a handsome man of about thirty, with a mischievous smile and serious eyes. I gathered the impression that he had probably spent an aimless and pleasure-filled youth and was about ready to settle down. He told me, over a decanter of topaz wine from his own vineyards, that he was liquidating his uncle's library in order to modernize the château and the farm lands around it. He intended buying American agricultural machinery, to simplify the problems of his wheat, and to devote more time to marketing the wines of his château vineyards, which he thought had never been properly appreciated outside the village. He even had—for a Frenchman—heretical ideas about advertising his wines.

The Aldine folio . . . the *Hypnerotomachia Poliphili*?

The young man's face darkened.

"I'm afraid you'll have to wait for Maître Cardonnet," he said. "He's the village notary and the executor of my uncle's estate. I think he'd give anything to block the sale, as he doesn't approve of my plans for modernization. He has the library under lock and key, but I'm sure he'll let you see the Aldine folio when he comes to dinner this evening. . . . Oh, Jeannette!"

A young woman was coming down the stairs near where we sat—a small, trim young woman with wavy chestnut hair and blue eyes and a pleasantly impertinent nose. She had the tiniest feet I ever saw, and a lovely pair of ankles that showed below the smock she was wearing. She seemed to be a few years younger than François.

"Mademoiselle Lacour, this is Mr. Bender, an American bibliophile," said François. "He is particularly interested in the Aldine folio. When will Maître Cardonnet come from the village?"

"Not before six o'clock," the girl said.

"Mademoiselle Lacour is my secretary," François continued. "I stole her from a rare book dealer, near the Odéon, to come here and catalogue my uncle's library. I had a hard time persuading her to leave Paris, but she finally took pity on my ignorance and came to my rescue. I don't know what I should do without her."

He looked at her solemnly as he said these last words, and he did not smile. She smiled in reply, but wistfully. There was adoration in her eyes and a deep, vague fear, as though she felt she had no right to a great happiness that had come to her and was afraid it might be snatched away at any moment. I could well believe that François spoke the truth in more than one sense when he said he did not know what he would do without Jeannette Lacour. And her manner eloquently proclaimed that she certainly could not do without him.

There was nothing for it but wait until Maître Cardonnet arrived. He came promptly at six—and brought two guests with him. Or rather one of the guests did the bringing—in a huge and shiny black Hispano-Suiza. The car belonged to Dr. Hugo Storch, a pink-faced old man, slightly stooped but vigorous-looking despite his thick white hair. Dr. Storch was a Swiss rare-book dealer who said he had driven up from Paris to bid on the Beaumur library.

The other passenger, who sat beside the notary, was a cadaverous, dissipated-looking individual who I learned was a Monsieur Jules Pujot, a distant cousin of René François' late lamented uncle. The air was electric with hostility as Pujot and François greeted each other. They did not even shake hands. I did not have to be clairvoyant to see instantly that Pujot had come to Beaumur to make trouble.

The notary himself was a plump, pompous, owl-faced little man with a beard. He rolled his R's and droned his O's with a rich Burgundian accent as he officiously took charge of everything, even the rooms that Pujot and Dr. Storch were to occupy. He had Dr. Storch drive his car right into the courtyard of the château, since there was no garage. François introduced me to the notary and explained that I was interested in the Aldine folio.

"After dinner!" declared Maître Cardonnet. "Dr. Storch, too, wished to see the collection, and I have agreed to show it to him later. I have taken the liberty of asking him to stay at the château, as it is quite possible there will be no auction tomorrow after all."

"No auction?" François was aghast.

"Your cousin Jules Pujot is entering a claim against the estate," Maître Cardonnet declared. "I may have to put everything under seals until the matter is decided."

"But Cousin Jules was provided for in my uncle's testament. . . ."

"He has further claims," the notary insisted. "I suggest a family council tomorrow morning. Your cousin's lawyer will come from Dijon, and we will see among us whether the sale shall go on."

"But it must go on," François protested. "There will be buyers from Paris. There is already Mr. Bender from America and now Dr. Storch. . . ."

"The law is the law," the notary pontificated. "I did not make the laws and I cannot change them. We will see. Is that roast lamb I smell cooking, my dear René?"

My glance shifted from the eager face of the notary, to the sallow, leering features of Cousin Jules Pujot, whose sleek hair was plastered down so tightly that it resembled a toupée; then to the tensely grave eyes of René François and the attractive anxiety of Jeannette Lacour, who had just come in to say that dinner would be served in five minutes. Only the bland pink face of Dr. Hugo Storch was relaxed.

The dinner, despite the excellent menu and the fragrant wine, was thoroughly disagreeable. Scarcely a word was spoken to break the spell of hostility that hung over the board. The frigid gloom of the vast, cavernous dining hall was lighted only by candelabras. I could feel the goose-flesh rising along my arms, despite the wine, and was on the point several times of suggesting that someone touch a match to the mountain of logs and fagots stacked in the great fireplace. I restrained myself because

I could not be sure that my discomfort was caused by the chill of the autumn evening or by some dreadful premonition.

The butler was passing a huge wheel of Brie cheese when the cadaverous Jules Pujot brought the antagonisms into the open. He leaned across the table to François and said:

"Cousin René, you would like very much for me to go away from Beaumur and not interfere with the sale of your library, wouldn't you?"

François did not reply. He did not even look at Pujot. He pressed his lips together until they were white. Pujot leaned back and laughed.

"Your answer is yes," Pujot said. "You want me to go away very much. Just *how* much, Cousin René?"

"I think," René François replied at last in a tight voice, "that if you tried to stop the sale, I would gladly kill you."

"Come now, Cousin René," Pujot sneered. "That is hardly a practical suggestion. I have a much better plan. While driving up from Maître Cardonnet's office, Dr. Storch told me that he was particularly interested in one volume that you have here—a very valuable volume."

"The Aldine folio of the *Hypnerotomachia Poliphili*," said Dr. Storch. "If it is the book I believe, and in perfect condition, I am ready to pay 400,000 francs for it this evening—in cash."

"Cash?" The notary's bushy eyebrows went up. "Is it prudent, Doctor, to carry—?"

"I always pay in cash," said Dr. Storch.

"If the folio is in perfect condition, I should be glad to raise Dr. Storch's figure by 50,000 francs," I said.

"The auction will take place tomorrow," François declared.

"It will not take place," Pujot contradicted. "That is just the point, Cousin René. Unless you agree to my plan, I shall tie up the estate—for years, perhaps. You know how slow the courts are."

"And your plan, monsieur?" François, deadly pale, refused to address Pujot as "cousin."

"Simplicity itself," Pujot said. "You will make me a present of this Aldine folio. I will sell it to Dr. Storch. Tonight I will go with Maître Cardonnet and sign a release to all claims against the estate. Tomorrow I will go away, and you will be rid of me forever."

François pushed back his chair with a grating sound. He said: "You realize what you are asking? You realize that nearly half a million francs—?"

"I realize everything," said Pujot calmly. "I have had a most unfortunate season at the Deauville Casino. I am badly in need of half a million francs immediately. And you, on the other hand, are badly in need of clear title to the rest of the estate. Is it a bargain?"

François glared. I thought he was going to leap across the table and strangle his cousin. Instead, he fairly shouted: "That is blackmail!"

Pujot shrugged. "It is good business," he said, "for both of us."

"This is idle talk," interrupted Maître Cardonnet, undoing the napkin which was fastened about his neck with a small gold clasp. "Let us go into the library and I will allow these gentlemen to examine the book in question."

The notary unlocked the library door with one of a bunch of heavy, old-fashioned keys. With another key he unlocked a bookcase of massive, iron-bound oak. Still another key opened an inner panel.

I did my best to hide my enthusiasm when I finally held the Aldine folio in my hands. I turned to the colophon, to look at the anchor and dolphin of Aldus, and the date: Venice, 1499. I turned to the notorious woodcut of the Worship of Priapus, which was either torn or defaced in every copy I had seen previously. This one was perfect, in all its extravagant anatomical detail. The volume was indeed a beautiful item.

Dr. Storch, too, evidently thought so. I could hear him making pleased, clucking sounds with his tongue as he looked over my shoulder. I turned, and when I saw the eager gleam in the eyes of the white-haired bibliophile, I made a mental note to raise the ante New York had authorized, if necessary to meet the doctor's bid, by another fifty or seventy-five thousand francs. I felt justified in doing so on my own responsibility.

"I will buy it," Dr. Storch declared. "Now."

Maître Cardonnet immediately took the book from my hands.

Dr. Storch had taken an astounding wallet from his pocket and was riffling through a sheaf of the huge, tissue-thin, pastel-tinted diplomas which used to be ten-thousand-franc bank notes when France was France.

The bearded little notary's eyes bulged as he watched the bibliophile handle the money.

"I will pay 500,000 francs—cash—tonight," Dr. Storch announced. "Tomorrow my bid will be less."

"Whatever your bid is, I will top it," I said.

"There will be no bidding whatsoever," declared Jules Pujot, "unless Dr. Storch's offer is accepted tonight. What about it, Cousin René?"

"I will not submit to blackmail," François replied. His white lips scarcely moved as he spoke.

"Suit yourself." Pujot shrugged. "It's your funeral, cousin."

"I'm not so sure of that," François muttered.

Dr. Storch replaced his wallet.

"Pardon me, Doctor," Maître Cardonnet said, "but don't you think it would be more prudent to leave that money in my safe tonight? A large sum like that, you know—"

"Nonsense." Dr. Storch chuckled tolerantly. "I am used to carrying substantial sums with me. And I am prepared to defend its safety." He patted his coat pocket—and his expression changed. He plunged his hand into the pocket and withdrew it—empty. The astonishment in his eyes changed to challenge. His teeth clicked. "I have been robbed!" he announced. "Someone has stolen the pistol I always carry with me."

"Perhaps you left it in your room," suggested François. He looked at Jeannette Lacour, whose lips were parted in an expression of anguish.

"I did not leave it in my room. I always carry it on me. It has not left my person for twenty years."

"I will notify the gendarmerie," said the notary.

"It is not necessary," said Dr. Storch. "I will retrieve it myself. I have an idea where it has gone."

"But you will leave the money in my safe meanwhile? . . ."

"That, too, is unnecessary." The old man's eyes flashed. "I can still defend myself, as anyone who doubts will discover."

"That settles it." The little notary crossed the room with pompous steps, replaced the Aldine folio in the oaken cabinet, locked all the doors, and pocketed the heavy keys. "What *Chinoiseries* are taking place here tonight, I do not know. But I intend to find out. You will leave the library, please. All of you. I am spending the night here."

Maître Cardonnet locked the library and installed himself in a big chair directly in front of the door. He brought up a small table, a bottle of brandy, and a candlestick. As I looked at the brandy and the already flushed face of the well-fed notary, I wondered how good a sentinel he was going to make.

The rest of us went to bed on the second floor. Dr. Storch had the room at the head of the stairs. Jeannette was in the next room, between the doctor and René François. Here the corridor made a right-angle turn, around which I was to sleep. Beyond me was the cadaverous Jules Pujot.

I took off my shoes, coat, and necktie, but did not undress further, as I knew I should not sleep in my present state of mind. For a long time I stood at the window, which looked into the courtyard. There was a fountain pool there, with a group of weather-beaten statuary posing in the dim moonlight. I could not see the entire courtyard; the entrance, where Dr. Storch's car was parked, was hidden from me, and for some subconscious reason I wished that I had been given the room occupied by Pujot, who could undoubtedly see as far as the entrance. I could not have said just what or whom I expected to come through that entrance.

As I stood there, the patch of light coming from Pujot's window disappeared from the flags of the courtyard, and a moment later, the light went out in Dr. Storch's window. The rooms of Dr. Storch, Jeannette Lacour, and René François all opened on a narrow balcony along which ran a stone balustrade. I continued to watch the two lighted windows and before long I saw Jeannette come into François' room. The window was closed and I could not hear what they were saying, but from their gestures, they were engaged in some heated discussion. After a few minutes the girl left, and François opened his window and put out the light. The girl's light, too, vanished a moment later.

I continued to stand at the window, waiting—although I did not know for what. I smoked a dozen cigarettes. Then I stretched out on the bed, and lay a long time in the dark, listening to the night noises of the château—the cracking of furniture, the creaking of a weather cock somewhere overhead, the flutter of a bat's wings against the eaves. I thought I heard footsteps in the corridor, but I could not be sure, as they were faint, stealthy, steps, like the whisper of bare feet. Then I heard an abrupt sound outside—a *ping*! followed by a tinkle—as though a bottle had broken on the flagstones.

I sprang up, peered into the courtyard. It was empty in the cold moonlight.

I waited, but nothing happened. I again stretched out on the bed—for how long I do not know. It may have been ten minutes, it may have been an hour. It seemed an eternity. And again I heard what I thought must be footsteps, the furtive, mysterious whisper of passing feet. I got up and pressed my ear against the door, in order to hear better. This time I was practically sure I heard someone pass.

I fumbled in my valise for a small flashlight, cautiously opened the door. There was no one in the hall. I walked out quietly, listened again. I thought I heard someone moving in François' room, but there was no light under the door. Carefully and fearfully, my heart beating so that I was certain it raised echoes in the vaulted old corridor, I went down the stairs.

To avoid the long walk around, I cut across the courtyard to the wing that held the library. Maître Cardonnet still sat in his sentry chair before the door, but, as I had thought he might, he had fallen asleep. His head was back and his short gray beard pointed directly at me. Then, all at once, I was not so sure that he was asleep. The yellow flame, which had gutted away half the candle, cast a strange, lifeless glow on his face, and accentuated its immobility.

I approached quickly, and even as I stood over him, I was struck by the peculiar, death-like aspect of his owl-like face. I felt my insides turning slowly to water. At that moment the notary gave a brief, reassuring snore. I was about to laugh at myself when my nostrils were assailed by a sickening, sweetish odor which I recognized at once. It was an odor that explained the unnatural impression of the notary's stupor: Chloroform! Beside him was a handkerchief. I picked it up and sniffed. Chloroform, all right. But it was the notary's own handkerchief and bore his embroidered initials.

I shook the little man. He did not awake. I was about to shake him again when I saw the door of the library slowly opening behind him.

I flattened myself against the wall. I watched the door opening, inch by inch, fascinated, yet dreading the moment when I should see whose hand was moving it. I believe I actually held my breath for what seemed hours while the mere crack of darkness grew silently wider and wider. Then I gasped.

Standing in the doorway was Jeannette Lacour, fully dressed. She stared at me without blinking. Her pale young face was expressionless, but her small poised body was trembling.

With a nod she beckoned me into the library. I stepped around the sleeping notary.

"Strike a match," she whispered.

Instead, I brought out my flashlight, pressed the switch. Her fingers closed around my hand, directed the beam across the room until the circle of light framed the notary's clumsy keys dangling from the lock of the oaken cabinet.

It didn't occur to me at that moment that her presence there was any more guilty than my own, and I whispered, "Is it gone?"

"I don't know," she replied. "I haven't looked. I'd just come in when I heard you outside. I thought I'd better have a witness."

I opened the cabinet. The Aldine folio was gone.

As I was checking through the other incunabula, to make sure the volume had not merely been moved, Jeannette was telling me in a few sketchy phrases that she had come down because she thought she heard footsteps coming and going in the upper hall and decided to investigate.

"We'd better rouse the notary," I said, when I was sure the Aldus was not there.

We tried, but in vain. He stirred uneasily, muttered a few senseless syllables, then relapsed into his coma. I felt his pulse, looked at his color again, and decided he had not been given a toxic dose and would probably awaken before long.

"We'd better wake René," the girl said.

I said I thought he was probably already awake, as I had heard someone moving in his room when I came down.

"We must tell him what's happened, anyway," she said.

We started across the courtyard when Jeannette clutched my arm with a hard, startled grasp. I turned my head in time to see what seemed to be the shadow of a man disappearing from a patch of moonlight into the blackness of the main gateway.

"Who is it?" I whispered.

"I don't know," she replied. "No one, probably. Just my imagination."

I was sure then that her movement had been one of recognition and that she was more terrified than ever. Her hand was trembling violently on my arm, and there was hopeless dread in her small, moonlit face.

"I'm sure I saw the shadow of a man," I said.

"Then you stay here and keep watch. I'll go back, the long way around, and tell René what's happened."

Without waiting for me to reply, she vanished.

I poked around among the shadows of the courtyard, but saw no sign of the intruder. I was still prowling when I heard what was unmistakably the sound of a pistol shot.

An instant later there was a second shot.

The queer echoes from the towers and sides of the courtyard made it impossible for me to determine from which direction the reports had come, but I at once ran back into the château. The notary had roused slightly, and was sitting up, but he was still stupefied. He could not reply to the questions I flung at him.

I ran back across the courtyard and climbed the stairs three at a time. At the top of the stairway I nearly collided with François, who grabbed me and shouted; "Where's Jeannette? Where's Miss Lacour?"

I told him I didn't know.

"Don't lie to me!" he shouted. "I saw you with her just a moment ago. I saw you together, standing in the courtyard in the moonlight."

"But she left me to come to you. Perhaps she's in her room."

"Her door is locked. She doesn't answer. I've knocked and shouted." Then, breaking off suddenly, he pushed past me and went down the stairs like a madman.

I saw a door opening farther down the corridor. The tousled white head of Dr. Storch appeared. He blinked sleepily at me as he asked: "What's happening? Did I hear shooting?"

"I think you did."

"Just a moment," he said. He went back into his room, leaving the door open, and I saw him take his fat wallet from under his pillow and tuck it into a pocket in his flannel nightgown.

As he came out again, the great bell at the gateway of the château was filling the halls with clanging echoes.

By the time we got downstairs, François was talking to a brigadier from the Beaumur gendarmerie, and another man in civilian clothes. With a start, I recognized the civilian as Inspector Paul Mordant.

"Why, hello, my dear Bender," the Inspector said. "Enjoying a quiet visit in the country?"

"What miraculous system of mental telepathy brings you here just at this moment?" I demanded.

"No telepathy," the Inspector said. "I stumbled on a bit of information in Paris this afternoon that made me think my presence in Beaumur might be useful. So I came. What has happened?"

"The Aldine folio has been stolen," I blurted, "and there have been shots fired."

"Shots? Where?"

"I don't know. But I think the reports came from the upper floor."

"*Voyons voir*," the Inspector said. He left the brigadier with the groggy notary and climbed the stairs with me, François, and Dr. Storch, who apologized for his nightgown.

He first made a leisurely, deliberate examination of Dr. Storch's room, shaking up the bed, looking behind tapestries and pictures, doing many little things that seemed senseless to me.

"Been housecleaning since you took over the château from your uncle haven't you, Monsieur François?" he said.

"Last week," François admitted.

Inspector Mordant winked at me. "Forgive me for showing off my powers of observation, my dear Bender," he said pointing to an age-darkened oil painting on the wall. "But I drew my conclusion from the fact that this portrait has been moved recently. Even you can see the difference in color of the pale oblong on the wall, just to the right, where it formerly hung."

He stooped, ran his finger along the baseboard below the painting, rubbed a little white plaster dust between his thumb and forefinger, and went on with his examination of the room.

"I see no sign of an Aldine folio here," he said. "Who is in the next room?"

"Miss Lacour." François pronounced the name with difficulty. He was suffering visibly.

"Ah, yes. Jeannette Lacour." Inspector Mordant smiled. "The name is familiar."

Getting no response to his knocks, the Inspector tried several pass keys and opened the door with the fourth. The room was in a state of disorder, indicating a hurried departure. There was clothing scattered on the bed and chairs, as though hurriedly pulled from hooks in the huge *armoire à glace* which stood open. A half-packed suitcase had been abandoned in one corner. Of Jeannette there was no sign.

"She—she's gone!" François stammered.

"She will return," said Inspector Mordant smugly. "The Beaumur gendarmerie is co-operating with me to guard all roads leading to the château and I am sure they will intercept her. I took the liberty, monsieur, of assuming that you would want no one to take leave of the château tonight."

He made no attempt to examine Jeannette's room.

"Obviously," he said, "if there was anything of importance

here, such as an early Venetian book, it would have been taken along by mademoiselle when she left. Whose room is next?"

François gulped. "Mine," he said.

Inspector Mordant opened the next door—and stopped short on the threshold.

Looking over his shoulder, I saw, sprawled on the floor at the far side of the room, just under the window, the body of Jules Pujot. I say body, because even to my unpracticed eye, it was evident at once that Pujot was dead.

Inspector Mordant pulled the door closed immediately, turned, gave orders to the brigadier downstairs. A few moments later two gendarmes had arrived to take charge of François, Dr. Storch, and even the notary, who had now revived sufficiently to sputter protests. Then the Inspector, the brigadier, and I went inside François' room to look at the body again.

Pujot had been shot squarely in the middle of his forehead. There was a dark, neat hole, with no marks of powder burns, and practically no bleeding except for a slight trickle at one corner of the mouth. After making a minute examination of the body, Mordant straightened up and said: "And now, my dear Bender, while I continue my work, you will tell me the whole story. I know you have a good memory and I want to hear about every minute of your stay at the château. Begin at the beginning."

I told him everything as I have related it here—the arrival of Dr. Storch and Pujot with the notary, the conversation during that dreadful dinner, the reactions of François and Jeannette to Pujot's blunt blackmailing proposal, the business of Dr. Storch's money and gun, the order in which the lights went out in the windows, the footsteps in the corridor, my discovery of the drugged notary—and Jeannette in the library.

As I spoke, Inspector Mordant was literally taking the room apart. He moved furniture, dismantled the bed, looked behind every picture, examined every inch of woodwork with a small magnifying glass. And yet I knew that his remarkable bivalent mind, while intent on his own investigation, was recording every word of my recital. He interrupted me only once: after my description of finding Jeannette in the library, in which I perhaps injected considerable of my own feeling that the girl was there for the same reason I was.

"You rather like Mademoiselle Lacour, don't you, my dear Bender?" He chuckled. "I don't blame you. She is most fascinating. But don't jump too readily to the conclusion that she is as innocent as she seems."

"What do you mean?"

"Nothing, perhaps. Just watch her face when she sees me again. Of course, she will not be surprised, this time, and will show greater control."

"This time?" I asked.

Mordant nodded. "My ringing of the bell at what seemed to you a psychological moment was no miracle, Bender," he said. "I confess I arrived earlier in the evening and was making a quiet, unofficial inspection of the château. I was the shadow you saw in the courtyard—and Mademoiselle Lacour evidently recognized me. So I thought I had better go out again and make an official entrance. I—"

"Then you came here tonight because of Jeannette Lacour?"

"I think so," the Inspector said quietly.

I would not have thought it possible for René François to turn any paler, but he did.

Inspector Mordant made just as thorough an examination of my room as he did of the two others. He was looking at Pujot's

ground floor in which he could lock up the chatelain and his guests while he continued his investigation.

"I should lock you up, too, Bender," he said, "except that I would much rather have you with me so that I can keep an eye on you."

I was with him when he found the fragments of the chloroform phial which I had heard smash in the courtyard. And I watched him retrieve the gun—Dr. Storch's pistol, it developed—from the fountain pool. Two cartridges had been fired.

"This checks with your story, Bender," he said. "Two shots. Why do you suppose, then, that there is only one bullet wound in Pujot's body?"

"The first shot must have missed," I suggested.

"Very logical. And yet I found no trace of the other bullet in François' room. I must have another look."

"It could have gone through the window," I said. "You remember I saw François open the window before he put out the light."

"And yet the window was closed when we found the body," Mordant said.

"François could have closed it while I was downstairs in the library and I would not have seen it," I said.

"Extremely logical," Mordant admitted. "Look here, Bender, why don't you try to get a little sleep? I'm going to mobilize the gendarmerie to help me look for the Aldine folio in the rest of the château—just in case Mademoiselle Lacour is telling the truth. If she did not take it, it is still here somewhere. I'll call you if anything exciting turns up."

He did not call me, and I must have slept soundly for two or three hours, because it was daylight when I awoke. I found Mordant sitting alone in the dining hall, sipping coffee.

"Good morning, Bender," he said. "I am in a quandary. I find no trace of the Aldine folio, so I am forced to conclude that the girl smuggled it out of the château. Otherwise how else could anyone hope to get it out of here? And yet I am practically convinced that the girl did not murder Jules Pujot. I—You're shivering, Bender."

"This place is an icebox," I said. "Mind if I light the fire?"

The Inspector had no objection, so I approached the huge grate with a lighted match. I was just about to touch the flame to the fagots when I dropped the match and uttered a loud exclamation. Tucked away among the twigs I saw a familiar-looking binding. I was reaching for it, when the Inspector brushed me aside and removed the book himself—a folio-size volume.

I tried to look over his shoulder as he excitedly turned the pages, but he waved me away. "Be a good fellow, Bender," he said, "and get me some water. Yes, water. Now."

I brought him a decanter. Immediately he spread the volume, and doused the center pages with water. He separated five or six pages to make sure they were properly soaked.

Puzzled, I asked: "But isn't that the Aldus, Inspector? It's in Latin, it is of the period, and—"

Mordant snapped the volume shut. "You haven't seen a thing, Bender," he said. "And you haven't heard anything. Now be a good fellow and tell the brigadier to bring everyone in here at once. Everyone. Then you'll hear all the answers."

As I left the room I looked back and saw Inspector Mordant replacing the big volume in the fireplace.

It was a tense, sullen group that filed into the dining hall. There were a few muttered "good-mornings," and more than a few hostile glances, but the only one who addressed Mordant directly was Dr. Storch. With a shudder, the white-haired old man said: "Aren't you cold, Inspector? Can't we have a little fire?"

I looked aghast at Mordant, who was nonchalantly sipping his coffee. He seemed positively chipper, as he nodded to me. When I hesitated, he said: "Go ahead and touch a match to it, Bender. The fire is already laid."

I obeyed. But it was with a sick feeling that I watched the first flames curl up past the spot where I had seen Mordant place the folio.

"And now," said Inspector Mordant, "I must ask all of you for further co-operation in the solution of this mystery."

"There is no mystery!" declared Maître Cardonnet, who was his pompous self again. "René François threatened to kill Pujot last night. We all heard him. He merely carried out his threat. Who else had any reason to kill Pujot?"

"You did," said Inspector Mordant simply.

"I? That's preposterous."

"I did a little polite burglary in your office on my way here last night, Maître Cardonnet," said Mordant. "Running over your papers, I found a letter from a rare-book dealer in London, offering you 50,000 francs' bonus if you would procure for him the Aldine folio at a reasonable figure."

"I—I—yes, that's true," stammered the notary. "But I did not even reply to the ridiculous offer. And certainly I would not kill a man for 50,000 francs."

"Suppose Pujot, too, knew of this offer. Suppose he tried to blackmail you, that you quarreled, and that he was killed."

"But I had been chloroformed."

"You were apparently chloroformed. There was an odor of

chloroform—on your own handkerchief. Why your own handkerchief, Maître Cardonnet?"

"Well, I . . . I may have been dozing. It would have been easy for the thief to take the handkerchief from my pocket."

"And it would also have been easy for you to pretend being drugged, to cover up the fact that you had stolen the book."

"Do you dare accuse me, Inspector?" The notary's beard bristled.

"I accuse nobody—yet. I merely point out all the possibilities. . . . Bender, do you smell leather burning?"

I had been standing with my back to the fire. I couldn't bear to watch the flames destroying the precious folio. I said yes. Then I turned to see Dr. Storch make a dash toward the hearth.

"Look, Inspector!" he cried. "There's a book in there. A large volume."

There was an excited rush for the fireplace. Eager hands tried to smother the flames. Others raked from the embers the smoking, smouldering object Dr. Storch had indicated. It was indeed the book, but the binding and pages had been charred beyond recognition. Inspector Mordant gently spread the blackened, crumbling remains on the hearth.

"You're an expert, Dr. Storch," he said. "What can you tell us from this?"

Dr. Storch screwed a glass into one eye and pored over the burned volume. "What a pity!" he said. "What a tragic loss! The Aldine folio has been destroyed."

"You are sure, Dr. Storch?"

"Positive."

With a brusque gesture, Inspector Mordant brushed away a sheaf of ashes to reveal the steaming half of an unburned page which was still damp. "What luck!" he said. "Here is an unmarred portion of the type page. Do you still think it is the work of Aldus, Dr. Storch?"

"No doubt about it," was the reply.

Inspector Mordant straightened up. His right hand dipped into his pocket emerged with a revolver. His left reached for Dr. Storch's white hair, yanked furiously. The snowy shock came off cleanly, revealing a gleaming bald pate.

"Emil Daur!" exclaimed Inspector Mordant. "You should have stuck to robbing art galleries, Emil. Your knowledge of type faces is faulty. The type on this page was designed by Garamond, fifty years after Aldus the Elder. See, Bender. Look at the serifs. Look at the capital letters. Unmistakably the hand of Garamond."

"Perhaps I may have been mistaken," admitted the bald-headed man whom Mordant now called Emil Daur. "But that is no reason for subjecting me to the indignities of—"

"No use pretending further, Emil," Mordant said. "It was a clever scheme, but it failed. You placed this nondescript Garamond folio in the fireplace, expecting it to be so completely ruined that we would all believe it was the Aldine folio, and stop searching further. That would allow you to carry off the genuine volume without interference. Brigadier, did you examine the Hispano-Suiza in the courtyard last night? Neither did I. We were both fools. Better have a look now. I'm certain you will find—Stop him, Brigadier!"

The man who had posed as Dr. Storch bolted for the door. Mordant did not shoot because Jeannette and François were in the line of fire. The fugitive was quickly overpowered, however, by three gendarmes.

"And now, Emil," said Inspector Mordant, "perhaps you would like to tell us what you have done with Dr. Hugo Storch."

The bald-headed book thief lapsed into surly silence. As I watched his pink nostrils quivering with suppressed rage, I remembered that Mordant had asked me on the terrace of the Café Grolier if I had seen Emil Daur at "Sotheby's."

"Very well, Emil," the Inspector continued. "If you won't tell us, I'll tell *you*. You killed him. Otherwise you would not have his automobile and the money that Dr. Storch always carried on his person. Too bad for you that you were not satisfied with the money, and had to test your professional skill on the Aldus. And once embarked on a career of homicide, you had to kill Jules Pujot, too."

"You can't prove it."

"Certainly, I can," said Inspector Mordant. "I knew last night that you had killed Pujot, but I postponed arresting you until I had found out what you did with the book. You shot Pujot, with the pistol you pretended was stolen, in your own room. The first shot missed and lodged in the wall. You moved a painting to hide the hole—but you did not notice the white plaster dust that fell from the hole. I did.

"When François, alarmed by the shots, left his room, you dragged Pujot's body along the balcony and pushed it into François' room by the open window. Then you closed the window in order to forestall any suggestion that the body had been introduced from outside. You did not expect me here, and you thought the local gendarmes would readily believe François guilty in view of his public threat against Pujot's life last night."

"I had no reason to kill Pujot," muttered Emil Daur.

"You had very good reason," Mordant countered. "Pujot's

window was the only one that commanded a perfect view of the Hispano-Suiza parked in the courtyard. I think we may assume, therefore, that Pujot saw you hiding the stolen book in the car, and—"

"Here's the book, Inspector," said the Brigadier, coming in with the Aldus. "It was tucked under the upholstery."

"There, you see," said Inspector Mordant triumphantly. "Pujot, who appears to have had no small talent for blackmail, must have come to you and demanded his price for silence. Probably he demanded the half-million francs you had foolishly displayed last night, threatening exposure. You could not afford to remain in the power of a blackmailer, because of what you have done to Dr. Storch, so you killed Pujot. You killed him, not to save the half-million francs, but to save your skin. You failed, Emil. Monsieur de Paris is going to have your head anyhow. What have you done with Dr. Storch, Emil?"

"Find out for yourself," growled Emil Daur.

Mordant did find out—before noon. He spent the rest of the morning at the Beaumur gendarmerie, making long-distance calls to Paris. It took only a few hours for the Sûreté to discover the body of Dr. Storch, packed in his own trunk, in the check-room of the Gare de Lyon.

Daur had evidently followed Dr. Storch after the old bibliophile had drawn the money from his bank, and had strangled him in his room at the Ritz. Since Dr. Storch had already given notice that he was leaving, it was easy for Daur to phone the hotel office to have the baggage—and the body—carted to the station. Then, to delay the discovery that Storch had disappeared, the murderer decided to impersonate him for a while, and drove his car to Beaumur. Once at the château, he could not resist the challenge to his professional skill. He had to tempt fate by stealing the Aldine folio.

I might add that I finally got the book for 500,000 francs. I think I could have had it for less, as there was little bidding, but I knew I was getting good value and I considered the extra money as a sort of wedding present for René François and Jeannette Lacour. After all, my firm could afford it!

DEATH WALKS IN MARBLE HALLS

Lawrence G. Blochman

The majority of Lawrence G(oldtree) Blochman's (1900-1975) more than fifty books and hundreds of short stories were adventure and popular fiction, often set in the Far East. His mysteries featured two series characters, Inspector Leonidas Prike in India and Dr. Daniel Webster Coffee in the fictional midwestern town of Northbank, but most of his novels and stories were stand-alones, as is "Death Walks in Marble Halls."

Blochman's original title for the story was "Death from the Sanscrit" but it had been commissioned by *The American Magazine* and the fiction editor did not like the title, giving it this one. Six years later, it was reprinted in *Ellery Queen's Mystery Magazine* and Frederick Dannay didn't like *that* title so, as he so often did, changed it to "Murder Walks in Marble Halls." Shortly after its first appearance, Twentieth Century-Fox acquired the rights and didn't like the title, either, so filmed it as *Quiet Please, Murder* (1942), directed and with a screenplay by John Larkin; it starred George Sanders, Gail Patrick, and Richard Denning.

In his introduction to the story's appearance in *EQMM*, Dannay recounts the humorous story of the film adaptation, suggesting that the title wasn't the only thing the studio didn't like. It changed all of the original characters as well as the plot, turning it from a mystery/detective story to a tale of psychological suspense, with the murderer's identity known from the outset. The only element of the story retained was the setting in a public library, though not the iconic and cavernous main branch of the New York Public Library on Fifth Avenue.

"Death Walks in Marble Halls" was originally published in the September 1942 issue of *The American Magazine*; it was published separately as a slim paperback by Dell in 1951.

Death Walks in Marble Halls

by Lawrence G. Blochman

Long before the storm broke, Phil Manning had an uneasy feeling that something unpleasant was about to happen. He had been jumpy ever since reading in the morning papers that Feodor Klawitz, the erudite screwball, was out on bail after having been arrested on charges of criminal libel preferred by H. H. Dorwin, a trustee of the public library. When Dorwin himself telephoned to say he was on his way over to discuss a matter of great importance, Manning's jumpiness increased by at least six latent jumps. And when his phone rang a second time, he winced and hit a handful of wrong typewriter keys.

Phil Manning did not believe in the occult or in premonitions. And as he had neither a hangover nor a guilty conscience, he decided he was suffering from an attack of the Deep-blue Willies (*Melancholia Bibliotecalis*), an occupational disease afflicting the staff of the Public Library on dark Winter days.

Even on the sunniest mornings of Spring there was a certain sepulchral chill about the marble grandeur of the library, and when the weather went into somber mourning for the dying year, the building was a positive mausoleum.

The phone rang again. The shaggy young man with the Willies reached for it apprehensively.

"Press relations. Manning speaking," he said.

"Phil, I've got to see you—right away!" It was Betty Vale's voice, usually guaranteed to restore fallen spirits with its cosmic music. Not today, though. Today it was without a single grace note. Today it was a taut, low-keyed call for help.

"What's happened, Betty?" Manning tried to fight off the sense of impending disaster with a facetious phrase. "Did somebody park a fire hydrant near your car again?"

"Don't joke, Phil." There was anguish in the tone. "Can you cross the street? I'm phoning from the cigar store at the corner."

"Why don't you come over here?" Manning asked. "I've got to wait for one of the trustees. H. H. Dorwin just phoned—"

"Dorwin?" The word was like a cry of pain. "I don't want to see Hugh Dorwin now, Phil. I can't."

"I didn't know he was a friend of yours," Manning said. "How—"

"I can't tell you about it now, Phil. And I'm afraid to come to the library. I'll wait here. You'll come when you can, Phil? Please."

"Of course, darling. Right away—if I can make it."

Manning banged down the phone and glanced at his typewriter, which had been automatically composing a press release on the library's exhibit opening the following week: The History of the Dog in America as Told by Contemporary Prints and Publications. The release could wait.

Uncoiling his long legs from the legs of the chair, Manning rose to his full six-feet-one and smoothed the sedentary wrinkles from his tweeds.

Suddenly Manning sat down again. This was indeed his off day. Dave Benson was flowing through the doorway, his white teeth flashing in an aggressive smile.

Manning never thought of Benson as walking; he moved as though the next step would see his pointed shoes gliding into a tango. The gait matched his double-breasted elegance, with its corner of blue-plaid handkerchief poking from his pocket to harmonize with his blue-plaid tie.

"Hi!" said Benson, turning on all his dark, slick-haired, self-conscious charm. "Where's Betty?"

He would ask that, Manning thought. Benson haunted Betty Vale like an unemployed ghost. He was always in the library if there was a chance of Betty's being there.

"Betty's gone to Bermuda for the onion season," Manning said. "And I'm leaving on the next plane myself. Goodbye, old man."

"Betty told me she was coming to the library this afternoon," Benson insisted through his white grin. "So I was thinking—"

"Stop boasting, Benson. And leave the door open as you go out. Goodbye." Benson's built-in smile slowly faded.

"Have it your own way," he said, fixing Manning with a curious stare. "But don't think Betty's going to thank you for this." He made his exit in two-four time.

Manning listened to his footsteps retreating down the marble corridor. He waited several minutes to give Benson plenty of chance to get out of range. Then he rose again quickly.

He was buttoning his coat when he heard the shot.

It was not a very loud report—a sharp explosion that made

hollow, singing echoes in the halls and galleries—and Manning did not recognize it immediately for what it was. After all, gun fire was not a usual sound in the public library. When the report was followed, however, by a cry, a shout, and the tattoo of running feet, Manning bolted from his office.

Fifty feet down the corridor he saw H. H. Dorwin flattened against the wall. Bullet-chipped flakes of marble from the bust of Sophocles above him were dusted over his well-tailored shoulders. His usually ruddy face was the color of the sculptured poet.

Halfway between Dorwin and the monumental staircase, a small target pistol lay on the floor. It was probably not more than .22 caliber.

Pounding down the stairs was big, white-thatched Tim Cornish, library guard, in pursuit of a shabby little man who had already reached the vast vestibule and was running for the street doors.

"You hurt, Mr. Dorwin?" Manning hesitated between joining the chase and helping the shaken trustee.

"Of course not!" Dorwin barked. "Manning, go after that guard! Don't let him turn the man over to the police!"

"But, Mr. Dorwin—"

"No cops!" Dorwin ordered, walking quickly down the corridor to pick up the pistol. "Bring him back here. Bring them both back here, Manning. And hurry."

Manning hurried. He went down the steps three at a time.

Once outside, he broke into a brisk trot, seeking Cornish and the threadbare fugitive among the throngs of women hurrying along the avenue, round-shouldered with the cold despite their furs.

Manning caught sight of Cornish near the corner. The guard had collared the seedy-looking assailant, apparently without a struggle. When Manning motioned, Cornish started toward him, his captive meekly in tow.

The man who had shot at Dorwin wore no overcoat, and his teeth were chattering. He was an unprepossessing specimen, thin and gray-haired. At first glance he seemed typical of the cold-weather derelicts now deserting the icy streets for the library, the homeless bums whose damp clothing gave off animal odors when it began to steam in the warmth of the reading rooms. When he came closer, however, Manning revised his estimate. The shabby stranger was young, despite the two-day stubble of graying beard on his tragically lined face; and his eyes were keen and intelligent.

"Maybe I ought to carry him," said the guard. The threadbare captive looked very small beside Tim Cornish. Tim was a big man, almost as big as Manning, with a Mark Twain mustache, hair like silver, and feet like a copper. Tim had in fact been pretty much all copper for most of his twenty-five years as library guard. Only after twenty years had he become aware of the millions of volumes which surrounded him daily. Three years ago he had discovered Shakespeare.

"You don't look like a gunman," Manning said to the seedy man beside him. "Why did you want to shoot H. H. Dorwin?"

There was no reply. They went up the steps to the portico.

"It was just the flash and outbreak of a fiery mind," said Tim. "A savageness in unreclaimed blood. That's from *Macbeth*, Mr. Manning."

The silent little man spoke at last. "It's from *Hamlet*," he said.

"I said *Hamlet*, didn't I?" Tim demanded. He tightened his

grip on his captive and pushed him indignantly through the entrance stile. The metal bar came between them and stuck—only for a fraction of a second. In the brief instant the man who had shot at Dorwin wrested himself free and ran.

Tim Cornish ran after him, with Phil Manning one click of the turnstile behind.

They ran past the elevators and up the steep vaulted stairway of the North Wing. On the first landing they stopped to pant in consternation. The seedy little would-be assassin was gone.

The stairways in the North Wing were a complex system of superimposed and parallel X's, a maze of crisscrossing marble tunnels, like false passages to detour ghouls from a Pharaoh's sepulchre. From the landing Manning and Cornish could continue upward by alternate branches of the X, either to the Music Room office, or to the elevators on the second floor; they could go down again by another leg of the stairway to the main floor. There was no way of knowing which of the three the fugitive had taken.

"Look, Tim," Manning said. "You stay on the scent. I'll warn the guards at all the doors."

When he returned to his office, after giving the description of the missing derelict to the guards at all the doors, Manning nearly collided with a young woman who was coming out. She was a sinuous little thing, lusciously proportioned and suspiciously blonde. She was probably pretty, although at the moment her sensuous features were distorted by an expression of dismay—or perhaps it was embarrassment at the brusqueness of the unexpected encounter. Manning did not remember having seen her before, although she was hatless and evidently worked in the library. As she muttered a hasty "Sorry," he thought her lips were white along their cosmetic edges. He was watching her hurry down the corridor, when Dorwin's voice from inside the office called, "Well?"

H. H. Dorwin had recovered his composure—at least outwardly.

"Where's Underwood?" he asked.

"Who's that, sir?"

"Underwood. James Underwood, the man I told you to bring here."

"He's still loose somewhere in the library, Mr. Dorwin. He won't get out of the building, though. Hadn't we better get the police?"

"No," snapped Dorwin. "The poor devil probably's sorry already for what he did."

"I see," said Manning, although he didn't.

"He has a brilliant mind, that Underwood," Dorwin went on. "Used to work for me, in my private library, cataloguing my first editions and incunabula. Resigned about a year ago, for some strange reasons of his own. Had a hard time of it ever since. On W.P.A. for a while, and I don't know what else. Been hanging around my place the last week, but I've been too busy to see him. I suspected he wanted his job back, and sent word I didn't have anything for him. Hard luck went to his head, I guess."

Dorwin paused expectantly. Manning didn't know what comment was expected of him. He said: "That young woman who just left here—was she looking for me?"

"No," said Dorwin quickly. Then he added, "She's a catalogue girl—new here. Doesn't know her way around yet, apparently. By the way, Manning, what happened to your notice on those Russian manuscripts I gave the library? They've been catalogued since Autumn and I haven't seen a word about them anywhere."

"There's a notice in next month's Bulletin, Mr. Dorwin," Manning replied. "Is that what you wanted to see me about?"

"There was something else," said Dorwin. He hesitated, got up, and went to the window. For a minute he seemed intent on the first flakes of snow swirling through the gloom.

His silhouette was slim and clean-lined against the window, particularly for a man in his fifties—the lusty fifties. He was a snappy dresser, too, for a banker and patron of the arts. Or for a collector. Dorwin was very much a collector. He collected interlocking directorates and symphony orchestras, tax-exempt securities and first editions, old masters and young blondes.

An unpleasant thought squirmed through Manning's mind. Betty Vale was on the blonde side. Betty Vale had admitted out of a clear sky that she knew Hugh Dorwin and didn't want to see him. And Betty Vale was scared of something . . .

"You know about my fuss with Feodor Klawitz?" Dorwin demanded suddenly without turning around.

"I know about it roughly," Manning said.

"How well do you know the man?"

"Well . . ." Manning hesitated. He knew Feodor Klawitz as a baldheaded, horse-faced eccentric who spent most of his waking hours in the library, except for three nights a week when he broadcast over a small local radio station. It was a strange program, part news, part personalities, all lugubriously learned and much of it violently scurrilous. Manning had always thought Klawitz a little mad, an opinion which had been strengthened the day he was arrested. The warrant had been served on Klawitz in the Map Room, and he had immediately gone berserk, throwing maps and charts about, pelting the librarian and the arresting officer with Persia, Baluchistan and Bokhara . . .

"I know him to speak to; that's about all," Manning said. "And of course I know him by sight—if he happens to be wearing a familiar wig."

"Wig?" Dorwin echoed.

"I thought everybody knew Klawitz wears a different toupee to suit his mood," Manning explained. "He wears a dignified gray wig when he's feeling severe and scholarly, a sleek black one for moments of glamor and romance, a reddish thatch when he feels argument and eloquence coming on."

"The fool libeled me again on his broadcast last night," Dorwin said. "Hadn't been out of jail two hours before he was calling me a lecherous plutocrat. Then at midnight I got a special delivery letter—anonymous, of course—saying that Klawitz had barely started on me. Said he'd rip my character completely to shreds, unless I did this or that, libel charge or no libel charge."

Dorwin turned around at last. He turned quickly, savagely. His face had gone white again.

"Damn it, Manning," the trustee said. "Nobody can blackmail me!"

"Do you think he . . . Do you think Klawitz had anything to do with this man Underwood taking a shot at you today?" Manning asked.

"I wouldn't put it past him," Dorwin said. "Klawitz is capable of anything. But I just wanted you to know, Manning, that I'm not backing down. I'm not dropping the libel charges against Klawitz. I'm telling you this, because in trying to get at me again, Klawitz may hurt you, Manning."

Manning moistened his lips. "Betty Vale?" he asked.

"I won't mention names, Manning. I'm a little old-fashioned

that way. Whatever my bachelor habits may be, I still observe the old niceties. I just want to tell you that . . . that no matter what Klawitz may say, you mustn't lose your faith in . . . in anyone."

The interview was interrupted by the sudden appearance of Tim Cornish. The guard was panting slightly as he announced: "We haven't found him yet, Mr. Dorwin. But we will. He's still in the library."

"Yes. Well, bring him to the Trustees' Room when you find him." Dorwin picked up a large portfolio which Manning had not noticed before. It was a deep-red portfolio fastened with blue tapes. "I'll be there in half an hour," he added. "There's a Trustees' meeting."

"Don't you think you'd better wait here, Mr. Dorwin?" Tim suggested. "Do you think it's a good idea to go wandering around while that guy—?"

"I'm not afraid, Tim." Dorwin looked at the red portfolio with a curious expression of alarm in his eyes. He started to say something, then changed his mind. He tucked the portfolio under his left arm—gingerly, as though it contained something highly explosive. "I'm not afraid of *him*," he said, patting his right coat pocket. "I've got the man's gun."

He strode out. Tim watched him admiringly. "He's right," Tim said. "Cowards die many times before their death, Mr. Manning."

Manning smiled. "*Hamlet*, Tim?"

"*Julius Caesar*, Mr. Manning. By the way, I've got a note for you." He fished a folded piece of paper from his pocket.

Manning quickly unfolded the paper. On it, Betty Vale's handwriting said: "Come to the Oriental Room as soon as you can! Please!! I'll wait for you there."

Thrusting the note into his pocket, Manning hurried past the guard without a word. He heard Tim say, "We'll have that guy rounded up in no time, Mr. Manning. Don't worry."

Manning waved an acknowledgement, and strode down the marbled whiteness of the crypt-like corridor. He turned into the long, low hall that housed the Oriental catalogue, passed the doors of the Slavonic and Hebrew rooms. His heart beat faster as he approached the entrance to the Oriental library. Not only was he anxious about Betty Vale's mysterious difficulties, but the Oriental Room was a sentimental symbol to him. It was here that he had rediscovered Betty.

They had been college sweethearts once, before Betty left the co-educational school for a Vermont college where a girl could study not only Greek philosophy and English poetry, but the Dance with a capital D. After that a million dollars and the Atlantic Ocean had come between them. The million was Edward Vale's—Betty's father's—the result of a smart advertising campaign for Vale Headache Powders, while Manning was learning the newspaper business in New York. And a million dollars can change almost anyone's social outlook, particularly in regard to a $60-a-week reporter; at least it would seem so to the reporter. The Atlantic Ocean came in when Manning was awarded a scholarship at Louvain—a year of study cut short by the blitzkrieg which blasted him out of the Louvain Library into the driver's seat of an ambulance—a year in which he and Betty did not even correspond.

Even after he was chased home with a Nazi bullet in his thigh and had settled down to his new job at the public library, he made no effort to get in touch with her. He was afraid of that million dollars.

He thought he had forgotten her, until the day, several months ago, he had found her in the Oriental Room, poring over the words of Kalidasa. He was pleased and puzzled—puzzled that he should be so pleased to learn that she was not yet married, even more puzzled that a pretty blonde with a rich father should be concerned with a Sanskrit poet fifteen centuries dead.

The answer to the first puzzle was not hard to find. The second, however, was more difficult. Betty Vale could be charmingly secretive. She seemed genuinely glad to pick up their old comradeship where they had left off, but she liked to talk more about the past than about the present.

If there had been any doubt in Manning's mind that she was in trouble, it was disspelled when he saw her face.

"I was scared to death you wouldn't come," she said.

"You're scared to death, all right, but you can't blame it on me, darling." He smiled desperately into her frightened eyes. "What happened?"

"I don't know where to begin."

"An anonymous letter?"

The girl gasped. Her eyes were almost round above her broad, high cheek bones. They were long eyes, normally—almost Oriental, if they hadn't been so blue. "How did you know?" she asked.

"A guess." Manning shrugged. He was not quite sure why he had not told her about H. H. Dorwin's anonymous letter—or the shot that hit Sophocles instead of Dorwin. He said: "Tell me about it."

Betty Vale pushed one hand into her muff, drew out a crumpled piece of paper. "It came in this afternoon's mail," she said.

Manning smoothed out the paper and read:

"If you don't stop seeing Hugh Dorwin, someone will stop you—and by the most primitive and certain means."

The message was printed in crudely-formed block letters that did not fit the precise phrasing.

"*Have* you been seeing Dorwin?" Manning asked.

"This past week, yes."

"Then I can give you some very simple advice: Don't see him any more."

"But I must see him this afternoon, Phil. I *must*."

"And let him make passes at you?"

"It's . . . it's not that."

The girl moistened her lips. Her long lashes fanned her cheek. She said in a low voice: "I've got to see him, that's all."

"That's a quick switch," Manning said. "When you phoned me, you didn't want to see him at all. You said you were even afraid to come to the library."

"I *was* afraid. Of that man."

"Underwood?"

"I don't know his name. The shabby man who needed a shave—and an overcoat. I was on my way to the library when I saw him go in. So I phoned you instead. But when I saw the guard arrest him, I thought it would be safe to come."

"The guard didn't arrest him," Manning said. "If it's Underwood you're talking about, he's still loose—in the library."

"He's—?" The girl started to rise, but sank back limply in her chair. "Oh, Phil."

Manning reached for her hand. It was cold and trembling.

"Why are you afraid of Underwood?" he asked.

"I think he wrote that letter."

"You don't know his name, but you think he wrote you a threatening letter. Why?"

"I saw him several times loitering outside of Hugh Dorwin's house on Fifth Avenue," Betty said. "Day before yesterday, when I came out, he was standing there, shivering in his thin coat. I almost felt sorry for him—until he looked into my face. Phil, his eyes! They're desperate, terrible eyes! They're—I can't explain, but they frightened me."

"That's the only reason you have for thinking Underwood wrote you an anonymous letter—the expression in his eyes?"

"Who else could it have been, Phil? No one else knew about my going to Dorwin's. And this man waiting outside there . . ."

Manning pulled thoughtfully at the lobe of one ear. It all sounded very strange—yet there were plenty of strange things going on in the library today. Betty was certainly holding something back—perhaps because she was still scared.

"Look, darling," Manning said, squeezing the girl's hand reassuringly. "I'm not going to ask you any more questions until I'm sure your Mr. Underwood is somewhere else. Wait here until I take a quick turn around the plant. The guards have probably rounded him up by this time."

Betty returned the pressure of his hand, but said nothing. . . .

The guard outside the Trustees' Room said: "Tim just went upstairs, Mr. Manning. He heard that man he's looking for is on the third floor."

Manning set out in pursuit.

As he climbed the stairs he noted that the afternoon darkness was as thick as night, and that the snow was falling in earnest outside.

Manning was wondering whether Tim had turned north toward the Music Room or south toward the map room, when he caught sight of Tim's white hair at the far end of the catalogue room, straight ahead. He followed.

He strode through the two-storied hush of the vast nave where men and women moved among high tables, like a swarm of termites boring into the six million listing-cards impaled on metal spindles in the long oak drawers. He lost track of Tim among the people digging out their references to Anaphylaxis, Brazilian Railroads, and Chaucer. When he reached the queue waiting to present call-slips to the pneumatic-tube station at the central desk, he decided that Tim must have disappeared into the great transept of the two reading rooms beyond the catalogue. He would find out which one.

He first circled the North Room, skirting the tall cliffs of encyclopedias and reference books. He saw no trace of Tim—or of James Underwood.

He passed the delivery desk—a corral of carved oak separating the two reading rooms—with its red lights flashing the numbers of books just arrived from the stacks by tiny elevator. He sidled through a parked caravan of low hand-trucks loaded with volumes returning to the stacks, each ticketed with pink or white slips to announce its destination. He stepped into the South Reading Room and was about to repeat his circular voyage of exploration when two arresting objects sprang simultaneously into his field of vision.

The first, the trim figure of a woman rushing excitedly toward him, he saw only vaguely. Even when she stopped beside him, seized his arm, and made a small, half-strangled sound in her throat, he did not really look at her. His eyes were focused in horrid fascination on the narrow gallery which ran along the entire side of the immense room, halfway up the precipice of books.

H. H. Dorwin was standing unsteadily on the gallery, the door of the spiral staircase open behind him.

Blood was streaming down Dorwin's left cheek, and his face was a ghastly mask. He took two disjointed steps, like a man walking in his sleep, tottered an instant, then collapsed. He toppled over the iron railing, struck the top of the jutting bookcases below, pitched across a dictionary stand, and crashed heavily on a reading table.

Three nuns and half a dozen students arose in shocked surprise, backed away from the sprawled figure on the table, and screamed in unison.

Pandemonium swept through the South Reading Room like a rising wind. The small noises of startled readers pushing back their chairs swelled to a roar. The shrieks of the terrified nuns struck human echoes from the far tables. The august silence shrouding the ornate gilded ceiling was ripped to shreds by a bedlam of voices raised above a murmur for the first time in nearly half a century. There was a movement of vicious curiosity toward the broken form on the reading table, a movement of terror away from it, a surge of panic toward the passage to the Catalogue Room.

Three library guards blocked the exit. One of them was Tim Cornish who had instantly sensed the situation and was lustily engaged in restoring order. His big voice droned through the din, calling: "Everyone be seated, please. Do not try to leave the room."

Tim's metallic monotone roused Phil Manning from his brief stupefaction. Turning his eyes from the man on the table, he realized that the woman who had gripped his arm was Betty

Vale. She clutched her muff closely against her breast with tense white fingers, and the hand on his arm shook violently.

"You and your rendezvous," Manning said. "Why didn't you stay put?"

The girl stared at him, wordlessly, her lips frozen in a small, scarlet, horrified O.

"Did you get to see Dorwin?" Phil asked.

"No. That is, not until he . . . Not until just now."

"How much of this did you see happen?"

"Just what you saw—and that was too much. I'm all cold and hot inside. I'm afraid I'm going to—"

"Sit down here, darling. No, here. Turn your back. Now listen hard and talk fast, because you'll probably have to be on your own for a while. You can tell me the whole story as soon as I can get you away from here. Meanwhile, tell me this: Why were you meeting Dorwin?"

"Well, Hugh said he wanted to explain about somebody trying to involve me in a scandal—some radio gossip."

"What scandal?"

"There isn't any, Phil. Not really. But I did go to Hugh Dorwin's alone—at night. And there was this awful man, this Underwood, watching me come out. Then there's that letter . . . Phil, I don't know what my father would do if I got mixed up in—"

"In a murder? You're already in it, from all the signs. And you're just afraid of your father?"

The girl shook her head. "Somebody killed Hugh Dorwin," she said. "Suppose it's the person who wrote me that letter? Suppose he thinks I *am* mixed up with Dorwin? Suppose he wants to kill me, too?"

Manning suddenly remembered the curious change in Dorwin's face as he picked up the big portfolio just as he left the office, not long ago. He asked: "Do you know anything about a portfolio—a large red portfolio tied with blue tapes?"

The girl made a queer, moaning sound.

Manning remembered that Dorwin had said: "Klawitz may hurt you. Klawitz may try to use a woman's name." Perhaps the portfolio contained old love letters. Or innocent letters that might be misconstrued. Dorwin had said: "You mustn't lose your faith in anyone." Well, he wouldn't. But he would have to find that red portfolio before the police did. If there was any incriminating evidence in it, anything that might link the girl to Dorwin, he would get rid of it. Meanwhile he would have to keep Betty out of the hands of the police. He wouldn't try to abet a guilty-looking escape, naturally, but he would like to delay the inevitable questioning as long as possible, to give him time to establish her innocence.

"Just remember one thing," he said. "Forget about Dorwin. If anybody asks you, you came here to meet me after work. We were going out for a drink together. Come on."

Manning glanced at the crowd around H. H. Dorwin. The rear ranks parted to let a man come through. The man had a professional air about him and was probably a doctor.

Tim still guarded the only exit from the reading room. He was thoroughly enjoying the exercise of authority, and his Mark Twain mustache seemed to have assumed a martial twist. It was more like a Marshal Foch mustache, as he gave orders to his constantly arriving reinforcements. Half a dozen of his fellow guards had taken up their posts at strategic points, and several special investigators whose normal duties were to watch for vandals and book thieves had come into the room.

Manning took Betty's arm and guided her toward Tim. Two uniformed policemen from a squad car came up behind the guard as Manning and the girl approached.

"Sorry, Mr. Manning." Tim continued to bar the way. "Nobody's allowed to leave. The police are here."

Another squad of bluecoats came through from the Catalogue Room in single file. Manning watched them out of the corner of his eye as he asked Cornish: "Is he here, Tim?"

"I'm not sure," the guard replied. "Berger thought he saw him come in."

"If he's not here, somebody else had the same idea," Manning said.

"I know," Tim Cornish stepped closer to whisper in Manning's ear: "There's Klawitz, Mr. Manning."

Manning started. "Where, Tim?"

"Over there, halfway across the room—reading just like nothing happened."

Manning looked in the direction indicated by Tim's nod. Eight tables away, apparently oblivious of the hubbub around him, Feodor Klawitz was serenely poring over a book. The burnished curve of his naked pate, gleaming in the light of the overhead fixtures, was the only spot of calm in the room. A beribboned monocle screwed disdainfully into one eye, his ivory jowls devoid of any show of emotion, Klawitz quietly turned a page.

"I think we can leave Mr. Klawitz to the police, Tim. By the way, who called the cops?"

"I did, Mr. Manning."

"I'll be with you in a minute, Tim—if you need me," he said. "Come on, Betty."

The girl came with him silently.

"Listen hard," Manning said, as they walked between the reading tables. "What you have to do now is this: Make yourself as inconspicuous as possible until I find out what happened to that red portfolio of yours. When I locate it, we can discuss future strategy. Yes?"

"Of course—if you say so."

"Then find yourself a seat down at the south end of the room. Slip into the American History Collection if you can do it neatly. Wait until I come for you—and stick to your story."

He gave the girl's arm an affectionate pinch and watched her walk away.

When he turned back to Tim Cornish, the police were arriving in force.

The uniformed detectives were already widely deployed about the reading room, dripping melted snow all over the erudite terrain. A platoon of specialists tramped in, unslinging cameras, tripods, and cases of clue-gathering apparatus. They were all obviously awaiting instructions from a small, inoffensive-looking man in mufti, who in turn was intently watching a husky, big-boned, bushy-haired medical examiner make a preliminary survey of the Dorwin corpse.

Manning skirted the center of police operations, hoping against hope that he could start his surreptitious search for the red portfolio without attracting attention. He was wrong.

"Hey, you!" The small man in mufti halted him with a slight side motion of his head. "Where do you think you're going?"

"I'm Philip Manning. I'm a member of the library staff. I don't think I got your name."

The small man grunted. "Kenneth Kilkenny, Homicide Squad." The detective did not look at Manning as he talked. The snow-filled crease of his slouch hat fed a rivulet that trickled off the brim to extinguish his cigarette, thus complying with library regulations. He continued to watch the medical examiner. "I don't think we need you, Manning," he said.

"I think you do," Manning contradicted. "I saw the whole show. You'll want me to go over the scene with you."

Kilkenny grunted again. "Wait till Doc Rosenkohl gets through here," he said.

"I'm through, Kenny—and you can turn your bloodhounds loose," the medical examiner said.

"What do I look for, Rosie—swords, pistols, or a blunt instrument?" the detective asked him.

"The man's been stabbed through the left eye," Dr. Rosenkohl replied. "But I can't tell you until after the autopsy if that's what killed him."

A pair of scissors could have done it, Manning thought; or some tool from the bindery downstairs.

"Whatever it was, we'll find it," Kilkenny declared. "How soon can you get into him, Rosie?"

"I'll ride down to Bellevue with him now, if you want," said the medical examiner.

"You'd better, Rosie. I can't keep a thousand bookworms here all week. I never saw so many suspects at one murder since Madcap Maisie Clark got shot on the stage of Bensky's Burlicue Theatre. What's the capacity here?"

"Nearly eight hundred seats in both North and South Reading Rooms," Manning replied. "There are probably about two hundred people in this room."

"Any way to get from one room to the other except through that passage at the end there?"

"A member of the staff could go through the delivery-desk enclosure, but nobody else could," Manning said. "I've been here from the moment Mr. Dorwin toppled off the balcony, and I know Tim Cornish has had the exit blocked from the first, so there's been no chance of anyone leaving the South Room."

"We'll let the folks in the North Room go as soon as I've talked to the staff," Kilkenny said.

"Here's something, Kenny," said Dr. Rosenkohl. He handed over the .22 caliber pistol the late H. H. Dorwin had picked up off the floor while Cornish was pursuing Underwood down the stairs. "Found it in his pocket," the medical examiner added.

Kilkenny sniffed the muzzle. Holding the butt through a handkerchief, he examined the gun. "One shot gone," he said.

"And here's something else." Dr. Rosenkohl made the announcement with the triumphant ring of a prospector pouncing on a nugget. He pried open the dead man's fingers. Dorwin's hand had been clasped upon a roughly-triangular scrap of paper.

The ragged edge of the hypotenuse, which was about four inches long, indicated that the fragment might have been torn from the corner of a heavy sheet of white paper. On it was drawn in light-blue ink a series of curious signs and symbols: Shaded curves, strange curlycues, angles, lines, dots, and tiny circles, all in queer combinations. Manning looked at the paper anxiously over the detective's shoulder.

"Hieroglyphics!" Kilkenny declared. "Maybe I'd better start looking for Egyptians!"

"It could be Sanskrit," said Dr. Rosenkohl.

At the word Sanskrit something cold turned over very slowly inside Phil Manning. He peered more closely at the scrap of paper in the detective's hand. Below the cabalistic symbols something had been written in pencil and then rubbed out. It was a single word, something that might be "Dharini" or "Dhavini" or something equally without sense. Manning was pretty sure the strange characters were not Sanskrit, but the restless lump of cold continued to stir in his viscera. He lifted his gaze, seeking Betty Vale.

He saw her almost at once, and the sight of her gave him another unpleasant turn. She was standing at the far end of the room, where he had told her to go, but she was talking to a dark, slick-haired young man who was quite unessential to Manning's personal happiness: Dave Benson.

"Okay, Manning," said Detective Kilkenny, breaking in on Manning's thoughts, "I'm ready to hear your story of what happened."

Manning took a last look at Betty Vale, at her silken legs extending below her beaver coat. They were pretty legs, exciting legs—but there was no doubt that the muscles of the calves, however graceful, were exceedingly well developed. He wondered whether Kilkenny, after he had followed the inevitable course of his investigation, would recognize them as the legs of a dancer.

The tumult and the shouting in the South Reading Room had long since subsided to an uneasy murmur. The late H. H. Dorwin had departed on a stretcher. Another platoon of police had arrived, headed by several gold badges, and including policewomen for searching female suspects. The gold badges had already established headquarters at the table nearest the exit and had started their preliminary questioning of the bookish horde before passing them out.

"All right. Spill it," said Kilkenny. "Where were you standing and just what did you see?"

Manning led the detective to the spot from which he had witnessed Dorwin's plunge.

As he listened, Kilkenny seemed to be memorizing the geography of the South Reading Room. His eyes roved over the west wall, which was a mass of books for its entire length and to a height of about twenty feet, where the great arched windows began. There were twelve tiers of bookshelves—the upper six reached from the gallery which jutted out above the lower six. A staff desk and four equally-spaced doors were all that broke the straight sweep of the gallery, which was just wide enough to allow the doors to be swung inward. Under the gallery was a supplemental bank of shelves, a long three-tiered bookcase which stood well out from the wall and ran the entire length of the room like a counter as high as the top button of a man's vest. There was only one door behind this counter, the one which opened into the short spiral staircase leading to the gallery. The detective interrupted Manning to point to this door, which was about thirty feet south of the oak-barred grating that marked the end of the delivery enclosure.

"When Dorwin took his nose-dive, was that door open?" Kilkenny asked.

"It was ajar, as I remember," Manning replied. "It stood open only a foot or so—not enough for me to see into the stairway."

"You didn't see anybody come out?"

"No."

"What are those other doors up there on the gallery? Do they lead to other stairways?"

"No, they just open on little two-by-four balconies on the outside of the building. They're opened in summer for ventilation."

"The outside balconies are big enough for a man to hide on, aren't they?"

"Yes," said Manning, "but the bronze outside doors are kept locked."

"We'll check, anyhow. Is there any other way to reach the gallery except by that spiral staircase?"

"No . . . except for the cat-walk along the top of that wooden colonnade in front of the delivery desk. It connects with the gallery on the other side of the room. But anyone using that would be in plain view, and I can swear that nobody else was in sight on the gallery or the cat-walk when Dorwin toppled over the railing."

"Then how did the murderer get out of the spiral staircase, since nobody saw him?"

"I don't know," said Manning—but he did know. He had figured it out while he was talking to Kilkenny. It was the only way possible. The murderer, bent double, could come out of the half-open door without being seen, because he—or she—would have been hidden by the parapet of the outer line of bookcases. While all eyes were on the spectacle of Dorwin's plunge from the gallery, he could make his crouching way half the length of the room behind the protection of this low wall of books. When he straightened up, he would be merely someone looking for a book, far from the scene of excitement.

There was no use of giving this theory to Kilkenny now, however. Manning needed an excuse for getting around a bit, to look for that red portfolio.

"I'd better look around on the gallery," he said.

"And what do *you* expect to find on the gallery, Manning?"

"Brain prints." Manning was improvising. "I thought if we looked at the books on this section of the balcony, we might get a line on what sort of man Dorwin was meeting."

Kilkenny pondered briefly. "Can't hurt anything, I guess," he said. "I'll go up with you."

Manning took two steps and then stopped. Halfway across

the room he saw the shabby, unshaven little man whom Dorwin had called James Underwood. Underwood looked furtively about him as he talked, scarcely moving his lips, to a young woman in blue—a sinuous, luscious-looking blonde whom Manning recognized with a start as the woman he had nearly bowled over at the door to his office.

"What did you see?" Kilkenny said.

"The murderer," Manning blurted.

"Where?"

Manning hesitated no longer. "Right over here." He wheeled, starting off with long strides.

"Point him out." Kilkenny walked rapidly beside Manning—until Manning stopped again.

"Funny," he said. "He was standing right there a few seconds ago. He's gone now."

"How do you know he's the murderer? Did you see him kill Dorwin?"

"No, but he took a shot at Dorwin this afternoon, so I assume—"

"You don't have to assume. I can call headquarters and get all the details."

"Headquarters won't have the details," Manning said. "The police weren't called."

"Dorwin got shot at, and he didn't call the police? Say, what are you—?"

"I don't know why," Manning said. "But that gun you found in Dorwin's pocket is the one this man shot at him with. I saw Dorwin pick it up."

"But the man who did it disappeared in thin air?"

"He must be here," Manning insisted. "I just saw him."

"You wouldn't be trying to pull a fast one, would you, Manning?"

"Of course not," Manning replied.

"Then come on," said the detective. "If there really is a guy who shot at Dorwin, he won't get out of the room. I'll have time for him later."

The marble steps that spiraled upward about the short twist of aluminum-painted frame were densely populated by police technicians. Two men were dusting powdered graphite on the walls, and two others were busy with oblique lighting and a long-nosed fingerprint camera. They stood aside to let Kilkenny and Manning past.

"Getting much?" Kilkenny asked.

"Nothing to speak of," said the man with the camera. "We dusted that bronze outside door on the landing, but it hasn't been opened."

"You didn't find anything that might have been dropped?" Manning asked. "No weapon, for instance?"

"Nope. Nothing."

And there was no place within the staircase that the red portfolio could have been secreted.

Manning and the detective stepped out on the gallery. Manning immediately turned his attention to the six tiers of bookshelves to the right of the door. Ostensibly he was examining the titles of the volumes so that he could tell the detective the sort of man Dorwin had been meeting. Actually he was looking to see if the red portfolio had been concealed among the books, or behind them. He was having no luck.

"Good lord! Indians!"

The exclamation came from Detective Kilkenny, who was on his knees, peering at the bottom row of books on the opposite side of the door.

"There's been a scalping," the detective added, taking a pair of tweezers from his pocket. He removed a handsome thatch of wavy red hair which was caught on the edge of the books and had been half hidden by the open door.

"Klawitz!" declared Manning.

"You mean the guy on the radio?"

"That's right. Klawitz, the Highbrow's Winchell. He has at least a dozen toupees he wears to match his moods. Apparently he's in a naked mood today. That's him down there in Seat 274."

Kilkenny looked over the railing at the polished scalp of Fe-odor Klawitz, who was still engrossed in his reading.

"Was this baldy-locks a good friend of the deceased?" he asked.

"Friend? I should say not. Dorwin was trying to get Klawitz jugged for libel."

"He was, eh?" Kilkenny pursed his lips reflectively. "I think we better ask him how he came to forget his pretty auburn hair up here. Come along and prompt me, Manning."

Manning followed the detective down the winding stairs, stepping over and around the technicians. The portfolio probably wouldn't be on the gallery anyhow, because the murderer himself had not appeared there. Manning was convinced, however, that the murderer had wrested the portfolio from Dorwin's hands at the time the trustee was killed. There seemed no other explanation for the scrap of paper in the dead man's fingers—unless, of course, it had been placed there deliberately to misdirect suspicion.

The detective marched straight to Klawitz's table.

"You're Feodor Klawitz?" said Kilkenny.

Klawitz looked up haughtily. He adjusted his monocle as though to say: Naturally, everyone knows who I am.

"You act pretty damn cool and collected for a man about to be arrested for murder," Kilkenny continued.

"Murder?" Klawitz echoed coldly.

"Sure, murder. I guess you've been so deep in your books that you don't even know that H. H. Dorwin was just killed here."

"Oh, that!" The corners of Klawitz's mouth turned down in a sarcastic crescent. "Neither the life nor death of H. H. Dorwin is of any particular importance compared to the work I am now doing. I am preparing to deliver the message of Demosthenes to the American people."

Kilkenny turned to Manning. "Who's this guy Demosthenes?"

"A Greek gent who died about two thousand years before the American people were invented," Manning replied. "Mr. Klawitz probably got his message by direct wire from the Hereafter."

"Bosh!" said Klawitz, flipping over a few pages. "Listen to this: 'There is one safeguard known generally to the wise, which is an advantage and security to all, but especially to democracies as against despots. What is it? Distrust!' True, Demosthenes was trying to rouse the Athenians from their supine smugness, trying to warn them against that other treaty-breaker, Philip of Macedon. But his Philippics are just as applicable today to—"

"Hey, wait a minute," Kilkenny cut in. "Don't change the subject. The dead man I'm interested in ain't a Greek. He's H. H. Dorwin. You killed him, Klawitz."

"Bosh! I'm not given to physical violence."

"You were violent enough in the Map Room, Mr. Klawitz," Manning said.

"I'm sorry about that," said Klawitz, without changing his disdainful expression. "I lost my temper. The stupid librarian insisted—"

"Is this yours?" Kilkenny suddenly produced the auburn toupee.

Klawitz again adjusted his monocle. "Yes," he said, extending his hand to take the wig. "Thank you very much."

"Nothing doing." The detective withdrew the toupee. "Know where I found this, Klawitz?"

"No."

"On the gallery—where Dorwin was killed."

"Really?"

"How did it get there?"

"Dropped from my pocket, undoubtedly. It frequently happens when I bend over. I must find a better way of carrying it."

"So you admit you were on the gallery, do you?"

"Yes, of course. I went there to get a book early this afternoon."

"Klawitz, you went there to meet Dorwin."

"Bosh! I should go nowhere on earth to meet Dorwin. I—" He removed his monocle and smiled with great self-satisfaction. "Now I understand," he said. "You're from the police, of course, and you want to know who killed Dorwin. You've come to the right person. I can give you a strong hint: Look for a woman, preferably a blonde woman. Dorwin was death on women so it is poetic justice that the reverse should ultimately prove true."

"You got any particular blonde in mind?" To Kilkenny, Klawitz was at last beginning to talk sense. Blondes were more comprehensible than Demosthenes.

"Yes," said Klawitz. "There was a blonde young woman on

the gallery this afternoon shortly before Dorwin's death. I remember seeing her cross on that walk above the delivery desk."

Kilkenny looked at Manning.

"Was she one of the library staff?" Manning asked, feeling distinctly uncomfortable.

"Possibly. I've noticed her about frequently these past few days. A rather pretty girl. . . ."

Manning began to perspire.

"She's small and somewhat plump."

Manning felt better.

"When you arrest her, I shall be glad to identify her," Klawitz said. "But now you really must pardon me. I have a broadcast to prepare."

He was again deep in his Philippics.

Kilkenny's jaw set at a threatening angle. Then he relaxed and wagged his thumb at Manning.

"I'll needle him again later," the detective said as he walked away. "And if he's lying about that blonde on the cat-walk, he'll do his next broadcast from Centre Street."

Manning hoped Klawitz was not lying about the blonde. She might well be the sinuous, sensuous, scared little blonde—"a new catalogue girl," Dorwin had called her—who had nearly collided with him coming out of his office and whom he had seen talking to Underwood.

Inasmuch as Detective Kenneth Kilkenny did not insist on his further collaboration on the problem of the blonde on the cat-walk, Manning returned anxiously to the bookshelves at the foot of the spiral stairway. He glanced once toward the south end of the reading room, where he had last seen Betty Vale. She was nowhere in sight, now. There was no one at the south end;

the last nervous remnants of the crowd had congregated near the tables where the gold badges were conducting their inquisition, letting the innocents go home. Betty was probably beyond the open doorway which led into the small adjoining room that housed the American History Collection. Just as probably Dave Benson was with her. Manning didn't relish the idea, yet there was still the matter of the red portfolio with the blue tapes. Reluctantly he returned to the Bibliography shelves, began feverishly pulling out books.

He was halfway through the rows of Whitaker's Circulative Book List when he heard a woman scream.

The scream came from the far southern end of the room. It was muffled. All character was wrung from the voice by shrill, dry-throated terror. Yet, though he had never heard Betty scream, Manning was sure it was the voice of Betty Vale.

A crowd began to surge back toward the southwest corner of the Reading Room, where a short, straight stairway led down to the stacks. Manning followed the sudden movement of people toward the corner. His knees were of flabby cardboard, yet he forced them to function. He was only a few steps behind the hurrying Cornish, far ahead of Detective Kilkenny.

A woman was sprawled on the steps, her blonde head near the locked metal-grid door at the bottom. She was lying in a position of final abandon. Her sheer-stockinged legs pointed toward Manning, one knee crooked slightly with tragic jauntiness. The hem of her skirt was lifted diagonally across her bare thighs to spread its blue pleats over the stairs like an open fan. One arm reached back and down, in the direction her ash-blonde hair seemed to flow in silent, motionless ripples; the other arm was bent, with the back of her hand pressed across her forehead as though to ward off a blow. Her sensuous features were frozen in a grimace of dismay—the same expression that Manning had seen on her face when he almost collided with her outside his office door.

Tim Cornish went down the steps and picked up the girl tenderly in his arms.

Manning backed out through the crowd just as he saw Kilkenny edging in from the other side.

Betty Vale, as he had suspected, was just around the corner of the American History Collection partition. She stood very straight and her face was white. Dave Benson had his arm around her.

"You didn't scream," Manning said to her.

"She screamed," Benson volunteered. "She screamed bloody murder."

"She didn't scream," Manning insisted. "Remember that, Betty. You didn't scream. That other girl screamed."

"The other girl couldn't scream," Betty said. "She was already . . . She was lying on the stairs when I saw her."

"Did you see her fall?"

"No. She was just lying there. I started out, looking for you or Dave, when I saw her. I was afraid to stay in here alone any longer. Who is she, Phil?"

"I don't know," Manning said. "Where was Benson? I thought he was with you?"

"I was looking for you, Master Mind," Benson said. "I thought it was time you used your influence to get the little girl out of this place—but you were busy with the boys in blue."

"I'll take care of the little girl," Manning replied.

"If you let the cops start on her, she'll be here all night," Benson said. "They'll find out she knew Dorwin."

"You know a lot about cops for a musician," Manning said.

"Look." Benson turned on his prop smile. "I played the fiddle for pennies when I was eight years old. I got run off of all the good street corners in Manhattan, and half the apartment house courtyards. By the time I was twelve I knew more cops than anybody in a library will ever know. I didn't learn music out of books. I—"

"Did you know the girl on the stairs?" Manning interrupted.

"Never saw her before—until just now with Betty."

Manning saw Tim Cornish motioning to him. He reached out to touch Betty Vale's cold cheek and said: "I'll be right back, darling. And remember—you didn't see anything and you didn't scream."

"Look, Manning, you'd better—"

"I'll take care of her," said Manning. He walked off to join the guard who was hovering at the fringe of the crowd around the figure of the blonde in the blue dress.

"The detective wants to talk to you," Cornish said.

Manning pushed through to Kilkenny who was looking at the body of the blonde in blue, stretched on a table.

Kilkenny summoned Manning with a wag of his thumb. "Broken neck," he said. "The guard here says she worked in the library. What's her name?"

"I don't know her name," Manning replied. "She's new here. I think she was a catalogue girl."

"Get her name for me," Kilkenny demanded. "Maybe when we know her name we'll know whether she fell down the stairs or got pushed down."

Kilkenny was walking toward the delivery enclosure, toward

the tables where the gold badges were still questioning people. Manning walked beside him.

"She didn't fall down," Manning said.

"She wore damned high heels."

"Why don't you ask Klawitz if—"

"I'm ahead of you, Manning. Klawitz just looked at her. He says she was the blonde on the cat-walk, all right."

"And you still think she fell down the stairs?"

"Why not? Klawitz thinks she killed Dorwin. She could have been trying to sneak out in a hurry."

"That door at the foot of the stairs is locked," Manning said.

"If she worked in the library, she'd have a key, wouldn't she?" Kilkenny asked.

"She might. Mind if I guess, too?"

"Go on and guess."

"I'll guess you ought to start looking for a thin, shabby-looking man in a shiny blue serge suit," Manning said. "He's about five-feet-four. He's got prematurely gray hair that needs cutting, and a two-day stubble on his face. His eyes—"

"I was wondering if you were going to bring him up again, Manning." The detective stopped walking, turned on Manning with bland warning in his grin. "Why didn't you tell me his name was Underwood?"

"How did you know?"

"I get around," said Kilkenny.

"So you've arrested Underwood?"

"Why arrest him? He didn't kill anybody. He couldn't have. He wasn't in the reading room."

"I'm pretty sure I saw him."

"Must of been two other guys," said the detective. "Underwood offered to give himself up to one of our boys in the outside corridor—clear outside the Catalogue Room. Said he knew he'd be suspected eventually so he wanted to tell his story now. They brought him inside and I heard him talking to the lieutenant."

"Underwood is the man who took a shot at Dorwin this afternoon," Manning said, "with that gun you found in Dorwin's pocket."

"You see him shoot?"

"Well, no," Manning admitted. "But I heard the shot. I saw the gun on the floor, where Underwood dropped it, and I saw Underwood running away."

"That's what Underwood said you'd say," Kilkenny observed. "He claims he was coming in the library to get out of the cold, when he heard the shot. He saw Dorwin and he saw the gun on the floor—so he ran. He used to work for Dorwin about a year ago—had some sort of row with him, in fact—so his first impulse was to scram. When he got thinking about it, he came back to tell his story."

"And you let him go—just on his own story?" Manning was incredulous.

"We didn't let him go all the way. He's still in the library. The lieutenant didn't give him a pass for the street door."

"Good," said Manning. "Because that gun—"

"That gun's the reason the lieutenant believes him," Kilkenny broke in. "We're not amateurs, Manning. We traced the number. The gun belongs to a woman. It's covered by a pistol permit issued a year ago to a lady called Viola Smith, who lived with her papa and mama, Mr. and Mrs. H. R. Smith at 120 East 18th Street."

"That's funny," Manning said.

"In case you can't guess," Kilkenny continued, "I'll tell you that some of my boys are digging up the vital statistics on Miss

Smith at this very moment. Now what about the blonde in blue?"

"Here's the man who can tell you about her," Manning replied. He indicated a round little man who was approaching with Tim Cornish. "This is Mr. Leonard of the cataloguing department."

Mr. Leonard was slightly green around the gills, and his bulging eyes announced that he had already seen the blonde in the blue dress. He stammered with excitement as he said to the detective:

"It—it's the girl who came to work last week. Mr. Dorwin recommended her. She—"

"What's her name?" snapped Kilkenny.

"W-why her name was Viola Smith," said Mr. Leonard.

Manning chuckled. "Still think Miss Smith fell down the stairs, Kilkenny?" he asked.

Kilkenny did not answer—perhaps because at that moment a plainclothesman handed him a leaf from a notebook.

As Kilkenny glanced at the sheet of paper, the plainclothesman said: "I just come from Dorwin's office, Kenny. I copied this dope off his desk pad. It's his engagements for today."

"Okay, thanks," said Kilkenny. He stuffed the paper into his pocket—but not before Manning, staring over his shoulder, had read the line: "Betty Vale—4:30 p.m., Library."

Manning moistened his lips. "You don't need me any more now, do you, Kilkenny?"

"You'll stay right with me now," Kilkenny declared. "You've got ideas on this whole business—too many. Come on."

The detective led Manning into the delivery enclosure. The thick, colored trays in which the books came up in the elevators from the stacks were piled on the tables, but the desk staff and the book-laden hand-trucks had been cleared out. The police had evidently shut down the reference department for the night, and Kilkenny was using the delivery desk for his own research.

Three librarians were awaiting Kilkenny, and when Manning saw them, he knew what they had been doing. One of the men was Dr. Flack, whose full black beard was as much an ornament to the Library as his knowledge of Egyptology. The second was Dr. de Winnah, who had only a half-portion of whiskers, but who was a well-known Orientalist. The third was Dr. Bellows, who had no beard and no neck, but had plenty of forehead and oversized eyes which looked even more tremendous through his thick spectacles. Dr. Bellows collected rare dialects of the Near East. Obviously the three experts had been studying the cryptic symbols on the scrap of paper found in the dead hand of H. H. Dorwin.

"Well, gents?" said Kilkenny. "What's the lowdown on the hieroglyphics?"

"They're not hieroglyphs—definitely," Dr. Flack stated.

"And obviously the characters are not cuneiform," added Dr. Bellows.

"There is a slight resemblance to Phoenician in this letter—and this," intoned Dr. de Winnah. "However, I imagine the similarity is purely accidental."

"In other words, you birds are stumped," said Detective Kilkenny. "What do you make of the hen tracks, Manning?"

"Just that," Manning replied. "Phone-booth etchings. Keep-on-ringing-them arabesques."

"I don't quite agree with you, Manning," said Dr. Flack. "There seems to be too much of a plan to allow for a subconscious explanation."

"I suggest the characters may be mathematical or scientific symbols of some sort," said Dr. de Winnah. "Engineering, perhaps."

"Why not try the technical librarians?" said Dr. Bellows.

"I'll try every expert you've got here and then send uptown to Columbia for more if you fellows can't crack it," Kilkenny said.

"I'll crack it," Manning volunteered. He held out his hand. "Let's have the puzzle."

"No soap," said Kilkenny.

"You don't think I can crack it?"

"Sure you can, Manning. But without the diagrams. You'll do it with mirrors."

"Do I get half an hour?"

"I'll give you an hour."

"And the right to circulate?"

"Inside the building. I don't want you to leave the building."

"I just want to get to my office on the second floor. Okay?"

Kilkenny chewed an imaginary toothpick for a few seconds. Then he took a card from his pocket, scribbled on it, and handed it to Manning without a word.

Manning instantly left the oaken corral of the delivery desk and headed south for Betty Vale. He had not taken twenty steps before his path crossed the suavely-gliding course of Dave Benson.

"Hi!" said Benson, with a challenging smile. "Did you fix it for the little girl?"

"She's fixed, all right," Manning replied.

"Then she can leave now with me?"

"She'd better not."

"I expected something like that." Benson expanded his white smile by a full inch. "I'll go to bat for her myself."

"Lay off, will you, Benson?" Manning gripped the musician's

arm. "Betty's in a spot. You know that. So don't even call attention to the fact that she's here."

"Betty's old man knows the District Attorney," Benson said. "I'm going out and start the wheels within wheels."

"The hell you're going out."

"Sure I am." Benson flourished a police pass. "I've just been through the works. All tests strictly negative. Goodbye, Manning."

Manning watched Benson's rhythmic exit. Then he resumed his quest for Betty Vale.

The south end of the Reading Room was deserted again. The mortal remains of Viola Smith, the blonde catalogue girl with a pistol permit, had been spirited away by the medical examiner's office. Two moulage men, with their plaster-dusted fingers and shellac sprayers, came out of the stairway to the stackrooms—apparently empty-handed. Manning waited until they sauntered off. Then he found Betty, still waiting anxiously just around the corner in the American History Collection.

She arose eagerly, but before she could speak, he said hurriedly: "Listen hard, because the police will be looking for you in about half a sec. I've got to know a lot of things before they monopolize you."

"But how—?"

"They've got Dorwin's desk pad. We'll go where we won't be disturbed until I'm good and ready."

"Where, Phil?"

"Take my arm and follow, darling."

Betty obediently hooked her slim fingers about his elbow. They walked to the head of the descending stairs to the stacks. Manning stopped.

"Turn around," he said. "And when I give the word, go down quickly but deliberately."

"Go down—*there*?" Betty's eyes widened. She stared as though she still saw the crumpled body of the blonde in blue sprawled on the steps.

Manning didn't reply at once. He carefully surveyed the room, watching until he thought no one at the other end of the room was looking in his direction. Then he said quietly, "Now."

Betty moved swiftly down the steps. Manning was right behind her, his keys already in his hand. He unlocked the metal-grid door, pushed the girl into the bookstacks ahead of him, closed the door.

He felt Betty recoil against him as though she were shying from the sudden vista of whiteness: the white corridor stretching far between the white end-panels of the steel bookcases, the low white ceiling with its long row of lights, the white marble floor.

"Now," he said. "I want the whole story."

"Of what, Phil?"

"Everything. Let's start with Dhavini."

Betty gasped. "You mean Dharini?"

"All right, Dharini. Who is she?"

"She's King Agnimitra's senior queen. You've been snooping."

"Do you know where I got the name Dharini—even if I got it wrong?"

"Certainly," the girl replied. "From Kalidasa's *Malavika and Agnimitra*."

"No. From a scrap of paper that H. H. Dorwin held in his hand when he was killed. I recognized your writing—the *r* that looks like *a v*—and vice versa. There were hieroglyphics on the paper, too."

Betty paled. She thrust her hands deep into her muff and fixed Manning with round, frightened eyes.

"Did the scrap of paper come from that red portfolio Dorwin was carrying?" Manning continued.

"It—it might have. I guess it did."

"I don't know what happened to the portfolio or when and where it's going to turn up," Manning said. "But sooner or later Detective Kilkenny is going to find out that the hieroglyphics are ballet-dancer's shorthand. Then, when he runs down all the ramifications and finds out that one leads to you, he's going to ask a lot of questions. I want the answers now. Who—?"

"Phil, where in the world did you learn to read choreographic notation?"

"In the Louvain Library. I happened to have a job there re-cataloguing Feuillet, Magny, Guillemin, and the other old masters who invented ways of writing down dance steps with conventional symbols."

"You're wonderful, Phil."

"Save those lovely lapel drawings, darling. So the Kalidasa research was for a ballet?"

"An original oriental ballet—called *Malavika*. I'm going to dance the title role."

"You also did the choreography, apparently. Who did the music?"

The girl lowered her eyes. "Dave," she said.

"Benson!" Manning made an aspirin grimace. "And did Benson by any chance give Dorwin the score of *Malavika* this afternoon?"

"He did not. I did—day before yesterday." Betty looked Manning full in the eyes.

"Why?" Manning demanded.

"Because Hugh Dorwin was going to put up the money to produce the ballet," the girl said. "He was going to put up twenty thousand dollars."

Manning frowned. "That doesn't make sense," he said. "Your Old Man makes a million dollars out of other people's headaches, and still you go to Dorwin for a measly twenty grand. Why?"

"Father doesn't want any ballets in the family," Betty said. "He doesn't approve of careers for women. Not for me, anyhow. He thinks woman's place is on the society page. That's why I haven't even told him I was going to that ballet school in the Village. That's why I didn't even tell you."

"I thought it was because Dave Benson played piano down there," Manning said. "Was it Benson's idea to get Dorwin to angel the ballet?"

"Well, yes. Dave thought if the ballet could be produced and made a hit, Father wouldn't oppose my career any more."

"And might even accept Benson as a son-in-law?"

"Phil, you're being catty. Dave's been terribly sweet."

"All right, he's been terribly sweet," Manning said. "And he went to H. H. Dorwin for the sugar?"

"Yes. He knew Hugh Dorwin was a patron of the arts, but he didn't know he was an old friend of the Vale family. When Hugh heard my name, he immediately offered to put up the money—and I began to get scared. I hurried out to see Hugh, to explain that Father didn't know anything about *Malavika*. I asked Hugh to keep my secret until opening night."

"And H. H. Dorwin made passes at you," Manning suggested.

"Only with his eyes, Phil. But I was afraid of the gleam. I was afraid—well, that his interest wasn't entirely artistic. I told him so. I told him I wanted his help only on a basis of artistic merit. I insisted on bringing him the score, the choreography, the maquettes—in the red portfolio. He was going to give me a decision today. And then I got that anonymous letter . . ."

She looked at Manning with eyes as big as sapphires in Cartier's window. They had been that way just a few seconds before Dorwin died.

"Did Benson know you were meeting Dorwin here today?" Manning asked.

"I don't think so. . . ." The girl spoke hesitantly. "Dave knew that Hugh was to put up the money today, but I don't think I told him where I was meeting Hugh. Phil! What do you mean?"

"Maybe Dorwin was going to change his mind. Maybe he didn't like Benson's score."

"That's no reason for murder, Phil. Dave and I have confidence in the ballet. We know it will get backing on its own. The music is really superb. Everyone who's heard it is crazy about it."

"Who, for instance?"

"Well, a man from Transcontinental Broadcasting heard Dave run over the score on the piano. You know, Dave won second prize with a quartet in the Transcontinental chamber music competition last week. He's got talent, Phil."

"He's got something, all right," said Manning glumly. "Does the name Viola Smith mean anything to you?"

"Nothing."

"All right. Now I have an idea. You wait for me here in the stacks," said Manning.

The girl looked about her uneasily. "Alone?" she asked.

"You won't be alone. You have all the wisdom of the ages to keep you company—sixty-seven miles of it."

Betty smiled nervously. She looked down through the narrow ventilating slits in the marble floor at the base of each stack—narrow glimpses of more stacks on the floor below in monotonous and diminishing repetition, like reflections in a double mirror.

"The catacombs of learning." She shuddered. "Will you be long?"

"I hope not. I just want you to stay out of sight for a little while longer—and still you can truthfully say you hadn't left the building. If you run into some member of the staff, refer them to me. And don't wander too far, because there are seven floors of these stacks, and I might not find you again for years."

"And what if you *don't* find me?"

"I'll find you, darling."

"Phil . . ." The girl lifted her face. Manning bent quickly and kissed her.

He walked away rapidly, the exciting fragrance of her kiss sweet on his lips, the desperation of her fear cold in his heart.

Manning left the stacks through the second-floor exit which led through the headquarters of the cataloguing staff, where hundreds of new listings were indexed and cross-indexed daily. Viola Smith had been working here, making new cards to be added to the millions already on file, but Manning did not tarry. His own office was just down the corridor.

His office was dark as he entered. Groping for the light switch, he could see the falling snow turn to flakes of whirling gold in the glow of the windows across the courtyard. He sat at his desk, lost in thought for a moment. Then he picked up the telephone and called a friend of his in the publicity department of Transcontinental Broadcasting.

"Hello, Joe. This is Phil Manning. Did a man named Dave Benson win a prize in your chamber music contest last week?"

"Benson's real enough," the voice replied. "He won the hundred bucks, all right. Only—What's the library want to know about him, Phil?"

"It's not the library. Just personal curiosity. What's wrong?"

"Nothing's wrong. As a matter of fact, I just got up a release on Benson this afternoon, but I don't know if the front office is ready to put it out yet. Can I call you back, Phil?"

"Do that," said Manning. Instead of waiting, however, he returned to the third floor.

Manning saw Kilkenny and half a dozen other men clustered about a scared, esthetic-looking youth with blue eyes and wavy blond hair.

The detective wagged an imperative thumb at Manning.

"I think we got something here," Kilkenny said. "It says its name is Dexter P. Dexter, Junior. It had a stiletto in its pocket."

"I explained all that," protested the blond young man, pursing his lips. "It's a 15th Century Italian stiletto. There's a coat-of-arms engraved on the hilt. I was doing some heraldic research on the coat-of-arms for a client of mine. I'm a genealogist."

"Mr. Dorwin was stabbed through the left eye with a weapon narrow enough to pierce the—" Kilkenny consulted the back of an envelope. "—the sphenoidal fissure," he continued, "entering the brain to cause death by cerebral hemorrhage. I just got the autopsy report from Dr. Rosenkohl. Dorwin could have lived long enough to stagger up a few stairs and out to the balcony, Rosie says, but he couldn't have yelled, because the motor-speech centers were damaged. This Mr. Dexter with the stiletto knew Dorwin."

"I never saw the man in my life," objected Dexter P. Dexter, Junior in a thin treble.

"You had correspondence with him, Mr. Dexter. You tried to sell him a phoney family tree, complete with coat-of-arms."

"Well, yes," admitted Dexter, blushing. "I did offer to do some genealogical research for him. I thought I had traced his forebears."

"And Dorwin wrote back that he was a self-made man," said Kilkenny. "He said that most of his ancestors never had a decent coat, let alone a coat-of-arms—and that he was going to have you kicked out of the National Genealogical Society and maybe get you jugged for using the mails to defraud. We got copies of the correspondence."

Dexter P. Dexter, Junior lowered his long lashes and pressed his esthetic fingers nervously against his temples. "Evidently I was working on the wrong Dorwin family," he said. "We all make mistakes."

Kilkenny turned abruptly to Manning. "What about those hen-tracks you were going to translate for me?" he demanded.

"No luck yet," Manning replied.

"Then quit trying. I got the answer right here. Those funny marks are what ballet dancers use to write down their jumps and swan-dives. It's like a code."

"No fooling!" said Manning.

"And that's one reason I'm sort of interested in Mr. Dexter, here. He looks like an adagio dancer to me."

"How did you find out about the code?"

"Your music librarian was up here just now and spotted it."

"Very smart of you to send for him," said Manning.

"Hell, I didn't send for him," the detective admitted. "He really came up to tell us that Dorwin was in the Music Library about five minutes before he was killed."

"What was he doing there?"

"He just walked in, picked up an envelope off the librarian's desk, and walked out again. He was alone, the librarian said, and he had a red portfolio under his arm."

"Where did the envelope come from?" Manning asked.

"Somebody left it on the desk while the librarian was busy somewhere else. He didn't see who it was. It was addressed to Dorwin, and the librarian was going to send it over to the Trustees' Room when Dorwin came in and got it. What was in the red portfolio, Manning?"

"Knowing Dorwin, I'd guess etchings," Manning said.

The telephone on the delivery desk rang. A policeman answered and motioned to Kilkenny.

The detective took the instrument, said "Hello, Brannigan," then, except for an occasional grunt, lapsed into scowling silence. When he came back to Manning his face was grim.

"Did you know Viola Smith was married?"

"No."

"Smith was her maiden name," said Kilkenny. "Legally she was Mrs. James Underwood."

"Good God."

"She and Underwood used to work for Dorwin in his private library up on Fifth Avenue. A year ago Dorwin thought up some cute extra assignments for Mrs. U. to do after hours, and Underwood resigned for both of 'em. Dorwin accepted Underwood's resignation, but kept his wife on the payroll. He just shifted her down here a week ago. I don't know why—yet. But the thing begins to make sense now. The old story: Irate Husband Kills Guilty Pair."

"Any more theories, Kilkenny?" Manning sat down.

"Yes." The detective looked at Manning narrowly. "Where's this Betty Vale?"

Manning made what he thought was a gesture of astonishment. "Why ask me?"

"Because she's a friend of yours. The Oriental expert with the goat whiskers said you were with her in the Oriental Library this afternoon."

"That was hours ago."

"She was supposed to meet Dorwin at four-thirty. Did she?"

"Not that I know of. Anyhow, why waste your time on Miss Vale, when you let James Underwood roam the library? Haven't you even tried—?"

Manning broke off suddenly. The lights winked out.

Somewhere in the darkness there was a flurry of sound—running feet, something overturned, an avalanche of books falling, an agonized series of gasps. The noises seemed to come from somewhere close by, perhaps the North Reading Room.

Manning sprang up, his scalp tingling. Through the blackness of the Catalogue Room he could see figures hurrying through the oblong of light that was the door to the third-floor atrium. Flashlight beams stabbed the darkness, swinging, darting forward, converging.

When the lights came on again, Detective Kilkenny was wrestling with a man with sleek black hair.

Even before the black hair slid off to reveal a shiny bald pate, Manning recognized Feodor Klawitz and one of his toupees.

"What," demanded the detective, forcing Klawitz into a chair, "do you think you're doing?"

"But I told you I must leave here."

"And I told you you couldn't," countered Kilkenny.

"But my broadcast—"

"Cancelled," said the detective.

From the next room, Manning heard excited voices. He left Klawitz and the detective, rushed through the passageway at the end of the delivery-desk enclosure.

In a corner of the North Reading Room, men were bending over something near the Photostat Desk, their flashlights focused on the floor.

As Manning approached, someone switched on the heavy chandeliers overhead.

There, propped up against the Photostat Desk, his eyes bulging, his uniform coat ripped open, his white hair disheveled, was Tim Cornish.

The motionless figure of the big guard was surrounded by a litter of papers. The Photostat Desk behind him was a picture of disorder. Drawers had been pulled out and obviously ransacked. Filing cards were strewn over the floor.

Kilkenny came in from the South Reading Room, accompanied by another plainclothesman.

"Nobody could of got out, Kenny," the other detective said. "Not even in the dark nobody could of got out. I was right in the doorway all the time."

"People could have gone back and forth between the North and South Rooms in the dark," Manning suggested. "People by the name of Klawitz, for instance."

"Shut up!" said Kilkenny. "Cornish is coming around."

Tim slowly raised his hand to his head. He blinked. Then he tried to get up.

Two uniformed policemen helped him to his feet. He leaned weakly against the desk, looked from one to the other, then grinned at Manning.

"The law hath not been dead, though it hath slept," Tim said, touching the ends of his white mustache.

"All's well that ends well, Tim," said Manning. He was genuinely relieved. He had thought Tim was the third corpse of the day.

"Wrong, Mr. Manning. *Measure for Measure.*"

"What happened, Tim?"

"Nothing," said the guard. "That is, I don't know exactly. I heard somebody in here—prowling around back of the Photostat Desk, I thought. When I started in to investigate, the lights went out. I felt somebody brush past me, and I grabbed him. Then something cracked me in the head, and I guess I was out for a minute. I think he hit me with a book."

"With a complete Shakespeare," Manning smiled.

"Whoever it was practically undressed you, Cornish," said Detective Kilkenny. "Did he steal anything?"

"Probably not." Cornish felt of his pockets. "Who steals my purse steals—Hey! My keys!"

Keys! Manning's glance swept to the northwest corner of the vast room where, within the glass-walled enclosure of the Theatre Collection, a short, straight stairway led steeply downward. Like the parallel staircase in the South Reading Room, these steps ended at a metal-grilled door to the stackrooms. With Tim Cornish's keys, the killer could open this door—and Betty Vale was in the stacks!

Manning felt the cold perspiration beading his forehead. He said: "Maybe you left the keys in your civvies, Tim."

"I don't think so, Mr. Manning."

"I'll run down and take a look. I'll get the super to open your locker for me." Manning turned questioning eyes to Kilkenny. "Or will it menace the public safety, Chief?"

"Okay. Go on." Kilkenny fixed Manning with a curious stare. "But make it snappy."

Manning hurried out through the Catalogue Room, his heart pounding. He did not go directly to the stacks by the stairs in the corner, because he did not want Kilkenny to know where he was going. It was foolish, perhaps, not to make Kilkenny an out-and-out ally. Now that the killer was probably in the stacks, keeping the police out might be exposing Betty Vale to needless danger. Yet Manning was determined to play his hand alone until he had found the red portfolio with the blue tapes—until he was certain that its discovery would not point a guilty finger at Betty Vale. And he knew now where the portfolio was.

It had to be there, he told himself, as he went down the marble stairs to the second floor. The portfolio had to be in the stacks. That was the only explanation of its disappearance—promptly and completely—from the South Reading Room.

Manning swore at himself for not having thought of it sooner. He was so used to seeing book-laden hand-trucks in the delivery enclosure that he had not noted particularly that one of them had been standing against the oak-barred grating that separated the delivery desk from a corner of the South Reading Room. The grating was only a few steps from the door to the spiral stairway, so that the person who killed Dorwin could have reached it, hidden by the parapet of the outer bookshelves, to push the portfolio—and the weapon—through the oaken bars into one of the book trucks. And Kilkenny, considering the delivery enclosure not to be part of the South Reading Room, had allowed the trucks to be removed. They were in the stack rooms now.

And the murderer evidently considered the time had come to retrieve the evidence—or rather to make doubly sure that it would never be found. Why else would he have stolen a guard's keys? Yes, he was certainly in the stacks, although Manning could not see how he hoped to locate the particular truck, once it had left the delivery enclosure. Manning was not sure he himself could find the right truck in all the six floors and many miles of stacks. It would be a hopeless task. Unless—

Yes, Manning remembered seeing pink tickets on at least one book truck that stood near the delivery desk that afternoon. Books tagged with pink slips were duplicates, of which sufficient copies were already in the reference department. Books tagged with pink slips went directly to the Duplicate Cage in Stack Six, to await transfer to other libraries. Books tagged—

Manning broke into a run. Stack Six was where he had left Betty Vale!

His footsteps made rapid, hollow echoes, like frightened heartbeats, as he entered the stacks. He went directly to the Duplicate Cage, glanced through the metal grille, then passed on. He would come back later. First he hurried to the aisle in which he had left Betty.

She was not there.

The familiar whiteness of the stacks suddenly lost its neat impersonality. The row on row of bookcases were grim bastions behind which lurked unknown perils.

"Betty."

Manning called softly. There was no response, but the sound

of his own voice steadied him. He walked slowly down the center aisle, stopped, and called again.

Again there was no answer—but this time Manning heard something that made his scalp crawl: a muted footstep.

It was the merest whisper of leather on marble, but it told a story of stealth. It was not the light, clicking, high-heeled step of a woman, but a broad, solid, full-soled tread. And the sound seemed to come from the stairs which led down to Stack Five on the floor below.

Quietly, quickly, Manning made for the stairway, went down.

There was no one in Stack Five, either—no one in sight, although the rank after rank of bookcases were a maze that might conceal a battalion. He stood a moment looking about him, his spirits oppressed by the lowness of the white ceiling, the danger of ambush in the vast labyrinth of books. Then he heard the scrape of shoe leather again.

This time the sound seemed to come from directly below him. He dropped to his knees, peered through the ventilating slot. He saw a shadow pass—a dark flicker on the floor below that was gone before he could hope to identify it.

He hurried down to Stack Four.

He had never before noticed the peculiar silence of the stack rooms at night. It was a tomb-like hush, and yet it was alive.

Someone seized Manning's arm.

He whirled, his nerves taut, his fists clenched, his free arm drawn back to strike. Then he went limp.

"Betty!" he breathed.

The girl clung to him. "You're just in time," she said. "One more minute and I'd have gone crazy."

"Why didn't you stay in Stack Six where I left you?"

"I was scared, Phil. I heard somebody walking, and I thought it was you coming back. I started out to meet you—and then I discovered that instead of following someone, I was being followed. I couldn't see anyone, but I could hear him walk a little, then stop—walk again and stop. So naturally my only thought was to get away . . ."

"But everything's all right now?"

"Of course."

"Then let's go back upstairs to Six," said Manning. "I think I know what happened to your portfolio."

Betty held tightly to his arm all the way to the Duplicate Cage. Manning opened the metal door. The little room was packed with hand-trucks. The pink dupe clips decorating the volumes gave a flag-bedecked gaiety to the musty place. Manning rolled out the two carts nearest him.

"There it is!" Betty started forward.

"Don't touch it!"

Manning, too, saw the red covers. He spread a handkerchief over his fingers before grasping the portfolio. As he lifted it from the truck, something fell to the floor with a metallic clang.

"I'll be damned!" he exclaimed. "So that's what stabbed Dorwin."

He bent over a long, slender brass rod with a milled knob at one end. The other end bore dark stains, which might be blood.

"What is it?" Betty asked.

"A spindle from a catalogue drawer," Manning replied. "Funny . . ." He frowned. "It's not from the Public Catalogue Room, either."

"How do you know, Phil?"

"The spindles in the main catalogue drawers aren't like this one," Manning said. "They're smooth all the way up, and you can pull them out by pressing a catch at the end of the drawer. This one is threaded near the knob, so it has to be unscrewed to come out. I wonder—"

Manning interrupted himself to open the portfolio. The blue tapes were untied, so that the red halves fell apart readily—at a torn page of choreographic symbols.

"Dorwin must have just opened it here when he was stabbed," said Manning. Carefully touching only the edges, he flipped over pages of costume sketches, designs for scenery, page after page of cryptic choreographic notation, the ruled sheets of music manuscript . . .

Suddenly he stood up.

"Betty, darling," he said. "I want you to get out of here right away. Do you know where the library print shop is?"

"No."

"It's in the basement. Would you be afraid to go there?"

"Alone?"

"It will be safer than the stacks, unless I miss my guess. And unless the police have shut it up, it will be full of printers working on the next issue of the *Bulletin*."

"All right. I'll go."

"Good. Just ask the foreman for the page proofs on the Dorwin article that I sent him a memo about. Tell him to give you all the pages, including the reproductions of the Russian manuscripts. And don't come back here. Bring them to my office. I'll be there by the time you get there."

He led the girl to the ornate bronze-barred door that led from Stack Six into the vaulted hall of the Oriental catalogue. He watched her walk off toward the arcade of the second floor balcony that looked out on the semicircular abarabesque of the great window of the vestibule.

Then he locked the door and hurried back to the red portfolio. He was looking through its loose pages again when something struck him a crashing blow at the base of his skull.

He pitched forward, sprawled face downward.

Detective Kenneth Kilkenny looked at the crumpled paper the Assistant Medical Examiner placed in front of him. He read the typewritten lines:

> "I received your message, but circumstances which I will explain when I see you make it impossible for me to come to the Music Room at the hour you mentioned. However, I will meet you on the West Balcony of the South Reading Room as soon as you can come."

The signature was a scrawl which Kilkenny could not decipher. Nobody, Kilkenny was convinced, could make anything of the scrawl except Dorwin, who knew the person he had asked to meet him. "Where'd you say this came from, Rosie?" the detective asked.

"Dorwin's trousers pocket," said Dr. Rosenkohl. "Don't know how I missed it the first time over, except it was wadded into a corner. I thought you'd want it, because the typewriter ought to be easy to trace. The second leg of the small *n* is badly nicked."

"I'll say it's going to be easy to trace," Kilkenny agreed. "I got the companion piece to it."

He produced an envelope addressed: "H. H. Dorwin, Esq. To be called for." The second leg of the small *n* in "Dorwin" was nicked.

"One of the boys just dug it out of a wastebasket in this guy Manning's office," Kilkenny added.

"Where's Manning?"

"He don't know it, but he's going to be with us very shortly," said the detective. "I just—Well, well, well, well! Look who's here."

Tim Cornish marched up to the delivery desk, leading a shabby little man in a blue serge suit.

"Here's your James Underwood, Mr. Kilkenny," the guard said. "I caught him in the stacks."

Kilkenny stared at Underwood. The gray-haired derelict was trembling like a man with fever. The tragic lines of his face were etched deeper than ever, and his dark, intelligent eyes were blurred with misery.

"So that's where he was hiding," said Kilkenny.

"I knew he'd be in the stacks as soon as I found my keys were gone," Tim Cornish said. "I couldn't think of any other reason he'd want my keys. So I went clear down and started up from the bottom floor. In Stack Three I discover the king of shreds and patches, just as I'd figured."

"I didn't take your keys," said Underwood at last. "I told you three times that my wife let me into the stacks. I was waiting for her to come and get me."

"He claims he doesn't know his wife is dead," Cornish said.

"I don't believe it. You're telling me this to confuse me . . . to make me give her away. . . ."

"I think you'd better come with me to the morgue, Underwood," said Dr. Rosenkohl.

"Wait a minute, Rosie. I'm not through with him yet," Kilkenny objected. "Why did your wife let you into the stacks, Underwood?"

"I . . . I threatened her," said Underwood. "We were both in the reading room when Dorwin was killed, so I knew that after the shooting of this afternoon, I'd have to get out somehow."

"You told me you had nothing to do with the shooting," Kilkenny said.

"I lied," Underwood admitted. "But I'm not lying now. When Dorwin was killed I told Viola she'd have to get me out through the stacks or I'd—"

Underwood stopped.

"Or you'd tell the police that she was Dorwin's mistress?" Kilkenny prompted.

"Then you knew?"

"We know everything," said Kilkenny. "How long ago did Dorwin give her the brush-off? Two weeks?"

"He asked her to move out of his house about two weeks ago," Underwood replied. "He got her this job in the library. I swallowed my pride and asked her to come back to me, but she was still crazy about Dorwin. She wrote anonymous letters to some girl she thought was taking her place."

"Was the girl's name Vale?"

"I believe it was. Yes. Betty Vale. And Viola wrote threatening notes to Dorwin, saying she'd give their whole history to Feodor Klawitz, who would broadcast it on the radio. She was really beside herself. That was when I decided that the best thing would be to shoot Dorwin."

"And so when you missed, you stabbed him instead?" Kilkenny suggested.

"I swear I didn't! You can hang me for it, and I suppose I'd deserve it, since I did mean to kill him—but as soon as the gun went off I knew I could never take a man's life."

"What about a woman's? What about Viola Smith?" Tim Cornish demanded.

"Why would I kill Viola?" Underwood's voice was a wail. "I loved her."

"That's why," said Kilkenny. "You were jealous. So you killed her and her lover. How did you happen to have her gun?"

"I took it with me when we separated a year ago," Underwood said. "But I didn't kill her. I didn't kill anybody."

"Did she know you shot at Dorwin with her gun?"

"Yes, I told her. I—I threatened to say she was the one who shot at him—unless she let me through the stacks. I didn't want to be found inside the reading room."

"How'd you get back in the stacks?" Kilkenny interrupted.

"I left a door ajar."

"Sounds to me like the lie direct, or at least the lie with circumstance," volunteered Tim Cornish. "Why would this Viola Smith help you out if she thought you killed the man she loved?"

"She knew I didn't kill Dorwin," said Underwood.

"How did she know that?"

"She saw the man who killed him."

"She—*what*?"

"Viola told me she was on the catwalk above the delivery desk just before Dorwin staggered out on that gallery. From her vantage point she could see down behind that outer row of bookshelves—and she saw a man come out of the door to the circular staircase, crouching down so he wouldn't be seen from the floor. She—"

"Who was it?" Kilkenny demanded.

"She didn't know him. He looked up, and she thinks he saw her. But she didn't recognize him. She didn't think she'd ever seen him before."

"Why didn't she tell us all this?" the detective asked.

"She was going to tell you," Underwood said. "She was—God, she *is* dead! I believe it now! She's dead—and that's why."

"Don't let him put on an act for you, Mr. Kilkenny," Tim Cornish said. "I still think he's got plenty to tell about what he was doing in the stacks. Take him down those steps where Viola Smith got her neck broke. Take him down those steps to the stacks and see how he acts."

"That's an idea," Kilkenny agreed. "I got a good mind to take 'em all down there. Brannigan, herd your people over to the head of those stairs, in the corner there. Come on, Cornish."

Phil Manning was stunned as he fell. Even the painful impact of his face against the marble floor did not rouse him from his dazed moment of paralysis. He felt someone leap astride his back, but he could not summon his muscles to action. Before he could fight his way back to full consciousness, long, hard fingers closed about his throat in a tight, strangling grip.

He struggled, but feebly. He could feel his strength ebbing into the agony of darkness, the emptiness of death seeping into his tortured lungs. The claws tightened on his windpipe, digging into his throat.

With a last desperate effort he squirmed, twisted, jabbed back and upward with his elbow. A grunt told him he had struck home. The crushing pressure on his windpipe relaxed for an instant. Air rushed into his aching lungs.

He heard an echo—or was it an echo?—of his involuntary cry.

A sudden lightness on his back told him his assailant had fled.

He heard the confused tramp of many footsteps.

He breathed again and again, hungrily savoring the delicious air. He got painfully to his feet. When he turned around, he saw what seemed to him a crowd pouring out of the stairway from the South Reading Room.

He recognized Detective Kenneth Kilkenny with his gun drawn. He saw Feodor Klawitz, Dr. Rosenkohl, Dave Benson, Tim Cornish, Underwood, the genealogical Dexter P. Dexter, and half a dozen policemen in and out of uniform.

"I might have known it would be you, Manning," said Kilkenny. "You better have a good story."

"I've been catching up on my reading," said Manning.

"You've been catching hell," said Tim Cornish. "You hurt, Mr. Manning?"

"Ay, beyond all surgery, Tim. Would you mind running down to the print shop to see if Betty Vale is all right? I just sent her—"

"I want to talk to that Vale dame myself," Kilkenny interrupted. "I just found out she's a dancer."

"Forget about the girl, Kilkenny. I've dug up the evidence that's going to crack your case," Manning said, "Here's the weapon that killed Dorwin."

"What is it?"

"The spindle from a catalogue drawer."

"Looks sort of long for a dagger," Kilkenny said. "How about it, Rosie?"

"It could have done the trick, all right," said Dr. Rosenkohl, "particularly if the murderer held it short when he jabbed."

"And here's the rest of the page of hieroglyphics to match the torn handful Dorwin was grabbing when he was killed," Manning said.

Kilkenny squinted at the open portfolio on the floor.

"Maybe," he growled reluctantly. "But before I let you sidetrack me again, Manning, I—"

"I'll need only one word to explain this mess," Manning broke in.

"The next word out of you," said Kilkenny, "is going to be written on a typewriter. Bring 'em along, Brannigan. And you, Cornish, show me how to get out of this place. I want to go to Manning's office."

A few minutes later Manning was seated in front of his own typewriter, taking dictation from Detective Kilkenny.

"I received your message," he wrote, "but circumstances which I will explain when I see you—"

"Well, well, well, well!" crowed Killkenny over his shoulder. "That's plenty. The letter *n* has a nick in the second leg. What were the circumstances?"

"There weren't any circumstances," Manning replied. "And there was no nick in the second leg. There was a sock in the head."

"The note that decoyed Dorwin to the gallery to be killed was written on your typewriter. Who wrote it?"

"The man who killed Dorwin, obviously."

"In other words, you admit you killed Dorwin," said Kilkenny.

"I admit nothing of the kind. I admit I dawdled somewhat over lunch today, so that someone might have come into my office and used the typewriter while my assistant and I were out."

"But that wouldn't explain why the envelope addressed to Dorwin was found in your wastebasket."

"Wouldn't it?" Manning frowned. He looked at the dozen people the detective had crowded into his little office. He studied the faces of Klawitz, Underwood, Dexter P. Dexter, Tim Cornish, as though seeking the answer to the question uppermost in his mind: What could be keeping Betty Vale?

The telephone rang. Manning reached for it automatically.

Kilkenny immediately imprisoned his hand before he could lift the receiver.

The detective nodded to another instrument on the next desk.

"Same circuit?" he asked.

"Yes."

"Okay. Answer."

As Manning said "Hello," the detective took up the second phone.

"Hello, Phil. This is Joe Dollar at Transcontinental Broadcasting," said the voice on the wire. "I called to tell you we're putting out that story after all."

"What story?" Manning asked.

"The one I called you about, half an hour ago."

"You didn't call me, Joe."

"The hell I didn't. Are you swacked, Phil? I told you—"

"You didn't tell me, Joe. Somebody else must have answered my phone. Let's have a repeat."

"Say, now that I think of it, your voice did sound funny," Dollar said. "But after all, I had your number, and whoever answered not only gave a good imitation of your voice, but he seemed to know what I was talking about."

"What were you talking about, Joe?"

"That chamber music competition you asked about. I phoned you that a music professor at some freshwater college out in Iowa wrote in to say Benson's quartet was a cold steal from an obscure Bohemian composer named Fibich who died in 1900. The front office was going to keep mum about it, which was what I called to tell you. Then the legal department said we'd better confess we were fooled and make another award, otherwise the Iowa professor might raise a stink and then all the other contestants could sue us. So—Hey, what's going on down there? An air raid?"

Manning did not reply. He dropped the phone and sprang up.

Once again the unfamiliar thunder of gunfire echoed through the marble halls of the library. There were two shots—not the sharp crack of a .22 this time, but the deep-throated roar of a .45, followed by the shrill whine of a ricochet.

Almost instantly Betty Vale ran unsteadily into the little office, white faced and round-eyed with terror. She dropped some papers in front of Manning, then collapsed in a chair, buried her face in her hands and sobbed.

Manning was beside her at once. "What happened?" he said.

"I—I stopped at a phone booth downstairs to call my father," the girl said through her fingers.

"And they shot at you, just because you tried to phone?"

"They—they didn't shoot at me. I was coming up the stairs when the shooting started."

At that moment the target of the police guns appeared in the doorway: Feodor Klawitz, flanked by two bluecoats, with Tim Cornish bringing up the rear.

"He was trying to run out on us," Tim announced, "We stopped him."

"It's an outrage!" declared Klawitz. His effort to look imperious was balked by the fact that his toupee was badly askew over one eye. "I was merely on my way to my broadcast," he said. "I told you that I have never missed a broadcast in my life."

"And I told you you were going to miss this one," said Detective Kilkenny. "Sit down there. You're lucky you didn't stop one of those slugs. And you, Manning, get away from that girl. I got things to ask her."

Manning did not move. He turned to Cornish and said: "Tim, I'm not speaking to Mr. Kilkenny since he wounded my feelings by suspecting me unjustly, so will you tell him I suggest he scurry right out and arrest Mr. David Benson for first-degree murder—if he can catch him."

"Benson, my eye!" said Kilkenny. "I may be dumb, but not that dumb. I don't see how you can fit this guy Benson into the picture."

"I'll draw the diagrams," Manning volunteered. "Open that red portfolio you picked up in the stacks. No, here—to the first page of the music. It's supposed to be an original score that Benson wrote for a ballet that Dorwin was going to finance—$20,000 worth. Now look at this proof-sheet. It's a reproduction of the first page of an unpublished manuscript, a tone-poem by the late Russian composer Scriabin, called *Dance*. Except for the title, Benson's music is a note-for-note steal from Scriabin. Benson evidently found the manuscript in the Music Library and had it photostated; that would explain the raid on the photostat desk which Tim Cornish interrupted. Benson was out to destroy the records. He thought he could get away with stealing the music, since it had never been published. Unfortunately he didn't know that the Scriabin manuscript was part of a collection of Russian manuscripts which H. H. Dorwin himself had presented to the library. That fact had not yet been announced. But Dorwin, of course, recognized the music, and was about to expose Benson as a phony."

"You mean he'd kill a man just to save his reputation as a composer?" Kilkenny objected.

"There was the matter of twenty grand."

"Not with Dorwin dead, there wouldn't have been twenty grand," the detective said.

"With Dorwin dead, the ballet might still pass as a Benson original. He could find another sucker to put up the money."

"He'd already found the money," Betty Vale volunteered. "My father had already put up another twenty thousand. He just told me so on the phone. Dave sold him the idea that if the ballet were produced, it would be a flop—and that I would be cured of wanting a career in the ballet. It was a secret, of course—so that I wouldn't know my father was scheming to give me a lesson in failure, supposedly; actually, so that neither my father nor Hugh Dorwin would know that they were both being used. Dave must have planned to clear out with the whole forty thousand, once he got his hands on the money."

"Nice guy," said Kilkenny.

"Dorwin was to give his decision on the money to Miss Vale this afternoon," Manning continued. "He must also have planned to show up Benson as a transposer, rather than a composer. Evidently the rendezvous was in the Music Library, where Dorwin would confront Benson with the original Scriabin manuscript, and his identical copy. However, the choice of the rendezvous was the tip-off to Benson. He knew that if Dorwin exposed him, he would have no chance of getting away with the money he had already collected from Betty's father. Therefore he wrote that note on my typewriter, and left it on the desk of the music librarian to lure Dorwin into the spiral staircase of the South Reading Room where he could be murdered in privacy."

"Are you sure Dave planned all this in advance, Phil—in cold blood?" Betty Vale asked.

"He must have," Manning replied. "That catalogue spindle he used to stab Dorwin comes from the music catalogue. It's a different type from the spindles in the general catalogue. Therefore Benson must have unscrewed it at the time he delivered the note. He probably carried it under his coat to the spiral staircase, to wait for Dorwin.

"When Dorwin opened the portfolio that contained the plagiarized music—he must have opened it since the tapes were untied when I found it, and since a torn fragment of the portfolio's contents was in his hand when he died—Benson knew the game was up and stabbed Dorwin through the eye.

"Benson ran down the circular stairs, carried the portfolio and the metal spindle to the delivery enclosure, concealed, as he thought, by the outer row of bookshelves, and shoved them through the oaken bars into a hand-truck bound for the stacks. A moment later Dorwin staggered out on the gallery and fell dead.

"We know from Klawitz's story that Viola Smith crossed on the raised cat-walk just before Dorwin tumbled off the gallery. We know from Underwood's story that Viola Smith, from her point of vantage, had seen the murderer come out of the staircase—and that he had looked up and seen her looking at him. He would naturally want to get rid of this only witness at the first opportunity, which was when Miss Smith—or Mrs. Underwood—started back up the steps on which she was killed, just after opening the stackroom door for her husband. Benson must have pushed her down the steps."

"That doesn't explain how the envelope addressed to Dorwin was found in your wastebasket, Manning," Detective Kilkenny said.

"I'll have to guess at that one," Manning said. "But it's a reasonable guess. After your people gave Benson a pass to leave the reading room, he must have gone back to the Music Library to make sure he had left no incriminating evidence. He had not been there since Dorwin picked up the note, remember. Suppose Dorwin had opened the note outside the Music Library and dropped the envelope. Probably he did—and probably Benson picked it up and brought it to this office to deposit in my wastebasket, in order to prompt your boys to match the typewriting with my machine. I'm pretty sure of this, because somebody was in this office within the last hour to intercept a call from my friend at Transcontinental Broadcasting."

"And what makes you think it was Benson who took the call?" Kilkenny demanded, chewing on his imaginary toothpick.

"Two things," said Manning. "First, up to that point, Benson had no reason to think he was suspected. But the call from Joe Dollar would let him know that I was not only on his trail, but also that I'd hit on something that would tie in with his motive for murder: Benson's penchant for stealing other men's music. Second, Benson had a police pass that let him go free of the library. Why would he come back, since the most incriminating piece of evidence seemed well hidden among more than two million books? It must have been that he learned that the evidence contained in the red portfolio was at least suspect. He would have learned by that phone call that I was digging in his garden of plagiarism.

"That's why he came back to ransack the Photostat Desk, to destroy the records of the fact that he had asked for copies of the Scriabin manuscript. That's why he knocked out Tim to steal his keys—to get into the stacks and try to find and obliterate the score for *Malavika*. And that's why, when he found me poring over the red portfolio, he set out to kill me, too. Which reminds me, Kilkenny, that, much as it hurts me, I must thank you for barging in when you did to scare him off. I was a goner. You saved my life."

"Think nothing of it," said Kilkenny. "I guess I'm indebted to you, too, for clearing up a few minor points. There's one more thing, though. Who put out the lights?"

"I did," volunteered Feodor Klawitz. "I wanted to get out for my broadcast. I—" He glanced at his watch. "Ten o'clock! I must get to the studio. Will you permit it, Inspector?"

"Inspector, my eye!" said Detective Kilkenny. "But go ahead. I guess I can always put my hands on you if I need you. Beat it."

Klawitz tucked a book under his arm and left.

"You might even put your hands on Benson, if you hurry," Manning said. "He's probably still hiding in the stacks, after taking a crack at me—although he's had time to get out, thanks to that pass you gave him, Kilkenny."

"He's still in the building, Kenny," Brannigan said. "I just checked with the men on the exits. Nobody's gone out in the last half-hour."

"Then he'll go out wearing bracelets," Kilkenny said. "Brannigan, run up and tell the lieutenant I need fifty more men to comb the building. Meanwhile we'll do a little preliminary combing ourselves. Get moving, men."

"Wait a minute, Kilkenny," Manning said.

"Now what do you want?"

"A pass," said Manning, "for Miss Vale and myself. There's a murderer at large in the library, and he might not like Miss Vale and me any more. I'm taking her out of here."

"Okay," said the detective. He scribbled something on a piece of paper, handed it to Manning, and went out.

Betty Vale watched him go. She stood silent, as though stunned. There was an expression of deep hurt in her eyes. Manning put his arms around her gently.

"Phil, I feel as though Dave had murdered part of me, too," she said slowly. "Knowing that Dave could kill two people is ghastly, of course, but somehow the thing that hurts most is knowing that he could use my faith in him to . . . to . . . Oh, Phil, I feel—well, empty inside. . . !"

"You're probably hungry," Manning said. "Shall we eat?"

"How can you talk of food now, Phil?"

"We might try a little liquid nourishment. I'd like to drink to *Malavika*."

"Poor Malavika. I'm afraid she won't marry King Agnimitra after all!"

"Why not? Personally I think the recasting will be a great improvement. Music by Alexander Scriabin. Choreography by Elizabeth Vale Manning. It will look fine on the program."

"Phil!"

"I'll get my hat and coat," said Manning.

He opened the door to the coat closet—and took a startled step backward.

Betty Vale gasped.

Dave Benson stood in the closet, his usual smile flashing ominously. His hands were pushed into the pockets of his coat. The right pocket, stiffly distended by something long and cylindrical, pointed at Manning.

"Raise your hands! Both of you!" Benson spoke quickly between his white teeth.

"Dave, you wouldn't dare—"

"Won't I?" said Benson. He stepped from the closet and moved between Manning and the door. Manning recognized his own hat and overcoat on Benson. "What can I lose?" Benson demanded.

"What can you gain, Dave?" The girl stared at him with hard-eyed, tight-lipped fury. Her voice was vibrant with cold, deep rage.

"Freedom," said Benson. "I'm going to get out of here. And you're coming with me, Betty." His left hand pulled the brim of Manning's hat lower over his eyes. "Where's that police pass Kilkenny just gave you, Manning?"

"Wouldn't you like to know," said Manning.

"I'm through talking," Benson said. "I'll count to three. It's your last chance. One!"

"Go to hell," said Manning.

Benson did not hear Feodor Klawitz come in behind him. Neither did he see what it was that Klawitz poked into the small of his back. He felt, however, the hard, sharp pressure. He went suddenly limp.

"Hands up, you plagiaristic swine!" Klawitz roared. "You stealer of golden notes, you despoiler of the dead Scriabin's tomb—"

Benson's arms went up promptly. Klawitz lifted the book, the corner of which he had poked into Benson's back. The book crashed down on Benson's head.

"Grave robber!" said Klawitz.

Silently, neatly, like the cloth figure in a puppet show, Benson folded up. He bent first at the knees, then at the hips—rhythmically, elegantly, as became a Benson.

With a yell Manning sprang on the prostrate Benson. His hand dove into Benson's right pocket—and came out holding a large fountain pen.

"The four-flusher!" he said sheepishly.

The yell brought Kilkenny, Cornish, and three policemen

piling into Manning's office. Handcuffs glittered about Benson's wrists almost before Manning had got to his feet again.

"What good angel brought you back, Klawitz?" Manning asked, as he gratefully pumped the hand of the horse-faced radio commentator.

"Angel!" snorted Klawitz. "A stupid policeman. He wouldn't let me out without a pass. He sent me back to get a pass from the Inspector."

"Give him a pass, Kilkenny," Manning said. "Quick—or he'll miss his broadcast."

Once outside the library, Phil Manning and Betty Vale hurried along the street, blinded by the big, wet, stinging snowflakes.

As they sank into curbside drifts and stumbled out again, a tall, familiar figure stalked up beside them.

"What a guy, this Benson, eh, Mr. Manning?" said Tim Cornish. "A man whose blood is very snow-broth; one who never feels the wanton stings and motions of the sense. Know what that's from?"

"No," said Manning. "But I've got one for you, Tim. 'A little warmth, a little light of love's bestowing—' Know the next line, Tim?"

"Gosh, I don't seem to remember. Is that Shakespeare, Mr. Manning?"

"It's George Louis Palmella Busson Du Maurier, and it's from *Trilby*, Tim."

"And the next line, Mr. Manning?"

"'And so, goodnight,' Tim."

QL 696 .C9
Anthony Boucher

William Anthony Parker White (1911-1968) is better known under the pseudonyms he used for his career as a writer of both mystery and science fiction, Anthony Boucher and H. H. Holmes. Under his real name, as well as under his pseudonyms, he established a reputation as a first-rate critic of opera and literature, including general fiction, mystery, and science fiction. He also was an accomplished editor, anthologist, playwright, and an eminent translator of French, Spanish, and Portuguese, becoming the first to translate Jorge Luis Borges into English.

He wrote prolifically in the 1940s, producing at least three scripts a week for such popular radio programs as *Sherlock Holmes*, *The Adventures of Ellery Queen*, and *The Case Book of Gregory Hood*. He also wrote numerous science fiction and fantasy stories, reviewed books in those genres as H. H. Holmes for the *San Francisco Chronicle* and *Chicago Sun-Times*, and produced notable anthologies in the science fiction, fantasy, and mystery genres.

All of Boucher's Golden Age mystery novels were published in the 1930s and 1940s, beginning with *The Case of the Seven of Calvary* (1937), which was followed by four novels featuring Los Angeles private detective Fergus O'Breen, including *The Case of the Crumpled Knave* (1939) and *The Case of the Baker Street Irregulars* (1940). As H. H. Holmes, he wrote two novels in which an unlikely detective, Sister Ursula of the Sisters of Martha Bethany, assists Lieutenant Marshall of the Los Angeles Police Department: *Nine Times Nine* (1940) and *Rocket to the Morgue* (1942), which was selected for the Haycraft-Queen Definitive Library of Detective-Crime Mystery Fiction. His much-loved character Nick Noble, a sad drunk who frequently brushes a non-existent fly from his nose, appeared in numerous short stories.

As Boucher (rhymes with "voucher"), he served as the long-time mystery reviewer of *The New York Times* (1951-1968, with eight hundred fifty-two columns to his credit) and *Ellery Queen's Mystery Magazine* (1957-1968). He was one of the founders of the Mystery Writers of America in 1946. The annual World Mystery Convention is familiarly known as the Bouchercon in his honor, and the Anthony Awards are also named for him.

"QL 696 .C9" was originally published in the May 1942 issue of *Ellery Queen's Mystery Magazine.*

QL 696 .C9

Anthony Boucher

THE LIBRARIAN's body had been removed from the swivel chair, but Detective Lieutenant Donald MacDonald stood beside the desk. This was only his second murder case, and he was not yet hardened enough to use the seat freshly vacated by a corpse. He stood and faced the four individuals, one of whom was a murderer.

"Our routine has been completed," he said, "and I've taken a statement from each of you. But before I hand in my report, I want to go over those statements in the presence of all of you. If anything doesn't jibe, I want you to say so."

The librarian's office of the Serafin Pelayo branch of the Los Angeles Public Library was a small room. The three witnesses and the murderer (but which was which?) sat crowded together. The girl in the gray dress—Stella Swift, junior librarian—shifted restlessly. "It was all so . . . so confusing and so awful," she said.

MacDonald nodded sympathetically. "I know." It was this girl who had found the body. Her eyes were dry now, but her nerves were still tense. "I'm sorry to insist on this, but. . ." His glance surveyed the other three: Mrs. Cora Jarvis, children's librarian, a fluffy kitten; James Stickney, library patron, a youngish man with no tie and wild hair; Norbert Utter, high-school teacher, a lean, almost ascetic-looking man of forty-odd. One of these. . .

"Immediately before the murder," MacDonald began, "the branch librarian Miss Benson was alone in this office typing. Apparently" (he gestured at the sheet of paper in the typewriter) "a draft for a list of needed replacements. This office can be reached only through those stacks, which can in turn be reached only by passing the main desk. Mrs. Jarvis, you were then on duty at that desk, and according to you only these three people were then in the stacks. None of them, separated as they were in the stacks, could see each other or the door of this office." He paused.

The thin teacher spoke up. "But this is ridiculous, officer.

Simply because I was browsing in the stacks to find some fresh ideas for outside reading. . ."

The fuzzy-haired Stickney answered him. "The Loot's right. Put our stories together, and it's got to be one of us. Take your medicine, comrade."

"Thank you, Mr. Stickney. That's the sensible attitude. Now Miss Benson was shot, to judge by position and angle, from that doorway. The weapon was dropped on the spot. All four of you claim to have heard that shot from your respective locations and hurried toward it. It was Miss Swift who opened the door and discovered the body. Understandably enough, she fainted. Mrs. Jarvis looked after her while Mr. Stickney had presence of mind enough to phone the police. All of you watched each other, and no one entered this room until our arrival. Is all that correct?"

Little Mrs. Jarvis nodded. "My, Lieutenant, you put it all so neatly! You should have been a cataloguer like Miss Benson."

"A cataloguer? But she was head of the branch, wasn't she?"

"She had the soul of a cataloguer," said Mrs. Jarvis darkly.

"Now this list that she was typing when she was killed." MacDonald took the paper from the typewriter. "I want you each to look at that and tell me if the last item means anything to you."

The end of her list read:

Davies: MISSION TO MOSCOW (2 cop)
Kernan: DEFENSE WILL NOT WIN THE WAR
FIC
MacInnes: ABOVE SUSP
QL 696 .C9

The paper went from hand to hand. It evoked nothing but frowns and puzzled headshakings.

"All right." MacDonald picked up the telephone pad from the desk. "Now can any of you tell me why a librarian should have jotted down the phone number of the F.B.I.?"

This question fetched a definite reaction from Stickney, a sort of wry exasperation; but it was Miss Swift who answered, and oddly enough with a laugh. "Dear Miss Benson. . ." she said. "Of course she'd have the F.B.I.'s number. Professional necessity."

"I'm afraid I don't follow that."

"Some librarians have been advancing the theory, you see, that a librarian can best help defense work by watching what people use which books. For instance, if somebody keeps borrowing every work you have on high explosives, you know he's a dangerous saboteur planning to blow up the aqueduct and you turn him over to the G-men."

"Seriously? It sounds like nonsense."

"I don't know, Lieutenant. Aside from card catalogs and bird-study, there was one thing Miss Benson loved. And that was America. She didn't think it was nonsense."

"I see. . . And none of you has anything further to add to this story?"

"I," Mr. Utter announced, "have fifty themes to correct this evening and. . ."

Lieutenant MacDonald shrugged. "O.K. Go ahead. All of you. And remember you're apt to be called back for further questioning at any moment."

"And the library?" Miss Jarvis asked. "I suppose I'm ranking senior in charge now and I. . ."

"I spoke to the head of the Branches Department on the phone. She agrees with me that it's best to keep the branch closed until our investigation is over. But I'll ask you and Miss

Swift to report as usual tomorrow; the head of Branches will be here then too, and we can confer further on any matters touching the library itself."

"And tomorrow I was supposed to have a story hour. Well at least," the children's librarian sighed, "I shan't have to learn a new story tonight."

Alone, Lieutenant MacDonald turned back to the desk. He set the pad down by the telephone and dialed the number which had caught his attention. It took time to reach the proper authority and establish his credentials, but he finally secured the promise of a full file on all information which Miss Alice Benson had turned over to the F.B.I.

"Do you think that's it?" a voice asked eagerly.

He turned. It was the junior librarian, the girl with the gray dress and the gold-brown hair. "Miss Swift!"

"I hated to sneak in on you, but I want to know. Miss Benson was an old dear and I . . . I found her and . . . Do you think that's it? That she really did find out something for the F.B.I. and because she did. . . ?"

"It seems likely," he said slowly. "According to all the evidence, she was on the best of terms with her staff. She had no money to speak of, and she was old for a crime-of-passion setup. Utter and Stickney apparently knew her only casually as regular patrons of this branch. What have we left for a motive, unless it's this F.B.I. business?"

"We thought it was so funny. We used to rib her about being a G-woman. And now. . . Lieutenant, you've got to find out who killed her." The girl's lips set firmly and her eyes glowed.

MacDonald reached a decision. "Come on."

"Come? Where to?"

"I'm going to drive you home. But first we're going to stop

off and see a man, and you're going to help me give him all the facts of this screwball case."

"Who? Your superior?"

MacDonald hesitated. "Yes," he said at last. "My superior."

He explained about Nick Noble as they drove. How Lieutenant Noble, a dozen years ago, had been the smartest problem-cracker in the department. How his captain had got into a sordid scandal and squeezed out, leaving the innocent Noble to take the rap. How his wife had needed a vital operation just then, and hadn't got it. How the widowed and disgraced man had sunk until. . .

"Nobody knows where he lives or what he lives on. All we know is that we can find him at a little joint on North Main, drinking cheap sherry by the water glass. Sherry's all that life has left him—that, and the ability to make the toughest problem come crystal clear. Somewhere in the back of that wino's mind is a precision machine that sorts the screwiest facts into the one inevitable pattern. He's the court of last appeal on a case that's nuts, and God knows this one is. QL 696 .C9. . . Screwball Division, L.A.P.D., the boys call him."

The girl shuddered a little as they entered the Chula Negra Café. It was not a choice spot for the élite. Not that it was a dive, either. No juke, no B-girls; just a counter and booths for the whole-hearted eating and drinking of the Los Angeles Mexicans.

MacDonald remembered which booth was Nick Noble's sanctum. The little man sat there, staring into a half-empty glass of sherry, as though he hadn't moved since MacDonald last saw him after the case of the stopped timepieces. His skin was dead white and his features sharp and thin. His eyes were of a blue so pale that the irises were almost invisible.

"Hi!" said MacDonald. "Remember me?"

One thin blue-veined hand swatted at the sharp nose. The pale eyes rested on the couple. "MacDonald. . ." Nick Noble smiled faintly. "Glad. Sit down." He glanced at Stella Swift. "Yours?"

MacDonald coughed. "No. Miss Swift, Mr. Noble. Miss Swift and I have a story to tell you."

Nick Noble's eyes gleamed dimly. "Trouble?"

"Trouble. Want to hear it?"

Nick Noble swatted at his nose again. "Fly," he explained to the girl. "Stays there." There was no fly. He drained his glass of sherry. "Give."

MacDonald gave much of the same précis that he had given to the group in the office. When he had finished, Nick Noble sat silent for so long that Stella Swift looked apprehensively at his glass. Then he stirred slightly, beckoned to a waitress, pointed to his empty glass, and said to the girl, "This woman. Benson. What was she like?"

"She was nice," said Stella. "But of course she *was* a cataloguer."

"Cataloguer?"

"You're not a librarian. You wouldn't understand what that means. But I gather that when people go to library school—I never did, I'm just a junior—most of them suffer through cataloguing, but a few turn out to be born cataloguers. Those are a race apart. They know a little of everything, all the systems of classification, Dewey, Library of Congress, down to the last number, and just how many spaces you indent each item on a typed card, and all about bibliography, and they shudder in their souls if the least little thing is wrong. They have eyes like eagles and memories like elephants."

"With that equipment," said MacDonald, "she might really have spotted something for the F.B.I."

"Might," said Nick Noble. Then to the girl, "Hobbies?"

"Miss Benson's? Before the war she used to be a devoted birdwatcher, and of course being what she was she had a positively Kieran-esque knowledge of birds. But lately she's been all wrapped up in trying to spot saboteurs instead."

"I'm pretty convinced," MacDonald contributed, "that that's our angle, screwy as it sounds. The F.B.I. lead may point out our man, and there's still hope from the lab reports on prints and the paraffin test."

"Tests," Nick Noble snorted. "All you do is teach criminals what not to do."

"But if those fail us, we've got a message from Miss Benson herself telling us who killed her. And that's what I want you to figure out." He handed over the paper from the typewriter. "It's pretty clear what happened. She was typing, looked up, and saw her murderer with a gun. If she wrote down his name, he might see it and destroy the paper. So she left this cryptic indication. It can't possibly be part of the list she was typing; Mrs. Jarvis and Miss Swift don't recognize it as library routine. And the word above breaks off in the middle. Those letters and figures are her dying words. Can you read them?"

Nick Noble's pallid lips moved faintly. "Q L six nine six point C nine." He leaned back in the booth and his eyes glazed over. "Names," he said.

"Names?"

"Names of four."

"Oh. Norbert Utter, the teacher; James Stickney, the nondescript; Mrs. Cora Jarvis, the children's librarian; and Miss Stella Swift here."

"So." Nick Noble's eyes came to life again. "Thanks, MacDonald. Nice problem. Give you proof tonight."

Stella Swift gasped. "Does that mean that he. . . ?"

MacDonald grinned. "You're grandstanding for the lady, Mr. Noble. You can't mean that you've solved that damned QL business like that?"

"Pencil," Nick Noble said.

Wonderingly, Lieutenant MacDonald handed one over. Nick Noble took a paper napkin, scrawled two words, folded it, and handed it to Stella. "Not now," he warned. "Keep it. Show to him later. Grandstanding. . . ! Need more proof first. Get it soon. Let me know about test. F.B.I."

MacDonald rose frowning. "I'll let you know. But how you can. . ."

"Goodbye, Mr. Noble. It's been so nice meeting you."

But Nick Noble appeared not to hear Stella's farewell. He was staring into his glass and not liking what he saw there.

Lieutenant MacDonald drew up before the girl's rooming house. "I may need a lot of help on the technique of librarianship in this case," he said. "I'll be seeing you soon."

"Thanks for the ride. And for taking me to that strange man. I'll never forget how. . . It seems—I don't know—uncanny, doesn't it?" A little tremor ran through her lithe body.

"You know, you aren't exactly what I'd expect a librarian to be. I've run into the wrong ones. I think of them as something with flat shirtwaists and glasses and a bun. Of course Mrs. Jarvis isn't either, but you. . ."

"I do wear glasses when I work," Stella confessed. "And you aren't exactly what I'd expected a policeman to be, or I shouldn't have kept them off all this time." She touched her free flowing hair and punned, "And you should see me with a bun on."

"That's a date. We'll start with dinner and—"

"Dinner!" she exclaimed. "Napkin!" She rummaged in her handbag. "I won't tell you what he said, that isn't fair, but just to check on—" She unfolded the paper napkin.

She did not say another word, despite all MacDonald's urging. She waved goodbye in pantomime, and her eyes, as she watched him drive off, were wide with awe and terror.

Lieutenant MacDonald glared at the reports on the paraffin tests of his four suspects. All four negative. No sign that any one of them had recently used a firearm. Nick Noble was right; all you do is teach criminals what not to do. They learn about nitrite specks in the skin, so a handkerchief wrapped over the hand. . . The phone rang.

"Lafferty speaking. Los Angeles Field Office, F.B.I. You wanted the dope on this Alice Benson's reports?"

"Please."

"O.K. She did turn over to us a lot of stuff on a man who'd been reading nothing but codes and ciphers and sabotage methods and explosives and God knows what all. Sounded like a correspondence course for the complete Fifth Columnist. We check up on him, and he's a poor devil of a pulp writer. Sure he wanted to know how to be a spy and a saboteur, but just so's he could write about 'em. We gave him a thorough going over, he's in the clear."

"Name?"

"James Stickney."

"I know him," said MacDonald dryly. "And is that all?"

"We'll send you the file, but that's the gist of it. I gather the Benson woman had something else she wasn't ready to spill, but if it's as much help as that was. . . Keep an eye on that library though. There's something going on."

"How so?"

"Three times in the past two months we've trailed suspects into that Serafin Pelayo branch, and not bookworms either. They didn't do anything there or contact anybody, but that's pretty high for coincidence in one small branch. Keep an eye open. And if you hit on anything, maybe we can work together."

"Thanks. I'll let you know." MacDonald hung up. So Stickney had been grilled by the F.B.I. on Miss Benson's information. Revenge for the indignity? Damned petty motive. And still. . . The phone rang again.

"Lieutenant MacDonald? This is Mrs. Jarvis. Remember me?"

"Yes indeed. You've thought of something more about—?"

"I certainly have. I think I've figured out what the QL thing means. At least I think I've figured how we can find out what it means. You see. . ." There was a heavy sound, a single harsh thud. Mrs. Jarvis groaned.

"Mrs. Jarvis! What's the matter? Has anything—"

"Elsie. . ." MacDonald heard her say faintly. Then the line was dead.

"Concussion," the police surgeon said. "She'll live. Not much doubt of that. But she won't talk for several days, and there's no telling how much she'll remember then."

"Elsie," said Lieutenant MacDonald. It sounded like an oath.

"We'll let you know as soon as she can see you. O.K., boys.

Get along." Stella Swift trembled as the stretcher bearers moved off. "Poor Cora. . . When her husband comes home from Lockheed and finds. . . I was supposed to have dinner with them tonight and I come here and find you. . ."

Lieutenant MacDonald looked down grimly at the metal statue. "The poor devil's track trophy, and they use it to brain his wife. . . And what the hell brings you here?" he demanded as the lean figure of Norbert Utter appeared in the doorway.

"I live across the street, Lieutenant," the teacher explained. "When I saw the cars here and the ambulance, why naturally I. . . Don't tell me there's been another. . . ?"

"Not quite. So you live across the street? Miss Swift, do you mind staying here to break the news to Mr. Jarvis? It'd come easier from you than from me. I want to step over to Mr. Utter's for a word with him."

Utter forced a smile. "Delighted to have you, Lieutenant."

The teacher's single apartment was comfortably undistinguished. His own books, MacDonald noticed, were chosen with unerring taste; the library volumes on a table seemed incongruous.

"Make yourself at home, Lieutenant, as I have no doubt you will. Now what is it you wanted to talk to me about?"

"First might I use your phone?"

"Certainly. I'll get you a drink meanwhile. Brandy?"

MacDonald nodded as he dialed the Chula Negra. Utter left the room. A Mexican voice answered, and MacDonald sent its owner to fetch Nick Noble. As he waited, he idly picked up one of those incongruous library books. He picked it up carelessly and it fell open. A slip of paper, a bookmark perhaps, dropped from the fluttering pages. MacDonald noticed typed letters:

430945q57w7qoOoqd3. . .

“Noble here.”

“Good.” His attention snapped away from the paper. “Listen.” And he told the results of the tests and the information from the F.B.I. and ended with the attack on Mrs. Jarvis. Utter came to the door once, looked at MacDonald, at the book, and at the paper. “And so,” MacDonald concluded, “we’ve got a last message again. ‘Elsie. . .’”

“‘Elsie. . .’” Nick Noble’s voice repeated thoughtfully.

“Any questions?”

“No. Phone me tomorrow morning. Later tonight maybe. Tell you then.”

MacDonald hung up frowning. That paper. . . Suddenly he had it. The good old typewriter code, so easy to write and to decipher. For each letter use the key above it. He’d run onto such a cipher in a case recently; he should be able to work it in his head. He visualized a keyboard. The letters and figures shifted into

reportatusualplace. . .

Mr. Utter came back with a tray and two glasses of brandy. His lean face essayed a host’s smile. “Refreshments, Lieutenant.”

“Thank you.”

“And now we can—Or should you care for a cheese cracker?”

“Don’t bother.”

“No bother.” He left the room. Lieutenant MacDonald looked at the cipher, then at the glasses. Deftly he switched them. Then he heard the slightest sound outside the door, a sigh of expectation confirmed and faint footsteps moving off. MacDonald smiled and switched the glasses back again.

Mr. Utter returned with a bowl of cheese wafers and the decanter. “To the success of your investigations, Lieutenant.” They raised their glasses. Mr. Utter took a cautious sip, then coolly emptied his glass out the window. "You outsmarted me, Lieutenant," he announced. "I had not expected you to be up to the double gambit. I underrated you and apologize." He filled his own glass afresh from the decanter, and they drank. It was good brandy, unusually good for a teacher's salary.

"So we're dropping any pretense?" said MacDonald.

Mr. Utter shrugged. "You saw that paper. I was unpardonably careless. You are armed and I am not. Pretense would be foolish when you can so readily examine the rest of those books."

Lieutenant MacDonald's hand stayed near his shoulder holster. "It was a good enough scheme. Certain prearranged books were your vehicles. Any accidental patron finding the messages, or even the average librarian, would pay little attention. Anything winds up as a marker in a library book. A few would be lost, but the safety made up for that. You prepared the messages here at home, returned them in the books so that you weren't seen inserting them in public. . ."

"You reconstruct admirably, Lieutenant."

"And who collected them?"

"Frankly, I do not know. The plan was largely arranged so that no man could inform on another."

"But Miss Benson discovered it, and Miss Benson had to be removed."

Mr. Utter shook his head. "I do not expect you to believe me, Lieutenant. But I have no more knowledge of Miss Benson's death than you have."

"Come now, Utter. Surely your admitted activities are a catamount to a confession of—"

"Is *catamount* quite the word you want, Lieutenant?"

"I don't know. My tongue's fuzzy. So's my mind. I don't know what's wrong. . ."

Mr. Utter smiled, slowly and with great pleasure. "Of course, Lieutenant. Did you really think I had underrated you? Naturally I drugged both glasses. Then whatever gambit you chose, I had merely to refill my own."

Lieutenant MacDonald ordered his hand to move toward the holster. His hand was not interested.

"Is there anything else," Mr. Utter asked gently, "which you should care to hear—while you can still hear anything?"

The room began a persistent circular joggling.

Nick Noble wiped his pale lips, thrust the flask of sherry back into his pocket, and walked into the Main library. At the information desk in the rotunda he handed a slip of paper to the girl in charge. On it was penciled

QL 696 .C9

The girl looked up puzzled. "I'm sorry, but—"

"Elsie," said Nick Noble hesitantly.

The girl's face cleared. "Oh. Of course. Well, you see, in this library we. . ."

The crash of the door helped to clear Lieutenant MacDonald's brain. The shot set up thundering waves that ripped through the drugwebs in his skull. The cold water on his head and later the hot coffee inside finished the job.

At last he lit a cigarette and felt approximately human. The big man with the moon face, he gathered, was Lafferty, F.B.I. The girl, he had known in the first instant, was Stella Swift.

". . . just winged him when he tried to get out of the window," Lafferty was saying. "The doc'll probably want us to lay off the grilling till tomorrow. Then you'll have your murderer, Mac, grilled and on toast."

MacDonald put up a hand to keep the top of his head on. "There's two things puzzle me. A, how you got here?"

Lafferty nodded at the girl.

"I began remembering things," she said, "after you went off with Mr. Utter. Especially I remembered Miss Benson saying just yesterday how she had some more evidence for the F.B.I. and how amazed she was that some people could show such an utter lack of patriotism. Then she laughed and I wondered why and only just now I realized it was because she'd made an accidental pun. There were other things too, and so I—"

"We had a note from Miss Benson today," Lafferty added. "It hadn't reached me yet when I phoned you. It was vaguely promising, no names, but it tied in well enough with what Miss Swift told us to make us check. When we found the door locked and knew you were here. . . ."

"Swell. And God knows I'm grateful to you both. But my other puzzle: Just now, when Utter confessed the details of the message scheme thinking I'd never live to tell them, he still denied any knowledge of the murder. I can't help wondering. . . ."

When MacDonald got back to his office, he found a memo:

> The Public Library says do you want a book from the Main sent out to the Serafin Pelayo branch tomorrow morning? A man named Noble made the request, gave you as authority. Please confirm.

MacDonald's head was dizzier than ever as he confirmed, wondering what the hell he was confirming.

The Serafin Pelayo branch was not open to the public the next morning, but it was well occupied. Outside in the reading room there waited the bandaged Mr. Utter, with Moon Lafferty on guard; the tousle-haired James Stickney, with a sergeant from Homicide; Hank Jarvis, eyes bleared from a sleepless night at his wife's bedside; and Miss Trumpeter, head of the Branches Department, impatiently awaiting the end of this interruption of her well-oiled branch routine.

Here in the office were Lieutenant MacDonald, Stella Swift, and Nick Noble. Today the girl wore a bright red dress, with a zipper which tantalizingly emphasized the fullness of her bosom. Lieutenant MacDonald held the book which had been sent out from the Main. Nick Noble held a flask.

"Easy," he was saying. "Elsie. Not a name. Letters L. C. Miss Swift mentioned systems of classification. Library of Congress."

"Of course," Stella agreed. "We don't use it in the Los Angeles Library; it's too detailed for a public system. But you have to study it in library school; so naturally I didn't know it, being a junior, but Mrs. Jarvis spotted it and Miss Benson, poor dear, must have known it almost by heart.

MacDonald read the lettering on the spine of the book. "U.S. Library of Congress Classification. Q: Science."

Stella Swift sighed. "Thank Heavens. I was afraid it might be English literature."

MacDonald smiled. "I wonder if your parents knew nothing of literary history or a great deal, to name you Stella Swift."

Nick Noble drank and grunted. "Go on."

MacDonald opened the book and thumbed through pages. "QL, Zoölogy. QL 600, Vertebrates. QL 696, Birds, systematic list (subdivisions, A-Z)."

"Birds?" Stella wondered. "It was her hobby of course, but. . ."

MacDonald's eyes went on down the page:

e.g., .A2, Accipitriformes (Eagles, hawks, etc.)
.A3, Alciformes (Auks, puffins)
Alectorides, *see* Gruiformes

"Wonderful names," he said. "If only we had a suspect named Gruiformes. . . Point C seven," he went on, "Coraciiformes, see also. . . . Here we are: Point C nine, Cypseli. . ."

The book slipped from his hands. Stella Swift jerked down her zipper and produced the tiny pistol which had contributed to the fullness of her bosom. Nick Noble's fleshless white hand lashed out, knocking over the flask, and seized her wrist. The pistol stopped halfway to her mouth, twisted down, and discharged at the floor. The bullet went through the volume of L. C. classification, just over the line reading

.C9, Cypseli (Swifts)

A sober and embittered Lieutenant MacDonald unfolded the paper napkin taken from the prisoner's handbag and read, in sprawling letters:

STELLA SWIFT

"Her confession's clear enough," he said. "A German mother, family in the Fatherland, pressure brought to bear. . . . She was the inventor of this library-message system and running it unknown even to those using it, like Utter. After her false guess with Stickney, Miss Benson hit the truth with St . . . the Swift woman. She had to be disposed of. Then that meant more, attacking Mrs. Jarvis when she guessed too much, and sacrificing Utter, an insignificant subordinate, as a scapegoat to account for Miss Benson's further hints to the F.B.I. But how the hell did you spot it, and right at the beginning of the case?"

"Pattern," said Nick Noble. "Had to fit." His sharp nose twitched, and he brushed the nonexistent fly off it. "Miss Benson was cataloguer. QL business had to be book number. Not system used here or recognized at once, but some system. Look at names: Cora Jarvis, James Stickney, Norbert Utter, Stella Swift. Swift only name could possibly have classifying number."

"But weren't you taking a terrible risk giving her that napkin? What happened to Mrs. Jarvis?"

Noble shook his head. "She was only one knew you'd consulted me. Attack me, show her hand. Too smart for that. Besides, used to taking risks, when I. . ." He left unfinished the reference to the days when he had been the best damned detective lieutenant in Los Angeles.

"We've caught a murderer," said Lieutenant MacDonald, "and we've broken up a spy ring." He looked at the spot where Stella Swift had been standing when she jerked her zipper. The sun from the window had glinted through her hair. "But I'm damned if I thank you."

"Understand," said Nick Noble flatly. He picked up the spilled flask and silently thanked God that there was one good slug of sherry left.

FOOT IN IT

James Gould Cozzens

Although born in Chicago, James Gould Cozzens (1903-1978) was an easterner, growing up on New York's Staten Island, then attending the Kent School in Connecticut before going to Harvard, from which he dropped out after his first book, *Confusion* (1924), was published during his sophomore year. He quit to write his second novel, then spent a year in Cuba teaching the children of Americans working there. He moved to New Jersey where he spent most of the rest of his life, apart from service in the U.S. Army Air Force during World War II, as far out of the public eye as J.D. Salinger and Greta Garbo.

His more mature work made regular appearances on the bestseller lists, beginning with *The Just and the Unjust* (1942), a crime novel of such excellence that it was selected for the Haycraft-Queen list of cornerstone mystery titles. His military novel, *Guard of Honor* (1949), won the Pulitzer Prize as the best novel of the year—recognition that critics of the time felt was long overdue, regarding it as perhaps the best novel to come out of the war. *By Love Possessed* (1961) was a massive bestseller, nominated for a Pulitzer Prize and adapted into a popular motion picture that starred Lana Turner, Jason Robards, and Efrem Zimbalist, Jr.

As an author whose primary characters were white men of middle or upper middle class, he was attacked as being an old-fashioned religious conservative by such left-wing critics as Dwight MacDonald (in *Commentary*) and Irving Howe (in *The New Republic*), destroying his literary reputation, although Cozzens was apolitical and not religious. Frequently mentioned as a possible Nobel Prize candidate in the 1940s and 1950s, he is largely forgotten and unread today.

"Foot in It" was originally published in the August 1935 issue of *Redbook Magazine*; it was reprinted in the June 1950 issue of *Ellery Queen's Mystery Magazine* with the more familiar (and better) title "Clerical Error."

Foot in It

James Gould Cozzens

THERE WERE three steps down from the street door. Then the store extended, narrow and low between the book-packed walls, sixty or seventy feet to a little cubbyhole of an office where a large sallow man worked under a shaded desk-lamp. He had heard the street door open, and he looked that way a moment, peering intently through his spectacles. Seeing only a thin, stiffly erect gentleman with a small cropped white mustache, standing hesitant before the table with the sign *Any Book 50 Cents*, he returned to the folded copy of a religious weekly on the desk in front of him. He looked at the obituary column again, pulled a pad toward him and made a note. When he had finished, he saw, upon looking up again, that the gentleman with the white mustache had come all the way down the store.

"Yes, sir?" he said, pushing the papers aside. "What can I do for you?"

The gentleman with the white mustache stared at him keenly. "I am addressing the proprietor, Mr. Joreth?" he said.

"Yes, sir. You are."

"Quite so. My name is Ingalls—Colonel Ingalls."

"I'm glad to know you, Colonel. What can I—"

"I see that the name does not mean anything to you."

Mr. Joreth took off his spectacles, looked searchingly. "Why, no, sir. I am afraid not. Ingalls. No. I don't know anyone by that name."

Colonel Ingalls thrust his stick under his arm and drew an envelope from his inner pocket. He took a sheet of paper from it, unfolded the sheet, scowled at it a moment, and tossed it onto the desk. "Perhaps," he said, "this will refresh your memory."

Mr. Joreth pulled his nose a moment, looked harder at Colonel Ingalls, replaced his spectacles. "Oh," he said, "a bill. Yes. You must excuse me. I do much of my business by mail with people I've never met personally. 'The Reverend Doctor Godfrey Ingalls, Saint John's Rectory.' Ah, yes, yes—"

"The late Doctor Ingalls was my brother. This bill is obviously an error. He would never have ordered, received, or wished to read any of these works. Naturally, no such volumes were found among his effects."

"Hm," said Mr. Joreth. "Yes, I see." He read down the itemized list, coughed, as though in embarrassment. "I see. Now, let me check my records a moment." He dragged down a vast battered folio from the shelf before him. "G, H, I—" he muttered. "*Ingalls*. Ah, now—"

"There is no necessity for that," said Colonel Ingalls. "It is, of course, a mistake. A strange one, it seems to me. I advise you strongly to be more careful. If you choose to debase yourself by surreptitiously selling works of the sort, that is your business. But—"

Mr. Joreth nodded several times, leaned back. "Well, Colonel," he said, "you're entitled to your opinion. I don't sit in judgment on the tastes of my customers. Now, in this case, there seems unquestionably to have been an order for the books noted from the source indicated. On the fifteenth of last May I filled the order. Presumably they arrived. What became of them, then, is no affair of mine; but in view of your imputation, I might point out that such literature is likely to be kept in a private place and read privately. For eight successive months I sent a statement. I have never received payment. Of course, I was unaware that the customer was, didn't you say, deceased. Hence my reference to legal action on this last. I'm very sorry to have—"

"You unmitigated scoundrel!" roared Colonel Ingalls. "Do you really mean definitely to maintain that Doctor Ingalls purchased such books? Let me tell you—"

Mr. Joreth said: "My dear sir, one moment, if you please! Are you in a position to be so positive? I imply nothing about the purchaser. I mean to maintain nothing, except that I furnished goods, for which I am entitled to payment. I am a poor man. When people do not pay me, what can I do but—"

"Why, you infamous—"

Mr. Joreth held up his hand. "Please, please!" he protested. "I think you are taking a most unjust and unjustified attitude, Colonel. This account has run a long while. I've taken no action. I am well aware of the unpleasantness which would be caused for many customers if a bill for books of this sort was made public. The circumstances aren't by any means unique, my dear sir; a list of my confidential customers would no doubt surprise you."

Colonel Ingalls said carefully: "Be good enough to show me my brother's original order."

"Ah," said Mr. Joreth. He pursed his lips. "That's unfair of you, Colonel. You are quite able to see that I wouldn't have it. It would be the utmost imprudence for me to keep on file anything which could cause so much trouble. I have the carbon of an invoice, which is legally sufficient, under the circumstances, I think. You see my position."

"Clearly," said Colonel Ingalls. "It is the position of a dirty knave and a blackguard, and I shall give myself the satisfaction of thrashing you." He whipped the stick from under his arm. Mr. Joreth slid agilely from his seat, caught the telephone off the desk, kicking a chair into the Colonel's path.

"Operator," he said, "I want a policeman." Then he jerked open a drawer, plucked a revolver from it. "Now, my good sir," he said, his back against the wall, "we shall soon see. I have put up with a great deal of abuse from you, but there are limits. To a degree I understand your provocation, though it doesn't excuse your conduct. If you choose to take yourself out of here at once and send me a check for the amount due me, we will say no more."

Colonel Ingalls held the stick tight in his hand. "I think I will wait for the officer," he said with surprising composure. "I was too hasty. In view of your list of so-called customers, which you think would surprise me, there are doubtless other people to be considered—"

The stick in his hand leaped, sudden and slashing, catching Mr. Joreth over the wrist. The revolver flew free, clattered along the floor, and Colonel Ingalls kicked it behind him. "It isn't the sort of thing the relatives of a clergyman would like to have made public is it? When you read of the death of one, what is to keep you from sending a bill? Very often they must pay and shut up. A most ingenious scheme, sir."

Mr. Joreth clasped his wrist, wincing. "I am at loss to understand this nonsense," he said. "How dare you—"

"Indeed?" said Colonel Ingalls. "Ordinarily, I might be at loss myself, sir; but in this case I think you put your foot in it, sir! I happen to be certain that my late brother ordered no books from you, that he did not keep them in private or read them in private. It was doubtless not mentioned in the obituary, but for fifteen years previous to his death Doctor Ingalls had the misfortune to be totally blind. . . . There, sir, is the policeman you sent for."

THE MISSING SHAKESPEARE MANUSCRIPT

Lillian de la Torre

Although she worked in several literary fields, the contribution to detective fiction made by Lillian de la Torre (Bueno McCue) (1902-1993) took pride of place in her oeuvre when she imagined how Dr. Samuel Johnson would have handled mysteries. Fortunately, just as Dr. Watson served Sherlock Holmes as the narrator and chronicler of his adventures, Johnson, too, had the perfect biographer in James Boswell.

A life-long devotee of mystery fiction, a scholar of history and crime, and with great passion for the theater, de la Torre began her literary career with well-researched narratives of famous murder cases of the past, such as *Elizabeth Is Missing* (1945) about the notorious Elizabeth Canning Case; *Villainy Detected* (1947), an anthology of eighteenth-century crime; *The Heir of Douglas* (1952), a study of one of the greatest scandals of eighteenth-century England; and *The Truth about Belle Gunness* (1955), unveiling an American serial killer for modern readers.

Combining her affection for history, crime, and the theater, de la Torre wrote an enthusiastically reviewed one-act play, *Goodbye, Miss Lizzie Borden* (1948).

The profound research into old crimes that captivated de la Torre were turned into fiction when she had an argument in which she defended the detective story, pointing out that a good fictional detective has many of the attributes possessed by Dr. Johnson. She then presented the primary elements of famous (and some not-so-famous) historical murders, thefts, kidnappings, and other crimes to Johnson to explain.

Most of the stories about Johnson were originally published in *Ellery Queen's Mystery Magazine* before being collected in book form. The books in the series are *Dr. Sam: Johnson, Detector* (1946), a *Queen's Quorum* title; *The Detections of Dr. Sam: Johnson* (1960); *The Return of Dr. Sam: Johnson* (1985); and *The Exploits of Dr. Sam: Johnson, Detector* (1987).

"The Missing Shakespeare Manuscript" was first published in *Dr. Sam: Johnson, Detector* (New York, Alfred A. Knopf, 1946). It had been acquired and edited previously by *Ellery Queen's Mystery Magazine* but was not published until the July 1947 issue.

The Missing Shakespeare Manuscript

Lilian de la Torre

(Stratford-on-Avon, 1769)

'Twas Dr. Sam: Johnson, in the end, who restored the missing Shakespeare manuscript at the Stratford Jubilee in the year 1769; though in the beginning he would not so much as look at it. In that rainy September, he preferred to hug the fire at the Red Lion Inn.

There he stood, bulky and immovable, holding forth his large, well-shaped hands to the glow of the coals and turning a deaf ear to my perswasions. But if he was stubborn, I was pertinacious.

"Do, Dr. Johnson," I urged, "give me your company to Mr. Ararat's though you come but to scoff."

"I shall not remain to pray, I promise you," rejoined the great *Cham* of literature intransigeantly.

"So much is unnecessary," I replied, "but indeed I have promised we would meet there with Dr. Percy and his young friend Malone, the Irish lawyer."

"This is very proper for Thomas Percy and his scavenging friends," remarked Dr. Johnson, lifting his coat-tails before the blaze, "for they are very methodists in the antiquarian *enthusiasm*. But truly this is ill for a scholar, to run with the vulgar after a parcel of old waste paper."

"Sir, sir," I protested, "the antiquarian zeal of Mr. Ararat has preserved to us a previously unknown tragedy of Shakespeare, 'Caractacus; or, the British Hero'."

"Which little Davy Garrick is to represent in the great amphitheatre tomorrow night. Let him do so. Let us see him do so. Let us not meddle with the musty reliques of the writing desk."

"Musty!" I cried. "Let me tell you this is no musty old dog's-eared folio that has lost its wrappings for pyes or worse, like the ballad-writings Percy cherishes, but a manuscript as fair and unblemished, so Dr. Warton assures me, as the day it came from the bard's own hand. By singular good luck Mr. Ararat is of antiquarian mind, and the manuscript was preserved from a noisome fate in the out-house."

"That it was preserved for Garrick to play and Dodsley to

publish, this is luck indeed; but now that the playhouse copies are taken off, it may end in the out-house for all of me," replied my learned friend. "No, sir; let a good play be well printed and well played; but to idolize mere paper and ink is rank superstition and idolatry."

"Why, sir, you need not adore it, nor look at it if you will not; but pray let us not disappoint Dr. Percy and his young friend."

Dr. Johnson's good nature was not proof against this appeal to friendship; he consented to walk along with me to Mr. Ararat's.

I made haste to don my hat and be off before anything could supervene. As we set off on foot from the yard of the Red Lion, my revered friend peered at me with puckered eyes.

"Pray, Mr. Boswell," he enquired in tones of forced forbearance, "what is the writing inserted in your hat?"

I doffed the article in question and gazed admiringly at the neatly inscribed legend which adorned it.

"CORSICA BOSWELL," read off my learned friend in tones of disgust. "Corsica Boswell! Pray, what commodity are you touting, Mr. Boswell, that you advertize the world of your name in this manner?"

"A very precious commodity," I retorted with spirit, "liberty for down-trodden Corsica. Do but attend the great masquerade tonight, you shall see how I speak for Corsica."

"Well, sir, you may speak for whom you will, and advertize Stratford of your name as you please. For me, let me remain *incognito*. I should be loath to parade about Stratford as DICTIONARY JOHNSON."

"Say rather," I replied, "as SHAKESPEARE JOHNSON, for your late edition of the Bard must endear you to the town of his birth."

"I come to Stratford," remarked Dr. Johnson with finality, "to observe men and manners, and not to tout for my wares."

"Be it so," I replied, "here is material most proper for your observation."

As I spoke, we were crossing the public square, which teemed with bewildered Stratfordians and jostling strangers. The center of a milling crowd, a trumpeter was splitting the air with his blasts and loudly proclaiming:

"Ladies and gentlemen! The famous Sampson is just going to begin—just going to mount four horses at once with his feet upon two saddles—also the most wonderful surprizing feats of horsemanship by the most *notorious* Mrs. Sampson."

A stringy man and an Amazon of a woman seconded his efforts by giving away inky bills casting further light on their own notorious feats. As we strolled on, we met a man elbowing his way through the press beating a drum and shouting incessantly:

"The notified Porcupine Man, and all sorts of outlandish birds and other beasts to be seen without loss of time on the great meadow near the amphitheatre at so small a price as one shilling a piece. Alive, alive, alive, ho."

Behind him came a man leading a large bin, and a jostling crowd following. Dr. Johnson smiled.

"This foolish fellow will scarce make his fortune at the Jubilee," he remarked. "Who will pay a shilling to see strange animals in a house, when a man may see them for nothing going along the streets, alive, alive, ho?"

As we walked along, Dr. Johnson marvelled much at the elegant art of the decorations displayed about the town. The town hall was adorned with five transparencies on silk—in the center Shakespeare, flanked by Lear and Caliban, Falstaff and Pistol. The humble cottage where Shakespeare was born, gave me those feelings which men of enthusiasm have on seeing remarkable places; and I had a solemn and serene satisfaction in contemplating the church in which his body lies.

Dr. Johnson, however, took a more lively interest in the untutored artistry of the townsfolk of Stratford, who had everywhere adorned their houses, according to their understanding and fantasy, in honour of their Bard. We read many a rude legend displayed to the glorification of Shakespeare and Warwickshire. We beheld many a crude portrait intended for the great playwright, and only a few less libels on the lineaments of David Garrick, as we strolled down to Mr. Ararat's.

"This is Garrick's misfortune, that as steward of the Jubilee, he is man of the hour," remarked Dr. Johnson, "for the admiration of Warwickshire has done him no less wrong than the lampoons of London."

"In Shakespeare he has a notable fellow-sufferer," I replied.

JOHNSON "You say true, Bozzy. Alack, Bozzy, do my eyes inform me true as to the nature of the small building, set apart, which someone has seen fit to adorn with the honoured features of the Bard?"

BOSWELL "Your eyes inform you truly. We are approaching the stationer's shop of Mr. Ararat, whose zeal for Shakespeare extends even to adorning the exterior of his out-house with the counterfeit presentment of the Bard."

JOHNSON "Better his face without than his works within."

BOSWELL "Sir, the antiquarian zeal of Mr. Ararat, 'tis said, extends even so far, for he provides for the convenience of his household a pile of old accounts of wonderful and hoary antiquity. The Stratfordians are long dead and gone who bought the paper for which the reckoning still awaits a last usefulness."

JOHNSON "Let Mr. Ararat keep Thomas Percy out of here.

Last year he published the Earl of Northumberland's reckonings for bread and cheese from the year 1512; next year, unless he's watched, I'll be bound, he'll rush to the press with a parcel of stationer's accounts he's *borrowed* from Ararat's out-house."

BOSWELL "Sir, you wrong Thomas Percy. He's a notable antiquarian and his works are much sought after."

JOHNSON "He's a snapper-up of unconsidered trifles, and that young Irishman who's followed him hither is no better. Sir, be it a Shakespeare manuscript or a publican's reckoning, just so it be old, I'd watch it narrowly while Percy is about."

Speaking thus, we turned the corner, when the full complexity of Mr. Ararat's decorative scheme struck us at once. Limned by an unskillful hand, the characters of Shakespeare's plays crowded the ancient facade, dominated under the gabled roof by the lineaments of the Bard, for which the portrait on the necessary-house was clearly a preliminary study. Hamlet leaned a melancholy elbow on the steep gable of the window, Macbeth and Macduff fought with claymores over the front door, a giant warrior guarded the corner post, all endued with a weird kind of life in the gray glare of the sky, for a storm was threatening.

"Ha," said Dr. Johnson, "who is this painted chieftain? Can it be Cymbeline?"

"No, sir, this is Caractacus, hero of the new play just recovered."

JOHNSON "Why has he painted himself like an Onondaga?"

BOSWELL "Sir, he is an ancient Briton. He has painted himself with woad."

JOHNSON "Will little Davy Garrick paint himself blue?"

BOSWELL "I cannot say, sir, though 'tis known he means to present the character in ancient British dress."

JOHNSON "This is more of your *antiquarianism*. Let Davy

Garrick but present a *man*, he may despise the fribbles of the tiring-room."

As we thus stood chatting before the stationer's shop, a strange creature insinuated himself before us. From his shoulder depended a tray full of oddments.

"Toothpick cases, needle cases, punch ladles, tobacco stoppers, inkstands, nutmeg graters, and all sorts of boxes, made out of the famous mulberry tree," he chanted.

"Pray, sir, shall we venture?"

"Nay, Bozzy, the words of the bard are the true metal, his mulberry tree is but dross. You seem determined to make a papistical idolator of me."

"Yet perhaps this box—" I indicated a wooden affair large enough for a writing-desk—"this box is sufficiently useful in itself—"

With a resentful scowl the man snatched it rudely from my hand.

"'Tis not for sale," he mumbled, and ran down the street with his boxes hopping.

"Are all the people mad?" quoted Dr. Johnson from the "Comedy of Errours"; and the shop bell tinkled to herald our entrance into the stationer's shop of Mr. Ararat.

Behind the counter in the dim little shop stood a solid-built man in a green baize apron. He had a sanguine face and thin, gingery hair. This was Mr. Ararat, stationer of Stratford, Shakespearean enthusiast, and owner of the precious manuscript of "Caractacus; or, the British Hero." He spelled out the sign on my hat and gave me a low bow.

"Welcome, Mr, Boswell, to you and your friend."

We greeted Mr. Ararat with suitable distinction. Being made known to Dr. Johnson, he greeted him with surprised effusion.

"This is indeed an unlooked-for honour, Dr. Johnson," cried Mr. Ararat.

"Percy is late," I observed to Dr. Johnson.

"Dr. Percy was here, and has but stepped out for a moment," Mr. Ararat informed us.

We whiled away the time of waiting by examining the honest stationer's stock, and Dr. Johnson purchased some of his laid paper, much to my surprise to good advantage. As the parcel was wrapping Thomas Percy put his long nose in at the door, and followed it by his neat person attired in clerical black. He laid his parcel on the counter and took Dr. Johnson by both his hands.

"We must count ourselves fortunate," he cried, "to have attracted Dr. Johnson hither. I had feared we could never lure you from Brighthelmstone, where the witty and fair conspired to keep you."

"Why, sir, the witty and fair, if by those terms you mean to describe Mrs. Thrale, took a whim that the sea air gave her a megrim, and back she must post to Streatham; and I took a whim not to wait upon her whims, so off I came for Stratford."

"We are the gainers," cried Percy.

Dr. Johnson's eye fell on the counter, where lay his package of paper and the exactly similar parcel Percy had laid down. He picked up the latter.

"Honest Mr. Ararat does well by us Londoners," he remarked, "to sell us fine paper so cheap."

"Yes, sir," replied Percy, possessing himself of his parcel with more haste than was strictly mannerly, "you see I know how to prize new folios as well as old, ha ha."

He gripped his parcel, and during the whole of our exciting

transactions in the house of Mr. Ararat it never left his hands again.

At that moment the shop-bell tinkled to admit a stranger. I saw a fresh-faced Irishman with large spiritual eyes the colour of brook water, a straight nose long at the tip, and a delicate smiling mouth. He was shabbily dressed in threadbare black. The new-comer nodded to Percy, and made a low bow to my venerable friend.

"Your servant, Dr. Johnson," he exclaimed in a soft mellifluous voice. "Permit me to recall myself—Edmond Malone, at your service I had the honour to be made known to you some years since by my countryman Edmund Southwell."

"I remember it well," replied Dr. Johnson cordially, "'Twas at the Grecian, in the Strand. I had a kindness for Southwell."

"He will be happy to hear it," replied Malone.

'Twas thus that I, James Boswell, the Scottish advocate, not quite twenty-nine, met Edmond Malone, the Irish lawyer, then in the twenty-eighth year of his age, who was destined to become—but I digress.

Our party being complete, we repaired into the inner room and were accommodated with comfortable chairs. Seated by the chimney-piece was a boy of about sixteen, a replica of old Mr. Ararat, with a rough red mop of hair and peaked red eyebrows. He looked at us without any expression on his round face.

"'Tis Anthony," said his father with pride, "Anthony's a good boy."

"What do you read so diligently, my lad?" enquired Dr. Johnson kindly, peering at the book the boy held. "Johnson's *Shakespeare!* I am honoured!"

"Nay, sir, 'tis we who are honoured," said Malone fervently.

"To inspect the Shakespeare manuscript in the company of him who knows the most in England of the literature of our country and the plays of the Bard, to read the literature of yesterday in the presence of Dictionary Johnson, who knows the age and lineage of every English word from the oldest to the word minted but yesterday, this is to savour the fine flower of scholarship."

The red-haired boy turned his eyes toward Dr. Johnson.

"Pray, sir," replied Dr. Johnson, "don't cant. In restoring a lost play this worthy boy has deserved as well as I of his fellow-Englishmen."

"Anthony's a good boy," said his father with pride, "he knows the plays of Shakespeare by heart, 'Caractacus' included."

I looked at Anthony, and doubted it.

"Shall you make him a stationer, like his fathers before him?" enquired Dr. Percy politely.

"No, sir," replied Ararat, "he's prenticed to old Mr. Quiney the scrivener over the way. Here, Anthony, fetch my strong-box, we'll show the gentleman what they came to see."

Anthony nodded, and went quickly out of the room.

"This is a great good fortune," said Dr. Percy eagerly, "to see the very writing of Shakespeare himself. We are your debtors that it has been preserved."

"'Tis nothing," but old Ararat began to swell like a turkey-cock. He launched into the story: "The first Anthony Ararat was a stationer in Stratford, like me, and Will Shakespeare was his neighbour. Anthony saved his life in the Avon, and in recompense he had of Will the manuscript of this very play, 'Caractacus; or, the British Hero', to be his and his children's forever. Old Anthony knew how to value it, for he folded it in silk, and laid with it a writing of how he came by it, and laid it away with his accounts and private papers."

"Then how came it to be lost?" enquired Dr. Percy.

"'Twas my grandmother, sir, who took the besom to all the old papers together, and bundled one with another into the shed, and there they lay over the years with the lumber and the stationer's trash. I played in there when I was a boy, and so did Anthony after me. I remember, there was paper in there my father said his grandfather had made when he was prenticed in the paper-mills. But I never turned over the old accountings, nor paid them any heed. But to make a long story short, gentlemen, come Jubilee time I thought to turn an honest penny letting lodgings, so I bade Anthony turn out the lumber in the shed and make a place where the horses could stand. Anthony turned out a quantity of waste paper and lumber, and my mother's marriage lines that went missing in the '28, and the manuscript of 'Caractacus', wrapped in silk as the first Anthony had laid it by. He had the wit to bring it to me, and I took it over to old Mr. Quiney the engrosser, and between us we soon made out what we had. Warton of Trinity rode over from Oxford, and Mr. Garrick came down from London and begged to play it . . ."

The words died in his throat. I followed his gaze toward the inner door. There stood young Anthony, pale as death. Tears were streaming down his wet face. Angrily he dashed the drops from his shoulder. In his hand he held a brass-bound coffer, about the size of the mulberry-wood box the pedlar had snatched from us. Wordlessly, though his throat constricted, he held out the strong-box toward his father. It was empty. We saw the red silk lining, and the contorted metal where the lock had been forced.

The manuscript of "Caractacus" had vanished quite away.

Old Ararat was beside himself. Thomas Percy was racked

between indignation and pure grief. Only Dr. Johnson maintained a philosophical calm.

"Pray, Mr. Ararat, compose yourself. Remember the playhouse copies are safely taken off. You have lost no more than a parcel of waste paper."

"But, sir," cried Malone, "the very hand of the Bard!"

"And a very crabbed hand too," rejoined Johnson, "old Quiney over the way will engross you a better for a crown."

"But, pray, Dr. Johnson," I enquired, "is not its value enormous?"

"Its value is nil. 'Tis so well-known, and so unique, that the thief can never sell it; he can only feed his fancy, that it is now his. Let him gloat. 'Caractacus' is ours. Tomorrow we shall see Garrick play the British hero; the day after tomorrow it will be given to the world in an elegant edition. The thief has gained, Mr. Ararat has lost, nothing but old paper."

But Percy and the Ararats thought otherwise. We deployed like an army through the domain of the good stationer, and left no corner unsearched. We had up the red satin lining of the coffer; we turned over the stationer's stock-in-trade; we searched the house from top to bottom; all to no purpose. In the end we went away without finding anything, leaving young Anthony stupefied by the chimney-piece and old Ararat red with rage and searching, blaming the whole thing on the Jubilee.

We were a dreary party as we walked back to the Red Lion in the rain. Percy and Malone stalked on in heart-broken silence. Having given his parcel into Percy's keeping, Dr. Johnson swayed along muttering to himself and touching the palings as we passed. Alone retaining my wonted spirits, I broached in vain half a dozen cheerful topicks, and at last fell silent like the rest.

Arrived in the court-yard of the Red Lion, Dr. Johnson took his parcel from Percy's hand and vanished without a word. I lingered long enough to take a dram for the prevention of the ague. Percy and Malone were sorry company, quaffing in silence by my side, and soon by mutual consent we parted to shift our wet raiment.

In the chamber I shared with Dr. Johnson (dubbed, according to the fancy of Mr. Peyton the landlord, after one of Shakespeare's plays, "Much Ado about Nothing") I found my venerable friend, shifted to dry clothing, muffled in a counterpane and staring at the fire.

I ventured to enquire where in his opinion the sacred document had got to.

"Why, Bozzy," replied he, "some Shakespeare-maniac has got it, you may depend upon it, or as it might be, some old-paper maniac. Some scavenging antiquarian has laid hold of it and gloats over it in secret."

"I cry your pardon," said Dr. Percy, suddenly appearing at our door. He was white and uneasy still. In his hand he carried a parcel.

"Pray, Dr. Johnson, do you not have my parcel that I brought from Mr. Ararat's?"

"I, Dr. Percy? I have my own parcel." Dr. Johnson indicated it where it lay still wrapped on the table.

Percy seized it, and scrutinized the wrappings narrowly. "You are deceived, Dr. Johnson. This parcel is mine. Here is yours, which I retained in errour for my own. I fear I have disarranged it in opening. Pray forgive me. I see you have opened mine more neatly."

"'Tis as I had it of you," replied Dr. Johnson.

"You have not opened it!" cried Percy. "Well, Dr. Johnson,

now we each have our own again, and no harm's done, eh? We lovers of good paper have done a shrewd day's bargaining, have we not, ha ha ha!"

"I will wager mine was the better bargain," said Dr. Johnson good-humouredly. "Come, open up, let us see."

"No, no, Dr. Johnson, I must be off," and Percy whipped through the door before either of us could say a word.

"Now," remarked Dr. Johnson, "'tis seen that Peyton was well advised to name our chamber 'Much Ado about Nothing'."

The rain continued in a dreary stream, so that boards had to be laid over the kennel to transport the ladies dry-shod into the amphitheatre; but for all that, the great masquerade that night was surely the finest entertainment of the kind ever witnessed in Britain. I was sorry that Dr. Johnson elected to miss it. There were many rich, elegant, and curious dresses, many beautiful women, and some characters well supported. Three ladies personated Macbeth's three witches with devastating effect, while a person dressed as the devil gave inexpressible offence.

I own, however, that 'twas my own attire that excited the most remark. Appearing in the character of an armed Corsican chief, I wore a short, dark-coloured coat of coarse cloth, scarlet waistcoat and breeches, and black spatterdashes, and a cap of black cloth, bearing on its front, embroidered in gold letters, VIVA LA LIBERTA, and on its side a blue feather and cockade. I also wore a cartridge-pouch, into which was stuck a stiletto, and on my left side a pistol. A musket was slung across my shoulder, and my black hair, unpowdered, hung plaited down my neck, ending in a knot of blue ribbands. In my right hand I carried a long vine staff, with a bird curiously carved at the long curving upper end, emblematical of the sweet bard of Avon. In this character of a Corsican chief I delivered a poetical address on the united subjects of Corsica and the Stratford Jubilee.

I cannot forbear to rehearse the affecting peroration:

> *"But let me plead for* LIBERTY *distrest,*
> *And warm for her each sympathetick Breast:*
> *Amongst the splendid Honours which you bear,*
> *To save a Sister Island! be your Care:*
> *With generous Ardour make* US *also* FREE;
> *And give to* CORSICA, *a* NOBLE JUBILEE."

As I came to an applauded close, I heard a resonant voice at my elbow.

"Pray, Bozzy," demanded Dr. Johnson, peering at me with disfavour, "what is the device on your coat? The head of a blackamoor upon a charger, garnished with watercress?"

"That, sir," I replied stiffly, "is the crest of Corsica, a Moor's head surrounded by branches of laurel. But what brings you from your bed, whither you were bound when I left you?"

"Sir," replied Dr. Johnson, "somebody in Stratford is in possession of the missing manuscript of Mr. Ararat. Here I have them all gathered under one roof, and all out of character, or into another character, which is just as revealing. I am here to observe. Let us retire into this corner and watch how they go on. To him who will see with his eyes, all secrets are open."

"Toothpick cases, needle cases, punch ladles, tobacco stoppers, inkstands, nutmeg graters, and all sorts of boxes, made out of the famous mulberry tree," chanted a musical voice behind us. We turned to behold the very figure of the man with the tray. His brilliant eyes twinkled behind his mask.

"Goods from the mulberry tree," he chanted, "made out of old chairs and stools and stained according, toothpick cases, needle cases, punch ladles—"

A blast from a trumpet cut him off. Beside him stood a second mask, garbed "like Rumour painted full of tongues," impersonating Fame with trumpet and scroll.

"Pray, sir," said Dr. Johnson, entering into the spirit of the occasion, "let us glimpse your scroll, whether our names be not inscribed thereon."

The mask withheld the scroll, and spoke in a husky voice: "Nay, sir, my scroll is blank."

"Why, sir, then you are the prince of cynics. What, not one name? Not *Corsica* Boswell? Not Garrick? Not Shakespeare? Sir, were I to betray this to the Corporation, you should stand in the pillory."

"Therefore I shall not reveal myself—even to Dr. Johnson—" replied the mask in his husky voice. He would have slipped away, when one of those spasmodic movements which cause my venerable friend so much distress hurled to the ground both trumpet and scroll. In a contest of courtesy, Fame retrieved the trumpet and my venerable friend the scroll.

"You say true," remarked the last-named sadly, re-rolling the scroll, "on the roster of Fame, my name is not inscribed."

He restored the scroll with a bow, and Fame made off with the mulberry-wood vendor.

"I interest myself much in the strange personages of this assemblage," remarked my philosophical friend. "Alack, there's a greater guy than you, *Corsica* Boswell, for he's come out without his breeches."

I recognized with surprize the fiery mop and blank face of young Ararat, whom I had last seen that morning weeping for the lost manuscript. He was robed in white linen, and carried scrip and claymore. He wore no mask, but his face was daubed with blue.

"'Tis Anthony," said I, "he personates Caractacus, the British hero. Sure he trusts in vain if he thinks to conceal his identity behind a little blue paint."

"To the man with eyes, the heaviest mask is no concealment," replied Dr. Johnson; "sure you smoaked our friends with the scroll and the mulberry wood in spite of their valences."

"Not I, trust me. Fame's husky voice was no less strange to me than the wizened figure of the pedlar."

"The husky voice, the bent figure, were assumed for disguise," replied Dr. Johnson, "but Percy's long nose was plain for all to see, and Malone's mellifluous tones were no less apparent. They thought to quiz me; but I shall quiz them tomorrow."

I was watching young Ararat, with his father the center of a sycophantic group of masks who made lions of them. Young Anthony was as impassive as ever, but his face was as red as his father's. Lady Macbeth plucked at his elbow; the three Graces fawned upon him; in the press about him. I saw the trumpet of Fame and the tray of the mulberry pedlar.

"A springald Caractacus," remarked Dr. Johnson, following my gaze, "how long, think you, could he live in equal combat if his life depended on that dull-edged claymore?"

"Yet see," I commented severely, "how the ladies flatter him, whose only claim on their kindness amounts to this, that through no merit of his own he found a dusty bundle of papers in his father's shed."

"While those who can compose, ay and declaim, verses upon *liberty*," supplied Dr. Johnson slyly, "stand neglected save by a musty old scholar."

"Nay, sir," I protested; but Dr. Johnson cut me off:

"Why, sir, we are all impostors here. Fame with an empty scroll, mulberry wood cut from old chairs and stools! Sir, I have canvassed the abilities of the company, and I find that but one sailor out of six can dance a horn-pipe, and but one more box his compass. Not one conjuror can inform me whether he could tell my fortune better by chiromancy or catoptromancy. None of four farmers knows how a score of runts sells now; and the harlequin is as stiff as a poker. So your Caractacus is an impostor among impostors, and we must not ask too much of him."

I looked at the press around the finder and the owner of the missing manuscript, buzzing like bees with talk and laughter. There was a sudden silence, broken by a bellow from old Ararat. The buzzing began again on a higher note, and the whole swarm bore down on our corner, old Ararat in the lead. He brandished in his hand an open paper.

Wordlessly he extended the paper to my friend. Peering over his shoulder, I read with him:

> "Sir,
>
> The manuscript of Caractacus is safe, and I have a mind to profit from it in spite of your teeth. Lay £100 in the font at the church, and you shall hear further.
>
> Look to it; for if the value of the manuscript is nil, and profits me nothing, as God is my judge I will destroy it. I do not steal in sport.
>
> I am,
>
> Sir,
>
> Your obliged humble servant,
>
> *Ignotus*"

"The scoundrel!" cried old Ararat. "Where am I to find £100?"

"This is more of your antiquarianism," I remarked, "like a knight of old, the miscreant holds his captive to *ransom*."

Dr. Johnson turned the letter in his hands, and held it against the lights of the great chandelier. 'Twas writ in a fair hand on ordinary laid paper, and sealed with yellow wax; but instead of using a seal, the unknown writer had set his thumb in the soft wax.

"Why," says he, "the thief has signed himself with *hand* and *seal* indeed. Now were there but some way to match this seal to the thumb that made it, we should lay the robber by the heels and have back the manuscript that Shakespeare wrote."

"Alack, sir," I replied, "there is no way."

"Nevertheless, let us try," said Dr. Johnson sturdily. "Pray, Mr. Malone, set your thumb in this seal."

"I?" said the mulberry-wood pedlar, drawing back.

"I will," said I, and set my thumb in the waxen matrix. It fitted perfectly. The eyes of the maskers turned to me, and I felt my ears burning. Dr. Johnson held out the seal to old Ararat, who with a stormy mutter of impatience tried to crowd his huge thumb into the impression. 'Twas far too broad.

Dr. Johnson tried in turn the thumb of each masker. The ladies' thumbs were too slender, Malone's too long; but there were many in the group that fitted. Dr. Johnson shook his head.

"This is the fallacy of the undistributed middle term," said he. "Some other means must be found than gross measurement, to fit a thumb to the print it makes. Pray, how came you by this letter?"

"'Twas tossed at my feet by someone in the press," replied old

Ararat. "Come, Dr. Johnson, advise me, how am I to come by £100 to buy back my lost manuscript?"

"A subscription!" cried Fame. "The price is moderate for so precious a prize. I myself will undertake to raise the sum for you."

So it was concerted. Dr. Johnson enjoined secrecy upon the maskers, and Fame with his visor off, revealed as Dr. Percy indeed, bustled off to open the subscription books.

We lay late the next day in the "Much Ado about Nothing" chamber. Dr. Johnson was given over to indolence, and declined to say what he had learned at the masquerade, or whether he thought that the mysterious communication held out any hope that the missing manuscript might be recovered.

The rain continuing, the pageant was dispensed with. We whiled away the hours comfortably at the Red Lion, while Percy and Malone spent a damp day with their subscription books. Representing the collection merely as "for the Ararats," they found the sum of £100 not easy to be amassed. Toward evening, however, they returned to the Red Lion with £87 in silver and copper, and Garrick's promise to make up the sum when the play's takings should be counted.

Dr. Johnson spurned at the idea of buying back mere paper and faded ink. In his roaring voice he *tossed* and *gored* Dr. Percy for his magpie love of old documents, adverting especially to Percy's recent publication of "The Household Book of the Earls of Northumberland."

"Pray, sir," he demanded with scorn, "of what conceivable utility to mankind can the 'Household Book' be supposed to be? The world now knows that a dead-and-gone Percy had beef to the value of twelve pence on a Michaelmas in 1512. Trust me, 'twill set no beef on the table of any living Percy."

The young Irish lawyer came to the unfortunate clergyman's defense, and fared no better. Johnson was in high good spirits as we dined off a veal pye and a piece of good beef (which the living Percy relished well).

We then repaired to the amphitheatre, where Percy had concerted to meet the Ararats with Caractacus's ransom.

Old Ararat would have none of Dr. Johnson's advice, to ignore Ignotus's letter. He was hot to conclude the business, and would hear of no other plan, than to deposit the £100 in the font as soon as the play should be over and the takings counted.

"Then, sir," said Dr. Johnson in disgust, "at least let us entrap Ignotus, and make him Gnotus. Mr. Boswell and I will watch by the font and take him as he comes for his ill-gotten gains."

"We must stand watch and watch," cried Percy. "Malone and I will relieve you."

"Nay, let me," cried old Ararat.

"So be it," assented Dr. Johnson; and we repaired to our respective boxes to see the play.

We shared a box with Percy and Malone. Dr. Johnson grunted to himself when David Garrick made his first entrance on the battlements, wearing white linen kilts and bedaubed with blue paint. In spite of this antiquarianism, I found myself moved deeply by the noble eloquence, the aweful elevation of soul, with which Garrick spoke the words of this play so strangely preserved for our generation. I was most affected by the solemn soliloquy which concluded the first act:

"O sovereign death,
Thou hast for thy domain this world immense:
Churchyards and charnel-houses are thy haunts,
And hospitals thy sumptuous palaces;

And when thou would'st be merry, thou dost chuse
The gaudy chamber of a dying King.
O! Then thou dost ope wide thy honey jaw
And with rude laughter and fantastick tricks,
Thou clapp'st thy rattling fingers to thy sides:
And when this solemn mockery is o'er,
With icy hand thou tak'st him by the feet,
And upward so, till thou dost reach the heart,
And wrap him in the cloak of lasting night."

As the act ended, from the stage box the Ararats, father and son, rose to share the plaudits of the huzzaing crowd.

"Davy Garrick," remarked Dr. Johnson in my ear, "has surpassed himself; and King is inimitable as the Fool."

The second act opened with another scene of King's.

"Alack," cries the lovelorn Concairn,
"Alack, I will write verses of my love,
They shall be hung on every tree . . ."

King turned a cart-wheel, ending with a resounding smack on the rump.

"Say rather," he cried, "they shall be used in every jakes, for by'r lakin, such fardels does thy prentice hand compose, they are as caviare to the mob. I can but compliment thee thus, they do go to the *bottom* of the matter."

The pit roared.

"Ha, what?" exclaimed Dr. Johnson. "Bozzy, Bozzy, where's my hat?"

"Your hat, sir? Why, the play is not half over." Dr. Johnson fumbled around in the dark.

"No matter. Do you stay and see it through. Where's this hat of mine?"

"Here, sir." I handed it to him.

"Whither do you go, sir?" enquired Malone eagerly.

"To do what must be done. Fool that I was, not to see—but 'tis not yet too late." Dr. Johnson lumbered off as the pit began to cry for silence.

We were on pins and needles in our box, but we sat through till Davy Garrick had blessed the land of the Britons and died a noble death, and we joined in the plaudits that rewarded the great actor and the great playwright and the finders of the manuscript. The Ararats were the cynosure of all eyes. It was long till we brought them away from their admirers and down to the church. Percy carried the £100 in a knitted purse. The rain had ceased, and a pale round moon contended with the clouds.

The solemn silence oppressed me as we pushed back the creaking door and entered, and my heart leaped to my mouth when a shadowy figure moved in the silent church. 'Twas Dr. Johnson. He had wrapped himself in his greatcoat, and armed himself with a dark lanthorn. I could smell it, but it showed no gleam.

Without ceremony old Ararat dropped the heavy purse in the empty font and carried young Anthony off for home, promising to return and relieve our watch. I envied Percy and Malone as they, too, departed, with the Red Lion's mulled ale in their minds. They promised to return in an hour's time. Dr. Johnson quenched the lanthorn, and we were left alone in the dark.

I own I liked it little, alone in the dark with the bones of dead men under our feet, and a desperate thief who knows how near? There was no sound. Dead Shakespeare lay under our feet, his effigy stared into the dark above our heads.

We sat in the shadow, back from the font. I fixed my eyes on its pale gleam, whereon the cloudy moon dropped a fitful light through the open door.

I will swear I saw nothing, no shadow on the font, no stealing figure by the open door; I heard nothing, I neither nodded nor closed my eyes. Dr. Johnson fought sleep by my side. The hour was gone, and he was beginning to snore, when the light of a link came toward us, and Percy and Malone came in with the Ararats. Johnson awoke with a snort.

"For this relief much thanks," he muttered. "What, all four of you?"

"Ay," returned Percy, extinguishing the link, "for the Ararats are as eager as we to stand the next watch."

"Let it be so," replied Dr. Johnson, approaching the font, "we will but verify it, that the money is here, and passes from our keeping into yours."

He bent over the font, and his voice changed. "Pray, gentlemen, step over here."

We did so as he made a light and opened his dark lanthorn.

The money was gone. In its place lay a pile of yellowed papers, thick-writ in a fair court-hand.

Beholding with indescribable feelings this relique of the great English Bard, I fell on my knees and thanked heaven that I had lived to see this day.

"Get up, Bozzy," said Dr. Johnson, "and cease this flummery."

"Oh, sir," I exclaimed, "the very handwriting of the great Bard of Stratford!"

"'Tis not the handwriting of the great Bard of Stratford," retorted Dr. Johnson.

Old Ararat's jaw fell. The boy Anthony opened his mouth

and closed it again. By the light of the lanthorn Dr. Percy peered at the topmost page.

"Yet the paper is old," he asserted.

"The paper may be old," replied Dr. Johnson, "yet the words are new."

"Nay, Dr. Johnson," cried old Mr. Ararat, "this is merely to affect singularity. Eminent men from London have certified that my manuscript is genuine, including David Garrick and Dr. Warton."

"Garrick and Warton are deceived," returned Dr. Johnson sternly. "'Caractacus; or, the British Hero' is a modern forgery, end no ancient play."

"Pray, sir, how do you make that good?" enquired Malone.

"I knew it," replied Dr. Johnson, "when I heard King use a word Shakespeare never heard—'mob'—a word shortened from 'mobile' long after Shakespeare died. Nor would Shakespeare have understood the verb 'to compliment'."

"Then," said I, "the thief has had his trouble for his pains, for he has stolen but waste paper indeed."

"Not so," replied Dr. Johnson, "the thief has come nigh to achieving his object, for the thief and the forger are one."

"Name him," cried Dr. Percy. All eyes turned to old Ararat. His face shewed the beginnings of a dumb misery, but no guilt. Anthony's face might have been carved out of a pumpkin.

"If," said Dr. Johnson slowly, "if there were in Stratford a young man, apprenticed to a scrivener and adept with his pen; a young man who has the plays of Shakespeare by heart; and if that young man found as it might be a packet of old paper unused among the dead stationers' gear; is it unreasonable to suppose that that young man was tempted to try out his skill at writing like Shakespeare? And when his skill proved more than adequate, and the play 'Caractacus' was composed and indited, and the Jubilee had raised interest in Shakespeare to fever pitch—what must have been the temptation to put forward the manuscript as genuine?"

"Yet why should he steal his own manuscript?"

"For fear of what has happened," replied Dr. Johnson, "for fear that Dictionary Johnson, the editor of Shakespeare, with his special knowledge might scrutinize the manuscript and detect the imposture."

Old Ararat's face was purple.

"Pray, sir," said Dr. Johnson, "moderate your anger. The boy is a clever boy, and full of promise. Let him be honest from this time forward."

Old Ararat looked at his son, and his jaw worked. "But, Dr. Johnson," cried Percy, "the hundred pounds!"

Anthony Ararat fell on his knees and raised his hand to Heaven.

"I swear before God," he cried vibrantly, "that I never touched the hundred pounds."

It was the first word I had heard out of Anthony. By the fitful light of the lanthorn I stared in amazement at the expressionless face. The boy spoke like a player.

"Believe me, father," cried Anthony earnestly, still on his knees by the font, "I know nothing of the hundred pounds; nor do I know how the manuscript came to be exchanged for the money, for indeed I never meant to restore it until Dr. Johnson was once more far from Stratford."

"He speaks truth," said Dr. Johnson, "for here is the hundred pounds, and it was I who laid the manuscript in the font."

He drew the purse from his capacious pocket and handed it to Dr. Percy.

"How came you by the manuscript?" asked Percy, accepting of the purse.

"It was not far to seek. The forger was the thief. It was likely that the finder was the forger. If Malone's panegyric on my learning frightened him into sequestering the manuscript to prevent it from falling under my eye, then it must have been hid between the time young Anthony left the shop and the time he returned with the empty coffer. He was gone long enough for Mr. Ararat to spin us his long-winded tale. In that space of time he hid the manuscript—surely no further afield than his father's out-buildings. When he came in to us his face and shoulders were wet with rain."

"Tears, surely?"

"Why, his eyes were full of tears. The boy is a comedian. But the drops on his shoulders never fell from his eyes; they were raindrops."

"But, Dr. Johnson," put in Edmond Malone, "we searched the out-buildings thoroughly, and the manuscript was not to be found."

"The manuscript," replied Dr. Johnson, "lay in plain sight before your eyes, and you passed it by without seeing it."

"How could we?" cried Malone, "we turned over the old papers in the shed."

"Did you turn over the other old papers?"

"There were no other old papers."

"There were," said Dr. Percy suddenly, "for when I visited the—the necessary-house, I turned over a pile of old accounts of the greatest interest, put to this infamous use by the carelessness of the householder. I—ah—" his voice trailed off.

"The forged sheets of 'Caractacus' were hastily thrust among them," said Dr. Johnson. "I guessed so much when I heard the allusion to the jakes as the destination of bad poetry. What more likely hiding-place for a day or two, till Dr. Johnson be far from Stratford once more? In short, I left the play and hurried thither, and found the pages undisturbed where young Ararat had thrust them into the heart of the pile."

"Yet if you only meant to sequester the writings, boy," said Dr. Percy sternly, "how came you to offer to barter them for money?"

Anthony rose to his feet.

"Sir," he said respectfully, "I never meant to touch the money. But Dr. Johnson saw clearly, and said so, that 'twas no theft for profit; and I feared that such thoughts might lead him to me. I saw a way by which a thief might profit, and I wrote the letter and dropped it at my father's feet that the deed might seem after all the work of a real thief. Consider my apprehension, sir," he turned to Dr. Johnson, "when you fitted my thumb into the impression it had made."

Dr. Johnson shook his head.

"Too many thumbs fitted it," he said. "Another way must be found to fit a thumb to its print. 'Twas so, too, with the paper. 'Twas clearly from your father's shop; but Percy and I and half Stratford were furnished with the same paper. Again the undistributed middle term."

"Pray, sir, how came you to spare me in your thoughts?" enquired old Ararat.

"I acquitted you," replied Dr. Johnson, "because after Malone's eulogy you never left my side; nor did your thumb fit the print in the wax."

"Pray, Dr. Johnson," added Malone, "coming down here from Mr. Ararat's necessary-house with the manuscript in your pocket, why did you play out the farce? Why not reveal all at once?"

"To amuse Mr. Boswell," replied my friend with a broad smile. "I thought an hour's watch by the bones of Shakespeare, and a dramatic discovery at its end, would give him a rich range of those sensations native to a man of sensibility, and enrich those notes he is constantly taking of my proceedings."

In the laugh that followed at my expense, the Ararats sullenly took themselves off, and we four repaired to the Red Lion.

"Sir," said young Malone, taking leave of us at the door of "Much Ado about Nothing," "this is a lesson in the detection of imposture which I will never forget."

"Sir," said Dr. Johnson, "you are most obliging. Be sure, sir, that I shall stand by you in your every endeavour to make known the truth. Pray, Dr. Percy, accept of the forged manuscript as a memento of the pitfalls of *antiquarianism.*"

Dr. Percy accepted with a smile, and we parted on most cordial terms.

"I blush to confess it," I remarked as we prepared to retire, "but I made sure that Dr. Percy was carrying stolen documents about with him in yonder folio-sized packet he was so particular with."

"So he was," remarked Dr. Johnson. "Therefore I exchanged packets with him. I knew with certainty then that Thomas Percy had not stolen the Shakespeare manuscript, for all his antiquarian light fingers."

"How so?" I enquired.

"Because I knew what he *had* stolen."

"What?"

"A household reckoning of the first Anthony Ararat, showing that the good stationer's family consumed an unconscionable quantity of small beer during the year 1614. The magpie clergyman had filched it from old Ararat's necessary-house!"

[Barring larceny, this is the story of William Henry Ireland and his amazing *Vortigern* (1796), transferred to Garrick's Shakespeare Jubilee, which Johnson did not really attend, but Boswell did, blatantly accoutered as described.]

STATE FAIR MURDER

Frank Gruber

In a field in which pulp writers needed to be churning out thousands of words a day in order to earn a living, few were as prolific as Frank Gruber (1904-1969) who, at the peak of his career, produced three or four full-length novels a year, many about series characters Johnny Fletcher and his sidekick, Sam Cragg, numerous short stories, many featuring Oliver Quade, "the Human Encyclopedia," and screenplays, including such near-classics as *The Mask of Dimitrios*, *Terror by Night* and, with Steve Fisher, *Johnny Angel*. He also wrote two dozen western novels.

In addition to a relentless work ethic and a fertile imagination, he developed an 11-point formula for his novels which certainly helped speed the writing process. In his autobiography, *The Pulp Jungle*, which is also an informal history of pulp magazines and the era in which they flourished, he outlined the formula for his mystery stories.

The successful adventure, he believed, needed a colorful hero, a theme with information the reader is unlikely to know, a villain more powerful than the hero, a vivid background for the action, an unusual murder method or unexpected circumstances surrounding the crime, unusual variations on the common motives of greed and hate, a well-hidden clue, a trick or twist that will snatch victory form the jaws of defeat, constantly moving action, a protagonist who has a personal involvement, and a smashing climax. These key points, of course, may well describe all of pulp fiction—and a lot of later adventure and crime stories as well.

The Oliver Quade series follows a formula in which the Human Encyclopedia and his constant sidekick, Charlie Boston, are broke and find a new venue to sell Quade's book, *Compendium of Human Knowledge* from a suitcase that the muscular Boston carries with him. Quade's loud voice, proclaiming himself to be the smartest man in the world, challenges his audience to ask him any question on any subject, and he answers correctly the most improbable and arcane queries thrown his way, after which he offers the books so that his listeners will be as smart as he is.

"State Fair Murder" was originally published in the February 1939 issue of *Black Mask*; it was first collected in *Brass Knuckles* (Los Angeles, Sherbourne Press, 1966).

State Fair Murder

Frank Gruber

HE WAS here again. He saw the bright new banners: *Minnesota State Fair*, and a wave of nostalgia swept through him. There was sunshine and the clacking of turnstiles. Along the Midway he saw the same faces, heard familiar voices; the Kewpie dolls the suckers never won gleamed from their shelves. He saw all of this and was glad that he was again a part of it.

And so he turned into the Education Building and found a bench and, mounting it, began talking in a voice that was louder than the noises of the huge building, that drowned even the clamor of the Midway and the yells of fifty thousand throats at the nearby speedway.

"I am Oliver Quade, the Human Encyclopedia!" he thundered. "I know the answers to all questions. I can answer anything anyone can ask, on any subject . . ."

A man rushed up and, grabbing Oliver Quade's coat, tugged furiously.

"You can't start that stuff in here!" he cried, in a thin, high voice. "I told you you had to work outside!"

A look of utter weariness came upon Oliver Quade's face. "Mr. Campbell," he said, "I do not think more of twenty-five dollars than you do of your right arm. Yet that is the sum I paid you and I insist therefore that I be allowed to work wherever I choose. And I choose this building."

"Quade," gritted Campbell, who was secretary of the Fair, "I dislike grease joints because they sell bad food and clutter up the grounds, yet I do not detest them one-hundredth as much as sheet-writers. And I would rather sleep in bed with a sheet-writer than live on the same street with a pitchman. And you, sir, are a pitchman. Do I make myself clear?"

So Oliver Quade took his case of books and went outside the Education Building. The noises of the Midway, the eighteen racing cars on the speedway, the fifty thousand persons in the grandstand could have been equalled only by eight tornadoes, three earthquakes and a 21-gun salute from the Pacific Fleet.

Yet Quade went into competition with it all—and held his own.

"I am Oliver Quade, the Human Encyclopedia," he roared

again. "I know the answers to all questions. I can answer anything anyone can ask me, on any subject—history, science, mathematics . . ."

An angry-looking man waved a book at Oliver Quade and yelled: "Who was the Republican nominee for president in 1848?"

"Ha," said Quade, "you jest. The Republican Party did not come into existence until 1860. Abraham Lincoln was its first nominee." He waved his arms dramatically and yelled at the throng that was gathering around him. "Now, try me on something else. Any subject, history, science, mathematics, sports—"

It was a hell of a time for murder.

The man who had asked the question about the Republican Party cried: "Ohmygawd!" and fell against Quade—dead.

Quade lowered the man to the ground and saw a little dart sticking in the small of his back. He picked up the book the man had dropped and noted the title: "*Arnold's American History.*"

"A ringer," he said.

And then—confusion.

For fifteen minutes the chief attraction of the fair was the corpse lying between the race track and the Education Building. A couple hundred of the Fair's special police made a solid, semi-circular fence.

Inside the circle twenty or thirty police from St. Paul milled about. Scattered among them were a half dozen private citizens. Oliver Quade was one of the unfortunates. A Lieutenant Johnson had him up against the Education Building and was giving him some law.

"I don't like your story," Lieutenant Johnson said for the fifth time.

"You don't, eh? All right. I'll give you a better one. A pink-eyed guy eight feet tall came along, riding a female zebra, with a six-shooter in each hand—"

"Wise guy, huh!" snarled the police lieutenant. "Wasn't there an audience around I'd paste you a couple."

"What'd you expect?" demanded Quade. "I'm a total stranger here. I was making a pitch to five hundred people and one of them got killed. I never saw the man before in my life. I'm just an innocent bystander."

The lieutenant knew that very well, but he hated to give up on Quade. He was the only tangible connection with a man who had been killed. He was the only one of all the persons who had been in the crowd who had remained to be grabbed by a policeman. Crowds are that way.

A sergeant came up with an open notebook. "Here's what we've got, Lieutenant. His name was L. B. Arnold and he was president of the Arnold Publishing Company, of Anoka. There was $36.53 in his pockets, besides some letters and papers. The dart, well, the doc says there was some strange poison on it, but he won't be able to say what it is until he makes a chemical analysis."

The lieutenant sawed the air impatiently. "All right, we'll go into that later." He turned back to Quade, glowering. "I could take you to Headquarters."

"What good'd it do you?"

"None, I guess. Where you staying?"

"At the Eagle Hotel in Minneapolis."

The lieutenant wrote it down. "Don't you check out of there without letting me know. And while you're here on the grounds check in at the secretary's office every couple of hours in case we want you."

"I'll do that," said Quade. "And Lieutenant, here's something. This book. I picked it up from the ground. It seems to have been the dead man's."

The lieutenant tore it from Quade's hands. But when he looked at the title, he sniffed. "Yeah, it was his, but it don't mean nothing. You heard the sergeant say he was president of the Arnold Publishing Company. They publish school books and they got an exhibit inside the building. I saw it myself. They got five hundred of these books."

"Then let me have this one. I'm interested in history."

"This is evidence. Go buy yourself a book."

Quade snorted and picked up his case, which contained a good many copies of the *Compendium of Human Knowledge*. He had hoped to sell these books here today. That was his business—selling these encyclopedias.

He bucked the throng held at bay by the circle of special police and broke through, to a lunch stand that was next door to the Education Building. There was a whole string of these grease joints along the Midway, some operated by professionals, some by amateurs. This one was an amateur's stand. It bore a banner: "South Side Church." A half-dozen attractive girls were inside the booth.

Quade caught the eye of the best looking girl. "Coke," he said.

The girl brought the bottle, opened it and put a straw in it. "You're the man—uh . . ."

"I am," said Quade, "but I didn't do it. This is Labor Day and I never kill a man on Labor Day. Haven't for years."

The girl was easy on the eyes. In her early twenties, blonde and rather tall. The white uniform she wore added to, rather than detracted from, her appearance.

He said, "My name's Oliver Quade."

She smiled, finally. "You announced it loud enough and often enough when you were making that—pitch, I guess you call it."

He grinned. "What's your name?"

She shook her head. "I have no name. I'm just one of the girls from the church. Reverend Larsen warned us—"

"That you were doing this for the church and not to get picked up by fresh young men."

"Exactly."

"All right. Let's keep it on a business basis then. You were listening to my pitch—"

"What else could I do? You drowned out even the noise from the grandstand."

He chuckled. "You can't make money by whispering. Look at your own business here. You've got a cleaner stand and serve better food than Joe Grein over there, but look at the way he drags them in."

She saw the logic of what he said and frowned. "What with that yelling of his and cane waving—"

"Cane," said Quade. "That reminds me. I'll see you later. I'll leave my case here, to make sure I come back."

He heaved it over the counter and set it by her feet, then grinned at her open-mouthed face and walked off quickly.

A hundred yards down the Midway Quade spotted a concession and muttered under his breath. He stopped behind a burly man in a checked suit, who was trying to drive a twenty-penny spike into a pine log. He wasn't having much luck with it. He swung lustily, but somehow the hammer always slipped off the nail, or struck it a glancing blow, bending it.

Quade made a clucking noise with his tongue and the big

man whirled. His angry face relaxed when he saw Quade. Then he winced.

"Uh, hello, Ollie. I was just comin'."

"Is that so, Mr. Boston?" Quade asked sarcastically. "Tell me, my friend, how much money have you spent here trying to win one of those lovely, lovely canes?"

Charlie Boston scowled. "Not much. Maybe a couple bucks."

"For a cane you could buy in town for thirty cents." Quade sighed and signalled to the concessionaire. "Hi, Johnny! Let me have your hammer a minute. I want to show this oaf how to drive in a nail."

The concessionaire chuckled. "I didn't know he was a pal of yours. He's gone for about four bucks. I'll give it back—"

"No, let him pay for his fun."

Johnny grinned crookedly. He tapped a spike about a half inch into the log, then handed Quade his own hammer. With one half the energy Boston had expended on a blow, Quade drove the nail two inches into the wood. With the second blow he sent it to within a half inch of the block. The third, a light one, drove the nailhead flush with the log.

Johnny Nelson sang out: "And the gentleman wins a cane!" He handed him a yellow stick. Quade winked at him, then pulled Boston away from the booth.

"Charlie," he chided the burly man, "how often have I told you not to try to beat the other fellow at his own game?"

"Aw, you don't have to rub it in," growled Boston. "Anyway, you were lucky, that's all. My hammer kept slipping."

"Of course it did. It was supposed to slip. The ball had been rounded on an emery wheel. You'll recall Johnny handed me his own private hammer. With it even you might have—"

"Why, the dirty crook!" Charlie Boston turned to plunge back to the cane concessionaire, but Quade grabbed his arm.

"We've no time for that. While you were frittering away your time I got mixed up in a murder mess."

Boston gasped. "Murder!"

"Yes. I was making a pitch and someone tossed a dart into a prospective customer's shoulder. There was poison on the dart."

"Is that what all that commotion was about awhile ago?" cried Charlie Boston. "Gawd! I saw everyone rushing but I figured it wasn't nothing more than a dip lifting someone's poke." He whistled as astonishment overwhelmed him. "A murder at your pitch!"

"While you were trying to win a cane!"

Boston sulked. "All right. All right."

"Got a job for you, Charlie. One that suits your peculiar talents. Next to the Education Building there's a grease joint, run by some girls from a church. Go down there with that nice, new cane of yours and give the girls your personality."

Boston looked suspiciously at Quade. "Is this a rib?"

"No. This murder happened right next door to them. Pump the girls. Find out if they saw anything. Wait there for me. I'll be back in a little while."

Boston walked off briskly. The assignment was one he relished. Quade shook his head dolefully after his pal and went off in the other direction.

A few minutes later he stopped at a tent concession. There was a board backdrop in the tent, over which was spread a sheet of canvas, with red hearts painted on it. One or two customers were throwing darts at the hearts.

"Abe," Quade said to the concessionaire, "did you lose a dart here today?"

Abe Wynn, a bald, fat man, grunted. "I lose a dozen every day. The yaps swipe 'em."

"The cops been here yet?"

Wynn winced. "No, but I heard—and I've been expectin' them. I don't know a damn thing. It happened at your pitch, huh?"

Quade nodded. He picked up a handful of darts and began tossing them at the red hearts. "And the dart had your trademark. I s'pose you wouldn't remember the people who tossed here today?"

"No. It's been a good day and there've been two-three hundred. Any one of them could have slipped a dart into his pocket. But, Ollie, you know damn well one of these darts wouldn't kill a man unless it struck a big vein or the heart."

"There was poison on it. A deadly poison."

"That lets me out, then. None of these darts have poison on them. I know because I wipe them with an oily rag every day to keep them from rusting."

"Well, I was just asking. If a Lieutenant Johnson talks to you, he's tough."

Quade worked his way to the front of the Fair Grounds, to the Administration Building. He located the secretary's office and had scarcely stepped inside, than Lieutenant Johnson grabbed him. "I was just going to look for you."

"Yeah?"

"Some people have been picked up. I want you to look them over and give me the nod if any of them were in that crowd when you were selling those books."

"There were five hundred. I wouldn't know them all."

"You might remember some of the faces. . . . In here."

In the secretary's office were eight or ten men and one woman. Quade's eyes ran quickly over the gathering. He whispered to Lieutenant Johnson. "The stocky fellow in the gray suit—I'm sure of him. And the girl, she was there for a minute, although I think she left before it happened."

The detective smacked his lips and stepped up to the middle-aged man in the gray suit. "Mr. Colby, you were Arnold's office manager, weren't you?"

Colby nodded. There was apprehension in his eyes. "I'm also a stockholder in the company. I thought a great deal of Arnold. I'm sure Ruth will bear me out in that." He nodded toward the girl.

The girl's eyes were tear-stained and she was wadding a moist handkerchief in a gloved hand. "My father always spoke very highly of Mr. Colby."

She was, then, the dead man's daughter. Which puzzled Quade. She had been in the crowd when he'd started, but she hadn't been with her father—and had left before he was killed. Or had she left?

Lieutenant Johnson was still working on Colby. "Today's a legal holiday. But you can save us time, Mr. Colby. We're putting an auditor into the business tomorrow. You can save yourself a lot of trouble right now by telling for how much you tapped the till."

Colby exclaimed angrily. "I resent that question. If I'm under arrest I demand to be allowed to telephone my attorney. If I'm not under arrest, I insist on courteous treatment."

"This is a murder case, Mr. Colby," snapped Johnson. "If my questions seem pointed, please bear in mind the gravity of the crime. It's my business to ask questions, so could you venture an opinion as to why someone would want to murder Mr. Arnold?"

"I could not," retorted Colby. "The Arnold Publishing Company is a corporation. L. B. owned sixty percent and I believe ten percent is in Miss Arnold's name. She will naturally inherit her father's stock. I stand to gain nothing by Arnold's death."

"Is that right, Miss Arnold?" the detective asked.

The girl nodded. "I believe so. Father told me only yesterday that the business was in bad shape."

"That's right!"

The exclamation came from a stocky man with huge, black eyebrows and a Hitler mustache. Lieutenant Johnson whirled on him. "Your name?"

"Wexler. Louis Wexler."

"You were a friend of Arnold's?"

"Creditor would be a better word. He owed me for printing."

Colby interrupted. "Do you have to advertise it to the world? You got plenty of money from Arnold over a period of years. That he was a little hard pressed at the moment . . ."

"Hard pressed?" cried Wexler. "What about me? I've got a plant and a payroll. I got to lay it out every week—"

"So you were sore at Arnold?" Lieutenant Johnson said softly.

Wexler glared at the detective, then seemed to realize that he had laid himself open. Abruptly, his manner changed. He even attempted a smile. "Just in a business way, you understand. After all, you don't kill a man who owes you money. You can't get it back, then."

Quade nudged the lieutenant. "Ask the girl why she slipped away from my pitch," he murmured.

Johnson inhaled softly. Then he pounced on Ruth Arnold. "You were at the scene of your father's murder. Did you leave before or after he was killed?"

Ruth Arnold's hand flew up to her mouth and her eyes popped wide open. The tall young man beside her gripped her arm. He scowled at the detective. "Ruth was with me all afternoon."

"Let her answer my question!" Johnson thundered.

"I left before," Ruth Arnold whispered.

"Why'd you leave—because you saw your father?"

That question scored, too. But the girl's supporter answered, "She left to meet me. It's all right, now, Ruth. They'll find it out anyway."

"That you and Miss Arnold are engaged?" cut in Oliver Quade.

The girl gasped, but the man beside her nodded. "Yes. Ruth's father objected to her having anything to do with me."

"What's your name?" demanded Johnson.

"Jim Stillwell."

Oliver Quade cleared his throat. "Lieutenant, if you don't mind, I'd like to ask Mr. Stillwell a question?"

Lieutenant Johnson shrugged. "Go ahead."

"All right, Mr. Stillwell, who was the first man in American history to win the Republican nomination for president?"

"What the hell!" snorted Lieutenant Johnson angrily. "You playing games?"

"No, I'm interested in history and I thought I'd ask—"

"I don't mind answering," said Jim Stillwell. "John C. Fremont, in 1856, was the first Republican nominee. Right?"

"Surprisingly, yes."

"You got any more questions?" the detective lieutenant asked, sarcastically.

"Yes, who was vice-president during Lincoln's first term?"

"Get out of here!" cried Johnson.

"In one minute. Did you find out what poison was on the dart?"

"Well, the doc says it was dipped in some hydrocyanic acid. But where the devil would they get that stuff?"

Quade said: "In a drugstore—or if a fellow was real smart he could go out into a cornfield where there was some Indian corn. He could pick out a stunted stalk, and in some crotch find enough hydrocyanic acid to kill fifty people. It forms in stunted Indian corn and—"

The lieutenant sawed the air. "Yeah, I know you're a smart guy. But get out of here!"

Quade left the room. On his way out, he picked up, from a desk, a copy of *Arnold's American History*.

At the grease joint operated by the girls from the church, he found Charlie Boston in command of the situation. He was leaning against the counter, twirling his new cane and chatting with a dark-haired girl.

"Hi, pal," he greeted Quade. "It's all fixed. This is Mildred Rogers. She's mine. Yours is the blonde. Her name's Linda Starr."

The blonde was the girl who had repelled Quade's advances a while ago. He shook his head at her. "So you'd accept a blind date—after turning down my own noble advances."

"You beat about the bush instead of getting down to business," she retorted. "Anyway, I'd seen you and I hadn't the blind date."

"Where'll we pick you up at seven-thirty?" he asked.

She gave him a number on South Lindell. "And if you don't show up, I'm knitting some ear muffs for my regular boy friend who's at West Point and I'd like to stay home an evening and finish them."

"Ear muffs are against army regulations," he replied. "So we'll be around at seven-thirty."

They moved away from the lunch stand and Quade whispered to Boston. "Well, what'd you find out?"

"Why, nothing. They didn't see a thing. But they are real nice girls and we didn't have anything to do this evening, anyway."

Quade swore softly. "Nothing except earn money. Do you realize that the four bucks you threw away trying to win that cane was our grub money? I had to shell out all of mine to pay for the Fair privileges."

"But it's only three o'clock. You can still make a pitch or two and get some money."

"I'm not in the mood, now."

Boston groaned. "So that's coming on again. You weren't in the mood all summer. That's why we're away up here in Minnesota at the last fair of the season and without a dollar of get-away money."

"Stop it, you're breaking my heart. All right, I guess I'll have to make a pitch. We can't stand up the dear girls!"

He made the pitch, but his heart wasn't in it. He sold four books at $2.95 each, working to a crowd of four hundred. Ordinarily, he would have disposed of twenty books to a crowd that size.

It was six o'clock when they climbed into the heap of tin and wheels they had parked in a parking lot outside the Fairgrounds.

On the eight-mile drive to Fourth and Hennepin in Minneapolis, Quade passed two red lights and almost ran over a traffic cop.

Charlie Boston groaned when the last blasts of the cop's whistle died out. "I think he got your number!"

"Is that so?" Quade asked, absent-mindedly.

Boston snarled. "If you're going to daydream, let me take the wheel. You know damn well our insurance lapsed on this buggy three months ago."

Quade roused himself. He grinned crookedly at Boston. "Charlie, tell me—who was Thomas Hart Benton?"

"I don't know. There was a Doc Benton in my home town of What Cheer, Iowa, but I don't think he had any relative by the name of Thomas Hart Benton."

Quade sighed. "Your abysmal ignorance is sometimes appalling, Charlie. Thomas Hart Benton was senator from Missouri from 1821 to 1851."

"If you knew, why did you ask me? I only carry your books. I don't read 'em."

"You'll read one this winter, in Florida, if I have the strength to make you. Now here's an American history I picked up today. A very interesting subject. Americans don't study it enough. Would you believe there were people who didn't know who won the War of 1812?"

"I'm one of them," said Boston, sarcastically. "But there's things I know you don't know. One of them is the swingeroo. We've got a date with a couple of jitterbugs tonight and you're going to be an awful disappointment to them."

"Why, Charlie, I'm sure that nice Linda girl would rather discuss cultural subjects than jump around a crowded dance floor."

"Nuts!" said Charlie Boston.

At Fourth and Hennepin, Quade made a left turn and drove the flivver two blocks south. Then he squeezed it in between a taxi and a fireplug.

They climbed out and went into the Eagle Hotel, a fourth-rate firetrap, that was patronized by lumberjacks, farm hands and traveling citizens who could not pay more than a dollar a day for a hotel room.

Quade called for his key and when the clerk handed it to him, he said jokingly: "Julius, in what year was fought the Battle of Hastings?"

Julius said: "1066. It established the supremacy of the Normans in England."

Quade gasped. "Why, Julius!"

The hotel clerk grinned. "Try me on Ancient history. I'm particularly good on Phoenician and Chaldean."

Quade fled to the elevators.

Up in their room, Quade took a quick shower, then brushed his suit and touched up his shoes with a towel. Boston went into the bathroom and when he came out, Quade was sprawled on the bed, reading *Arnold's American History.*

Boston scowled. "Why don't you take it along tonight?" he asked.

"A very good idea, Charlie." Quade rose and tucked the book under his arm. "Let's go."

Quade followed Hennepin to Lindell, then turned into the south boulevard and cruised along for more than a half-hour.

Finally he pulled up before a two-story frame house. "Here's the number."

He blew the horn and the girls, Mildred Rogers and Linda Starr, came out. They were dressed in semi-formal evening dresses. "Ha," said Quade, "you should have told us and we'd have got our dinner jackets out of the mothballs."

The girls were looking dubiously at the ancient flivver. Linda said, "I suppose your chauffeur has the limousine tonight?"

"Never judge a man by the car he drives," retorted Quade.

"Climb in and we'll be off to a nice Greasy Spoon and a quiet country road."

"The road's all right," retorted Linda Starr, "as long as you don't stop on it before we get to The Poplars, which is halfway between here and Lake Excelsior. And if you don't have at least three gallons of gasoline in the car and ten dollars, we don't step into this pile of junk."

"By a coincidence," laughed Quade, "we have just that much money. So climb in."

They arranged themselves in the flivver. Boston and Mildred in front and Quade with Linda in the rear. Linda saw the book in Quade's hands.

"Your homework?"

"My history lesson. D'you know, Linda, who won the Battle of Gettysburg?"

"The United States."

"Ha, I had in mind a more specific answer, such as which general."

"Abraham Lincoln."

"Perhaps we'd better skip the history lesson."

"Hooray! I never liked it myself. I always got D's. Now it's my turn. What do you think of Benny Goodman?"

He told her and she sulked all the way out to The Poplars, which turned out to be a huge roadhouse with great neon signs and a parking lot that already contained more than a hundred cars.

They went in and got a table for four and when they had seated themselves, Quade saw Colby, the manager of the Arnold Publishing Company. He was in a booth with a blonde; a blonde on the voluptuous side.

Colby's face looked a bit sick when he saw Quade. He whispered to the blonde, then signalled to a waiter. A moment later he paid the check and the two of them got up and started for the door.

Quade pushed back his chair. "Will you excuse me a moment?"

Without waiting for a reply, he followed Colby and the blonde. They got outside before he reached the door and when he stepped out into the night, he saw them moving in the ghostly light shed by the neon signs, toward the parking lot.

He went after them, calling, "Hey, Colby! Wait a minute!"

Instead of stopping, they started running.

"Damn!" Quade said. He bounded after the fleeing pair. When he reached the first line of cars, someone rose up out of the gloom. Quade, thinking it was the parking lot attendant, swerved to the left. A battering ram lunged out of the darkness and smacked him in the forehead. Quade went down like a log.

Some time later he crawled to his hands and knees. He shook his head and pain darted from his head down into his body. He winced and began swearing.

After a minute he climbed to his feet. He got out a packet of matches from his pocket and began lighting them. By their feeble light he searched the ground around where he had fallen. When he had used up the last of the matches he quit in disgust.

He returned to the roadhouse.

Linda Starr saw him first. "So he gave you what you deserved! Imagine trying to flirt with a man's girl!"

"And two shiners!" guffawed Charlie Boston.

Linda Starr opened her purse and handed Quade a small mirror. "Look at yourself!"

Quade looked and winced. The punch he had taken in the darkness had caught him right between the eyes, a little high or both eyes would already have been closed. As it was, they were decidedly puffy. They would be black by tomorrow.

"What did you do with your book?" Linda asked.

"Somebody swiped it. I was on the ground looking for it. That was a very interesting book."

"What was interesting about it?" asked Mildred Rogers. "I used the Arnold History in high school, only four years ago."

"Yes?" said Quade eagerly. "Then, do you remember—was William Clarke Quantrill a famous Confederate colonel?"

"I don't remember," frowned Mildred. "I guess I was like Linda about history."

"You girls!" said Quade bitterly.

Linda Starr reached again into her purse. "Here's something may interest you, Mr. Quade." She brought out a handkerchief, unrolled it on the table and revealed a feathered dart, with an inch and a half of pointed needle.

Quade exclaimed, "Where did you get that?"

"From the back drop of our lunch stand. Someone threw it at me. It missed my head by about one inch."

Quade inhaled sharply. "When did that happen?"

"Right after you two left this afternoon—after the murder."

"What is it?" Charlie Boston asked, reaching for the dart.

"Let it alone!" Quade slapped Boston's hand away before it could touch the dart. Then he picked it up himself, handling it gingerly. The point, for about a half-inch, was covered with a greenish, sticky substance.

He looked sharply at Linda. "Have you any idea what this stuff is on the point?"

Her eyes met his, steadily. "I handled it very carefully."

He stared at her. She was a flippant, light-headed girl. Or was she?

He asked softly: "When that murder happened this afternoon, were you looking?"

"I was," she replied. "The man who threw the dart was standing right at the edge of our stand."

"You saw his face?" Quade exclaimed.

"Unfortunately, no." She sighed. "I didn't pay any attention to him, until I saw his arm whip forward. And then he sprang quickly around the corner. I had no more than a glimpse of him. I don't think I could identify him."

"He wouldn't know that, though," said Quade, half-aloud. "And he must have seen me talking to you. He must've prepared two darts instead of only one in case he either missed the first time or had to get rid of a witness." He laughed shortly. "And Johnson, storming all around!"

"Look, Ollie," said Charlie Boston. "Are you playing detective again? You promised me the last time that you were through. We always come out the wrong end on it."

Quade looked around the table. "Well, you've had a drink apiece . . ."

"Why not?" retorted Boston. "You were gone twenty minutes. What'd you expect us to do, sit around twiddling our thumbs?"

"So, inasmuch as I don't want to embarrass the girls with my shiners, let's pull out."

"Let's," said Linda Starr.

Quade rolled the dart into Linda's handkerchief and stowed it carefully in his breast pocket. Then he called the waiter.

A few minutes later they reached the flivver in the parking lot. "I'll drive this time," Quade volunteered.

Boston had no objections. He was even enthusiastic about the suggestion as he climbed in the back with Mildred. When they were in the car, Quade whispered to Linda.

"Which way do I go to get to Anoka?"

"Left," she whispered back. "There's a cut-off road about two miles from here. It's about ten miles to Anoka. You're going to follow up on that—business?"

"Yes, but—sh!"

But they were whispering in the rear seat, too. And after a mile or so they were quiet. Linda moved closer to Quade. There was a chill in the September air and she shivered a little.

On the outskirts of Anoka, Quade pulled in at a filling station. "Got to get some gas," he announced.

Charlie Boston yawned elaborately. He did not even know where they were; did not care.

When the attendant had filled the tank, Quade went into the station with him and paid for the gas. Then he asked: "By the way, can you tell me how to get to the residence of L. B. Arnold?"

"Turn right on the second street. It's the big white house in the middle of the block."

"And Mr. Colby, who works for Arnold?"

"He lives at the hotel—the Fortner House."

"Thanks," Quade stepped to the door, then turned back. "Ever hear of a man named Wexler?"

"Yeah, sure, he owns the printing plant here. It's on the other side of town."

Quade went back to the car. Linda nudged him gently and looked inquiringly at him. But he shook his head. He turned the car right in the second block and drew up before the Arnold house. He climbed out alone.

Jim Stilwell opened the door to Quade.

"What do you want?" Stilwell demanded truculently.

"I'd like to ask Miss Arnold a question. She lives here, not you. Or have you moved in since her father got killed?"

Stilwell blocked the doorway. "You're not a cop. It's none of your business. Miss Arnold's gone through enough today. Clear out of here."

Quade heard movements in the house behind Stilwell. He tried to push past Ruth Arnold's fiance. Stilwell snarled and swung his fist. Quade ducked and used his head as a battering ram. He drove the young fellow into the house, but Stilwell was only recently out of college and had evidently played football. He chopped down and hit Quade on the back of his neck, smashing him to the floor.

Quade clawed at the big fellow's ankles. He heard Charlie Boston coming up the porch stairs and tried desperately to hang on until he got there. Stilwell drew back his foot to kick Quade and then Charlie Boston roared. Quade rolled aside in time to hear a loud smack. It was followed by a thump.

When he got to his feet, Jim Stilwell was sitting on the floor and Charlie Boston stood over him.

"Come on, get up!" Charlie invited.

"O.K., Charlie!" said Quade. Then to Stilwell, "I only wanted to ask Miss Arnold a couple of questions."

Ruth Arnold was already in the vestibule, gasping at Stilwell on the floor. "What—what happened?"

"Nothing much, Miss Arnold. I just want to ask you a question."

"He isn't a cop, Ruth!" exclaimed Stilwell. "You don't have to tell him anything."

"You don't," admitted Quade, "but it will save you trouble if you do. How much insurance did your father carry?"

"Not much, only about five thousand dollars."

"See, wise guy," exclaimed Stilwell. "You think Ruth killed him."

Quade shook his head. "I know she didn't. I'm merely trying to establish a motive for the real killer."

"Well, you'll have to look somewhere else. Ruth didn't kill her father, not for a measly five thousand dollars insurance!"

"I'd forgotten!" said Ruth Arnold. "Before the Depression, when business was good, Father took out a fifty-thousand-dollar insurance policy as president of the Arnold Publishing Company. That policy is still in effect, but it wouldn't help me any at all, because the insurance money would go into the firm which isn't doing well at all."

"You could liquidate, couldn't you?"

"Perhaps, but I wouldn't. Father was proud of the business. When he took out that insurance policy, the company did a million-dollar business. It's gone away down, but Father always said it would come back, some day."

Quade nodded. "Thank you, Miss Arnold." He turned and walked out of the house.

Out by the flivver, Linda Starr said, "So you got a few more wallops? Nice going." He grinned and slammed into the car.

In the rear, Charlie Boston growled, "That's what we usually get when we play detective."

Quade drove back to the main street of the little town. He turned right in the next block and stopped before the hotel.

"I won't need you this time, Charlie," he said, as he climbed out.

In the lobby, he went into the telephone booth. He picked up the phone and said, "Will you give me Mr. Colby's room."

A moment later Colby's voice said, "Yes?"

"This is Lieutenant Johnson of the St. Paul Police Department," Quade said in a muffled voice. "I want to ask you one question."

"Go ahead," Colby said wearily.

"Was William Clarke Quantrill a Confederate colonel of cavalry?"

He heard Colby inhale sharply before replying. "No. He was a Missouri guerilla who pretended—"

"Thank you, Mr. Colby," Quade said and hung up. He ran out of the hotel and said to Charlie Boston and the girls, "There's a restaurant across the street. Let's get that dinner we didn't get at the roadhouse."

"What's the matter with you, Ollie?" exclaimed Boston. "Why should we eat in a dump like this after we walked out on that swell joint?"

"The food's good here—I hope," said Quade. "Come on, Linda."

Linda came willingly, but Charlie Boston and Mildred still complained when they went into the restaurant. Quade selected a table near the window and seated himself so he could look out.

They ordered, and just as the waitress brought the food, Quade got up, abruptly. "Excuse me a minute." He went out of the restaurant.

Across the street, Colby was walking rapidly northward. Quade followed on his own side of the street. In the next block, Colby stopped at the door of a two-story brick building. After a moment he went inside, and a light appeared in a window.

Quade crossed the street. Standing on his toes, he peered into the lighted room. It was furnished as an office with shelves of books on three sides. It was unoccupied. He moved to the door and found it unlocked. Drawing a deep breath, he opened the door and went inside.

He heard noise in the room beyond the lighted office. A drawer squeaked and, as Quade stopped and listened, he heard the rustle of paper.

He took a couple of quick steps across the office and entered the room beyond.

"Hello, Mr. Colby," he said. A bundle of long, narrow sheets of paper fell from Colby's hands.

"You!" Colby gasped. "How'd you get here?"

Quade said, "What do you know about Quantrill, Mr. Colby?"

The expression of fright on Colby's face disappeared, and was replaced by a snarl.

"So it was you!"

Quade pointed to the long sheets of paper which were scattered on the desk before Colby. "Checking up on the galley proofs? So you were in on it?"

"I don't know what you're talking about."

"History," said Quade. "Specifically, *Arnold's American History*, the favorite in hundreds of high schools. I should say *was* because the last edition is *not* a favorite. It contains too many historical inaccuracies, such as, Quantrill being a Confederate colonel of cavalry, and Zachary Taylor being the first Republican candidate for president."

"Stupid proofreaders!" exclaimed Colby.

"And because of the proofreaders' blunders, you came down in the middle of the night to find the galley proofs? What are you going to do with them?"

"He wasn't going to do anything with them," said a soft voice behind Oliver Quade.

Quade sighed. He moved carefully to one side and then turned. "Hello, Mr. Wexler," he said.

There was a .32 automatic in Louis Wexler's hand. He said, "Colby should have given it to you earlier tonight."

"At the Poplars when he took the book from me?"

"Yes, then." Wexler shook his head. "That just goes to show you, Colby, even the smartest plans can go screwy."

Colby scowled. "I don't know what you're talking about, Wexler."

"Oh, it's all right now, Colby," said Quade. "You can let your hair down. This is just among us. It's possible for an editor to get historical inaccuracies into a book, but a printer couldn't do it alone, because the editor, who knows such things, reads the proofs. So I knew you had to be in on it."

Wexler nodded admiringly. "You see, Colby, your scheme was no good. It's a good thing I muscled in on you."

"That explains one of the little things that puzzled me," said Quade. "I could figure out that the Arnold Publishing Company had been staggering for some years because Arnold was conservative and didn't want to take any chances. Mr. Colby wanted more money, so he thought if he helped to make things even worse, the creditors would force the business into bankruptcy and then he, Colby, would buy it in, at a bargain price. But Arnold got wise to Mr. Colby's little plan, and so did you, Wexler. But why did *you* kill him, Wexler?"

"That's a little secret between me and Colby," said Wexler. "But I don't mind letting you in on it. It's not going any further! Arnold owed me a little money, not much. He could have cleaned it up if his last book had gone over. And then, what? I discover Mr. Arnold's manager, Mr. Colby, has been changing history. You wouldn't think, would you, Mr. Quade, that I am an expert on history? Yeah, it's a hobby with me.

"So what? So I talk to Mr. Colby and he mentions that Mr. Arnold has a fifty-thousand-dollar corporation policy. It don't do Colby any good, though. If Arnold dies, the money goes to the company. Arnold's girl owns seventy per cent of the stock. She can liquidate the business—in which case Colby gets three-four thousand as his share.

"Or she can run the business indefinitely. In which case Colby gets nothing. . . . But suppose Arnold Publishing Company owes their printer forty thousand and Arnold dies? What happens then? The insurance is paid to the company and the company pays its creditors."

Wexler chuckled. "And I am the chief creditor. I get the money and split with Colby—on account of I wouldn't be such a big creditor if Mr. Colby don't doctor up the company's books."

"A very nice scheme," said Quade. "But what about the insurance company—weren't you afraid of them?"

"Naw. What can they suspect? That Mr. Colby killed Mr. Arnold? No, because he owns only thirty per cent of the stock. Arnold's daughter inherits sixty and already owns ten. *She's* the likely suspect, but the insurance company wouldn't dare say a nice girl would kill her father. Me, why would *I* kill Arnold? The insurance company don't even know I exist."

"But you're the chief creditor of the firm. Most of the money the insurance company pays the Arnold Publishing Company goes to you."

"Ah, that's the sharp point. The insurance company don't know I am a creditor. Naw, they don't know that, because Mr. Colby, he don't say nothing. Not right away. Later on—well, Mr. Wexler liked Mr. Arnold so much he didn't want to press for payment of his bill right away. So in two-three months, when the cops and the insurance company have forgotten all about things, Arnold Publishing pays its bills. . . . It's really all very simple. I'm sure there won't be another human encyclopedia up in this neck of the woods, then, to figure out this and that."

"No," said Quade, "but it so happens I have three friends outside. They're up the street waiting for me."

A startled look leaped into Colby's eyes. "You're lying!" he said, but there was uncertainty in his tone.

"Am I?" smiled Quade. "You forget I was at The Poplars with a group."

"To hell with that," Wexler said.

"You can't kill him, Wexler!" exclaimed Colby. "Not here. I—"

Wexler looked coldly at Colby. "Ah, you're afraid of that, Colby. Afraid when there's the least little chance of getting your toes in it. All right, go outside and see if those friends of his are waiting."

"They're in the restaurant across from the hotel," said Quade.

Colby ran out of the proofroom. Quade heard the door outside slam. He thought Wexler might be scared enough to let him have it now.

"While we're waiting, Quade," said Wexler, "I could be more relaxed if you'd raise your hands."

Quade brought his hands up to shoulder level. Then he sniffed and reached carefully for the white handkerchief in his breast pocket.

"Careful!" cautioned Wexler.

"Yeah, sure!" Quade drew out the handkerchief and showed Wexler the dart inside.

"Remember this?" he asked. "You threw it at the girl in the lunch counter."

"Drop it!" cried Wexler. "Drop it, or I'll plug you!"

"You can shoot," said Quade, "and there's a possibility the wound won't be fatal, but a scratch of this, Wexler—well, you put the poison on it yourself. And I can surely hit you with it."

He gripped the poison dart between thumb and forefinger. A quick flip and it would zip at Wexler. The distance was too short to miss.

Perspiration broke out on Wexler's forehead. "Drop it, Quade!" he cried hoarsely.

He knew his own poison, but he knew that he had everything to lose and nothing to gain—except a few more months of life. Was it enough?

Surrender meant but a stay of death.

Quade was still casual outwardly, but inwardly he was like a coiled spring. He had to read Wexler's intentions from his face, and act a fraction of a second before the killer.

"All right," said Wexler, "you win."

He lied. He was lowering his gun, but Quade saw it in his eyes. He was going to shoot. He was going to gamble on getting in the surprise, vital shot.

"Fine," said Quade. He took a step back, smiled—and dropping his hand to the proofreader's desk, lifted it up and shoved it at Wexler in a tremendous heave. At the same instant, he threw himself frantically sidewards and forward.

Thunder rocked the little room. The bullet from the automatic missed Quade's face by less than one-sixteenth of an inch. He felt the wind as it zipped past him.

Then Wexler was down under the desk and Quade was swarming over it, slamming at the printer with his fist that was not encumbered by the dart. He put everything he had into the blow and it connected solidly with Wexler's jaw.

Wexler collapsed.

When he recovered a few seconds later, Quade had the automatic. There were tears in Wexler's eyes as he looked up at Quade. "The dart . . ." he muttered. It was sticking in his throat.

"Oh, that," said Quade. He grinned crookedly and gave it a flip. It stuck in the overturned desk. "Why, you see, Wexler, I didn't want to carry a thing around in my pocket with poison on it, for fear I might accidentally stick myself with it—so I carefully wiped the poison from it."

Louis Wexler screamed incoherently.

The outside door slammed open, feet pounded through the office. Quade whirled, the automatic gripped in his fist. But it wasn't Colby; it was Charlie Boston.

"Ollie!" Boston cried. "I heard a shot and I knew you had something to do with it."

"I did," said Quade. "But did you see a man running outside?"

"Yeah. He bumped into me and got tough. The squirt! I knocked him cold with one punch!"

"Good, Charlie! Now go out and collar him before he comes around. The local law ought to come around any minute."

He came, a burly policeman with a huge revolver. With him came Linda Starr and Mildred Rogers.

Quade waved at the girls. "Be through here in a few minutes."

"No more history, Mr. Quade?" asked Linda.

"No more history. The lesson's finished for today."

THE EPISODE OF THE CODEX' CURSE

C. Daly King

Of the merely seven volumes of detective fiction that C(harles) Daly King (1895-1963) produced in his lifetime, his undoubted masterpiece is the short story collection *The Curious Mr. Tarrant.* Although King was an American, the book was first published in England in 1935 and was among the rarest mystery books of the twentieth century until Dover issued the first American edition as a paperback in 1977. It was selected by Ellery Queen for his *Queen's Quorum* as one of the 106 most important volumes of mystery short stories of all time, where it was described as containing "the most imaginative detective short stories of our time."

Trevis Tarrant, the amateur detective in the eponymous story collection, is a wealthy, cultured gentleman of leisure who believes in cause and effect; they "rule the world," he says. He takes it on himself to explain locked room mysteries and impossible crimes that involve such improbabilities as mysterious footsteps by an invisible entity heard even in broad daylight, horrible images of a hanged man haunting a modern house, headless corpses found on a heavily traveled highway, as well as dealing with apparent ghosts and other supernormal happenings. It entertains him to bring his gift of being able to see things clearly and solve mysteries by the use of inarguable logic. He is accompanied at all times by his valet, Katoh, a Japanese doctor and spy.

Born in New York City, King graduated from Yale University, received his master's degree in psychology from Columbia University, and a Ph.D. from Yale. With the advent of World War II, he stopped writing mysteries and devoted the rest of his life to his work in psychology. Because of their uneven nature and occasional long, boring passages, King's novels are not often read today, despite the ingenuity of their plotting, though *Obelists at Sea* (1932) and other of his novels have their champions. As a mystery writer, King is enigmatic, at times writing brilliantly with the verve and assurance of a master, at other times as frustrating as the club bore who tells the same stories over and over again, once inserting a fifteen-page treatise on economic theory into a detective novel for absolutely no reason.

"The Episode of the Codex' Curse" was first published in *The Curious Mr. Tarrant* (London, Collins, 1935).

The Episode of the Codex' Curse

C. Daly King

Characters of the Episode

JERRY PHELAN, the narrator
JAMES BLAKE, Curator of Central American Antiquities
MARIUS HARTMANN, a collector

ROGER THORPE, a Director of the Metropolitan Museum
MURCHISON, a Museum guard
TREVIS TARRANT, interested in the bizarre
KATOH, Tarrant's butler-valet

I HAD not wanted to spend the night in the Museum in the first place. It had been a foolish business, as I realised thoroughly now that the lights had gone out. A blown fuse, of course; but what could blow a fuse at this time of night? Still, it must be something of that nature, perhaps a short in the circuit somewhere. Murchison, the guard in the corridor outside, had gone off to investigate. Before leaving he had stepped in and made his intention clear; then he had closed the door, whose handle he had shaken vigorously to assure both of us that it was locked. The lock had had to be turned from the outside, for the door was without means of being secured from within. I was alone.

The room was in the basement. It was comparatively narrow and about fifty feet long; but, since it was situated at one of the corners of the great building, its shape was that of an L, with the result that, from where I sat near its only door, no more than half of the room could be seen. Of the three barred windows near its ceiling, the one in my half of the room was already becoming dimly visible as a slightly lighter oblong in the darkness.

The darkness had given me quite a jolt. Earlier, at half-past ten, when I had propped my chair back against the wall and settled down to read my way through the hours ahead with the latest book on tennis strategy, it had been very quiet; I had seen to it that the three windows were all closed and fastened, so that even the distant purr of the cars across Central Park had been inaudible. Murchison, from outside, had reported every hour, but of course he had other duties than patrolling this one corridor, although he was giving it most of his attention tonight. We had considered it better, when he was called away, to leave the door locked and this he had done on each occasion. At first he had unlocked it and either come in or lounged in the doorway when reporting, but lately he had been contenting himself with calling to me through the closed entrance.

The silence, which to begin with had been complete, seemed somehow to have gotten steadily more and more profound. Imperceptibly but steadily. Oppressive was the word probably, for by two a.m. I had the distinct feeling that it would have been possible to cut off a chunk of it and weigh it on a scale.

I am a person who is essentially fond of games and outdoor life generally; being cooped up like this was uncongenial as well as unusual. As the silence grew deeper and deeper and Murchison's visits farther and farther apart, the whole thing commenced to get on my nerves. Inside, I undoubtedly began to fidget. There was no possibility of backing out now, however. The diagrams showing just how one followed the ball to the net for volley (the proper time to do so being explicitly set forth in the text) made less claim upon my attention as the hours drew past. I had finally ended by closing the book and dropping it impatiently to the floor beside me.

Could there possibly be anything in this Curse business? Absurd! I stared across at the Codex lying on the little table near the closed door. What power for either good or evil could be possessed by some unknown Aztec, dead hundreds of years ago? It was an indication of my unaccustomed nerviness that I found it of comfort to reflect that I was in a world-famous Museum in the centre of modern New York, to be specific on upper Fifth Avenue; there must be a score of guards in the Museum itself, a precinct station was but a few blocks away, the forces of civilisation that never sleep surrounded me on all sides. I glanced at the Codex again and gave something of a start. Had it moved ever so slightly since I had looked at it before? Hell, this was ridiculous. Then the lights went out.

The effect in any case is startling and in the present instance it was doubly so. Nothing could have been more unexpected. Unconsciously, I suppose, one becomes accustomed to hearing the click of a button or a switch when lights are extinguished; even in a roomful of people, unexpected darkness descending suddenly causes uneasiness. And I was not in a roomful of people by any means. The unbroken silence preceding and following made a sort of continuity that ought to have prevented any abrupt change. Darkness, silently instantaneous, for a moment was unbelievable.

Murchison's voice through the door a minute later was, I admit, a bit of a relief. He opened the door, flashed his light about for a moment, then locked it again and hurried away.

The guard's light had shown the Codex quietly in its place on the table. Well, naturally; how could it have moved, since I had not been near it and no one else was in the room? A Curse from the dark past of Aztlan. The third night. Nonsense. Here was merely a matter of a short circuit. It suddenly occurred to me that that, too, might not be unimportant. Where there are short circuits, there are sometimes fires. The door was locked on the outside. I could break any of the windows, of course, if they couldn't be unfastened, but what then? All of them were guarded by sturdy iron bars set in the stonework of the building. It was plain enough that in any emergency I couldn't get out by myself.

I simply couldn't help thinking how often these coincidences seemed to happen. An ancient warning and a modern calamity.

It was a silly notion; it persisted in running through my head. In that inanimate manuscript written by dead Aztec hands there couldn't possibly be anything——

When I had come into town that morning, nothing had been further from my mind than spending the night in the Metropolitan Museum. At most I had anticipated no more than calling there for a few minutes around noon to take Jim Blake out to lunch. Blake is considerably older than I am, being in fact a friend of one of my aunts; our common interest, however, is not the aunt but the game of golf, as to which we are both enthusiasts. Thus, having some business in town, I thought I might run up and compare notes with him about a recently opened course in New Jersey which we had both played, though not together. Blake had been with the Museum for years and, I understand, is now the Keeper, or whatever they call it, of their Central American antiquities.

When I found him in his basement office, however, I discovered Marius Hartmann already with him, a fellow about my own age whom I knew slightly at college and never liked very much. A quiet, studious chap, though I suppose that's nothing against him. What I really disliked was his contempt for all sports, a matter he took little trouble to conceal. I had not seen him since graduation but had heard that he had come into a large inheritance and taken up collecting. This interest, I suppose, had brought him and Blake together but, not knowing of their acquaintance, I was considerably surprised to find him in the office.

He shook hands with me pleasantly enough but it was evident that his interest had been excited and was wholly taken up by the subject he had been discussing with Blake.

"Why, a Codex like that is priceless, literally priceless!" he exclaimed, as soon as the greetings were over. "Such a find isn't reported once in a century. And when it is, it's usually spurious."

Blake, leaning back in his chair with his feet resting on a corner of his desk, grunted acquiescence. "Fortunately there's no question of authenticity this time," he asserted. "Our own man found it, sealed away in a small stone wall-vault in the *teocalli*. More by chance than anything else, he says himself. The place where it was must have been rather like a safe; they never did find out how it was properly opened. It was partly broken open during the excavation work and when they saw that some sort of storage chamber had been struck, they finished it up with a pick. As I say, it was only a small receptacle, a few feet each way, I understand."

"I suppose that accounts for its preservation," Hartmann reflected. "Over seven hundred years, you say? It's a long time, that, but if this temple safe was sealed up—— Of course, we do know of manuscripts as old as seven hundred years. The oldest Codex I have is about four hundred," he added.

I thought it was high time to find out what a Codex is, so I asked.

"A Codex, Jerry," replied Blake with half a smile, "is a manuscript book. Strictly speaking, the thing we're talking about is not a Codex; it's written on stuff resembling papyrus and it is rolled rather than being separated into leaves and bound. But so many of these Central American records *are* Codices written by Spaniards or Spanish-speaking Aztecs after the conquest, that we have been calling this record a Codex, too."

"But seven hundred years?" I was puzzled.

"Oh, yes, it far antedates the conquest. In fact, it purports to have been inscribed by the Chief Priest of the nation at Chapultepec on the occasion of the end of one Great Cycle and the beginning of the next. 'Tying up the bundles of bundles of years,' they called it; a bundle, or cycle, being fifty-two years and a bundle of bundles being fifty-two cycles, or twenty-seven hundred and four years. The end of the particular Great Cycle in question has been pretty well identified with our own date, 1195 a.d."

Hartmann's eyes were glistening as he leaned forward. "What a treasure!"

"You knew of it some time ago, I believe?" Blake asked him.

"Yes. Yes, I did. Roger Thorpe, one of your directors, told me. I offered the Museum forty thousand dollars for it, through him, before it ever got here. Turned down, of course . . . But I had only the vaguest idea about the contents. It appears to be even more valuable than I realised; undoubtedly it contains an historical record of the whole preceding Great Cycle."

"More than that," Blake chuckled, "more than that. When this is published, it is going to make a sensation, you can be sure . . . I don't mind telling you in confidence that the Codex contains the historical high spots of the preceding five Great Cycles, including place names and important dates of the entire Aztec migration. In some way we have not been able to ascertain as yet, the occasion of its writing was even more impressive than the end of a Great Cycle; apparently it was the ending of an especially significant number of Great Cycles in their dating system. Possibly thirteen; we're not sure."

Frankly the subject wasn't of much interest to me. I couldn't work up the excitement that Hartmann obviously felt, and Blake, too, to a lesser degree. But I didn't want to mope in a corner about the thing. More to stay in the conversation than for any other reason, I asked what sort of writing was employed in the manuscript.

"Eh, what sort of writing? Why, picture writing, naturally. Much more developed than the American Indian, though; more like the Egyptian hieroglyphs. Some ideographs; Chapultepec, for example, which means 'grasshopper-hill,' is represented by a grasshopper on a hill. But there is a lot of phonetic transcription also, in which the symbols stand for their sounds rather than the objects pictured. The curious thing is that this Codex, by far the earliest Aztec manuscript we know of, uses a much more highly developed script than the later writings just preceding the conquest. It certainly makes the Popol-Vuh look just like what some of us have always suspected—the ignorant translation by a Spanish priest of traditions that had already been badly mangled and half forgotten by the natives themselves."

Marius Hartmann had been doing some rapid calculation. He said: "But if this covers five Great Cycles, it goes back thirteen thousand five hundred years or more from 1195. Thirteen thousand five hundred years! Why, that's—why——"

"Oh, yes," acknowledged Blake with an understanding grin. "It is indeed. You know the controversies concerning the origin of the Aztecs, the location of the original Aztlan from which they traditionally migrated. I've only had a chance for one look at the Codex myself but it appears to me to be a highly circumstantial history without any embroidery at all. The writer states definitely that Aztlan is nothing else than the Atlantis mentioned by Plato. He even gives the clear location of the ancestors of the Aztecs in one of the western, coastal provinces of the continent. After the catastrophe the survivors found themselves on the North American coast, apparently in the vicinity of what have now become the Virginia capes. From there, after the passage of thousands of years and through the operation of a good many different causes, their migrations finally carried them into central Mexico."

Hartmann's mouth was partly open and his eyes, I thought, would soon be popping out. "You—you believe this is an authentic record?" he stammered.

"I can only tell you this, but I really mean it. I've been here a good many years now, Hartmann, and so far as my own experience goes, it's the most authentic document that I have ever come across. I'd be perfectly willing to stake my reputation on it."

There could be no doubt about it; the man's eyes would pop out in another minute. That would never do.

I said, "How about getting some lunch? I'm empty as a football, for one."

The lunch was highly unsatisfactory from my point of view at any rate. Highly so. I had no opportunity to discuss the new course with Blake, or anything else about golf, for that matter. Marius Hartmann came with us; he stuck to Blake like a leech and there was no getting rid of him. Worse, they both continued to discuss the matter of the Codex with undiminished zeal. Most of the time I ate in silence and by the approach of the end of the meal I was pretty thoroughly fed up on everything connected with Aztecs.

It was during lunch that the question of the Curse came up. It appeared that the Codex really comprised two separate parts, although both were written on the same manuscript. The second part was the historical section already mentioned, while the first dealt with a religious ritual or training of some kind. "Curious," Blake observed, "very curious. The title of the first part is almost identical with the actual title of the Egyptian Book of the

Dead, *Pert em Hru,* 'Coming into Light.' The Aztec title is *Light Emergence,* but the contents are certainly not concerned with a burial ritual or anything like it."

Preceding this part of the Codex and introducing the entire manuscript, a species of warning had been placed. Blake quoted some of it. "Beware," it ran, "lest vengeance follow sacrilege. Who would read the Sacred Words, let him be instructed, for ignorance conducteth disaster. Quetzalcoatl, the Reminder, (goeth) in dread splendour. The desecration of Light-Words is an heavy thing; in an unholy resting-place the third night bringeth the Empty." And considerably more to the same general effect.

"It doesn't sound much like the Codex Chimalpopoca, does it?" ventured Hartmann.

"Not a bit. No, we have to do with something along different lines here. The Chimalpopoca is not much more than folklore at best, written some time after the conquest, even if it is in the native language. Our Codex is a genuine article; the man who wrote it was quite certainly the religious head and he had no doubts as to what he was writing about. Not only is the form of expression quite different but the content is, too; even the language is far more evolved. The author isn't guessing, in other words; he gives the strongest impression both of accuracy and of knowledge."

"How do you mean, Blake? Are you hinting that you take the opening Curse seriously?"

"Well, no. I didn't mean that exactly. I was referring more to the historical section and even to the ritual part itself. That seems to be a good bit more explicit, in parts at least, than most such compilations; from what I had a chance to read, one section appears to lead up to and introduce the following one, quite otherwise than in the usual haphazard collections. It gave me rather a strange feeling, just glancing through it. . . . As a matter of fact I've heard that you take such passages as the prefatory Curse more seriously than most of us."

Hartmann looked up from his salad. "As a matter of fact, I do. When I meet the real thing. Of course there was a lot of pseudo-magic in Greek times that couldn't affect a child. I mean the real thing," he repeated. "I can assure you that I'm much more sceptical about the dictum of a modern scientist than I am about that of a High Priest of, say, the Fourth Dynasty."

Blake smiled at our companion's earnestness. "Can't say I feel your way entirely. However, if that's your opinion, tonight is your night."

"Why? How is that?"

"'In an unholy resting-place the third night bringeth the Empty.' We've finally gotten the Codex to its permanent resting-place and I've no doubt at all that the writer would consider it unholy. To complete the point, tonight is the third one." He paused and smiled again. "If I took it literally, I'd expect the Codex to vanish or undergo spontaneous combustion or something of the kind before morning. I shouldn't feel any too pleasant myself, either, for I happen to be its custodian now."

"Oh, you're all right. It doesn't say anything about the custodian," Hartmann answered. I was surprised, I must admit, at the entire seriousness of his words, which were accompanied by no hint of a smile. "About reading it, that's another matter; I don't know whether I'd be prepared to try it or not, 'uninstructed.' But its custody, especially in an official capacity, will surely be harmless. It's not as if you had stolen it or even been the one to dig it up."

Blake looked a touch astonished himself, though not as

much as I was. He explained to me later that enthusiasts often get these notions. He had known a man once who had been determined to obtain an Egyptian mummy and had finally procured one which he kept in his library as his most prized possession; but he had assured Blake that were he ever prevented from doing a proper obeisance—"purification ceremony," he called it—night and morning upon entering the room, he would get rid of the mummy the same day. I, however, had not met this man and Hartmann's sentiments, I confess, were strengthening my disposition to consider him something of an ass. Too much learning—some old fellow said once, I think—is worse than not enough.

But he was continuing. "About tonight, though, that's a different thing. *If* it will really be the third night and *if* it was set forth literally in the warning just as you said, I should be frankly anxious, in your place. What precautions have you taken?"

"It's really the third night," Blake acknowledged. "And the threat, or whatever you want to call it, is not ambiguous; it is simply and literally that the third night will bring 'the Empty.' But, thank heaven, I haven't your idea about it and I'm not anxious at all. My word, if I worried about those things, I'd have been out of my mind long ago; I'm surrounded every working day by more curses and threats from the past than I can count. I just don't bother about 'em. To tell you the truth, I haven't taken any precautions," he finished, "and I don't intend to."

"Surely you've got it locked up somewhere?"

"Oh, surely. Your friend Thorpe, by the way, is of your mind; he seems quite worried over the matter. You ought to talk to him about it . . . Yes, it's down in one of the extra rooms in the basement, locked up naturally. No one could get at it down there. In the first place, a thief wouldn't know where to look for it, in the second, although the room isn't a bank vault by any means, it *is* locked; and in the third place, the usual patrols will be on duty near it anyhow. That's safe enough from my point of view."

"Oh, thieves." Hartmann snorted contemptuously. "I wouldn't be concerned about modern sneak-thieves; no market for such a thing, anyhow. I'm thinking of something quite different than that, I assure you."

"So is Thorpe apparently. I can't make him out this time. He has insisted upon putting the Codex into the same room every night with his precious statue from Palestine, until we are ready to put it on exhibition in the main halls. *I* believe he has some superstition about that statue; thinks it will be a guardian angel or something. He surprised me, really. You do too, if you're serious. What do you imagine could happen, thieves ruled out?"

The other man shrugged. "Nothing—possibly. These warnings don't materialise sometimes but in my opinion that is because we don't know enough to interpret them correctly. Neither you nor I have any definite knowledge as to what 'the Empty' means. Maybe your Codex will disappear tonight, although a thief would be the last thing I should look for in such a case. I don't know; but I am certain of this, that something, and something more or less unpleasant, will happen on the third night that that bit of ancient wisdom rests in a museum. . . . After all, a museum is simply an exhibition house for the ignorantly curious, or vice versa."

Blake grinned his appreciation. "No reflections, I take it? A lot of us have to earn our bread and butter, you know. . . . Well, why don't you sit up with it tonight and see what happens? I'll get you permission."

"Not a chance! I'm going to a ball at the Waldorf tonight; but if I had nothing to do, you can take it I wouldn't do that. I don't want to be anywhere near your Codex on the third night."

"I believe you're more than half in earnest," said Blake, regarding our companion with an estimating glance. "It's tosh, you know."

Hartmann suggested, "Ask Jerry. He has heard both sides." Turning to me. "What's your idea, old man; will anything happen, or won't it?"

It was an opportunity I couldn't resist. I said briefly, probably all too briefly, "*Nuts!*"

He leaned back, smiling as he lit a cigarette. "Nuts, eh? . . . Well, Jerry, I'll give you a thousand you won't stay up with the Codex and, further, if you do, that something will happen and you won't be able to prevent it . . . On?"

Doubtless I looked as bewildered as I felt at the offer. Before I could pull my wits together and reply, Blake volunteered: "Wish I could take you myself. As a matter of fact, though, I'm taking Jerry's aunt to the opera tonight and I don't intend to miss out on that. You might tell her sometime, Jerry, that I paid one grand, extra, for the pleasure of seeing her this evening."

"Sure, glad to." My impatience with the whole business had reached a crucial point and I was feeling fairly irked. Not a word about golf the entire time and in another minute or so I should have to leave. "Look here," I said, "I can't afford to take you for a thousand but you're on for a hundred. I'll spend the night with your damned Codex and nothing will happen to it at all or about it at all. So what?"

"So there's a hundred for me," came the exasperating answer.

"Nuts again. Draw your cheque."

Suddenly he was serious. "You mean this? You really intend to go through with it?"

"Naturally."

"All right. Now listen to me. A hundred isn't enough to make me want to have you take a risk. And you'll be taking one, no matter what you think about it. I'm sorry now that I made the proposition. I'd much rather call it off. Shall we?"

Let him crawl out like that? "Nothing doing, my lad. It was your suggestion. It's on now; I'm chaperoning the Codex tonight and collecting in the morning." If there's one thing I can't stand, it's these fellows who know more than everyone else about everything. Except golf, of course.

"As you will." He shrugged, as who remarks that sagacity is wasted on any but sages. "Do you mind, Jerry, if I call you up once or twice during the night? I'd feel a little easier."

"Call away. All you want."

"It can be arranged, Blake, can't it?"

"Easily. I'll have the phone in the room plugged through before I leave." He smiled broadly, with more pleasure than I could muster over the tedious performance. "I don't think, though, that I'll stay up fretting over Jerry," he added.

"No?" The tone had just that accent of the sceptical tinged with the supercilious that is appropriate, I suppose, to these occasions.

The waiter was bringing our check.

Late that afternoon Blake showed me the room. As I have said it was L-shaped. There was a roll-top desk in it and a flat one, both obviously unused. Several piles of bundles, pamphlets no doubt or some of the monographs the museum is frequently publishing, were stacked against the long back wall.

There were also a few small boxes, various odds and ends that accumulate in a disused apartment. The statue, still in its skeleton crate whose sides were covered with sacking, stood at the farther end of the room beyond the flat desk on which rested the telephone instrument. Life-size, apparently, to judge from the crate. "Thorpe's sweetheart," said Blake in a dry voice. "He won't even let us see it. It's a particularly nifty one of Astarte, I understand. Came in ten days ago from the Palestine expedition and he insists on unpacking it himself. Hasn't gotten around to it yet."

He laid the Codex on the small table in the other half of the room, near the entrance door. It was contained in a cylinder of wood, black with age, on one side of which two symbols, or letters, had been skilfully inlaid in white shell. "Sacred very-very," Blake translated them, explaining that the Codex was in its original package, as found. He had taken it carelessly from one of the drawers of his own desk.

As we turned to the door, he said: "Here's a note I've written for you to Murchison, the guard who will be on duty down here tonight. He's not here yet. And I'll introduce you to the supervisor as we go out, so there will be no trouble when you come in after dinner."

On the way up to the main entrance I surprised an unwonted expression on Blake's face. He said abruptly, "Of course, Jerry, I don't really know much about that Codex or its origin. Something might happen—I suppose. Watch your step. And if anything does begin to break, get out."

I stared at him in plain amazement. Through the big doors the sunlight was slanting cheerfully across Fifth Avenue. "Forget it. I'm making the easiest hundred bucks I've ever found. . . . Remember me to Aunt Doris."

There wasn't any sunlight now. I sat back on my chair, staring into black murk. I couldn't fool myself into believing that I was relaxed; I realised in fact, that my muscles were tensed as if for a spring. Not that I had any idea where to spring or for what purpose.

Funny, how thick the darkness seemed to be. One's eyes usually become accustomed to lack of light within a relatively short time, but the window continued as dim as at first, minute after minute. I couldn't see the table, only a few feet away. This darkness was like the silence—it had weight—it *pressed.* The cigarettes I had been smoking all evening, perhaps? That was a comforting thought and I clung to it as long as I could. Still, cigarette smoke doesn't show a preference, in a closed room, for one part rather than for another. I became more and more certain that the gloom was deeper in the corner where the Codex rested than anywhere else. Where the mischief was Murchison? How long *did* it take him to plug in a new fuse, anyhow?

A little rustle! Little enough, it would not even have been perceptible ordinarily; in the silence of the room it was not only perceptible but it just couldn't be put down to imagination. Thank God it didn't come from the direction of the table. It was only momentary and the silence resumed, as leaden as ever. *Had* I imagined it? As I strained my ears for a repetition, Blake's words occurred to me—"If anything breaks, get out." It also occurred to me that the Codex was between me and the door. The fact that the door was locked, if I remember correctly, didn't occur to me till later.

Why hadn't I brought a flashlight? I hadn't brought a thing, actually. A gun would have helped a lot, too. I'm a good shot with an automatic; but a good shot without an automatic is about as useful as a fine yachtsman in the subway. I couldn't blame myself for that, however. When I had left home in the morning I hadn't foreseen a night of conflict with the nebulous menace of a piece of manuscript.

I suppose your eardrums, if you are listening intently, become supersensitised. Something about "sets," I think. At any rate the noise that broke out was terrific; it seemed as if fifty devils had started screaming simultaneously. I don't know whether I yelled or not (probably did) but I gave such a jump that I upset the chair and found myself sprawling on the floor, supported by one foot, one knee, and one hand. As I scrambled to my feet, still instinctively crouching, I was too scared to do any thinking. It was only when the noise stopped and then began again, that I realised the telephone was ringing.

I was relieved. For the moment I just straightened up and felt like singing the first song that came into my head. Then I became annoyed, suddenly, at the infernal din the thing was making. I started toward the bend in the room and the instrument beyond it; and of course knocked a couple of bundles off the pile at the corner. With a hearty "Damnation!" I took up the receiver.

"Hallo."

"Hartmann speaking from the Waldorf. Jerry, is everything O.K. so far?"

That fellow certainly wouldn't find out how uncomfortable I was, if I could help it. I felt grateful to him, though, for the steadying effect of his silly voice. But I wasn't prepared yet for much talking. "Certainly. Why not?"

"You're sure? Nothing a bit out of the way has happened?"

"Well, the lights seem to be out for the moment."

"What? . . . My God! . . . "

I waited but there wasn't any more.

"What do you mean, my God?"

The quiet over the wire continued for so long that I began considering the possibility that he had left the phone. Then his voice came through excitedly.

"Jerry, get out of that room! Listen, Jerry, please, *please* will you get out? I'll pay you the hundred, I'll——. Get out now! Before it happens. Now!"

I'll admit I had a hard time answering that one, but I did. I said, "I won't get out at all. Anyhow, I can't; the door's locked——"

"Oh my God! You say the door's *locked*?" Hartmann's voice rose into a kind of wail that, under the circumstances, wasn't the pleasantest sound I could have thought of. "Jerry, Jerry! Listen to me; listen carefully. If you can't get out, you must do this. You must; understand, you must! Don't go near the Codex. Get as far away from it as you can, even if only across the room. And lie down on the floor. Do you hear me, Jerry? You must lie down on the floor; get as——"

Click.

And there I was, inanely banging the hook of the telephone up and down. It was dark as pitch in the room. There was silence over the wire. There isn't much that is deader than a dead telephone line, but somehow the silence over the wire didn't seem half as dead as the silence in the room.

I couldn't go one way, nor could I go the other. I stood there, with the telephone receiver still in my hand. The telephone had gone now, too. The lights had gone, the guard had gone, the telephone had gone; what price those "forces of civilisation"?

What is unavailable, it was being borne in upon me, might just as well not exist. . . . What could he possibly mean, about lying down? Why lie down? It didn't——

The lights came on.

Instantaneously. Just as they had gone off. Light is truly a blessed thing. I only realised that I had been trembling when I stopped, after the first dazzle was over. There were the blank walls, the two black windows, the piles of bundles, the crated statue. All motionless, with the stolidity of the prosaic. It was all right; it was all right, I repeated, it was all right. I drew a deep breath of the heavy air and expelled it in a long "whew." Automatically I put the receiver on the phone. I started back to my chair in the other part of the room.

Right then I got the biggest shock of my life. The table was absolutely bare. The Codex had vanished!

I jumped to the door and shook it; it was locked as tightly as ever. I turned and stood stock still, staring down at the table, disbelieving my eyes.

From somewhere I heard an unmistakable chuckle.

I whirled around. And saw him.

There he stood, leaning negligently against the corner of the wall where the room turned, and regarding me with amusement in his grey eyes. A tall, lean man in an ordinary tweed suit. A sensitive face, ending in a long, strong jaw.

A number of thoughts chased themselves through my head in the space of that first second. Amazement was one of them. How had he gotten in? And if he had (which was impossible, unless he could walk through locked doors), how had he managed to get behind me? He hadn't been in the other half of the room when I had put down the telephone receiver; and during my trip from the flat desk to the door, he could not have passed me, for the lights had been on then. Hostility was another of the thoughts. Had I not been overwrought by what had gone before, I might have reflected that, once in, he certainly couldn't get out again until the guard returned, and I might have acted differently. But as it was, I would probably have flung myself upon anything in the room that moved or betrayed an appearance of animation.

I flung myself upon the man at the corner, glad that he no more resembled an Aztec bird-god in armour than did any one else to be met with on Broadway in the daytime. Here was someone I could deal with adequately, at any rate.

It soon turned out that I was wrong in that, however. Unexpectedly as my sudden attack must have been, he slipped back in a quick turn and landed a powerful blow against my shoulder. I got in with a few then on my own account, while he contented himself with little more than parrying. Within a short time, however, he appeared to have come to the conclusion that I meant business. He stepped closer; just as I was launching a smash toward his chin, he ducked with an agility that caught me unprepared, grasped my arm in a grip like a vice, and twisted.

The arm was bent back behind me. My face was forced suddenly forward and collided smartly with a bony knee that moved into its path at the proper instant. Then the knee moved on and I was forced to the floor with my opponent kneeling over me. Pain shot along my arm from the wrist and began spreading over the shoulder. I grunted with it and tried in vain to twist away; all I accomplished was to rub my face along the floor until it was turned once more in the direction of the doorway.

I had just achieved this position, surely no improvement

upon its predecessor, when the door opened. Murchison stood in the entrance, his mouth partly open in amazement. But not for long. Like the other museum guards, he was a special officer and the gun that came up in his hand was business-like and steady. Although it was pointing too near my own head for comfort, I have seldom been more pleased with the sight of any weapon.

"Get up outta that," commanded Murchison. "Stand away."

They were the first words, except my short replies to Hartmann, that had been spoken in the room since he had left.

"Who is the man?" Murchison demanded.

I said: "I don't know. I never saw him before." I had gotten to my feet now and crossed over to the guard beside the doorway. Opposite us the fellow stood nonchalantly in the centre of the room, his hands in his coat pockets, and regarded us quizzically but with evident good humour. Murchison still had him covered.

"Don't worry, he's got the Codex," I went on grimly. "It was here when you left to see to the lights. When they came on, it was gone and he had gotten into the room somehow."

"Search him. . . . Up with your hands, my man."

I made the search, to which he acceded willingly enough, with that amused half-smile still on his lips. Most of it I conducted with the left hand, for my right arm was growing no less painful and was now beginning to swell. There was no sign of the Codex; and since it was a good two and a half feet long and a number of inches in diameter, it could scarcely have been concealed on his person. I found a bunch of keys and took from his coat pocket (where his own hand had so recently been) a wicked little automatic. I realised abruptly that he could easily have shot down Murchison, and myself too, a few seconds before. I looked at him perplexedly; this was certainly a funny sort of chap.

I tried his keys on the door immediately. None of them fitted and I tossed the bunch back to him. There was no other key on him. He said, "Thanks, old man," and pocketed them.

"Now," he went on, "you'll want to search the room. You have my word that I won't interfere, nor will I attempt to get away. Let's get it over with."

The easy sincerity in his voice impressed me, but Murchison, I noticed, continued to keep a wary eye on him. We began at the door and went completely through the room. Every bundle was moved, every box was opened, the desks were thoroughly searched and also moved about. No sign whatsoever of the Codex could we find.

When we came at last to the crated statue at the end of the room, there was a long slit down one side of the sacking. Before I could say anything, our prisoner remarked conversationally, "Yes, that's where I was. Of course. The lady with me looks hot but feels cold. If you have to lean against her for a few hours."

I hadn't an idea what he meant until I enlarged the slit somewhat and peered inside the crate. I recalled vaguely that Astarte was never considered as a symbol of the virginal and this conception, chiselled some thousands of years ago in Palestine, even from the small glimpse I could get, was sizzling. It struck me as a side thought that the basement was probably destined to be her permanent home at the Metropolitan.

The crate yielded nothing either. And that was the end. Definitely, the Codex had vanished from this locked room.

Our companion suggested calmly: "It's getting late and I should like to leave presently. Will you please call up Mr. Roger Thorpe on that telephone? The number is Butterfield 7-8344."

For want of anything better to do, the truth being that my mind was filled with bewilderment, I followed the suggestion. But I decided not to be too naïve about it. First I called Information and verified that the number was that of Roger Thorpe.

After a minute's ringing Thorpe himself answered the phone; and since he was already acquainted with the situation, it took little time to tell him what had happened. He received the news with rumbles of excitement. "Let me speak to Tarrant at once," he snorted through the receiver.

I placed the receiver against my side and turned about. "What is your name?" I asked the man across the room.

He was bending forward, lighting a cigarette. When he had finished, he said: "My name is Trevis Tarrant. Thorpe wants to speak with me?"

I handed the instrument over to him and heard him confirming the information I had just given. . . . "And kindly speak to this guard here, so I can go home. . . . Oh, forget it, Roger; and stop that snorting. You'll have it back by noon tomorrow, one o'clock at the latest. . . . Yes, I give you my guarantee."

More bewildered than ever, I hardly caught the end of Murchison's words through the instrument. The upshot, however, was a complete change in the guard's attitude. He now treated Tarrant with the utmost respect and seemed prepared to follow any directions the latter might give.

"Well," said Tarrant, "first of all I'll take back my little gun. And then I shall bid you goodnight, if you will be so good as to show me the way out. How is your arm, young man?"

I winced with pain as he touched it and his concern was apparent at once. "That's a bad wrench," he ejaculated. "Worse than I meant. See here, you must come along with me and spend the night. No, I insist. I can fix that arm up for you; I owe you that much at the very least. Yes, yes, it's decided; let us be getting along."

I was too tired and in too much pain to argue. I merely went with him.

We picked up a cab opposite the Museum and in a few minutes were set down before a modern apartment house in the East Thirties. As Tarrant opened the door of his apartment a little Jap butler-valet, spick-and-span in a white coat, came hurrying into the entrance hallway, despite the lateness of the hour.

"Katoh," Tarrant advised him, "this is Mr. Jerry Phelan. He will spend the rest of the night with us. Let us have two stiff whiskies for a nightcap, please."

In the lounge-like room, pleasant and semi-modernistic, which we entered, the butler was already coming forward with a tray of bottles, glasses, and siphon. The drinks were quickly mixed.

"Bless," said Tarrant raising his glass. He took a long pull. "Mr. Phelan is suffering from a severe ju-jitsu wrench in his right arm. See what you can do for him, Katoh."

Once again the man hastened away, to return in a moment with a small bottle of ointment. He indicated a couch upon which he invited me to rest and helped me out of my coat and shirt. The arm was now throbbing with pain and was almost unbearable when he first touched it. His fingers were deft, strong—and gentle; and within a short time the peculiar massage he administered began to have a soothing effect.

To distract my attention, Tarrant was talking. "Katoh is as well educated a man as either you or I," he was saying. "He is a doctor in his own country in fact. Over here he is a Japanese spy. I found that out some time ago."

Katoh, busy with the muscles of my shoulder, looked up and grinned impishly. "Yiss." He poured out more ointment. "Not to mention, pless. Not everybody so broad-minded."

"Oh, I don't mind a bit," my host assured me. "If he wants to draw maps of New York when he could buy much better ones from Rand McNally for fifty cents, it's entirely all right. . . . I heartily approve of spy systems that permit me to hire one of my equals as a butler. . . . A hobby of mine, as you saw tonight, is investigating strange or bizarre occurrences and he's sometimes invaluable to me there also. No; I'm not only amused by the spy custom but I am actually a beneficiary of it."

My arm was now so greatly improved that I was becoming aware of a tremendous fatigue. I sat up, mumbling my thanks, and finished off my drink. Tarrant said: "I think you'll sleep very well. Show him where to do it, Katoh."

I hardly saw the room to which the little Jap conducted me and where he assisted me out of my clothes and into a pair of silk pyjamas. The events of the evening had worn me out completely; I remember seeing the bed before me, but I don't remember getting into it.

At quarter of ten the next morning Katoh came into the room just as I was preparing to open one eye. As he advanced toward me, he grinned cheerfully and observed, "Stiff, yiss?"

In a moment I was sufficiently awake to perceive the justice of the remark. My whole arm and shoulder were incapable of movement and as I inadvertently rolled over on my side, I gave a grunt of pain.

"Pless."

The butler very gently removed my pyjama top and got to work with the same bottle of ointment. His ability was amazing; it could have been no more than a minute before the arm was limbering up. Within five minutes the pain had gone completely.

"All right now. You rub tonight, then all finish. Your shower ready, sair."

Tarrant was waiting for me in the lounge, beside a table upon which two breakfast places had been laid out. As soon as we had greeted each other I lost no time in attacking the ice-cold grapefruit before my place. I was hungrier, in fact, than I can ever remember being.

During an excellent repast, of which I evidenced my appreciation in the most practical way, little was said. But when we had finished the last cup of coffee and were leaning back enjoying that first, and best, cigarette of the day, Tarrant remarked: "I see you know Marius Hartmann."

This was surprising. I was sure I had not mentioned Hartmann to him during our brief acquaintance.

He smiled at my puzzled expression. "No," he remonstrated, "I am not trying to emulate Holmes and bewilder a Dr. Watson. His card dropped out of your pocket last night when Katoh helped you out of your coat. There it is, over on the smoking stand."

"Oh, I see. Yes, I know him, worse luck. And by golly I shall have to step round and see him this morning." I explained how I had come to be in the Museum the night before and related the matter of the wager. "So there it stands," I finished. "I'm out a hundred dollars I certainly never expected to lose."

"Bad luck," my host observed. "Still, it was a foolish bet to have made. As I believe I mentioned last night, I interest myself in the sort of peculiar affairs with which we had to do; and whatever else may be said about them, they always come out unexpectedly. Very poor subjects for wagers. I should never risk anything on them myself."

"I am altogether in the dark," I confessed. "I can't imagine what happened to the Codex. You—you don't think it's possible that that Aztlan Curse thing really worked, do you?" With the sunlight streaming in brightly I was viewing the matter quite differently than a few hours before. And yet, what could have happened?

"If you are asking whether I take a seven-hundred-year-old Mexican threat literally, I can tell you I don't. I have seen older warnings than that take a miss; very much older. You heard me talking to Thorpe over the phone; he was afraid something would happen and, at my suggestion, he smuggled me into the room in the basement to discover what it might be."

I grinned. "So I'm not the only one out of luck this morning."

"I'm afraid you are," Tarrant stated calmly. "In spite of your own unexpected presence which kept me much closer to the charmingly immoral Astarte than I had intended, I know exactly what occurred, and why."

"Well——"

"Yes, I think you are entitled to an explanation, but I should rather let you have it a little later. Before the morning is out, I'll be glad to tell you. Meantime, if you intend calling on Marius Hartmann, I should like to go with you, provided you have no objection. It happens that I should like to meet him and this will be a good opportunity, if you are sure you don't mind."

I expressed my entire willingness; indeed I was finding my new friend a pleasant companion. And presently we alighted in front of Hartmann's sumptuous apartment on upper Fifth Avenue, somewhat above the Museum.

His rooms were ornate, with the stuffiness of classic furnishing, and filled with *objets*, as I am sure he called them. We had little time to notice them, however, for he made an immediate appearance. His smile was just what I had expected, as he greeted me. "I take it you have come to make a little settlement? You're very prompt, Jerry."

With the best grace I could summon I admitted his victory; and seeing a spindly kind of desk against one wall, I sat down and wrote out a cheque for him without more ado.

As I got up and waved the paper in the air to dry it (the desk had a sand trough instead of a blotter), I remembered Tarrant with sudden embarrassment. Hartmann had so exasperated me that I had forgotten my manners. I stammered some apologies and made the introduction.

They shook hands and Tarrant appropriated the only decent chair in the room. "By the way, Mr. Hartmann," he asked, "how did you know so soon what happened at the Museum last night?"

"Eh? Oh, I telephoned Roger Thorpe first thing this morning and he told me all about it. I felt pretty sure something unusual would occur; the ancients possessed strange powers on this continent as well as in the East. But this is more remarkable than I imagined. Really inexplicable."

"Why, I wouldn't say that exactly." Tarrant crossed one long leg over the other, as he lounged back comfortably. "I was there myself last night during the—phenomenon and a rather simple explanation occurs to me."

"Is that so? You have discovered what type of power is in the Codex?" Hartmann leaned forward with every appearance of interest.

"There is undoubtedly a certain force in the Codex," my companion agreed, "though not quite the sort you are thinking of.

The recent phenomenon, however, was modern, very modern. And in a way estimable; scheduled simplicity is always a characteristic of the best phenomena. I almost regret that it didn't come off."

"How do you mean? I thought——"

"Oh, surely, the Codex vanished. But I have the strongest reasons to believe that it will return before one o'clock this afternoon. If you know what I mean?"

"But I don't know at all. I can't imagine. You suppose that in some way it became invisible last night and will materialise again today?"

"No, Mr. Hartmann," said Tarrant softly, "I do not look for anything so astonishing. The Codex will reappear in a much more prosaic manner, I expect. It would not surprise me, for instance, if it should be handed in at the entrance of the Museum by a messenger, addressed to the Curator of Central American Antiquities. Of course, it might be delivered otherwise, but that, I should think, would be perhaps the best way."

"You surprise me," Hartmann declared. "Why should such a thing happen?"

"Chiefly because a certain Deputy Inspector Brown is a great friend of mine. He is a very busy man, handling cases turned over to him by the District Attorney, signing search warrants, but I am sure he would be glad to take a few minutes any time to see me. Ours is a very close friendship; he has actually sent two of his men with me this morning, simply on the chance that I might have some unexpected use for them. . . . Yes, that, I think, is the real reason why the Codex may be expected to reappear before my time limit runs out. It would embarrass me somewhat if the prediction I made to Roger Thorpe should fail in any particular."

Hartmann had plainly been giving the words his serious attention. He said, "I see."

Tarrant got unconcernedly out of his chair and, on his feet, extended his right hand. "It has been a pleasure to make your acquaintance, Mr. Hartmann. I should be glad of your opinion about my little prediction. Of course, I can come back later—I should be delighted to see you again—but in that case I fear it will be too late to justify *all* my claims as prophet."

The other apparently failed to observe Tarrant's hand. He said, "I should really prefer not to interfere further with your day. Pleasant as your visit has been, I feel that we might not get on if we saw too much of each other. On the other hand, I may say I feel certain that so *brilliant* a man as you cannot be mistaken, especially when he has gone so far as to confide his expectations to one of the Museum Directors."

It was evidently our cue to leave and I followed Tarrant across the room puzzled by the enigmatic fencing with words to which I had been a witness. At the doorway he turned.

"Oh, I'm afraid I nearly forgot something, Mr. Hartmann. Experiments of the kind we engaged in last night naturally carry no other penalty than failure. There is, however, a small fine of one hundred dollars, to cover the necessary experimental expenses and I have arranged that my friend Phelan should be empowered to deal with it rather than my other friend, Inspector Brown. To save everyone's time and trouble. Brown, as I said, is so busy he has doubtless forgotten all about it by now and it would be a shame to impose on his time unnecessarily."

Marius Hartmann did a most surprising thing. He said, "I fear I shall be forced to agree with you again. Fortunately the matter is simple, as you have arranged it."

He took from his pocket the cheque I had given him and, tearing it into small bits, dropped them into a tall vase.

In the taxi, on the way downtown, I turned to Tarrant. "But what—how—what *is* this all about?"

Tarrant's expression was one of amusement. "Surely you realise that Hartmann has the Codex?"

"Well, yes; I suppose so. I couldn't make head or tail of most of the conversation, but when he tore up my cheque, I realised he must be on a spot somehow. But I don't see how he *can* have gotten hold of it. He was at the Waldorf telephoning me just before it disappeared. . . . Or was that a fake? Wasn't he at the Waldorf at all?"

"Oh, no," said Tarrant, "I'm sure he was at the Waldorf; and almost certainly had a friend with him at the telephone booth, to make sure of his alibi. His accomplice took the Codex, of course, and delivered it to him later."

"His accomplice?"

"Murchison, the guard. That is the only way it could have happened. The affair was run off on a time schedule. Murchison turned the lights off at an arranged time. A few minutes later Hartmann phoned, calling you into the other part of the room, and while you were talking to him, the guard quietly opened the door, secured the Codex in the dark and locked the door again. His cue to do so was the ringing of the telephone bell. I've no doubt Hartmann did everything he could to upset you while the lights were out so that you would be too nervous to connect anything you might hear with an ordinary opening of the door."

"Yes, he certainly did. He pretended to be frightened half out of his wits about me. Told me I must get as far away from the Codex as I could. But look here, Hartmann was the one to suggest that I be there, in the first place. Surely he wouldn't have done that, if——"

"A brilliant idea; he is really a smart chap. He didn't know I was going to be there; didn't know anything about me. But if no one was present, it is obvious the guard would be suspected, as the only person to have a key, and be grilled unmercifully. He might break down. But this way, here was someone else, present at Hartmann's own suggestion, who would give evidence that the door had not been opened at the crucial time. Provided everything worked out as planned. No, that was a clever notion of his."

"How could you figure all this out, when you were inside that crate, if I'm right, during the theft?"

"Why, it's the only way it *could* have happened. Although I didn't see it, I was there in the room and knew just what the conditions were. If you attack the problem simply with reason—dismiss the smoke screen, an Aztec Curse this time—there cannot be any other solution."

I thought that over. After a few moments I said: "That might do for Murchison. But how did you know who had bribed him?"

"Oh, that. Well, it was a longer shot. But Thorpe had some suspicions of him, to begin with. Hartmann had suggested the possibility of something supernatural about the Codex when his offer was turned down. And when he heard about the opening warning, he mentioned it again. He slipped there. Thorpe felt sure, though, that Hartmann wouldn't plan an ordinary theft; that was why he fell in with the idea that I should be smuggled in. I wasn't entirely certain, until he made that other slip, giving away his knowledge of what had happened, when he first saw you just now. I talked with Thorpe this morning myself and asked especially whether Hartmann had called him. He hadn't."

"The man's no better than a common thief. It will be a good thing to have him arrested." By golly, I never had liked that man; and for the first time I was beginning to feel my animosity justified.

"Wouldn't think of having him arrested," was Tarrant's calm comment.

"Why not? He's a thief," I repeated.

"Nonsense. The episode was more in the nature of good entertainment than theft. The Codex will be back unharmed within an hour, which in itself is a very mitigating circumstance. All that talk of mine about Inspector Brown was pure bluff. Arrest one of the future benefactors of the Museum? He'll be on the Board some day. Don't be silly.

"As for me," Tarrant concluded, "I should dislike greatly seeing him arrested. There are far too few such clever fellows at large as it is. With Hartmann confined there would be just one less chance for my own amusement."

THE ADVENTURE OF THE THREE R'S
Ellery Queen

It is fair to say that Ellery Queen was America's foremost practitioner of the fair play detective story, so much so that critic (and mystery writer) Anthony Boucher wrote that "Ellery Queen IS the American detective story."

In what remains one of the most brilliant marketing decisions of all time, the two Brooklyn cousins who collaborated under the pseudonym Ellery Queen, Frederic Dannay (born Daniel Nathan) (1905-1982) and Manfred B(ennington) Lee (born Manford Lepofsky) (1905-1971), also named their detective Ellery Queen. They reasoned that if readers forgot the name of the author, *or* the name of the character, they might remember the other. It worked, as Ellery Queen is counted among the handful of best-known names in the history of mystery fiction.

Lee was a full collaborator on the fiction created as Ellery Queen, but Dannay on his own was also one of the most important figures in the mystery world. He founded *Ellery Queen's Mystery Magazine* in 1941 and it remains, more than seventy years later, the most significant periodical in the genre. He also formed one of the first great collections of detective fiction first editions, the rare contents leading to reprinted stories in the magazines and anthologies he edited, which are among the best ever produced, most notably *101 Years' Entertainment* (1941), which gets my vote as the greatest mystery anthology ever published.

Dannay also produced such landmark reference books as *Queen's Quorum* (1951), a listing and appreciation of the 106 (later expanded to 125) most important short story collections in the genre, and *The Detective Short Story* (1942), a bibliography of all the collections Dannay had identified up to the publication date.

It is not surprising that Ellery Queen wrote a bibliomystery; the only surprise is that there weren't more. Dannay was such a great bibliophile, scholar, and collector of one of the greatest collections of detective fiction ever assembled. It now resides at the Ransom Center at the University of Texas.

"The Adventure of the Three R's" was originally published in the September 1946 issue of *Ellery Queen's Mystery Magazine*; it was first collected in *The Calendar of Crime* (Boston, Little, Brown, 1952).

The Adventure of the Three R's

Ellery Queen

HAIL MISSOURI! Which is North and also South, upland and river-bottom, mountain, plain, factory, and farm. Hail Missouri! For MacArthur's corncob and Pershing's noble mule. Hail! For Hannibal and Mark Twain, for Excelsior Springs and Jesse James, for Barlowe and . . . Barlowe? Barlowe is the site of Barlowe College.

Barlowe College is the last place in Missouri you would go to (Missouri, which yields to no State in the historic redness of its soil) if you yearned for a lesson in the fine art of murder. In fact, the subject being introduced, it is the rare Show Me Stater who will not say, with an informative wink, that Barlowe is the last place in Missouri, and leave all the rest unsaid. But this is a smoke-room witticism, whose origin is as murky as the waters of the Big Muddy. It may well first have been uttered by the alumnus of some Missouri university whose attitude toward learning is steeped in the traditional embalming fluid—whereas, at little Barlowe, learning leaps: Jove and jive thunder in duet, profound sociological lessons are drawn from "Li'l Abner" and "Terry and the Pirates," and in the seminars of the Philosophy Department you are almost certain to find Faith, as a matter of pedagogic policy, paired with Hope.

Scratch a great work and find a great workman.

Dr. Isaiah St. Joseph A. Barlowe, pressed for vital statistics, once remarked that while he was old enough to have been a Founder, still he was not so old as to have calcified over a mound of English ivy. But the good man jested; he is as perennial as a sundial. "Even a cynic," Dr. Barlowe has said, "likes his grain of salt." And the truth is, in the garden where he labors, there is no death and a great deal of healthy laughter.

One might string his academic honors after him, like dutiful beads; one might recount the extraordinary tale of how, in the manner of Uther Pendragon, Dr. Barlowe bewitched some dumfounded Missourians and took a whole series of substantial buildings out of their pockets; one might produce a volume on the subject of his acolytes alone, who have sped his humanistic gospel into the far corners of the land. Alas, this far more rewarding reportage must await the service of one who has, at the very least, a thousand pages at his disposal. Here there is space merely to record that the liveliness of Barlowe's alarming approach to scholarship is totally the inspiration of Dr. Isaiah St. Joseph A. Barlowe.

Those who would instruct at Barlowe must pass a rather unusual entrance examination. The examination is conducted *in camera*, and its nature is as sacredly undisclosable as the Thirty-Third Rite; nevertheless, leaks have occurred, and it may be significant that in its course Dr. Barlowe employs a 16-millimeter motion-picture projector, a radio, a portable phonograph, one copy each of The Bible, *The Farmer's Almanac*, and *The Complete Sherlock Holmes;* and the latest issue of *The Congressional Record*—among others. During examinations the voices of Donald Duck and Young Widder Brown have been reported; and so on. It is all very puzzling, but perhaps not unconnected with the fact that visitors often cannot distinguish who are Barlowe students and who are Barlowe professors. Certainly a beard at Barlowe is no index of dignity; even the elderly among the faculty extrude a zest more commonly associated with the fuzzy-chinned undergraduate.

So laughter and not harumphery is rampant upon the Gold and the Puce; and, if corpses dance macabre, it is only upon the dissection tables of Bio III, where the attitude toward extinction is roguishly empirical.

Then imagine—if you can—the impact upon Barlowe, not of epic murder as sung by the master troubadours of Classics I; not of romantic murder (Abbot, Anthony to Zangwill, Israel) beckoning from the rental shelves of The Campus Book Shop; but of murder loud and harsh.

Murder, as young Professor Bacon of the Biochemistry Department might say, with a stink.

The letter from Dr. Barlowe struck Ellery as remarkably woeful.

"One of my faculty has disappeared," wrote the president of Barlowe College, "and I cannot express to you, Mr. Queen, the extent of my apprehension. In short, I fear the worst.

"I am aware of your busy itinerary, but if you are at all informed regarding the institution to which I have devoted my life, you will grasp the full horror of our dilemma. We feel we have erected something here too precious to be befouled by the nastiness of the age; on the other hand, there are humane—not to mention legal—considerations. If, as I suspect, Professor Chipp has met with foul play, it occurred to me that we might investigate *sub rosa* and at least present the not altogether friendly world with *un mystère accompli*. In this way, much anguish may be spared us all.

"Can I prevail upon you to come to Barlowe quietly, and at once? I feel confident I speak for our Trustees when I say we shall have no difficulty about the coarser aspects of the association."

The letter was handwritten, in a hasty and nervous script which seemed to suggest guilty glances over the presidential shoulder.

It was all so at variance with what Ellery had heard about Dr. Isaiah St. Joseph A. Barlowe and his learned vaudeville show that he scribbled a note to Inspector Queen and ran. Nikki, clutching her invaluable notebook, ran with him.

Barlowe, Missouri, lay torpid in the warm September sunshine. And the distant Ozarks seemed to be peering at Barlowe inquisitively.

"Do you suppose it's got out, Ellery?" asked Nikki *sotto*

voce as a sluggish hack trundled them through the slumbering town. "It's all so still. Not like a college town at all."

"Barlowe is still in its etesian phase," replied Ellery pedantically. "The fall term doesn't begin for another ten days."

"You always make things so darned uninteresting!"

They were whisked into Dr. Barlowe's sanctum.

"You'll forgive my not meeting you at the station," muttered the educator as he quickly shut the door. He was a lean gray-thatched man with an Italianate face and lively black eyes whose present preoccupation did not altogether extinguish the lurking twinkle. Missouri's Petrarch, thought Ellery with a chuckle. As for Nikki, it was love at first sight. "Softly, softly—that must be our watchword."

"Just who is Professor Chipp, Dr. Barlowe?"

"American Lit. You haven't heard of Chipp's seminar on Poe? He's an authority—it's one of our more popular items."

"Poe," exclaimed Nikki. "Ellery, that should give you a personal interest in the case."

"Leverett Chisholm Chipp," nodded Ellery, remembering. "Monographs in *The Review* on the Poe prose. Enthusiasm and scholarship. That Chipp . . ."

"He's been a Barlowe appendage for thirty years," said the doctor unhappily. "We really couldn't go on without him."

"When was Professor Chipp last seen?"

Dr. Barlowe snatched his telephone. "Millie, send Ma Blinker in now. . . . Ma runs the boarding house on the campus where old Chipp's had rooms ever since he came to Barlowe to teach, Mr. Queen. Ah! Ma! Come in. And shut the door!"

Ma Blinker was a brawny old Missourian who looked as if she had been summoned to the council chamber from her Friday's batch of apple pies. But it was a landlady's eye she turned on the visitors from New York—an eye which did not surrender until Dr. Barlowe uttered a cryptic reassurance, whereupon it softened and became moist.

"He's an old love, the Professor is," she said brokenly. "Regular? Ye could set your watch by that man."

"I take it," murmured Ellery, "Chipp's regularity is germane?"

Dr. Barlowe nodded. "Now, Ma, you're carrying on. And you with the blood of pioneers! Tell Mr. Queen all about it."

"The Professor," gulped Ma Blinker, "he owns a log cabin up in the Ozarks, 'cross the Arkansas line. Every year he leaves Barlowe first of July to spend his summer vacation in the cabin. First of July, like clockwork."

"Alone, Mrs. Blinker?"

"Yes, sir. Does all his writin' up there, he does."

"Literary textbooks," explained Barlowe. "Although summer before last, to my astonishment, Chipp informed me he was beginning a novel."

"First of July he leaves for the cabin, and one day after Labor Day he's back in Barlowe gettin' ready for the fall term."

"One day after Labor Day, Mr. Queen. Year in, year out. Unfailingly."

"And here 'tis the thirteenth of September and he ain't showed up in town!"

"Day after Labor Day. . . . Ten days overdue."

"All this fuss," asked Nikki, "over a measly ten days?"

"Miss Porter, Chipp's being ten days late is as unlikely as—as my being Mrs. Hudson in disguise! Unlikelier. I was so concerned, Mr. Queen, I telephoned the Slater, Arkansas, authorities to send someone up to Chipp's cabin."

"Then he didn't simply linger there past his usual date?"

"I can't impress upon you too strongly the inflexibility of Chipp's habit-pattern. He did not. The Slater man found no sign of Chipp but his trunk."

"But I gathered from your letter, Doctor, that you had a more specific reason for suspecting—"

"And don't we!" Ma Blinker broke out frankly now in bosomy sobs. "I'd never have gone into the Professor's rooms—it was another of his rules—but Dr. Barlowe said I ought to when the Professor didn't show up, so I did, and—and—"

"Yes, Mrs. Blinker?"

"There on the rug, in front of his fireplace," whispered the landlady, "was a great . . . big . . . stain."

"A stain!" gasped Nikki. "A *stain?*"

"A bloodstain."

Ellery raised his brows.

"I examined it myself, Mr. Queen," said Dr. Barlowe nervously. "It's—it's blood, I feel certain. And it's been on the rug for some time. . . . We locked Chipp's rooms up again, and I wrote to you."

And although the September sun filled each cranny of the president's office, it was a cold sun suddenly.

"Have you heard from Professor Chipp at all since July the first, Doctor?" asked Ellery with a frown.

Dr. Barlowe looked startled. "It's been his habit to send a few of us cards at least once during the summer recess . . . " He began to rummage excitedly through a pile of mail on his desk. "I've been away since early June myself. This has so upset me I . . . Why didn't I think of that? Ah, the trained mind . . . Mr. Queen, here it is!"

It was a picture postcard illustrating a mountain cascade of improbable blue surrounded by verdure of impossible green. The message and address were in a cramped and spidery script.

July 31

Am rewriting my novel. It will be a huge surprise to you all. Regards—

CHIPP

"His 'novel' again," muttered Ellery. "Bears the postmark Slater, Arkansas, July thirty-first of this year. Dr. Barlowe, was this card written by Professor Chipp?"

"Unmistakably."

"Doesn't the writing seem awfully awkward to you, Ellery?" asked Nikki, in the tradition of the detectival secretary.

"Yes. As if something were wrong with his hand."

"There is," sniffled Ma Blinker. "Middle and forefinger missin' to the second joint—poor, poor old man!"

"Some accident in his youth, I believe."

Ellery rose. "May I see that stain on Chipp's rug, please?"

A man may leave more than his blood on his hearth, he may leave his soul. The blood was there, faded brown and hard, but so was Professor Chipp, though *in absentia*.

The two small rooms overlooking the campus were as tidy as a barrack. Chairs were rigidly placed. The bed was a sculpture. The mantelpiece was a shopwindow display; each pipe in the rack had been reamed and polished and laid away with a mathematical hand. The papers in the pigeonholes of the old pine desk were ranged according to size. Even the missing professor's books were disciplined: no volume on these shelves leaned carelessly, or lolled dreaming on its back! They stood in battalions, company after company, at attention. And they were ranked by author, in alphabetical order.

"Terrifying," Ellery said; and he turned to examine a small ledger-like volume lying in the exact center of the desk's drop-leaf.

"I suppose this invasion is unavoidable," muttered Barlowe, "but I must say I feel as if I were the tailor of Coventry! What's in that ledger, Mr. Queen?"

"Chipp's personal accounts. His daily outlays of cash . . . Ah. This year's entries stop at the thirtieth day of June."

"The day before he left for his cabin!"

"He's even noted down what one postage stamp cost him . . ."

"That's the old Professor," sobbed Ma Blinker. Then she raised her fat arms and shrieked: "Heavens to Bessie, Dr. Barlowe! It's Professor Bacon back!"

"Hi, Ma!"

Professor Bacon's return was in the manner of a charge from third base. Having pumped the presidential hand violently, the young man immediately cried: "Just got back to the shop and found your note, Doctor. What's this nonsense about old Chipp's not showing up for the fall brawl?"

"It's only too true, Bacon," said Dr. Barlowe sadly, and he introduced the young man as a full professor of chemistry and biology, another of Ma Blinker's boarders, and Chipp's closest faculty friend.

"You agree with Dr. Barlowe as to the gravity of the situation?" Ellery asked him.

"Mr. Queen, if the old idiot's not back, something's happened to him." And for a precarious moment Professor Bacon fought tears. "If I'd only known," he mumbled. "But I've been away since the middle of June—biochemical research at Johns Hopkins. Damn it!" he roared. "This is more staggering than nuclear fission!"

"Have you heard from Chipp this summer, Professor?"

"His usual postcard. I may still have it on me . . . Yes!"

"Just a greeting," said Ellery, examining it. "Dated July thirty-first and postmarked Slater, Arkansas—exactly like the card he sent Dr. Barlowe. May I keep this, Bacon?"

"By all means. Chipp not back . . ." And then the young man spied the brown crust on the hearthrug. He collapsed on the missing man's bed, gaping at it.

"Ellery!"

Nikki was standing on tiptoe before Chipp's bookshelves. Under *Q* stood a familiar phalanx.

"A complete set of *your* books!"

"Really?" But Ellery did not seem as pleased as an author making such a flattering discovery should. Rather, he eyed one of the volumes as if it were a traitor. And indeed there was a sinister air about it, for it was the only book on all the shelves—he now noted for the first time—which did not exercise the general discipline. It stood on the shelf upside down.

"Queer . . ." He took it down and righted it. In doing so, he opened the back cover; and his lips tightened.

"Oh, yes," said Barlowe gloomily. "Old Chipp's quite unreasonable about your books, Mr. Queen."

"Only detective stories he'd buy," muttered Professor Bacon. "Rented the others."

"A mystery bug, eh?" murmured Ellery. "Well, here's one Queen title he didn't buy." He tapped the book in his hand.

"*The Origin of Evil,*" read Nikki, craning. "Rental library!"

"The Campus Book Shop. And it gives us our first confirmation of that bloodstain."

"What do you mean?" asked Bacon quickly, jumping off the bed.

"The last library stamp indicates that Professor Chipp rented this book from The Campus Book Shop on June twenty-eight. A man as orderly as these rooms indicate, who moreover scrupulously records his purchase of a postage stamp, would scarcely trot off on a summer vacation and leave a book behind to accumulate eleven weeks' rental-library charges."

"Chipp? Impossible!"

"Contrary to his whole character."

"Since the last entry in that ledger bears the date June thirtieth, and since the bloodstain is on this hearthrug," said Ellery gravely, "I'm afraid, gentlemen, that your colleague was murdered in this room on the eve of his scheduled departure for the Ozarks. He never left this room alive."

No one said anything for a long time.

But finally Ellery patted Ma Blinker's frozen shoulder and said: "You didn't actually see Professor Chipp leave your boarding house on July first, Mrs. Blinker, did you?"

"No, sir," said the landlady stiffly. "The expressman came for his trunk that mornin', but the Professor wasn't here. I . . . thought he'd already left."

"Tell me this, Mrs. Blinker: did Chipp have a visitor on the preceding night—the night of June thirtieth?"

A slow change came over the woman's blotchy features.

"He surely did," she said. "He surely did. That Weems."

"Weems?" Dr. Barlowe said quickly. "Oh, no! I mean . . ."

"Weems," said Nikki. "Ellery, didn't you notice that name on The Campus Book Shop as we drove by?"

Ellery said nothing.

Young Bacon muttered: "Revolting idea. But then . . . Weems and old Chipp were always at each other's throats."

"Weems is the only other one I've discussed Chipp's nonappearance with," said the college president wildly. "He seemed so concerned!"

"A common interest in Poe," said Professor Bacon fiercely.

"Indeed," smiled Ellery. "We begin to discern a certain unity of plot elements, don't we? If you'll excuse us for a little while, gentlemen, Miss Porter and I will have a chat with Mr. Weems."

But Mr. Weems turned out to be a bustly, bald little Missouri countryman, with shrewdly-humored eyes and the prevailing jocular manner, the most unmurderous-looking character imaginable. And he presided over a shop so satisfyingly full of books, so aromatic with the odors of printery and bindery, and he did so with such a naked bibliophilic tenderness, that Nikki—for one—instantly dismissed him as a suspect.

Yep, Mr. Queen'd been given to understand correctly that he, Claude Weems, had visited old Chipp's rooms at Ma Blinker's on the night of June thirty last; and, yep, he'd left the old chucklehead in the best of health; and, no, he hadn't laid eyes on him since that evenin'. He'd shut up shop for the summer and left Barlowe on July fifteenth for his annual walking tour cross-country; didn't get back till a couple of days ago to open up for fall.

"Doc Barlowe's fussin' too much about old Chipp's not turnin' up," said little Mr. Weems, beaming. "Now I grant you he's never done it before, and all that, but he's gettin' old, Chipp is. Never can tell what a man'll do when he passes a certain age."

Nikki looked relieved, but Ellery did not.

"May I ask what you dropped in to see Chipp about on the evening of June thirtieth, Mr. Weems?"

"To say goodbye. And then I'd heard tell the old varmint'd just made a great book find—"

"Book find! Chipp had 'found' a book?"

Mr. Weems looked around and lowered his voice. "I heard he'd picked up a first edition of Poe's *Tamerlane* for a few dollars from some fool who didn't know its worth. You a collector, Mr. Queen?"

"A *Tamerlane* first!" exclaimed Ellery.

"Is that good, Ellery?" asked Nikki with the candor of ignorance.

"Good! A *Tamerlane* first, Nikki, is worth at least $25,000!"

Weems chuckled. "Know the market, I see. Yes, sir, bein' the biggest booster old Edgar Allan ever had west of the Mississip', I wanted to see that copy bad, awful bad. Chipp showed it to me, crowin' like a cock in a roostful. Lucky dog," he said without audible rancor. "'Twas the real article, all right."

Nikki could see Ellery tucking this fact into one of the innumerable cubbyholes of his mind—the one marked *For Future Consideration*. So she was not surprised when he changed the subject abruptly.

"Did Professor Chipp ever mention to you, Weems, that he was engaged in writing a novel?"

"Sure did. I told ye he was gettin' old."

"I suppose he also told you the *kind* of novel it was?"

"Dunno as he did." Mr. Weems looked about as if for some goal for his spittle, but then, with his indignation, he swallowed it.

"Seems likely, seems likely," mumbled Ellery, staring at the rental-library section where murder frolicked.

"*What* seems likely, Ellery?" demanded Nikki.

"Considering that Chipp was a mystery fan, and the fact that he wrote Dr. Barlowe his novel would be a 'huge surprise,' it's my conclusion, Nikki, the old fellow was writing a whodunit."

"No! A Professor of Literature?"

"Say," exclaimed Mr. Weems. "I think you're right."

"Oh?"

"Prof Chipp asked me—in April, it was—to find out if a certain title's ever been used on a detective story!"

"Ah. And what was the title he mentioned, Weems?"

"*The Mystery of the Three R's.*"

"Three R's . . . Three R's?" cried Ellery. "But that's incredible! Nikki—back to the Administration Building!"

"Suppose he was," said Professor Bacon violently. "Readin'! 'Ritin'! 'Rithmetic! Abracadabra and Rubadubdub. What of it?"

"Perhaps nothing, Bacon," scowled Ellery, hugging his pipe. "And yet . . . see here. We found a clue pointing to the strong probability that Chipp never left his rooms at Ma Blinker's alive last June thirtieth. What was that clue? The fact that Chipp failed to return his rented copy of my novel to Weems' lending library. Novel . . . book . . . *reading*, gentlemen! The first of the traditional Three R's."

"Rot!" bellowed the professor, and he began to bite his fingernails.

"I don't blame you," shrugged Ellery. "But has it occurred to you that there is also *a writing clue?*"

At this Nikki went over to the enemy.

"Ellery, are you sure the sun . . . ?"

"Those postcards Chipp wrote, Nikki."

Three glances crossed stealthily.

"But I fail to see the connection, Mr. Queen," said Dr. Barlowe soothingly. "How are those ordinary postcards a clue?"

"And besides," snorted Bacon, "how could Chipp have been bumped off on June thirtieth and have mailed the cards a full month later, on July thirty-first?"

"If you'll examine the date Chipp wrote on the cards," said Ellery evenly, "you'll find that the *3* of *July 31* is crowded between the *y* of *July* and the *1* of *31*. If that isn't a clue, I never saw one."

And Ellery, who was as thin-skinned as the next artist, went on rather tartly to reconstruct the events of the fateful evening of June the thirtieth.

"Chipp wrote those cards in his rooms that night, dating them a day ahead—July first—probably intending to mail them from Slater, Arkansas, the next day on his way to the log cabin—"

"It's true Chipp loathed correspondence," muttered Dr. Barlowe.

"Got his duty cards out of the way before his vacation even began—the old sinner!" mumbled young Bacon.

"Someone then murdered him in his rooms, appropriated the cards, stuffed the body into Chipp's trunk—"

"Which was picked up by the expressman next morning and shipped to the cabin?" cried Nikki.

And again the little chill wind cut through the office.

"But the postmarks, Mr. Queen," said Barlowe stiffly. "The postmarks also say July *thirty*-first."

"The murderer merely waited a month before mailing them at the Slater, Arkansas, post-office."

"But *why?*" growled Bacon. "You weave beautiful rugs, man—but what do they mean?"

"Obviously it was all done, Professor Bacon," said Ellery, "to leave the impression that on July thirty-first Professor Chipp was *still alive* . . . to keep the world from learning that he was really murdered on the night of June thirtieth. And that, of course, is significant." He sprang to his feet. "We must examine the Professor's cabin—most particularly, his trunk!"

It was a little trunk—but then, as Dr. Barlowe pointed out in a very queer voice, Professor Chipp had been a little man.

Outdoors, the Ozarks were shutting up shop for the summer, stripping the faint-hearted trees and busily daubing hillsides; but in the cabin there was no beauty—only dust, and an odor of dampness . . . and something else.

The little steamer trunk stood just inside the cabin doorway.

They stared at it.

"Well, well," said Bacon finally. "Miss Porter's outside—what are we waiting for?"

And so they knocked off the rusted lock and raised the lid—and found the trunk empty.

Perhaps not quite empty: the interior held a pale, dead-looking mass of crumbly stuff.

Ellery glanced up at Professor Bacon.

"Quicklime," muttered the chemistry teacher.

"Quicklime!" choked the president. "But the body. Where's the body?"

Nikki's scream, augmented a dozen times by the encircling hills, answered Dr. Barlowe's question most unpleasantly.

She had been wandering about the clearing, dreading to catch the first cry of discovery from the cabin, when she came upon a little cairn of stones. And she had sat down upon it.

But the loose rocks gave way, and Miss Porter found herself sitting on Professor Chipp—or, rather, on what was left of Professor Chipp. For Professor Chipp had gone the way of all flesh—which is to say, he was merely bones, and very dry bones, at that.

But that it was the skeleton of Leverett Chisholm Chipp could not be questioned: the medius and index finger of the right skeletal hand were missing to the second joint. And that Leverett Chisholm Chipp had been most foully used was also evident: the top of the skull revealed a deep and ragged chasm, the result of what could only have been a tremendous blow.

Whereupon the old pedagogue and the young took flight, joining Miss Porter, who was quietly being ill on the other side of the cabin; and Mr. Queen found himself alone with Professor Chipp.

Later, Ellery went over the log cabin with a disagreeable sense of anticipation. There was no sensible reason for believing that the cabin held further secrets; but sense is not all, and the already-chilling air held a whiff of fatality.

He found it in a cupboard, in a green steel box, beside a rusty can of moldering tobacco.

It was a stapled pile of neat papers, curled by damp, but otherwise intact.

The top sheet, in a cramped, spidery hand, said:

The Mystery of the Three R's
by
L. C. Chipp

The discovery of Professor Chipp's detective story may be said to mark the climax of the case. That the old man had been battered to death in his rooms on the night of June thirtieth; that his corpse had been shipped from Barlowe, Missouri, to the Arkansas cabin in his own trunk, packed in quicklime to avert detection *en route;* that the murderer had then at his leisure made his way to the cabin, removed the body from the trunk, and buried it under a heap of stones—these were mere facts, dry as the Professor's bones. They did not possess the aroma of the grotesque—the *bouffe*—which rose like a delicious mist from the pages of that incredible manuscript.

Not that Professor Chipp's venture into detective fiction revealed a new master, to tower above the busy little figures of his fellow-toilers in this curious vineyard and vie for cloud-space only with Poe and Doyle and Chesterton. To the contrary. *The Mystery of the Three R's* by L. C. Chipp, was a labored exercise in familiar elements, distinguished chiefly for its enthusiasm.

No, it was not the murdered professor's manuscript which was remarkable; the remarkable thing was the manner in which life had imitated it.

It was a shaken group that gathered in Chipp's rooms the morning after the return from the Arkansas cabin. Ellery had called the meeting, and he had invited Mr. Weems of The Campus Book Shop to participate—who, upon hearing the ghastly news, stopped beaming, clamped his Missouri jaws shut, and began to gaze furtively at the door.

Ellery's own jaws were unshaven, and his eyes were red.

"I've passed the better part of the night," he began abruptly, "reading through Chipp's manuscript. And I must report an amazing—an almost unbelievable—thing.

"The crime in Chipp's detective story takes place in and about a small Missouri college called . . . Barleigh College."

"Barleigh," muttered the president of Barlowe.

"Moreover, the victim in Chipp's yarn is a methodical old professor of American Literature."

Nikki looked puzzled. "You mean that Professor Chipp—?"

"Took off on himself, Nikki—exactly."

"What's so incredible about that?" demanded young Bacon. "Art imitating life—"

"Considering the fact that Chipp plotted his story long before the events of this summer, Professor Bacon, it's rather a case of life imitating art. Suppose I tell you that the methodical old professor of American Literature in Chipp's story owns a cabin in the Ozarks where his body is found?"

"Even *that?*" squeaked Mr. Weems.

"And more, Weems. The suspects in the story are the President of Barleigh College, whose name is given as Dr. Isaac St. Anthony E. Barleigh; a local bookshop owner named Claudius Deems; a gay young professor of chemistry known as Macon; and, most extraordinary of all, the three main clues in Chipp's detective story revolve about—are called—'Readin',' ''Ritin',' and ''Rithmetic'!"

And the icy little wind blew once more.

"You mean," exclaimed Dr. Barlowe, "the crime we're investigating—Chipp's own death—is *an exact counterpart of the fictional crime Chipp invented in his manuscript?*"

"Down to the last character, Doctor."

"But Ellery," said Nikki, "how can that possibly be?"

"Obviously, Chipp's killer managed to get hold of the old fellow's manuscript, read it, and with hellish humor proceeded to copy in real life—actually to duplicate—the crime Chipp had created in fiction!" Ellery began to lunge about the little room, his usually neat hair disordered and a rather wild look on his face. "Everything's the same: the book that wasn't returned to the lending library—the 'readin'' clue; the picture postcards bearing forged dates—the ''ritin'' clue—"

"And the ''rithmetic' clue, Mr. Queen?" asked Barlowe in a quavering voice.

"In the story, Doctor, the victim has found a first edition of Poe's *Tamerlane*, worth $25,000."

Little Weems cried: "That's ''rithmetic,' all right!" and then bit his lip.

"And how," asked Professor Bacon thickly, "how is the book integrated into Chipp's yarn, Mr. Queen?"

"It furnishes the motive for the crime. The killer steals the victim's authentic *Tamerlane*—substituting for it a facsimile copy which is virtually worthless."

"But if everything else is duplicated . . ." began Dr. Barlowe in a mutter.

"Then that must be the motive for Professor Chipp's own murder!" cried Nikki.

"It would seem so, wouldn't it?" Ellery glanced sharply at the proprietor of The Campus Book Shop. "Weems, where is the first edition of *Tamerlane* you told me Chipp showed you on the night of June thirtieth?"

"Why—why—why, reckon it's on his shelves here somewheres, Mr. Queen. Under *P*, for Poe . . ."

And there it was. Under *P*, for Poe.

And when Ellery took it down and turned its pages, he smiled. For the first time since they had found the skeleton under the cairn, he smiled.

"Well, Weems," he said affably, "you're a Poe expert. Is this an authentic *Tamerlane* first?"

"Why—why—why, must be. 'Twas when old Chipp showed it to me that night—"

"Really? Suppose you re-examine it—now."

But they all knew the answer before Weems spoke.

"It ain't," he said feebly. "It's a facsim'le copy. Worth about $5."

"The *Tamerlane*—stolen," whispered Dr. Barlowe.

"So once again," murmured Ellery, "we find duplication. I think that's all. Or should I say, it's too much?"

And he lit a cigarette and seated himself in one of Professor Chipp's chairs, puffing contentedly.

"All!" exclaimed Dr. Barlowe. "I confess, Mr. Queen, you've—you've baffled me no end in this investigation. All? It's barely begun! *Who* has done all this?"

"Wait," said Bacon slowly. "It may be, Doctor, we don't need Queen's eminent services at that. If the rest has followed Chipp's plot so faithfully, why not the most important plot element of all?"

"That's true, Ellery," said Nikki with shining eyes. "*Who is the murderer in Professor Chipp's detective story?*"

Ellery glanced at the cowering little figure of Claude Weems.

"The character," he replied cheerfully, "whom Chipp had named Claudius Deems."

The muscular young professor snarled and he sprang.

"In your enthusiasm, Bacon," murmured Ellery, without

stirring from his chair, "don't throttle him. After all, he's such a little fellow, and you're so large—and powerful."

"Kill old Chipp, would you!" growled Professor Bacon; but his grip relaxed a little.

"Mr. Weems," said Nikki, looking displeased. "Of course! The murderer forged the dates on the postcards so he wouldn't know the crime had been committed on June thirtieth. And who'd have reason to falsify the true date of the crime? The one man who'd visited Professor Chipp that night!"

"The damned beast could easily have got quicklime," said Bacon, shaking Weems like a rabbit, "by stealing it from the Chemistry Department after everyone'd left the college for the summer."

"Yes!" said Nikki. "Remember Weems himself told us he didn't leave Barlowe until July fifteenth?"

"I do, indeed. And Weems' motive, Nikki?"

"Why, to steal Chipp's *Tamerlane.*"

"I'm afraid that's so," groaned Barlowe. "Weems as a bookseller could easily have got hold of a cheap facsimile to substitute for the authentic first edition."

"And he said he'd gone on a walking tour, didn't he?" Nikki added, warming to her own logic. "Well, I'll bet he 'walked' into that Arkansas post-office, Ellery, on July thirty-first, to mail those postcards!"

Weems found his voice.

"Why, now, listen here, little lady, I didn't kill old Chipp—" he began in the most unconvincing tones imaginable.

They all eyed him with savage scorn—all, that is, but Ellery.

"Very true, Weems," said Ellery, nodding. "You most certainly did not."

"He didn't . . ." began Dr. Barlowe, blinking.

"I . . . didn't?" gasped Weems, which seemed to Nikki a remarkable thing for him to have said.

"No, although I'm afraid I've been led very cleverly to *believe* that you did, Weems."

"See here, Mr. Queen," said Barlowe's president in a terrible voice. "Precisely what do you mean?"

"And how do you know he didn't?" shouted Bacon. "I told you, Doctor—this fellow's grossly overrated. The next thing you'll tell us is that Chipp hasn't been murdered at all!"

"Exactly," said Ellery. "Therefore Weems couldn't have murdered him."

"Ellery—" moaned Nikki.

"Your syllogism seems a bit perverted, Mr. Queen," said Dr. Barlowe severely.

"Yes!" snarled Bacon. "What about the evidence—?"

"Very well," said Ellery briskly, "let's consider the evidence. Let's consider the evidence of the skeleton we found near Chipp's cabin."

"Those dry bones? What about 'em?"

"Just that, Professor—they're so very dry. Bacon, you're a biologist as well as a chemist. Under normal conditions, how long does it take for the soft parts of a body to decompose completely?"

"How long . . . ?" The young man moistened his lips. "Muscles, stomach, liver—from three to four years. But—"

"And for decomposition of the fibrous tissues, the ligaments?"

"Oh, five years or so more. But—"

"And yet," sighed Ellery, "that desiccated skeleton was supposed to be the remains of a man who'd been alive *a mere eleven weeks before*. And not merely that—I now appeal to your chemical knowledge, Professor. Just what is the effect of quicklime on human flesh and bones?"

"Well . . . it's pulverulent. Would dry out a body—"

"Would quicklime destroy the tissues?"

"Er . . . no."

"*It would tend to preserve them?*"

"Er . . . yes."

"Therefore the skeleton we found couldn't possibly have been the mortal remains of Professor Chipp."

"But the right hand, Ellery," cried Nikki. "The missing fingers—just like Professor Chipp's—"

"I shouldn't think," said Ellery dryly, "snapping a couple of dry bones off a man dead eight or ten years would present much of a problem."

"Eight or ten years . . ."

"Surely, Nikki, it suggests the tenant of some outraged grave . . . or, considering the facts at our disposal, the far likelier theory that it came from a laboratory closet in the Biology Department of Barlowe College." And Professor Bacon cringed before Ellery's accusing glance, which softened suddenly in laughter. "Now, really, gentlemen. Hasn't this hoax gone far enough?"

"Hoax, Mr. Queen?" choked the president of Barlowe with feeble indignation.

"Come, come, Doctor," chuckled Ellery, "the game's up. Let me review the fantastic facts. What is this case? A detective story come to life. Bizarre—fascinating—to be sure. But really, Doctor, so utterly unconvincing!

"How conveniently all the clues in Chipp's manuscript found reflections in reality! The lending-library book, so long overdue—in the story, in the crime. The postcards written in advance—in the story, in the crime. The *Tamerlane* facsimile right here on Chipp's shelf—exactly as the manuscript has it. It would seem as if Chipp collaborated in his own murder."

"Collab—I can't make hide nor hair of this, Mr. Queen," began little Mr. Weems in a crafty wail.

"Now, now, Weems, as the bookseller-Poe-crony you were the key figure in the plot! Although I must confess, Dr. Barlowe, *you* played your role magnificently, too—and, Professor Bacon, you missed a career in the theater; you really did. The only innocent, I daresay, is Ma Blinker—and to you, gentlemen, I gladly leave the trial of facing that doughty lady when she finds out how her honest grief has been exploited in the interest of commerce."

"Commerce?" whimpered Nikki, who by now was holding her pretty head to keep it from flying off.

"Of course, Nikki. I was invited to Barlowe to follow an elaborate trail of carefully-placed 'clues' in order to reach the conclusion that Claude Weems had 'murdered' Professor Chipp. When I announced Weems' 'guilt,' the hoax was supposed to blow up in my face. *Old Prof Chipp would pop out of his hiding place grinning from ear to silly ear.*"

"Pop out . . . You mean," gasped Nikki, "you mean Professor Chipp is *alive?*"

"Only conclusion that makes sense, Nikki. And then," Ellery went on, glaring at the three cowering men, "imagine the headlines. 'Famous Sleuth Tricked By Hoax—Pins Whodunit On Harmless Prof.' Commerce? I'll say! Chipp's *Mystery of the Three R's*, launched by such splendid publicity, would be swallowed by a publisher as the whale swallowed Jonah—and there we'd have . . . presumably . . . a sensational bestseller.

"The whole thing, Nikki, was a conspiracy hatched by the

president of Barlowe, his two favorite professors, and their good friend the campus bookseller—a conspiracy to put old Chipp's first detective story over with a bang!"

And now the little wind blew warm, bringing the blood of shame to six male cheeks.

"Mr. Queen—" began the president hoarsely.

"Mr. Queen—" began the bio-chemistry professor hoarsely.

"Mr. Queen—" began the bookseller hoarsely.

"Come, come, gentlemen!" cried Ellery. "All is not lost! We'll go through with the plot! I make only one condition. Where the devil is Chipp? I want to shake the old scoundrel's hand!"

Barlowe is an unusual college.

THE UNIQUE HAMLET
Vincent Starrett

(Charles) Vincent (Emerson) Starrett (1886-1974) produced innumerable essays, biographical works, critical studies, and bibliographical pieces while managing the "Books Alive" column for the *Chicago Tribune* for many years. His autobiography, *Born in a Bookshop* (1965), should be required reading for bibliophiles of all ages.

Starrett indisputably was one of America's greatest bookmen, as evidenced by his young daughter, who offered the best tombstone inscription for anyone who is a Dofab—Eugene Field's useful word—which is a "damned old fool about books," as Starrett admitted to being. When a friend called at his home, Starrett's daughter answered the door and told the visitor that her father was "upstairs, playing with his books."

He wrote numerous mystery short stories and several detective novels, including *Murder on "B" Deck* (1929), *Dead Man Inside* (1931), and *The End of Mr. Garment* (1932). His 1934 short story, "Recipe for Murder," was expanded to the full length novel *The Great Hotel Murder* (1935), which was the basis for the film of the same title and released the same year; it starred Edmund Lowe and Victor McLaglen.

Few would argue that Starrett's most outstanding achievements were his writings about Sherlock Holmes, most notably *The Private Life of Sherlock Holmes* (1933) and "The Unique Hamlet," described by Sherlockians for decades as the best pastiche ever written.

It was privately printed in 1920 by Starrett's friend, Walter M. Hill, in a limited hardcover edition of unknown quantity. It is likely that ten copies were issued for the author with his name on the title page. The number of copies published with Hill's name on the title page has been variously reported as thirty-three, one hundred, one hundred ten, and two hundred. It was selected for *Queen's Quorum*, Ellery Queen's selection of the 106 most important volumes of detective fiction ever written.

The Unique Hamlet

Vincent Starrett

To Sir Arthur Conan Doyle with admiration and apologies

I

"HOLMES," SAID I, one morning as I stood in our bay window, looking idly into the street, "surely here comes a madman. Someone has incautiously left the door open and the poor fellow has slipped out. What a pity!"

It was a glorious morning in the spring, with a fresh breeze and inviting sunlight, but as it was rather early few persons were astir. Birds twittered under the neighboring eaves, and from the far end of the thoroughfare came faintly the droning cry of an umbrella repair man; a lean cat slunk across the cobbles and disappeared into a courtway; but for the most part the street was deserted save for the eccentric individual who had called forth my exclamation.

My friend rose lazily from the wicker rocker, in which he had been lounging, and came to my side, standing with long legs spread and hands in the pockets of his dressing gown. He smiled as he saw the singular personage coming along. A personage indeed he seemed to be, despite his odd actions, for he was tall and portly, with elderly whiskers of the brand known as muttonchop, and he seemed eminently respectable. He was loping curiously, like a tired hound, lifting his knees high as he ran, and a heavy double watch chain of gold bounced against and rebounded from the plump line of his figured waistcoat. With one hand he clutched despairingly at his silk, two-gallon hat, while with the other he essayed weird gestures in the air in an emotion bordering upon distraction. We could almost see the spasmodic workings of his countenance.

"What under heaven can ail him!" I cried. "See how he glances at the houses as he passes."

"He is looking at the numbers," responded Sherlock Holmes, with dancing eyes, "and I fancy it is ours that will bring him the greatest happiness. His profession, of course, is obvious."

"A banker, I imagine, or at least a person of affluence," I hazarded, wondering what curious bit of minutiae had betrayed the man's business to my remarkable companion, in a single glance.

"Affluent, yes," said Holmes, with a mischievous grin, "but not exactly a banker, Watson. Notice the sagging pockets, despite the excellence of his clothing, and the rather exaggerated madness of his eye. He is a collector, or I am very much mistaken."

"My dear fellow!" I exclaimed. "At his age and in his station!

And why should he be seeking us? When we settled that last bill—"

"Of books," said my friend, severely. "He is a professional book collector. His line is Caxtons, Elzevirs, Gutenberg Bibles, folios; not the sordid reminders of unpaid grocery accounts and tobacconists' debits. See, he is turning in here, as I expected, and in a moment he will stand upon our hearthrug and tell us the harrowing tale of an unique volume and its extraordinary disappearance."

His eyes gleamed and he rubbed his hands together in profound satisfaction. I could not but hope that Holmes' conjecture was correct, for he had had little to occupy his mind for some weeks, and I lived in constant fear that he would seek that stimulation his active brain required in the long-tabooed cocaine bottle.

As Holmes finished speaking the man's ring at the doorbell echoed through the apartment; hurried feet sounded upon the stairs, while the wailing voice of Mrs. Hudson, raised in agonized protest, could only have been occasioned by frustration of her coveted privilege of bearing his card to us. Then the door burst violently inward and the object of our analysis staggered to the center of the room and, without announcing his intention by word or sign, pitched headforemost onto our center rug. There he lay, a magnificent ruin, with his head on the fringed border and his feet in the coal scuttle; and sealed within his lifeless lips the amazing story he had come to tell for that it was amazing we could not doubt, in the light of our client's extraordinary behavior.

Holmes quickly ran for the brandy bottle, while I knelt beside the stricken mountain of flesh and loosened the wilted neckband. He was not dead, and, when we had forced the nozzle of the flask between his teeth, he sat up in groggy fashion, passing a dazed hand across his eyes. Then he scrambled to his feet with an embarrassed apology for his weakness, and fell into the chair which Holmes held invitingly toward him.

"That is right, Mr. Harrington Edwards," said my companion, soothingly. "Be quite calm, my dear Sir, and when you have recovered your composure you will find us ready to listen to your story."

"You know me then?" cried our sudden visitor, with pride in his voice and surprised eyebrows lifted.

"I had never heard of you until this moment, but if you wish to conceal your identity it would be well for you to leave your bookplates at home." As Holmes spoke he handed the other a little package of folded paper slips, which he had picked from the floor. "They fell from your hat when you had the misfortune to tumble," he added, with a whimsical smile.

"Yes, yes," cried the collector, a deep blush spreading over his features. "I remember now; my hat was a little large and I folded a number of them and placed them beneath the sweatband. I had forgotten."

"Rather shabby usage for a handsome etched plate," smiled my companion, "but that is your affair. And now, Sir, if you are quite at ease, let us hear what it is that has brought you, a collector of books, from Poke Stogis Manor—the name is on the plate—to the office of Mr. Sherlock Holmes, consulting expert in crime. Surely nothing but the theft of Mahomet's own copy of the Koran can have affected you so amazingly."

Mr. Harrington Edwards smiled feebly at the jest, then sighed. "Alas," he murmured, "if that were all it were! But I shall begin at the beginning.

"You must know, then, that I am the greatest Shakespearean commentator in the world. My collection of *ana* is unrivaled and much of the world's collection (and consequently its knowledge of the true Shakespeare) has emanated from my pen. One book I did not possess; it was unique, in the correct sense of that abused word; it was the greatest Shakespeare rarity in the world. Few knew that it existed, for its existence was kept a profound secret between a chosen few. Had it become known that this book was in England any place, indeed its owner would have been hounded to his grave by American millionaire collectors.

"It was in the possession of my friend—I tell you this in the strictest confidence, as between adviser and client—of my friend, Sir Nathaniel Brooke-Bannerman, whose place at Walton-on-Walton is next to my own. A scant two hundred yards separate our dwellings, and so intimate has been our friendship that a few years ago the fence between our estates was removed, and each roamed or loitered at will about the other's preserves.

"For some years, now, I have been at work on my greatest book—my *magnum opus*. It was to be also my last book, embodying the results of a lifetime of study and research. Sir, I know Elizabethan London better than any man alive, better than any man who ever lived, I sometimes think—" He burst suddenly into tears.

"There, there," said Sherlock Holmes, gently. "Do not be distressed. It is my business to help people who are unhappy by reason of great losses. Be assured, I shall help you. Pray continue with your interesting narrative. What was this book—which, I take it, in some manner has disappeared? You borrowed it from your friend?"

"That is what I am coming to," said Mr. Harrington Edwards, drying his tears, "but as for help, Mr. Holmes, I fear that is beyond even you. Yet, as a court of last resort, I came to you, ignoring all intermediate agencies.

"Let me resume then: As you surmise, I needed this book. Knowing its value, which could not be fixed, for the book is priceless, and knowing Sir Nathaniel's idolatry of it, I hesitated long before asking the loan of it. But I had to have it, for without it my work could not be completed, and at length I made the request.

"I suggested that I go to his home, and go through the volume under his own eyes, he sitting at my side throughout my entire examination, and servants stationed at every door and window, with fowling pieces in their hands.

"You can imagine my astonishment when Sir Nathaniel laughed at my suggested precautions. 'My dear Edwards,' he said, 'that would be all very well were you Arthur Bambidge or Sir Homer Nantes (mentioning the two great men of the British Museum), or were you Mr. Henry Hutterson, the American railroad magnate; but you are my friend Edwards, and you shall take the book home with you for as long as you like.' I protested vigorously, I assure you, but he would have it so, and as I was touched by this mark of his esteem, at length I permitted him to have it his own way. My God! If I had remained adamant! If I had only—"

He broke off and for a moment stared fixedly into space. His eyes were directed at the Persian slipper on the wall, in the toe of which Holmes kept his tobacco, but we could see that his thoughts were far away.

"Come, Mr. Edwards," said Holmes, firmly. "You are agitating yourself unduly. And you are unreasonably prolonging our curiosity. You have not yet told us what this book is."

Mr. Harrington Edwards gripped the arm of the chair in which he sat, with tense fingers. Then he spoke, and his voice was low and thrilling:

"The book was a 'Hamlet' quarto, dated 1602, presented by Shakespeare to his friend Drayton, with an inscription four lines in length, written and signed by the Master, himself!"

"My dear sir!" I exclaimed. Holmes blew a long, slow whistle of astonishment.

"It is true," cried the collector. "That is the book I borrowed, and that is the book I lost! The long-sought quarto of 1602, actually inscribed in Shakespeare's own hand! His greatest drama, in an edition dated a year earlier than any that is known; a perfect copy, and with four lines in his handwriting! Unique! Extraordinary! Amazing! Astounding! Colossal! Incredible! Un—"

He seemed wound up to continue indefinitely, but Holmes, who had sat quite still at first, shocked by the importance of the loss, interrupted the flow of adjectives.

"I appreciate your emotion, Mr. Edwards," he said, "and the book is indeed all that you say it is. Indeed, it is so important that we must at once attack the problem of rediscovering it. Compose yourself, my dear sir, and tell us of the loss. The book, I take it, is readily identifiable!"

"Mr. Holmes," said our client, earnestly, "it would be impossible to hide it. It is so important a volume that, upon coming into possession of it, Sir Nathaniel Brooke-Bannerman called a consultation of the great binders of the Empire, at which were present Mr. Riviere, Messrs. Sangorski and Sutcliffe, Mr. Zaehnsdorf and others. They and myself, and two others, alone know of the book's existence. When I tell you that it is bound in brown levant morocco, super extra, with leather joints, brown levant doublures and flyleaves, the whole elaborately gold tooled, inlaid with 750 separate pieces of various colored leathers, and enriched by the insertion of eighty-two precious stones, I need not add that it is a design that never will be duplicated, and I tell you only a few of its glories. The binding was personally done by Messrs. Riviere, Sangorski, Sutcliffe, and Zaehnsdorf, working alternately, and is a work of such enchantment that any man might gladly die a thousand deaths for the privilege of owning it for five minutes."

"Dear me," quoth Sherlock Holmes, "it must indeed be a handsome volume, and from your description, together with a realization of its importance by reason of its association, I gather that it is something beyond what might be termed a valuable book."

"Priceless!" cried Mr. Harrington Edwards. "The combined wealth of India, Mexico, and Wall Street would be all too little for its purchase!"

"You are anxious to recover this book?" Holmes asked, looking at him keenly.

"My God!" shrieked the collector, rolling up his eyes and clawing the air with his hands. "Do you suppose—"

"Tut, tut!" Holmes interrupted. "I was only testing you. It is a book that might move even you, Mr. Harrington Edwards, to theft but we may put aside that notion at once. Your emotion is too sincere, and besides you know too well the difficulties of hiding such a volume as you describe. Indeed, only a very daring man would purloin it and keep it long in his possession. Pray tell us how you came to suffer it to be lost."

Mr. Harrington Edwards seized the brandy flask, which stood at his elbow, and drained it at a gulp. With the renewed strength thus obtained, he continued his story:

"As I have said, Sir Nathaniel forced me to accept the loan of the book, much against my own wishes. On the evening that I called for it, he told me that two of his trusted servants, heavily armed, would accompany me across the grounds to my home. 'There is no danger,' he said, 'but you will feel better,' and I heartily agreed with him. How shall I tell you what happened? Mr. Holmes, it was those very servants who assailed me and robbed me of my priceless borrowing!"

Sherlock Holmes rubbed his lean hands with satisfaction. "Splendid!" he murmured. "It is a case after my own heart. Watson, these are deep waters in which we are sailing. But you are rather lengthy about this, Mr. Edwards. Perhaps it will help matters if I ask you a few questions. By what road did you go to your home?"

"By the main road, a good highway which lies in front of our estates. I preferred it to the shadows of the wood."

"And there were some 200 yards between your doors. At what point did the assault occur?"

"Almost midway between the two entrance drives, I should say."

"There was no light?"

"That of the moon only."

"Did you know these servants who accompanied you?"

"One I knew slightly; the other I had not seen before."

"Describe them to me, please."

"The man who is known to me, is called Miles. He is clean-shaven, short and powerful, although somewhat elderly. He was known, I believe, as Sir Nathaniel's most trusted servant; he had been with Sir Nathaniel for years. I cannot describe him minutely for, of course, I never paid much attention to him.

The other was tall and thickset, and wore a heavy beard. He was a silent fellow; I do not believe he spoke a word during the journey."

"Miles was more communicative?"

"Oh yes—even garrulous, perhaps. He talked about the weather and the moon, and I forget what all."

"Never about books?"

"There was no mention of books between any of us."

"Just how did the attack occur?"

"It was very sudden. We had reached, as I say, about the halfway point, when the big man seized me by the throat—to prevent outcry, I suppose—and on the instant, Miles snatched the volume from my grasp and was off. In a moment his companion followed him. I had been half throttled and could not immediately cry out; when I could articulate, I made the countryside ring with my cries. I ran after them, but failed even to catch another sight of them. They had disappeared completely."

"Did you all leave the house together?"

"Miles and I left together; the second man joined us at the porter's lodge. He had been attending to some of his duties."

"And Sir Nathaniel—where was he?"

"He said goodnight on the threshold."

"What has he had to say about all this?"

"I have not told him."

"You have not told him!" echoed Sherlock Holmes, in astonishment.

"I have not dared," miserably confessed our client. "It will kill him. That book was the breath of his life."

"When did this occur?" I put in, with a glance at Holmes.

"Excellent, Watson," said my friend, answering my glance. "I was about to ask the same question."

"Just last night," was Mr. Harrington Edwards' reply. "I was crazy most of the night; I didn't sleep a wink. I came to you the first thing this morning. Indeed, I tried to raise you on the telephone, last night, but could not establish a connection."

"Yes," said Holmes, reminiscently, "we were attending Mme. Trontini's first night. You remember, Watson, we dined later at Albani's?"

"Oh, Mr. Holmes, do you think you can help me?" cried the abject collector.

"I trust so," declared my friend, cheerfully. "Indeed, I am certain that I can. At any rate, I shall make a gallant attempt, with Watson's aid. Such a book, as you remark, is not easily hidden. What say you, Watson, to a run down to Walton-on-Walton?"

"There is a train in half an hour," said Mr. Harrington Edwards, looking at his watch. "Will you return with me?"

"No, no," laughed Holmes, "that would never do. We must not be seen together just yet, Mr. Edwards. Go back yourself on the first train, by all means, unless you have further business in London. My friend and I will go together. There is another train this morning?"

"An hour later."

"Excellent. Until we meet, then!"

II

We took the train from Paddington Station an hour later, as we had promised, and began the journey to Walton-on-Walton, a pleasant, aristocratic village and the scene of the curious accident to our friend of Poke Stogis Manor. Holmes, lying back in his seat, blew earnest smoke rings at the ceiling of our compartment, which fortunately was empty, while I devoted myself to the morning paper. After a bit, I tired of this occupation and turned to Holmes. I was surprised to find him looking out of the window, wreathed in smiles and quoting Hafiz softly under his breath.

"You have a theory?" I asked, in surprise.

"It is a capital mistake to theorize in advance of the evidence," he replied. "Still, I have given some thought to the interesting problem of our friend, Mr. Harrington Edwards, and there are several indications which can point only to one conclusion."

"And whom do you believe to be the thief?"

"My dear fellow," said Sherlock Holmes, "you forget we already know the thief. Edwards has testified quite clearly that it was Miles who snatched the volume."

"True," I admitted, abashed. "I had forgotten. All we must do then, is find Miles."

"And a motive," added my friend, chuckling. "What would you say, Watson, was the motive in this case?"

"Jealousy," I replied promptly.

"You surprise me!"

"Miles had been bribed by a rival collector, who in some manner had learned about this remarkable volume. You remember Edwards told us this second man joined them at the lodge. That would give an excellent opportunity for the substitution of a man other than the servant intended by Sir Nathaniel. Is not that good reasoning?"

"You surpass yourself, my dear Watson," murmured Holmes. "It is excellently reasoned, and as you justly observe the opportunity for a substitution was perfect."

"Do you not agree with me?"

"Hardly, Watson. A rival collector, in order to accomplish

this remarkable coup, first would have to have known of the volume, as you suggest, but also he must have known what night Mr. Harrington Edwards would go to Sir Nathaniel's to get it, which would point to collaboration on the part of our client. As a matter of fact, however, Mr. Edwards' decision as to his acceptance of the loan, was, I believe, sudden and without previous determination."

"I do not recall his saying so."

"He did not say so, but it is a simple deduction. A book collector is mad enough to begin with, Watson; but tempt him with some such bait as this Shakespeare quarto and he is bereft of all sanity. Mr. Edwards would not have been able to wait. It was just the night before that Sir Nathaniel promised him the book, and it was just last night that he flew to accept the offer—flying, incidentally, to disaster, also. The miracle is that he was able to wait for an entire day."

"Wonderful!"

"Elementary," said Holmes. "I have employed one of the earliest and best known principles of my craft, only. If you are interested in the process, you will do well to read Harley Graham on "Transcendental Emotion," while I have, myself, been guilty of a small brochure in which I catalogue some twelve hundred professions, and the emotional effect upon their members of unusual tidings, good and bad."

We were the only passengers to alight at Walton-on-Walton, but rapid inquiry developed that Mr. Harrington Edwards had returned on the previous train. Holmes, who had disguised himself before leaving the train, did all the talking. He wore his cap peak backwards, carried a pencil behind his ear and had turned up the bottoms of his trousers; from one pocket dangled the end of a linen tape measure. He was a municipal surveyor to the life, and I could not but think that, meeting him suddenly in the road, I should not myself have known him. At his suggestion, I dented the crown of my derby hat and turned my coat inside out. Then he gave me an end of the tape measure, while he, carrying the other end, went on ahead. In this fashion, stopping from time to time to kneel in the dust, and ostensibly to measure sections of the roadway, we proceeded toward Poke Stogis Manor. The occasional villagers whom we encountered on their way to the station barroom, paid us no more attention than if we had been rabbits.

Shortly we came into sight of our friend's dwelling, a picturesque and rambling abode, sitting far back in its own grounds and bordered by a square of sentinel oaks. A gravel pathway led from the roadway to the house entrance, and, as we passed, the sunlight struck glancing rays from an antique brass knocker on the door. The whole picture, with its background of gleaming countryside, was one of rural calm and comfort; we could with difficulty believe it the scene of the sinister tragedy we were come to investigate.

"We shall not enter yet," said Sherlock Holmes, resolutely passing the gate leading into our client's acreage, "but we shall endeavor to be back in time for luncheon."

From this point the road progressed downward in a gentle incline and the trees were thicker on either side of the road. Holmes kept his eyes stolidly on the path before us, and when we had covered about one hundred yards he stopped. "Here," he said, pointing, "the assault occurred."

I looked closely at the earth, but could see no sign of struggle.

"You recall it was midway between the two houses that it happened," he continued. "No, there are few signs; there was no violent tussle. Fortunately, however, we had our proverbial fall of rain last evening and the earth has retained impressions nicely." He indicated the faint imprint of a foot, then another, and another. Kneeling down, I was able to see that, indeed, many feet had passed along the road.

Holmes flung himself at full length in the dirt and wriggled swiftly about, his nose to the earth, muttering rapidly in French. Then he whipped out a glass, the better to examine a mark that had caught his eye; but in a moment he shook his head in disappointment and continued with his examination. I was irresistibly reminded of a noble hound, at fault, sniffing in circles in an effort to reestablish the lost scent. In a moment, however, he had it, for with a little cry of pleasure he rose to his feet, zigzagged curiously across the road and paused before a hedge, a lean finger pointing accusingly at a break in the thicket.

"No wonder they disappeared," he smiled as I came up. "Edwards thought they continued up the road, but here is where they broke through." Then stepping back a little distance, he ran forward lightly and cleared the hedge at a bound, alighting on his hands on the other side.

"Follow me carefully," he warned, "for we must not allow our own footprints to confuse us." I fell more heavily than my companion, but in a moment he had me by the heels and had helped me to steady myself. "See," he cried, lowering his face to the earth; and deep in the mud and grass I saw the prints of two pairs of feet.

"The small man broke through," said Holmes, exultantly, "but the larger rascal leaped over the hedge. See how deeply his prints are marked; he landed heavily here in the soft ooze. It is very significant, Watson, that they came this way. Does it suggest nothing to you?"

"That they were men who knew Edwards' grounds as well as

the Brooke-Bannerman estate," I answered, and thrilled with pleasure at my friend's nod of approbation.

He lowered himself to his stomach, without further conversation, and for some moments we crawled painfully across the grass. Then a shocking thought came to me.

"Holmes," I whispered in horror, "do you see where these footprints tend? They are directed toward the home of our client, Mr. Harrington Edwards!"

He nodded his head slowly, and his lips were set tight and thin. The double line of impressions ended abruptly at the back door of Poke Stogis Manor!

Sherlock Holmes rose to his feet and looked at his watch.

"We are just in time for luncheon," he announced, and hastily brushed his garments. Then, deliberately, he knocked on the door. In a few moments we were in the presence of our client.

"We have been roaming about the neighborhood," apologized Holmes, "and took the liberty of coming to your rear entrance."

"You have a clue?" asked Mr. Harrington Edwards, eagerly.

A queer smile of triumph sat upon Sherlock Holmes' lips.

"Indeed," he said, quietly, "I believe I have solved your little problem, Mr. Harrington Edwards!"

"My dear Holmes!" I cried, and "My dear Sir!" cried our client.

"I have yet to establish a motive," confessed my friend, "but as to the main facts there can be no question."

Mr. Harrington Edwards fell into a chair, white and shaking.

"The book," he croaked. "Tell me!"

"Patience, my good sir," counseled Holmes, kindly. "We have had nothing to eat since sunup, and are famished. All in good time. Let us first dine and then all shall be made clear.

Meanwhile, I should like to telephone to Sir Nathaniel Brooke-Bannerman, for I wish him to hear what I have to say."

Our client's pleas were in vain. Holmes would have his little joke and his luncheon. In the end, Mr. Harrington Edwards staggered away to the kitchen to order a repast, and Sherlock Holmes talked rapidly and unintelligibly into the telephone for a moment and came back with a smile on his face, which, to me, boded ill for someone. But I asked no questions; in good time this amazing man would tell his story in his own way. I had heard all he had heard, and had seen all he had seen; yet I was completely at sea. Still, our host's ghastly smile hung in my mind, and come what would I felt sorry for him. In a little time we were seated at table. Our client, haggard and nervous, ate slowly and with apparent discomfort; his eyes were never long absent from Holmes' inscrutable face. I was little better off, but Holmes ate with gusto, relating meanwhile a number of his earlier adventures, which I may some day give to the world, if I am able to read my illegible notes made on the occasion.

When the sorry meal had been concluded, we went into the library, where Sherlock Holmes took possession of the big easy chair, with an air of proprietorship which would have been amusing in other circumstances. He screwed together his long pipe and lighted it with a malicious lack of haste, while Mr. Harrington Edwards perspired against the mantel in an agony of apprehension.

"Why must you keep us waiting, Mr. Holmes?" he whispered. "Tell us, at once, please, who—who—" His voice trailed off into a moan.

"The criminal," said Sherlock Holmes, smoothly, "is—"

"Sir Nathaniel Brooke-Bannerman!" said a maid, suddenly, putting her head in at the door, and on the heels of her announcement stalked the handsome baronet, whose priceless volume had caused all this stir and unhappiness.

Sir Nathaniel was white, and appeared ill. He burst at once into talk.

"I have been much upset by your call," he said, looking meanwhile at our client. "You say you have something to tell me about the quarto. Don't say—that—anything has happened—to it!" He clutched nervously at the wall to steady himself, and I felt deep pity for him.

Mr. Harrington Edwards looked at Sherlock Holmes. "Oh, Mr. Holmes," he cried, pathetically, "why did you send for him?"

"Because," said my friend, firmly, "I wish him to hear the truth about the Shakespeare quarto. Sir Nathaniel, I believe you have not been told as yet that Mr. Edwards was robbed, last night, of your precious volume—robbed by the trusted servants whom you sent with him to protect it."

"What!" shrieked the titled collector. He staggered and fumbled madly at his heart; then collapsed into a chair. "Good God!" he muttered, and then again: "Good God!"

"I should have thought you would have been suspicious of evil when your servants did not return," pursued Holmes.

"I have not seen them," whispered Sir Nathaniel. "I do not mingle with my servants. I did not know they had failed to return. Tell me—tell me all!"

"Mr. Edwards," said Sherlock Holmes, turning to our client, "will you repeat your story, please?"

Mr. Harrington Edwards, thus adjured, told the unhappy tale again, ending with a heartbroken cry of "Oh, Sir Nathaniel, can you ever forgive me?"

"I do not know that it was entirely your fault," observed

Holmes, cheerfully. "Sir Nathaniel's own servants are the guilty ones, and surely he sent them with you."

"But you said you had solved the case, Mr. Holmes," cried our client, in a frenzy of despair.

"Yes," agreed Holmes, "it is solved. You have had the clue in your own hands ever since the occurrence, but you did not know how to use it. It all turns upon the curious actions of the taller servant, prior to the assault."

"The actions of—" stammered Mr. Harrington Edwards. "Why, he did nothing—said nothing!"

"That is the curious circumstance," said Sherlock Holmes, meaningly.

Sir Nathaniel got to his feet with difficulty.

"Mr. Holmes," he said, "this has upset me more than I can tell you. Spare no pains to recover the book, and to bring to justice the scoundrels who stole it. But I must go away and think—think—"

"Stay," said my friend. "I have already caught one of them."

"What! Where?" cried the two collectors, together.

"Here," said Sherlock Holmes, and stepping forward he laid a hand on the baronet's shoulder. "You, Sir Nathaniel, were the taller servant; you were one of the thieves who throttled Mr. Harrington Edwards and took from him your own book. And now, Sir, will you tell us why you did it?"

Sir Nathaniel Brooke-Bannerman toppled and would have fallen had not I rushed forward and supported him. I placed him in a chair. As we looked at him, we saw confession in his eyes; guilt was written in his haggard face.

"Come, come," said Holmes, impatiently. "Or will it make it easier for you if I tell the story as it occurred? Let it be so, then. You parted with Mr. Harrington Edwards on your doorsill, Sir

Nathaniel, bidding your best friend goodnight with a smile on your lips and evil in your heart. And as soon as you had closed the door, you slipped into an enveloping raincoat, turned up your collar and hastened by a shorter road to the porter's lodge, where you joined Mr. Edwards and Miles as one of your own servants. You spoke no word at any time, because you feared to speak. You were afraid Mr. Edwards would recognize your voice, while your beard, hastily assumed, protected your face, and in the darkness your figure passed unnoticed.

"Having choked and robbed your best friend, then, of your own book, you and your scoundrelly assistant fled across Mr. Edwards' fields to his own back door, thinking that, if investigation followed, I would be called in, and would trace those footprints and fix the crime upon Mr. Harrington Edwards, as part of a criminal plan, prearranged with your rascally servants, who would be supposed to be in the pay of Mr. Edwards and the ringleaders in a counterfeit assault upon his person. Your mistake, Sir, was in ending your trail abruptly at Mr. Edwards' back door. Had you left another trail, then, leading back to your own domicile, I should unhesitatingly have arrested Mr. Harrington Edwards for the theft.

"Surely, you must know that in criminal cases handled by me, it is never the obvious solution that is the correct one. The mere fact that the finger of suspicion is made to point at a certain individual is sufficient to absolve that individual from guilt. Had you read the little works of my friend and colleague, here, Dr. Watson, you would not have made such a mistake. Yet you claim to be a bookman!"

A low moan from the unhappy baronet was his only answer.

"To continue, however: there at Mr. Edwards' own back door you ended your trail, entering his house—his own house—and spending the night under his roof, while his cries and ravings over his loss filled the night, and brought joy to your unspeakable soul. And in the morning, when he had gone forth to consult me, you quietly left—you and Miles—and returned to your own place by the beaten highway."

"Mercy!" cried the defeated wretch, cowering in his chair. "If it is made public, I am ruined. I was driven to it. I could not let Mr. Edwards examine the book, for exposure would follow that way; yet I could not refuse him my best friend when he asked its loan."

"Your words tell me all that I did not know," said Sherlock Holmes, sternly. "The motive now is only too plain. The work, Sir, was a forgery, and knowing that your erudite friend would discover it, you chose to blacken his name to save your own. Was the book insured?"

"Insured for £350,000, he told me," interrupted Mr. Harrington Edwards, excitedly.

"So that he planned at once to dispose of this dangerous and dubious item, and to reap a golden reward," commented Holmes. "Come, Sir, tell us about it. How much of it was forgery? Merely the inscription?"

"I will tell you," said the baronet, suddenly, "and throw myself upon the mercy of my friend, Mr. Edwards. The whole book, in effect, was a forgery. It was originally made up of two imperfect copies of the 1604 quarto. Out of the pair, I made one perfect volume, and a skillful workman, now dead, changed the date for me so cleverly that only an expert of the first water could have detected it. Such an expert, however, is Mr. Harrington Edwards—the one man in the world who could have unmasked me."

"Thank you, Nathaniel," said Mr. Harrington Edwards, gratefully.

"The inscription, of course, also was forged," continued the baronet. "You may as well know all."

"And the book?" asked Holmes. "Where did you destroy it?"

A grim smile settled on Sir Nathaniel's features. "It is even now burning in Mr. Edwards' own furnace," he said.

"Then it cannot yet be consumed," cried Holmes, and dashed into the basement. He was absent for some little time, and we heard the clinking of bottles, and, finally, the clang of a great metal door. He emerged, some moments later, in high spirits, carrying a charred leaf in his hand.

"It is a pity," he cried, "a pity! In spite of its questionable authenticity, it was a noble specimen. It is only half consumed, but let it burn away. I have preserved one leaf as a souvenir of the occasion." He folded it carefully and placed it in his wallet. "Mr. Harrington Edwards, I fancy the decision in this matter is for you to announce. Sir Nathaniel, of course, must make no effort to collect the insurance."

"I promise that," said the baronet, quickly.

"Let us forget it, then," said Mr. Edwards, with a sigh. "Let it be a sealed chapter in the history of bibliomania." He looked at Sir Nathaniel Brooke-Bannerman for a long moment, then held out his hand. "I forgive you, Nathaniel," he said, simply.

Their hands met; tears stood in the baronet's eyes. Holmes and I turned from the affecting scene, powerfully moved. We crept to the door unnoticed. In a moment the free air was blowing on our temples, and we were coughing the dust of the library from our lungs.

III

"They are strange people, these book collectors," mused Sherlock Holmes, as we rattled back to town.

"My only regret is that I shall be unable to publish my notes on this interesting case," I responded.

"Wait a bit, my dear Doctor," advised Holmes, "and it will be possible. In time both of them will come to look upon it as a hugely diverting episode, and will tell it upon themselves. Then your notes will be brought forth and the history of another of Mr. Sherlock Holmes' little problems shall be given to the world."

"It will always be a reflection upon Sir Nathaniel," I demurred.

"He will glory in it," prophesied Sherlock Holmes. "He will go down in bookish chronicle with Chatterton, and Ireland, and Payne Collier. Mark my words, he is not blind even now to the chance this gives him for sinister immortality. He will be the first to tell it." (And so, indeed, it proved, as this narrative suggests.)

"But why did you preserve the leaf from *Hamlet*?" I curiously inquired. "Why not a jewel from the binding?"

Sherlock Holmes chuckled heartily. Then he slowly unfolded the page in question, and directed a humorous finger at a spot upon the page.

"A fancy," he responded, "to preserve so accurate a characterization of either of our friends. The line is a real jewel. See, the good Polonius says: '*That he is mad, 'tis true: 'tis true 'tis pittie; and pittie it is true.*' There is as much sense in Master Will as in Hafiz or Confucius, and a greater felicity of expression . . . Here is London, and now, my dear Watson, if we hasten we shall be just in time for Zabriski's matinee!"

A VOLUME OF POE

Vincent Starrett

(Charles) Vincent (Emerson) Starrett (1886-1974), arguably America's greatest bibliophile, was named a Grand Master by the Mystery Writers of America in 1958, more for his countless essays, biographical works, critical studies, and bibliographical pieces on a wide range of authors and subjects, than for his mystery fiction, though he wrote six well-regarded detective novels and scores of mystery short stories. He also wrote numerous supernatural/fantasy stories, many of which were published in *Weird Tales* magazine and collected in *The Quick and the Dead* (1965).

His non-fiction appeared in numerous journals and magazines but most famously in the "Books Alive" column in the *Chicago Tribune*, which he wrote for twenty-five years. Many of his best articles were collected in such treasured volumes as *Buried Caesars* (1923), *Penny Wise and Book Foolish* (1929), *Books Alive* (1940), *Bookman's Holiday* (1942), *Autolycus in Limbo* (1943), *Books and Bipeds* (1947), and he wrote *Best Loved Books of the 20th Century* (1955), which covered fifty-two major works, and a memoir, *Born in a Bookshop* (1965), a must-read for bibliophiles.

He was a devoted collector of detective fiction and Sherlockiana, though an impecunious one who was forced to sell his collection and start over on numerous occasions.

It is not surprising, then, that several of his fictional works fall into the bibliomystery category. They are infused with that rare combination of enthusiasm for the sub-genre plus profound knowledge of the subject.

"A Volume of Poe" was originally published in the February 1929 issue of *Real Detective Tales and Mystery Stories*; it was first collected in *The Blue Door* (New York, Doubleday, 1930).

A Volume of Poe

Vincent Starrett

I

EMERGING FROM a small restaurant shortly after nine o'clock of an autumn evening—for it was his practice to dine later than a majority of his fellow citizens— Allardyce turned northward in Chicago's Broadway for two blocks, then bent his head beneath an awning, still unreefed, and entered the antique shop of his friend De Gollyer.

Over the door and on the window of De Gollyer's shop, in addition to the proprietor's remarkable name, were the words, in large capitals, OLD THINGS. In consequence of this, Allardyce had bestowed a similar appellation upon his friend by the simple expedient of dropping an *s*.

"Well, Old Thing," he observed briskly and as usual, when the bell above the door had tinkled twice (once when it opened and once when it closed), "how are—?"

He was about to ask foolishly and as usual, "How are *things?*" but interrupted himself as he discovered that De Gollyer had a customer. The relative dimness of Old Thing's bazaar made it difficult at times to be certain that De Gollyer was alone. The antique dealer was not fond of glaring lights; he said they hurt his eyes. A single light, well to the rear of the establishment, was all that he permitted himself. It illumined brilliantly one side of a cabinet of majolica horrors and about half a section of disreputable books, leaving the rest of the shop in an interesting and rather fantastic twilight that became dimmer as it approached the surrounding walls, except at the front, where the lights of the street outside helped the casual purchaser to enter without breaking his neck.

Allardyce, interrupting the jovial greeting, said, "Oh, I beg pardon!"—noting as he did so that De Gollyer's customer was a woman. A young woman, he assumed from her figure and carriage.

He removed his hat, hung it upon the head of a plaster Arab with striking effect, lighted a cigarette, and listened to what was going forward at the back of the shop. The hat was much too large for the Bedouin, who was merely a bust intended to horrify cultured visitors in middle-class drawing rooms.

"I'm sorry," the young woman was saying. "I have been told that it is worth at least a hundred dollars. I had hoped to get that for it."

Allardyce smiled a sympathetic smile. Apparently he had arrived at a critical moment. There was an odd coincidence in the situation. He had been hoping to get a hundred dollars himself for some days past; but a reluctant parent in the East was holding out on him. What under the canopy, though, was worth a hundred dollars to an antique dealer in upper Broadway? He heard the bass rumble of De Gollyer replying:

"I'm sorry, too, but upon my honor, if I had a hundred dollars to spare I'd shut up the shop and take a holiday."

Which was perfectly true, as Allardyce happened to know. De Gollyer paid his rent each month with old-fashioned punctiliousness, then began to save all over again for that long-deferred vacation.

"It may be worth a hundred," continued the dealer. "I'm not denying it. But I can't purchase at that sum, nor half that sum. Look here—I'll tell you what I'll do. Leave it with me, if you care to, and I'll try to interest someone in it. I have one or two customers who might care for it. Are you in a hurry to sell it?"

"I'm afraid I am." There was something between a laugh and a sob in the young woman's reply.

Somebody else, thought Allardyce, who needed a hundred dollars. Well, that made three of them—himself, De Gollyer, and the young woman with something to sell. Birds of a feather! He squinted back at her, trying to make out her features in the half darkness, but they were turned from him. De Gollyer's aquiline beak and high white forehead were all that was notably in evidence.

The antique dealer was answering. "Well," he was saying, "you'd better take it to one of the larger dealers down town tomorrow. I don't suppose you have to have the hundred tonight. Try Bancroft. He's a good man, and he'll treat you fairly. Here, I'll give you his card."

So it was a book, thought Allardyce. A bit shabby of De Gollyer not to have called him into the conference. Books were his own hobby, and he knew something about them, too. But then

De Gollyer, after all, knew very well that his friend Allardyce was not carrying a hundred dollars about in his vest pocket.

The fact was, De Gollyer had forgotten that his friend had entered the shop. Suddenly he remembered him. "Oh, I say," he went on hurriedly, "here's the very man. He can tell us what it's worth, anyway. Mr. Allardyce is a collector and an expert."

The collector and expert moved eagerly toward the light. He nodded his acknowledgment of the handsome introduction, then received the book from its owner's hand.

A pair of worried blue eyes looked into his own.

"I've been told," repeated the girl apologetically, "that it's worth a hundred dollars."

By George, she was lovely! If his own hundred had only arrived that morning he would have been tempted to purchase the book without looking at it. He felt her blush under his admiring scrutiny, and so he dropped his eyes to the volume.

"Yes," he agreed, after an instant, "there is no doubt of that. I should say it was worth *several* hundred dollars. Nothing extravagant, you know—but it's a rare book and its condition is very good."

It was a slender volume of poems by one Edgar Allan Poe, of the edition known to collectors as the *third*.

"It was my great-aunt's," she explained. "She took very good care of her books."

"Had it been a *first* edition, now, instead of a third," continued Allardyce with a smile, "it would have been worth several thousands."

"Good gracious!" said the owner of the volume. "You are sure it *isn't* a first?"

"Quite sure. There are less than a dozen firsts in existence."

He hesitated. "I think Mr. de Gollyer's advice is good, Miss—?" Again he hesitated, but she did not supply the name he had hoped to hear. "Yes, I think you had better take it to Bancroft, or leave it with Mr. de Gollyer to sell for you."

"I would give you a receipt for it, of course," added the shopkeeper.

After a moment she made up her mind. "Thank you," she answered. "I'll think it over tonight, and perhaps I shall bring it in again tomorrow."

She held out her hand for the book, nodded brightly to them both, and allowed the antique dealer to conduct her to the door. He was certain, he told her, that she would fall over a sofa or something if she attempted the dangerous passage without a guide.

Then again the doorbell tinkled. Allardyce, looking after her, saw her turn southward in Broadway and vanish beyond the line of the window. De Gollyer, standing for a moment at his shop door, saw her cross the street at the nearest intersection and walk eastward in the intersecting avenue. Others, no doubt, saw her, thereafter, without knowledge of what she carried, but with no less interest in her appearance. She was, as Allardyce had decided, a beautiful young woman.

For nearly an hour, then, the two men, so far apart in years, sat and talked in the semi-darkness of the establishment, and wondered why so attractive and respectable a young woman should suddenly require a hundred dollars.

"Do you know," said Allardyce at last, "I almost wish I had followed her. She may never return."

De Gollyer laughed in his beard. "It's this weird array of bottles and brasses and things," he observed. "These gargoyles and griffins, so to speak. They make romance out of sordid reality—

particularly at night. I often feel that way myself. But really, you know, she was only a pretty girl in need of a hundred dollars. The city is full of them, I imagine."

"They don't all own copies of the 1831 Poe," retorted Allardyce, rising to depart. "Well, I'll see you in the morning, Old Thing. I'm curious to know whether she comes back."

It was to be some days before he was to find out, however, for in the morning he pushed past a morbid throng outside the door of Old Thing's shop, to stare in horror at the murdered body of Old Thing on the floor inside, surrounded by tradesmen, broken china, and detectives.

II

Young Mr. Woolfolk (of the *Evening Globe)* alighted from his taxicab, paid off his driver, and pushed his way through the same throng, approximately twenty minutes later. Messrs. Slater and Considine (of the North Halsted Street police station) regarded him with tolerant dismay. They looked at each other and said, "Well, here's Woolfolk!" After which they looked at Allardyce seated in Old Thing's chair, a bit doubtfully, as if debating the advisability of ordering him under cover. He was their only clue and they were not inclined to share him.

It was Woolfolk's habit to appear upon the scene of a police activity only a few minutes after the police themselves. Nobody was certain how he did it; that is, how he discovered what was going on. It was assumed that he was more than a little friendly with someone at headquarters. He was an energetic and sometimes discomfiting newspaperman, and he had another habit that worried the police even more than his extraordinary timeliness: he had a habit of picking up valuable clues that the detectives in charge had overlooked. This, of course, in a reporter, is unforgivable.

The body of Old Thing had been removed from the floor and now lay upon an ancient settee that had been one of the antiques offered for sale in his shop. Young Mr. Woolfolk approached the settee and looked down upon the body.

"Well, well!" he observed. And after a moment he added: "Well, well, well!" He turned to Messrs. Slater and Considine. "What's been going on here?"

The latter shrugged. "It's evident, isn't it? His name's De Gollyer. This was his shop. He was found this way, this morning, by the neighbors."

"*This* way?"

"Dead, anyway. Murdered, I guess. There was a knife in his heart. He was on the floor, to begin with. The first men in here foolishly moved the body to this couch."

"By Jove!" exclaimed Woolfolk. "The neighbors looked in through the glass and saw him lying there, eh? Who found him, Considine?"

"The man next door," said Considine. "His name is Haines. He is a real-estate dealer."

"Realtor," corrected Woolfolk. "Robbery?" he asked after a moment.

"We don't know." It was Slater who answered. "The front door was open. Anybody could have walked in."

"Open!"

"Well, unlocked. Apparently he'd never locked up.

It must have happened some time late last night."

"Hm-m," commented the reporter. "No telling what might have been in a place like this." He glanced about him as he spoke. "It looks like a junk pile, but you never can tell. Where's the knife, Slater?"

"It's—*ah*—still in Mr. de Gollyer; but we've covered it up. We're waiting for the coroner."

"I see! Well, I'll wait, too." The newspaperman sidled up more closely to the two detectives. He lowered his voice. "Who's the pale young man in the rear?"

Considine hesitated, but Slater merely shrugged, then answered the question. Woolfolk would find out sooner or later, anyway, all that they knew. By telling him, they would be saving themselves a lot of questions. Also, when fairly treated, the reporter was sometimes inclined to play fair in return. He might turn up something of importance himself; something that the police could use.

"Charles Allardyce," replied the detective. "Friend of the dead man. He just happened to drop in. Knows nothing about the murder."

"So he says, eh? Are you sure?"

"Well, I'm sure enough. He seems honest and his story seems straight. Naturally, we're holding him for a while. He's perfectly willing to stay."

"May I question him?"

"You can't bulldoze him, if that's what you mean. But if he wants to answer your questions, it's all right with me."

"What did he tell you?"

"He was here with De Gollyer last night, until the old man closed the shop. He didn't actually see him lock up; but De Gollyer was getting ready to close when Allardyce left."

"Nobody else was in the shop?"

"He says not. Never a great many customers, he says. The old man was in good spirits, and he knew Allardyce was going to drop in this morning. No chance of it's being suicide apparently."

"Did De Gollyer have anything of value in the shop?"

"I asked him that. He says he doesn't think so. It's mostly old junk, as you say. Nothing in the place worth over ten dollars probably. You can see for yourself."

"Yeh," said Woolfolk, "but that doesn't mean anything. It's in places like this that you find the missing crown jewels and that sort of thing."

He directed his footsteps to the rear of the shop and sat down in a chair facing the shocked and bewildered Allardyce, who looked up with a faint smile.

"You're Mr. Allardyce," began the reporter. "My name is Woolfolk. *Globe* reporter. The police don't mind my talking to you, if *you* don't mind talking. May I ask you a few questions?"

The other hesitated. Then his shoulders moved slightly. "If you like," answered Allardyce. "I'm afraid there isn't much I can tell you. I told the detectives everything I know."

"I'd like to get it all in your own words," explained the reporter. "You were with Mr. de Gollyer last night, and left just before he closed, you said. Now what time would that be, Mr. Allardyce?"

"I came in a little after nine, and I stayed until about ten, I suppose; maybe ten-fifteen. It must have been ten-fifteen or thereabouts. I walked around afterward, for about half an hour, then went home; and I got home about eleven, I know."

"There wasn't anybody else in the shop in all that time?"

"While I was with him there wasn't anybody—no! Unless somebody was hiding somewhere."

But Allardyce had hesitated slightly before answering, and,

infinitesimal as had been the hesitation, the shrewd reporter had noted it. The police had asked the same question and the repetition had bothered Allardyce, who had answered the inquiry of the detectives with a prompt negative.

"You're sure of that, are you?"

"Quite sure."

Why under the sun, Allardyce wondered, hadn't he told the police at once about that girl who needed a hundred dollars? It was too late now. He must stand by his story to the end. An obscure emotion had decided him to conceal the fact of the girl's visit: an emotion born of a certain chivalry and of a conviction that she could have had nothing to do with the murder of his friend. She was not at all that sort of a person.

But the police, who had not seen her, would, he knew, take no such view of the situation. There would be trouble for her if he betrayed her and she was found.

He realized, too, that he would be in a troublesome position himself if she were to be discovered. It would then be known that he had lied, and to conceal a stranger. Or would it be believed that they were strangers? Good Lord, what a mess it might be! Possibly, even, the girl herself would come forward, once the story of the murder had been made public.

Well, it was too late now to change his tune.

Woolfolk was eyeing him curiously. "What did you and Mr. de Gollyer talk about?" asked the journalist suddenly.

Allardyce considered. He could hardly answer that question, either.

"A great many things, I imagine," he replied, at length. "Books, for one thing. There was certainly nothing said to suggest that Mr. de Gollyer was anticipating—*this*—if that is what you mean."

"I'll ask you the question now that is in all the detective novels," grinned Woolfolk. "Did he have any enemies?"

"None that I ever heard of. He may have had. I suppose everybody does. He never mentioned any to me. He didn't have a great many friends either. I suppose I was his closest friend—and we just struck up an acquaintance because I liked to drop in here. He was a rather lonely old man."

The reporter nodded, a gleam in his eye. "Yes," he said, "that's it—that's the mysterious part of it, Mr. Allardyce. Why should anybody want to murder a lonely, friendless old man? Unless—he had something valuable in the shop, and somebody knew it!" He leaned forward and gazed significantly into Allardyce's eyes. "Eh?"

But Allardyce only smiled. "That's absurd," he answered. "I don't pretend to be an expert; but *he* was—and I know he didn't have anything of the slightest value. If he had, he'd have sold it. He was generally a bit hard up."

"Maybe he had something valuable and didn't know it," persisted Woolfolk; but Allardyce again shook his head.

After a few more questions the newspaper man stood up. "Well, many thanks," he said. "Sorry to have had to bother you."

But he was not sorry. With the peculiar prescience of good reporters, he had had what he would have called a "hunch." He was entirely certain that Charles Allardyce was concealing some vital information. That one moment of hesitation had given him the idea, and it was enough. He was not prepared to believe that Allardyce himself had committed the murder—although it would not have shocked him to learn that such was the case—but that Allardyce suspected the identity of the murderer was, at the very least, a plausible notion that he intended to hold. If the police did not already suspect Allardyce, that was their own lookout. It was not Dane Woolfolk's intention—just yet, at any rate—to put the idea into their heads.

He returned to the detectives, asked innumerable leading questions, few of which could be answered, and at length subsided until the arrival of the coroner's assistants.

The examination of the body was brief. Suicide, thought the young doctor who made the investigation, was a possibility, but an unlikely one. There was every appearance of murder. The knife was obviously one that had been handy; it was the sort of thing that would be found in an antique shop. There had been a quarrel, possibly, and the knife—on a table nearby—had been snatched up and used with fatal effect. The young doctor was somewhat of a criminologist, and the two detectives—all that remained of the original half dozen that had taken possession of the shop—listened carefully.

"Did you ever see that knife around here, Mr. Allardyce?" asked Slater suddenly.

"No, I didn't." Allardyce was certain that he had not.

"Well, I suppose it might have been here, just the same," mused the detective. "I suppose you don't know everything the old man had around the place."

Allardyce did not agree with him. He thought he knew Old Thing's stock almost as well as had Old Thing himself. However, he said no more than was necessary.

There was some further questioning of the several tradesmen who had first entered the place, and at length the body was removed in a patrol wagon. A uniformed policeman was left in charge of the premises, and shortly thereafter Messrs. Slater and Considine also went away, accompanied by Allardyce. Woolfolk had left some time before, to hurry to a telephone.

On the sidewalk Allardyce asked: "What do you want me to do, Sergeant? Mind my own business?"

The detective grinned. "That's always a good idea. I suppose you can *go* home. We know who you are and where to reach you. You'll be wanted at the inquest, if for nothing else. I guess you won't run away."

"I certainly *won't*. There's nothing to run from."

"Well, if you get any ideas about this thing, let me hear them."

Looking very much like exactly what they were, Messrs. Slater and Considine sauntered off upon their routine inquiries in such matters as murder. The throng had gradually thinned. The shopkeepers had gone back to their business. Allardyce, left virtually alone upon the pavement, felt that a definite era in his life had ended. De Gollyer was dead and gone; the shop was irrevocably closed; and he was standing in sunlight that Old Thing would never see again. It was a bitter enough thought.

He left the sidewalk and cut diagonally across the street to the other side, and at the same instant Dane Woolfolk, who had been watching him from a nearby shop door, left his concealment and followed.

III

Charles Allardyce felt that, in all probability, he would make no great name for himself as a detective. Reading detective stories of an evening was a pleasant enough pastime, but detective novels, after all, are not textbooks of detection, save of fictional detection.

Allardyce made a small living out of a hired typewriter. He wrote city travelogues and little stories of the streets for a number of down-state papers, and at night he read detective stories with considerable ardor. Occasionally he broke into an Eastern weekly of no great importance, but of select circulation, with a poem that nobody understood. But he had no illusions about his ability as a detective. A reader might guess the name of a murderer on page 13 of a volume of 365 pages and still be a pretty poor sort of sleuth, he realized, in life. His cleverness would consist not in his ability to unravel a living tangle, but in his knowledge of the methods of certain mystery writers.

Nevertheless, Old Thing had been his friend, Old Thing had been murdered, and—in a melodramatic sense—Old Thing's corpse was crying for vengeance. He, Allardyce, had liked Old Thing. They had talked over mystery novels together, and had conspired together to solve the puzzles concocted by ingenious authors. In the circumstances, it was almost imperative that he, Allardyce, seek the murderer of Old Thing.

Why, then, he asked himself, did his first move in that direction involve the girl of the night before? He was certain that she was no murderess. The answer was that she was the only clue he had. The actual murderer might have been inspired to his deed after the girl's visit. There were men in the world who would commit murder for a dollar and a quarter, and there were certainly men in the world who would commit murder for a hundred-dollar book.

The questions to be answered, then, were:

Had the young woman of the night before returned to the shop after he, Allardyce, had gone away? If so, it could only have been to leave the volume for immediate sale.

Supposing this to have happened, had there been a third person present on the occasion of that second visit? If so, and that third person did not at once come forward, it was likely enough that he had excellent reason for declining to reveal himself. (If he *did* come forward, there might be trouble for Charles Allardyce, who, it would be assumed, had lied to the police.)

Had the young woman herself, after her second (conjectured) visit, spoken of the book and its (conjectured) transfer to someone else?

The questions were simple and obvious, and they all involved the girl and the book. If the girl and the book were not, however remotely, connected with the murder of Robert de Gollyer, then he, Allardyce, was on the wrong track and would have to start over again.

The starting point of an investigation was certainly Bancroft. If the girl who needed a hundred dollars had been to Bancroft, then there had been no second visit to De Gollyer. So to Bancroft Allardyce hastened, reaching the bookshop in the Loop shortly after ten o'clock.

He was exactly an hour too late.

"I'm sorry," said the bookseller, when he had listened to a fraction of the breathless story, "but she was here when I opened up at eight-thirty, and she was gone by nine. I bought her book and paid her for it. She had to catch a train, I think she said."

"Good Lord!" cried Allardyce. "She was leaving town?"

"So I gathered. She didn't specifically say so, but she did say that she was in a hurry to catch a train. The inference seemed obvious."

Allardyce was floored.

Yet, after all, the bookseller's simple statement had cleared the attractive girl of complicity in the murder, had it not? If she had sold her book to Bancroft, then she had not returned to De Gollyer. Not that he, Allardyce, had ever suspected her of complicity; but the bookseller's testimony might be useful if ever she were discovered.

Yet, for some reason, this girl was hurriedly leaving town.

"May I see the book?" he asked after a moment.

"Of course," said the bookseller; "but it's hardly likely that it's another book and another girl."

Allardyce hastily skimmed the yellowed pages. At the title page he stopped, puzzled. There was a small stain in the center of the page that he was certain had not been there the night before. It was a pinkish sort of stain, almost circular, and the exact center was of a heavier hue.

"That's odd," he said. "It looks like a blood stain."

Disturbed, he continued with his explorations, the bookseller looking over his shoulder. "I don't even know who she is," confided the investigator. "Well, there's no clue here apparently. Yes, there is! Here's a name on the half-title."

"And a date." The bookseller smiled a bit sardonically. "'Christmas, 1832.' Won't help you much, I'm afraid."

The signature was as old, exactly, as the date. Allardyce was silent for a moment.

"Still," he urged, "it might be her name also. The book was her great-aunt's, she said, and it may be that the old lady was on her father's side of the house and had the same name. Odd name, too, fortunately. *Courtneige*. There can't be many of them in town. English, I'll bet." He asked quickly: "Have you a telephone directory?"

Bancroft brought it out. "The only book in the place that isn't for sale," he smiled.

Allardyce fluttered the pages. *"Court, Courtel, Courtham, Courtin, Courtledge,"* he muttered, scanning the names. "Here it is! There are three of them. Look here, Mr. Bancroft, I'm going to tell you the whole story and see what you think."

He recounted everything that had happened, while the bookseller's eyes widened.

"If you had only called me up early this morning," said Bancroft, when he had finished, "I'd have been ready for her when she arrived. But the very fact that she came, it seems to me, proves that she *didn't* return to De Gollyer's."

"So it seems to me," agreed Allardyce, "and yet I've a feeling that that damned book is somewhere at the bottom of it all. She didn't volunteer anything that now looks suspicious, I suppose?"

"Not a thing. However, you'd better run down the history of that book. I won't feel easy about it myself until I know what happened." He glanced at the directory. "Any of your Courtneiges in the right neighborhood?"

"Yes, there is. One is on Hazel Avenue. It's an old-fashioned street, not far from where De Gollyer saw her turn. Well, there it is! *Anthony Courtneige.*"

"You're in luck," said the bookseller. "The odds were against it."

"I'm off at once," cried Allardyce. "Many thanks, Mr. Bancroft." He turned and hurried out of the shop.

As he left the door a second young man hastily drew back into a neighboring entrance. Immediately a considerable problem presented itself to the second young man: whether to continue to follow Allardyce or to enter the bookshop and learn the object of the visit.

"Blast it!" observed Dane Woolfolk profanely. But he decided to follow Allardyce. It was the safest bet.

Allardyce was heading for State Street. He was waiting on the corner. Was he waiting for a taxi? Mr. Woolfolk began to look around, himself. No, he was going to board a street car—the piker! Yes, he was taking a Broadway car. Again Mr. Woolfolk thought rapidly. There were disadvantages either way, but he felt that he would be better off in a taxi. He allowed the street car to leave the corner, then turned quickly to look for a cab. Allardyce would be going some distance, no doubt, since he was riding, and it would be easy enough for a taxi to overhaul the car.

A cab came cruising around the corner and he hailed it. In a few minutes he was jogging comfortably along in the wake of the street car, stopping when the car stopped and starting when it started.

It became evident rapidly that Allardyce was going back to the old neighborhood. It was a tiresome ride. The pursued man left the car at Montrose Avenue and walked east, Woolfolk still trailing easily in his taxi.

Courtneige, thought Allardyce as he walked, was a very pretty name, and it fitted a very pretty girl. He wondered what her first name might be and decided that it ought to be something old-fashioned, something like Sally. The name in the old book had been Sally, as it happened; and why should not the grand-niece wear her grand-aunt's name?

The house was small but charming, a two-story gabled structure of wood and stone, with ivy on its walls and a tiny stained-glass window at one side that obviously marked the landing of a stairway within. There was a handsome tree before the door, and a bit of a yard in the rear, in which some flowers were still blooming. A lantern hung above the front door, and on the central panel there was a small knocker fashioned in the semblance of one of the Lincoln Park lions.

Allardyce lifted the brass doodad and smote the lion in the

nose. He had not quite made up his mind what he would say to whoever answered his knock.

As it happened, he said nothing at all for a moment. Instead, he stood and stared blankly at the girl who, he had supposed, was by this time miles removed from Chicago.

Lord, what a situation! he thought.

For an instant she did not recognize him; then quite suddenly she did, and her face flushed. A little knot of puzzlement appeared between her eyes—they were blue, he noted, and disturbing. Then her face cleared.

"Oh, of course!" she smiled. "You have come from Mr. de Gollyer, I suppose."

Allardyce was staggered. Suddenly he found his tongue. "Good heavens!" he whispered. Haven't you *heard?*"

The little frown again appeared on her forehead. "My book?" she asked, a bit anxiously.

"May I come in?" asked Allardyce abruptly. "I assure you it's important—and very serious."

She swung the door open more widely and he entered the narrow hall and then, at her direction, passed into a living room at the front.

Without seating himself, he turned swiftly and demanded: "Answer me one question, please. Did you return to Mr. de Gollyer last night, after you had gone away the first time?"

Her face, by this time, had paled. "Yes," she answered, "I did. I went back about—about eleven o'clock, I should imagine. I told him that I would leave the book with him, and he promised to try and sell it for me today, so that I could have the money tonight. What has happened?"

"Who else was in the shop when you went back?" continued Allardyce hoarsely. "I'll tell you everything in a minute."

"There was nobody in the shop but Mr. de Gollyer and myself—nobody that I saw, anyway. Oh, I'm sure of it. He was just getting ready to close when I entered."

Allardyce sagged from shoulder to heel. He moved slowly to a chair and, without asking permission, dropped into it.

"I'm sorry, Miss— Is it *Courtneige?*"

She nodded, apprehension in her eyes.

"I'm sorry, Miss Courtneige, but I'm afraid we are both in for a lot of trouble. Mr. de Gollyer was murdered last night, shortly after you left the shop, and your book was stolen."

She too sank into a chair, and for a moment they stared into each other's eyes in silence. At length, "Tell me," she breathed; and suddenly a hot flush swept the paleness of her cheek so that it burned. "Do you mean," she asked quickly, "that they think—that the police—?"

"Think *you* did it?" he finished. "No, thank the Lord, they don't. They don't know anything about you—yet—Miss Courtneige. But—they may later on. I don't see how it can be kept from them. Listen!"

He told her the story from beginning to end, concluding with a recital of what he had learned at Bancroft's.

"Of course," he finished, "it was not you who sold the book to Bancroft."

"No," she agreed, "but who *was* it? What girl would want to murder that poor old man?"

He shrugged hopelessly. "You see the mess it is! You and I may not be the only persons who know that you were there. Suppose—just suppose—this other woman—this other girl—was hiding there all the time. *She* also might know, and to throw suspicion in another direction she might communicate anonymously with the police, telling them about your visit.

You see how it would look! I have already lied about you—by suppressing the fact of your visit. Why, it's even possible that someone passing the shop saw you the second time, or even the first. Oh, it's hopeless!"

After a moment he asked: "Why did you need a hundred dollars in a hurry?"

She flushed again. "For clothes," she replied frankly. "I don't mean that I'm destitute; but I had been invited to a weekend party in Wisconsin, and I wanted a new outfit. I couldn't afford it, I felt, but I was eager to go to the party. Then I thought of my book. If Mr. de Gollyer had sold it for me I should have bought my outfit tomorrow and taken the night train. I hadn't a great deal of time left."

"It's too bad," he observed perfunctorily, but she cut him short.

"I don't mind about the book—now." She hesitated a moment, then timidly asked: "Ought I to tell the police myself that I was there?"

"Yes," he said, "I suppose you ought. My lie to them is going to make it troublesome, but your frankness may save you from annoyance. I will simply say that I was so certain you couldn't have done it that I couldn't bring myself to betray you. Anyway, I didn't know who you were," he added, a bit argumentatively.

"Oh, I don't know *what* to do!" she cried.

An amused voice broke in suddenly, at the sound of which both sprang to their feet and whirled toward the doorway.

"I'll tell you exactly what to do," said the voice.

In the doorway leading from the hall to the living room stood a young man smiling an impudent smile.

"Woolfolk!" cried Allardyce.

"Right as rain," smiled the newcomer easily. "Permit me, Miss Courtneige. Dane Woolfolk of the *Globe.*"

Miss Courtneige caught her breath. Then her anger burst over him. "How dare you enter this house without knocking?" she demanded.

He smiled again with superb insolence. "Well," he drawled, "the door was half open anyway, and I thought it was an invitation for me to follow my friend Allardyce inside. Having heard most of what you have had to tell him, I am rather glad I did. But why be angry? You say you had nothing to do with the murder—at least, you suggest it by your attitude—so what is there for you to fear? I have arrived, it would seem, in very good time. You are both in doubt about the course to pursue, and here am I, a highly resourceful fellow, prepared to answer your doubts."

Allardyce stepped forward angrily. "Shall I throw him out, Miss Courtneige?" he asked.

"No, don't do that," answered the reporter with another grin. "In the first place, you might not be able to do it; and in the second place, what good would it do either of you? I would simply step to a telephone, tell the *Globe* everything I know, then let the police know about this new and very valuable clue."

"If I go to the police myself—at once—" began the girl, looking at Allardyce; but Allardyce shook his head.

"No, it wouldn't do. He's right. He's got the drop on us, so to speak. All right, Mr. Woolfolk, we are in your hands. What do you propose?"

Mr. Woolfolk rubbed his hands gleefully. "This," he replied. "I want a story—a good one—today. You two are the story. Now, I don't mind saying that I believe neither of you had anything to do with the murder of old De Gollyer. But for one day—today—I want it to appear that I have a warm clue, dug up exclusively by the *Evening Globe*. I will print one story about you, telling merely the facts, and letting the police and the public draw their own conclusions. I'll tell about Miss Courtneige's two visits to the antique shop, about Mr. Allardyce's gallant falsehood to protect the young lady, and about the disappearance of the book. Nothing libelous in that. For one day, it will appear that the *Globe* has run down the murderer. Tomorrow I shall tell the Bancroft side of it. Miss Courtneige will be seen by Bancroft, who will say positively that it was not she who sold him the book. Obviously, then, it was not she who murdered De Gollyer, and a nation-wide search begins, conducted by the *Globe*, for the young woman who impersonated Miss Courtneige in the Bancroft bookshop. The murderer, or murderess, will be run down and all will be well. I am, in other words, offering you all the facilities of the *Evening Globe*—a great newspaper—in clearing yourselves, in return for a story, the printing of which will place you for one day under suspicion. What do you say?"

A hot retort was on the lips of Allardyce, but the upraised hand of his companion stayed it.

"And if we refuse?" asked Miss Courtneige.

Woolfolk shrugged. "Well, I'll telephone the office, at once, everything that I have heard pass between you, this morning, and the police can dig up Bancroft for themselves."

The girl turned to Allardyce with an appraising glance at his tall frame. "*Can* you throw him out, Mr. Allardyce?" she asked.

"Oh, yes, indeed," said Allardyce.

"Then please *do!*"

IV

Come what would, thought Allardyce, as once again he made his way toward the bereft antique shop, he had gained something fine from the bloody tangle. If he had lost one friend, certainly he had gained another. Her first name, he had learned, was not Sally but Stella, and she was—well, she was wonderful!

Even now she was on her way in a taxicab to the North Halsted Street police station to tell her story. It had seemed the only thing to do. To wait until Woolfolk had broadcast it would have been madness. No doubt he, Allardyce, would now be arrested on suspicion—but what if he were? A man might lie to protect a girl without being a murderer, surely.

Would he be allowed to enter the shop? he wondered. Doubtless the uniformed policeman was still in charge. And if a clue to the murderer of Old Thing existed anywhere it was in the shop. The detectives had been lax enough; he had watched them. It was absurdly perfunctory, the way they poked about. Obviously, it was to them an unimportant murder.

Well, he owed it to Old Thing to make this effort. He owed it to Stella Courtneige, who might, after all, be held suspect, in spite of her blue and disturbing eyes. By George, he owed it to himself. There was no telling! One Charles Allardyce himself might be languishing behind iron bars by evening.

Inside the shop door, upon a rickety chair, sat the policeman who had been left in charge. He looked forlorn and unhappy. An expression of interest crossed his face as Allardyce approached the door.

"So it's you," he observed, as the bell tinkled and tinkled again at the entrance of the investigator.

"It's me, again," said Allardyce ungrammatically. "I want to look around a bit, if you don't mind. De Gollyer was a friend of mine, you know, and I'd like to get an idea whether anything is missing."

"Got permission?" asked the bluecoat.

"Slater told me to try out any ideas I had. This is one of

them." It was almost true. The detective had not intended, however, that De Gollyer's friend should reënter the shop upon a hunt for clues.

The policeman shrugged. "Hop to it, buddy," he said; "but if you can tell whether anything's missing from this place, you're a wonder."

Allardyce glanced down at the spot where Old Thing had fallen. The stain on the pine board made him shudder, and suddenly he was thinking again of the stain upon the title page of the volume in the downtown bookshop. Could it have been blood?

Certainly not De Gollyer's blood. How possibly could a single drop have fallen in the mathematical center of a page, when all else around had been imbued with Old Thing's life stream? There had been no sign of it upon the volume's cover; no sign on any other page. And again he would have sworn that the spot upon the title page had not existed the night before.

He recalled the appearance of the circular stain. Almost a perfect circle in its deeper hue, but splashed and somewhat lighter at its edges. Almost as if— By George, almost as if it had been *blotted!* Suppose it had been. . . .

A swift picture of what might have happened after the murder came to him, born of his imagination. Suppose—just suppose—the murderess herself to have been slightly wounded in the scuffle, or touched by some of De Gollyer's blood.

The book safely in her possession, wherever and however she had got it from the antique dealer, what would be her first thought? The big room was beyond all question in darkness, except for such light as might have filtered in from the street. How could she be sure that she had the right book?

Obviously, she would carry it to a light and look at the title page. And then, bending over it, suppose a drop of blood—?

Allardyce walked swiftly to the rear of the shop, where Old Thing's desk sat in its obscure corner. Even in daylight it was dark in that corner. He switched on the electric desk lamp, while the policeman at the front screwed about in his chair to see what was going on.

The papers on the desk had been jumbled and tossed chaotically by the desultory detectives, but none had fallen to the floor. Allardyce lifted and piled and piled and lifted. At length he found what he was looking for.

It was a yellow blotter and the stain upon it was very faint, but it was there. The stain that corresponded to that on the title page of the book of poems.

"What is it, buddy?" asked the fat man at the front. "Found something?"

"I've found a blotter," said Allardyce. "Take a look at it. I want you to know that I found it here—on Mr. de Gollyer's desk. See it? Well, there's a blood stain on it. There!"

"Hm-m!" mused the fat man. "It *might* be blood." He added after a thoughtful instant: "What of it?"

"Nothing yet; but I was looking for it. That's the point—I was *looking* for it. I'm taking it to Slater, see?"

"Take it along, take it along," said the policeman wearily.

But what, after all, he asked himself in the street, had he proved? Merely that the murderer (or murder*ess*) had spilled a drop of her blood upon a book? Was all human blood alike, he wondered, or was the blood of every individual distinctive and different? It was a point upon which his detective reading had not informed him.

Well, there was one other thing. He would have a talk with this realtor, Haines, who had found the body. His reading had informed him that the reek of perfumes was potent and powerful. Haines had been the first inside the shop. The murder had been committed by a girl. Might it not be that some lingering odor might have associated itself with Haines' entrance? Reminded of it, might not Haines recall the very odor? It was of such trifling clues as odors and bloodstains on yellow blotters that solutions were often builded.

At the door of the real-estate office next door he saw consciously for the first time that the name in gold upon the glass was not Haines but Dalgeish. He stared. What error was this? Possibly, however, Haines was merely one of the juniors. At any rate, this was certainly the place, for, glancing through the half-open door, he saw the very man he wanted.

Haines was seated at a desk, writing. His head was bent, but at the sound of the opening door he raised it. Yes, it was the very man, thought Allardyce. He recalled his face now, perfectly—a long face, a bit thin, a bit sallow, the eyelids slightly drooping, as if heavy with sleep. He recalled even the bit of court plaster that the man was wearing on his rather high cheek bone, although no single detail had stood out during the morning.

Good God! The bit of court plaster!

The idea struck Allardyce so suddenly and with such force that he stopped short in his tracks.

Was it possible? Oh, it was madness! A girl had committed the crime. A man might wear a bit of court plaster without being a murderer, just as a man might tell a falsehood without being a murderer. But a terrible conviction was growing in Allardyce's mind.

Haines, the man who had found the body of De Gollyer, stood beside him.

"Oh," he said, suddenly recognizing the individual who had entered. "You are—?"

"Mr. Allardyce, yes—you saw me this morning. I'm sorry to bother you, but—I was a friend of Old—of Mr. de Gollyer, you know, and I'd like—Do you mind if I ask you a few questions?"

The real-estate man hesitated. "I'm fairly busy," he answered, "but in this particular case, why I guess I can take some time off. What was it you wanted to know?"

Allardyce had by this time recovered his wits.

"Frankly," he explained, "I'm playing detective—with the permission of the police, of course—and I have a queer idea. I'm wondering if, when you entered the unlocked shop this morning, you were aware of any peculiar aroma or perfume?"

Romancing quickly, he explained his idea in more detail and waited almost respectfully for the man's answer.

But Haines had noticed nothing of the sort, and said so rather brusquely.

"Then I sha'n't bother you," said Allardyce, "for it appears that I'm wrong. You see, a woman did this thing, and—"

"The deuce!" cried Haines. "I hadn't heard that."

"Very few have heard it yet," said Allardyce, "and I must ask you to keep it a secret, if you don't mind; but that's the fact."

"Of course. I won't say a word. But who—if I may ask—is the woman? Or is that a secret, too?"

"It's so deep a secret," said Allardyce, "that—but no, I can say nothing about it. Please don't ask me. And thanks very much."

He left the shop hurriedly and almost ran to his small hotel, a few blocks distant, leaving the real-estate clerk staring up the street after him.

Once safely locked in his own room, the amateur detective rummaged frantically in a drawer until he had unearthed a long darning needle; then, standing before his miniature bookcase, he slowly drew forth a slender volume of Poe's Poems. It was not a rare edition, but in size and format it was not unlike the copy that had belonged to Stella Courtneige.

For a moment or two he practised opening the book to its title page and bending over it, as if to verify a date. Then, with an anticipatory grimace, he strode to the small mirror over his basin and plunged the bodkin into his cheek at the point where the bone was most prominent. For an instant he stood and watched the slow drop gather on the wound. When it was of sufficient size, as he judged, he again seized the volume and opened quickly to the title, bending over the book as before. An instant later the drop had fallen to the white page.

Allardyce waited another moment, then carefully blotted the spot on the page that he had marred. After that he stood back to admire his demonstration. He had not exactly reproduced the stain in Bancroft's book, but he had approximated it with surprising accuracy.

He pasted a bit of court plaster over his tiny wound and smiled at the effect in the glass. What a start he might give Haines by striding in on him, just that way, and slapping the volume of Poe down under his nose, its stained title page exposed to his guilty eyes!

But who was the woman?

Then his telephone bell rang sharply, and the voice of the clerk at the desk, when he had answered, rang like a death knell in his ears. "Two men are on their way up to see you, Mr. Allardyce. They told me not to announce them."

Slater and Considine! There could be no doubt about it. He was about to be arrested as—as what? Murderer, accessory, witness, or simple liar?

He hung up the receiver without speaking and strode to the

door. He flung it open. Slater and Considine were advancing up the hall.

"I thought it might be you," said Allardyce grimly.

They entered the room and he closed the door behind them.

"Am I under arrest?"

"Well, why not?" countered the detective called Slater.

Allardyce shrugged. "It's all right with me. Only I didn't do it."

"Nobody thinks you did," observed Slater.

"Then why am I under arrest? For failing to tell you about that girl?"

The detective smiled. "You're not exactly under arrest," explained Slater. "The fact is, we were sent over to give you hell for concealing important information, and then to ask you what else you had up your sleeve. The captain thinks you know more about this De Gollyer than you've told anybody yet."

"Where is Miss Courtneige?" asked Allardyce bluntly.

"She is off to the Loop, with one of our fellows. She's being taken to Bancroft's. Of course, if he says she isn't the girl who sold him the book there'll be no difficulty for her. Nobody thinks *she* did it, either."

Allardyce was relieved. "But, honor bright, I haven't an idea who killed the old man," he insisted. "The fact is, I've been working on the case myself."

"Umph!" grunted Considine. "Well," added Slater, "we're to take you to the captain, anyway."

Allardyce thought quickly. "Look here, Slater," he cried, "while you're taking me, the man who did it may be escaping. Maybe I'm an idiot, but I've got an idea about this murder, and it's this: a woman didn't do it!"

He burst out with the whole story while the detectives listened with mingled amusement and interest.

"Now," he concluded, "what do you think?"

"Haines, eh?"

"Yes!"

"Of course, he'd say he cut himself shaving."

"Rot! He couldn't cut himself that high up—not unless he was pretty nervous. And if he didn't commit the murder he had nothing to be nervous about."

"What do you want to do?" asked Considine.

"I want to confront him with this book. Slap it down under his nose and see what he does."

Slater grinned. "It might work, at that—if he's guilty, that is. What do you think, Tim?"

Considine thought there could be no harm in trying. "But I've got a better idea," he said. "Listen!"

V

Seated in a taxi, with steam up ready for departure, Considine and Allardyce waited for the reappearance of Slater. Across the street about three hundred feet distant was the office of the Dalgeish Realty Company. On the corner beyond it was a drug store. Into the drug store, a few moments before, the two in the taxi had seen Slater disappear.

Five minutes later the second detective came out and the taxi riders caught his signal. They transferred their attention to the front door of the realty company.

Then the door opened and a young man rushed out, carrying his hat in his hand. He looked wildly up and down the street for a taxi. It was an emergency that had not been overlooked. There was one waiting for him—directly ahead of that occupied by the detective Considine and his companion. The driver was instructed. He caught Haines' signal and swung his car across the street. Haines, cramming his hat onto his head, was seen to speak quickly with the driver and pile into the cab, which started southward at once.

"He's off to Bancroft's, all right," said Considine. "That settles it. He's our man. In half an hour we'll be hearing what happened last night."

They picked up Slater at the opposite curb and started in pursuit.

"Got him," said the other detective laconically, as he dropped into his seat. "I told him I was Bancroft, and it gave him quite a shock. What did I want? he asked. I said a young woman, who had given his name as a reference, had sold me a book this morning—a rare book—and it had turned out to be a fake. I said I wanted it taken up and my money returned quickly, or I would call the police.

"He didn't dare doubt it. He realized that there was only one thing to do: get Bancroft his money as fast as he could and take up that incriminating book."

At Addison Road the leading machine turned westward at a high speed, and the pursuing car followed at the same rate. Haines was obviously nervous. He kept looking back at the other taxi.

At Halsted Street the big bulk of the police station pushed itself up, and with a grinding of brakes the leading car stopped at the curb, to be instantly surrounded by a circle of men who ran out from the station.

Haines collapsed in the taxi. He almost had to be carried inside.

"What are you going to do with me?" he asked later.

"Hang you, I hope," responded the captain pleasantly. "Who was the girl who was your accomplice?"

"I won't tell you that. She's gone where you'll never find her. But I'll tell you something else. *She* murdered De Gollyer!"

"Quit your kidding!" said the officer in charge.

"She did," insisted Haines. "I only stood in the alley, at the back. She went inside. I owed her some money, for—for something—and I couldn't give it to her. I tried to borrow some from old De Gollyer last night, and he said he didn't have it. She was pushing me pretty hard. Well—I decided to rob the old man. I thought he was lying about not having any money. The girl was waiting for me. There's a window at the back of the antique shop that looks out on the alley. It's always open. De Gollyer slept in the shop. I was going to get in there, knock the old man unconscious, and take his money. But as I stood beside the window, listening, a girl came in. She had brought him a book to sell for her—a valuable book. They talked about it awhile, and he told her a bookseller named Bancroft would give her more money; but she said she'd trust him—De Gollyer—to sell it for her."

He shrugged. "It looked easier than swiping his money. I went back and told the girl about it, gave her my flashlight, and boosted her in through the window when we thought the old man was asleep. He wasn't asleep. He was smoking his pipe, in the dark, up at the front of the shop. He heard her coming and spoke to her. There was nothing else for it, and she grabbed a knife from a rack of things close by and let him have it. I was sore when I heard about it, but it was too late then. I told her what to do with the book, and how to get out of town. This morning I thought it would be a good idea to find the body myself and make the first report. I don't know how you heard about the book," he concluded bitterly.

"We've heard of a lot of things," answered Slater. "When you looked at that book last night, Haines, to be sure you'd found the right one, a drop of blood fell from your cheek onto the title page. De Gollyer had struggled with you and gashed your cheek with his nail. You've got a piece of plaster on it now. You carried the book to the old man's desk, and it was there the drop of blood fell. You hunted for a blotter and blotted the spot of blood. This is the blotter you used. Here is the corresponding stain. There may have been a girl with you in the alley—I don't know—but she had nothing to do with killing De Gollyer."

"It's a lie!" screamed the clerk. "You're trying to scare me."

"Well," said the captain, "I guess we're succeeding. There are two other points, Haines. The knife wasn't in De Gollyer's rack, for there isn't any rack, I believe, and anyway Mr. Allardyce knows everything he had in the place. Finally, when Sergeant Slater telephoned a little while ago I sent a man around to the undertaker's near here to check on something. He ought to be back at any minute."

The door of the private office opened and a plainclothes man strode in. He nodded significantly, and the captain continued his monologue.

"Finally, Mr. Haines, the small strip of your skin that De Gollyer gashed out of your cheek has just been found under the right thumbnail of the man you murdered."

A few minutes later, when they had taken the dejected murderer away, the captain turned upon Allardyce. There was a vast sternness on his countenance.

"So, Mr. Allardyce," he said, "I understand that you have been maltreating one of the city's most famous reporters!"

Allardyce flushed. "I'm afraid that's true," he admitted. "But, on my honor, he had it coming to him."

The captain's frown deepened. "You took the law into your own hands, I suppose you know, and can be punished for assault and battery?"

Allardyce stammered. "Well—he had no right in Miss Courtneige's home, and so I—"

"Did you throw him out on his ear?" snapped the captain.

"I'm afraid I did."

"Did you hit him first?" persisted the officer.

"Y-yes, I did. You see—"

Suddenly Captain Costigan was grinning amiably and rubbing his hands with an ecstatic washing movement.

"Well," he asserted, "that's the best news I've heard for a month of Sundays. You know, for years I've been wanting to take a poke at that cocky reporter, and have been afraid of what his damn' paper would do to *me*. I think, if you don't mind, I'll have to shake the hand that smashed Dane Woolfolk. Any time you want any favors around here, the station is yours."

Allardyce laughed joyously. "There's one I'd like now. You won't hold Miss Courtneige any longer than is absolutely necessary, will you?"

"Miss Courtneige," said the captain, looking at his watch, "has been at home now for nearly an hour. We released her as soon as Bancroft gave her a clean bill."

Then he watched the figure of Charles Allardyce passing rapidly through the front door.

"Well," he muttered, "that young man *is* in a hurry."

THE SHAKESPEARE TITLE-PAGE MYSTERY

Carolyn Wells

The prolific and bibliophilic Carolyn Wells (1869-1942) wrote and edited one hundred seventy books, of which eighty-two are mysteries, many of which had exceptionally ingenious plot ideas, and most of which are achingly dull—reason enough to ignore them. Still, it is difficult to understand that someone so enormously popular and prominent in her lifetime could be so largely forgotten and seldom unread today.

As famous as she was for her mystery novels, sixty-one of which featured the scholarly, book-loving Fleming Stone, she was equally noted in her time for such anthologies as *Nonsense Anthology* (1902), considered a classic of its kind, and her *Parody Anthology* (1904), which remained in print for more than a half-century. Wells also wrote the first instructional manual in the detective fiction genre, *The Technique of the Mystery Story* (1913). Her first mystery novel, *The Clue* (1909), was selected for the "Haycraft-Queen Definitive Library of Detective-Crime-Mystery Fiction."

Her affection for satires and parodies led her to write many of them herself, including *Ptomaine Street* (1921), a full-length parody of Sinclair Lewis, and several stories involving Sherlock Holmes, including "The Adventure of the 'Mona Lisa'" (1912) and "The Adventure of the Clothes-Line" (1915).

Wells was a dedicated rare book collector, as is evidenced in this story, which contains much bibliographic arcana. She had two major collections, one devoted to such high spots of literature as first editions of Walt Whitman's *Leaves of Grass* and Herman Melville's *Moby Dick*, the other dedicated to mystery fiction. Her collection went to auction shortly after she died.

"The Shakespeare Title-Page Mystery" was originally published in the Winter 1940 (volume 4, part 2), issue of *The Dolphin*, published by the Limited Editions Club.

The Shakespeare Title-Page Mystery

Carolyn Wells

THAT'S THE way with you collectors! You were just crazy with joy when you got a first *Leaves of Grass* in wrappers. And now you want a first *Venus*, and I don't suppose you care whether she has her wrapper on or not!"

"I do want a first *Venus and Adonis*, but I have not forgotten my other treasures—my true first—"

"I know, your fifty-five *Alice*—"

"No, Sherry," Herenden corrected him gently. "Fifty-five *Leaves* and sixty-five *Alice*. You know nothing of rare books."

"Rare! Rare!" Young Sherry Biggs enjoyed heckling those two famous collectors, Garrett Sheldon and Leigh Herenden, their host. "Why is a thing valuable because it's rare? An honest man is rare, does any one care for him? A good woman is rare, who collects those? O Boy! as Shakespeare says in *Merry Wives*, Three, four, thirty-six, you collectors are an unmixed evil. This craze for rare books breeds crime. You're always guarding against theft."

"No, Sherry," his host smiled at him, "you're wrong there. I've guarded my treasures once and for all. Want to see my book room?"

Like many another good American, whose wealth piled itself up after the manner of Ossa on Pelion, Leigh Herenden had built a house for himself on Long Island, and the library occupied a large wing. They had to go down two or three steps to it, as seems to be the case with most self-respecting libraries.

"Your stenographer is a pretty girl," Sherry Biggs noticed in passing.

"Muriel Jewell," Herenden said carelessly. "I have little to do with the girl. I've little to do, anyhow. Herbert Rand is my secretary, and Gorman is my confidential book-buyer."

"It must be nice," Sheldon said, musingly, "to have a lynx-eyed librarian like Gorman to nose out rare volumes for you. But somehow, I'd feel I was losing half the fun if I didn't make my own discoveries."

"Everyone to his taste," Herenden conceded, and his gray eyes were kindly, with no hint of criticism. "I know," he went on, "there is a noble sentiment that decrees, 'not the quarry, but the chase; not the laurel, but the race,' and yet, I do not enjoy poking around in the rare bookshops as much as I do having my quarry in hand."

He led the way into a steel-lined safe, the size of a small room, and showed Sherry its hidden devices to balk both the moth that corrupts and the thief who breaks through and steals. As Sheldon was about to leave, Herenden turned to him.

"I have an announcement to make this afternoon."

"I'll stay, then," his neighbor and rival collector decided. Garrett Sheldon had a feeling that the news would concern a new acquisition to the already famous Herenden library, and he prepared himself to feel jealous pangs, which he would conceal at all cost. . . .

"You know," Leigh Herenden began that afternoon, "that among other favorites, I am specializing in Shakespeare. And only now have I been able to find a first edition of *Venus and Adonis*."

Their excited hubbub of questions and exclamations obliged him to pause.

"Go on!" cried Sheldon, "don't stop at the most interesting point! Where did you get it? And—" he almost said, "how much did you pay for it?" but changed his question to—"how did you hear of it?"

"It was a heaven-sent boon," Herenden smiled happily. "I was asked if I wanted it, and I said I did."

"I'll bet there was something shady about your getting it!" Sherry Biggs exclaimed.

"Maybe." Herenden showed no offense. "If so, I sin in company with Cardinal Mazarin. I have read on good authority that 'a little pilfering here and there was never known to upset Mazarin—if the book he coveted was worthy of it.'"

Sherry turned up his youthful nose.

"Anybody would think it was a Gutenberg Bible you were talking about."

"A real first edition of *Venus and Adonis* is worth more than a Gutenberg Bible, if you are speaking of money value." Herenden gave Sherry a glance of reprimand.

"But I happen to know that the first and second editions of the book you are talking about are exactly alike, except for the date. Now, how can it matter which one you possess?"

"You know very well that, to a collector, age is the pre-eminent point of value. Age in a book is much the same as youth in a woman."

"Such a fuss about books!"

"But where is your book, Leigh?" asked Garrett Sheldon. "Seeing is believing."

"Sorry, but I can't show it today. It isn't yet tuned to the atmosphere of my collection. Come back Sunday night and see 'the first heir of my invention.' You'll covet it, I know."

"Hardly that! As I have one of my own. A real one."

"You have a first *Venus and Adonis*! I never knew that!"

"A fine copy, too."

"Bring it with you to the party tomorrow night. We'll show off together."

After the guests had gone, Herenden said to Gorman, his book-buyer and librarian, with a perplexed air, "Did you hear Sheldon say he had a first?"

"I did, Mr. Herenden, but it can't be possible."

"No, I suppose not. Of course, people in England are glad to sell their books over here just now. But another first *Venus*! It can't be."

"Unless somebody found a nest—"

"Don't be silly, Gorman. They didn't have nests in those days."

"No, sir. But Mr. Sheldon must have something. Could it be a faked copy?"

"Oh, no. That book is too well known to be faked. There were thirteen or more editions, and every copy is located. We know where each one is, though, of course, the later editions are of far less value. Keep the secret, Gorman—don't let anybody know where our book came from. Some day, perhaps I may tell."

"I've told no one, sir. Not even Rand knows where it came from."

"It is a wonderful find. Sheldon couldn't have got one the same way, could he?"

"Not likely. Such things don't happen often."

"And the lad is all right? He won't tell?"

"Oh, no! He won't even remember it."

"If ever the proper time comes, I shall tell the whole story, and give up the book. But you won't suffer, I promise you. All I've given you, you may keep, and I shall give you more if all goes well. I suppose I'm an accessory before the fact. Even so, I assume all responsibility, and if we are found out, no blame shall attach to you. You have confidence in Baines?"

"Oh, yes, sir. He has no idea it is a valuable book. He is more than satisfied with what you paid him."

"Am I interrupting a private confab?" Rand's cheery voice was followed by his appearance.

"Not at all," Herenden replied, a trifle coldly. "Come in. What is it?"

"Only this, Mr. Herenden. May I have the afternoon off? I've got the desk cleared and I'd like to go to the golf tournament; a friend of mine is playing today."

"Certainly, Rand. You are a wizard at finishing your work, I must say. By the way, Rand, can you be here tomorrow evening? I'm going to show my new *Venus* to some admiring friends, and you know where everything is."

"So does Gorman. But just as you say, Mr. Herenden."

Rand left them, and Gorman said, "Do you suppose he heard what we were saying? He's a quick fellow, and we were talking pretty plainly."

"Don't worry about it. And now I'm off to the golf tournament myself. Put the time lock on the safe, if you go out."

After Herenden had gone, Gorman went to the safe, where he could have found any book in the dark, had it been necessary. He took down the *Venus and Adonis*.

Back again in the library, he sat down to gloat over the acquisition—a small volume, measuring a bit over seven inches one way, and a trifle over five the other. Its cover was of old calf, worn and rubbed, a little soiled, and showing no title or legend of any kind.

Ralph Gorman was a practical man. He opened the book with intense interest but with no feeling of reverence, and read the title-page. *Venus and Adonis*. Then some lines in Latin, which he did not understand. Then the information that the book was printed by Richard Field—in 1593.

Just those four figures gave the tiny volume its worth. A fourth edition of the *Venus* had once sold at auction for $75,000. Rare books had gone up in price since then. And what would a first sell for? His eyes widened. He knew of several men in these United States who would gladly pay more—a great deal more—than $100,000 for this plain little book!

He put the precious volume back in the case which Herbert Rand had made for it. Rand was clever with books. He did any necessary repairing—Herenden knew better than to have any unnecessary repairing done—and he could collate with neatness and dispatch.

Gorman pored over Herenden's reference works on rare books. Yes, the second edition of the *Venus* was exactly the same as this first, save for the date, 1594, on the title page. The first edition was "printed with remarkable accuracy, doubtless from the author's manuscript." The only known copy was in the Bodleian Library at Oxford, and many facsimiles had been made from it.

Aha! thought Gorman, that's it! Mr. Sheldon has a facsimile and he thinks he can put it over on us! We'll see about that!

On Sunday evening the party came. Most of Leigh Herenden's friends were interested in books, for one reason or another, and many of the guests were collectors. Others were writers or playwrights or actors. They all knew enough of the situation to be eager to see the two books that were to be shown.

Garrett Sheldon came in, bringing a stranger, whom he introduced to Herenden. "Malcolm Osborne," he said, "and I warn you, Leigh, he knows his first editions from the ground up. He can decide which of us has the real first."

"Very kind of Mr. Osborne," Leigh said, politely. "You have your book with you, Sheldon? Gorman will bring mine."

As the librarian returned from the safe-room with Herenden's copy, Sheldon produced his volume.

"After you," Herenden said.

Sheldon opened a dark-red morocco case and took out his book.

It was impossible to misinterpret the murmur of surprised disappointment that rippled through the room. Two or three young people even laughed, but Garrett Sheldon winked at Herenden and said, "I assure you that this little book makes up in worth what it lacks in size."

As the crowd surged toward him, he handed the book to Leigh Herenden. And it certainly looked like the real first edition of *Venus and Adonis*. Gorman, standing by him, looked at it too, and they were both startled by the verity of it, or the perfection of imitation, whichever it might be.

"And now," said Sheldon, smiling, "where's yours, Leigh?"

Gorman, feeling queer, as he said afterward, passed Herenden's book to him. Removing the case, the host offered the volume to his guest.

Sheldon took it smilingly, looked it over rather carelessly, and placed it on the table beside the one he had brought.

"They look alike," he said slowly.

They did look alike—almost exactly. Two small, seemingly insignificant books, both bound in old calf, both dark brown and worn at the edges and corners. Nondescript affairs, with no physical charm or beauty.

"May I open this?" Herenden smiled.

"Indeed, yes. I'll look into yours, then we'll turn them over to Osborne, and ask his opinion."

Gorman stayed beside Herenden as they looked at the title-page. Both were amazed at its perfectness. Surely those figures were neither facsimiles nor fakes. Sheldon must have achieved the miracle of getting another first at the same time Herenden acquired his.

Sheldon and Osborne had their heads together over the other book.

"This is yours, Mr. Herenden?" and Osborne tapped the old brown binding.

"Yes, Mr. Osborne."

"You don't care to tell where you got it?"

"I'd rather not. You find no flaw in it?"

"Sorry, but I most decidedly do. It has an entire new title-page for one thing, there is a flyleaf missing, and it has been rebound. That's all I can see without a magnifying glass, but it is enough to prove to my mind that you were badly hoaxed. Have you had any other expert examine it?"

"No, but I have absolute confidence in it."

"Absolute confidence, Mr. Herenden, is a fine thing. I wish you had it in me, for what I tell you is true. While I hate to displease you, I think you should know the facts, whether you like them or not."

"You are quite right, Mr. Osborne, and I thank you. But I am sure this is boring our other guests. Shall we go to the living-room?"

After the guests had departed, Herenden turned to his librarian with a face of utter wonder.

"What does it mean, Gorman?" he said.

"I'd like to think there's been some jiggery-pokery and the books were switched—but that's impossible, Mr. Herenden."

"Yes; mine has been in the safe-room ever since I have had it. It *is* my book, isn't it, Gorman?"

"No doubt about it, sir. Here's your bookplate, that I put in myself. And here's that old inkspot on the back cover. It's faint, but we decided it was ink, didn't we?"

"Oh, yes, I remember. We decided that anything used to remove it would make a worse stain."

"Yes, sir. And Mr. Osborne says this whole title-page is new. It doesn't look so to me. But you must remember, sir, that when you—er—bought the book, you were given no guaranty of its genuineness—"

"That is quite true." Herenden smiled now. "All the same, I shall not rest until I am certain about the matter. I want to have another expert pass on it. Osborne may be all right, but there's no one in the world with the knowledge of old books that Kent has."

"Kent?"

"Yes. The English statesman. He's in this country now on diplomatic affairs, but if anything would interest him, this matter will. I'll set about getting him."

Herenden did set about it, and secured Godfrey Kent's promise to visit him and stay overnight. Herenden was so elated that he invited Sheldon to come and hear the final decision from the great man.

Sheldon came, and Herenden sent his car to meet Kent at train after train. He telephoned to New York and found that Godfrey Kent had left his hotel about five o'clock, intending to visit him. But the last train passed, and the Herenden chauffeur brought back an empty car.

"Some official business turned up, I suppose." Leigh Herenden hid his disappointment as Sheldon smiled and told him good night.

The next morning a visitor arrived early. Herenden hurried into his clothes and went down to meet him.

"I'm Pierson," the stranger announced, "of the New York Police. Do you know Godfrey Kent? He was found dead in the woods along the Palisades. Brutally murdered. He had your address in his pocket."

"What a terrible thing! It seems incredible." Herenden told how Kent had intended to visit him. "Gorman," he called, "Mr. Kent has been murdered."

"On account of the book?" Gorman said impulsively.

"What book?" the detective asked quickly. "The notes with your address seemed to refer to some play by Shakespeare."

"A poem." Herenden nodded, and told the story of his *Venus* with the doubtful title-page.

"May I see it?" Pierson compared the book with Kent's typewritten notes which were headed *Re V. and A.* "This says the true book must have two flyleaves in front, and two in back. I find only one in the back of your copy, Mr. Herenden."

"I fear my book is not a real first after all."

"When you got that book, Mr. Herenden," Gorman said, firmly, "it had two flyleaves in the back. Somebody must have torn one out!"

"Easy now, Mr. Gorman," Pierson said, in his common-sense way. "Someone has done more than damage a flyleaf. Now, if you will give me the name of Mr. Kent's New York hotel, it will help the Homicide Bureau. Confidentially, we think the murderer was a hired thug."

He left Herenden shuddering.

"I hope," Gorman said grimly, "that they get the fellow."

When Pierson came back to the Herenden house, he was greeted like a long-lost brother.

"Any luck?" Herenden asked, after the detective had been made comfortable in the library.

"The answer is yes. First of all, we have the hired gunman who murdered Mr. Kent. We haven't found out yet who is back of the crime, but we will. I have a pretty definite notion myself."

"What did you learn about the book?" Herenden could hold off no longer.

"I went to the Public Library and to several other libraries, and I can face the examiners as to Shakespeare's earliest printed work. I hate to hold out, Mr. Herenden, but I have suspicion of a crime against you. Let me get my bearings." Pierson rose. "This is your library. There is your safe-room. Here is your office. Now we make our real start. Which desk is whose? I must look into them all. Much may be learned from a desk."

Gorman became their usher, and Pierson worked methodically. He went through the desks quickly, yet seemed to see all their contents. He smiled at the stenographer's, which held a complete beautifying outfit and an old copy of *The Adventures of Sherlock Holmes*. Then he passed on to Rand's desk.

"Meticulous chap here, and a good bookkeeper. Not a blot nor erasure in his work. And his handwriting tells his character. See, not a flourish or unnecessary stroke. You trust him completely?"

"I'd trust Rand and Gorman with my life, liberty, and pursuit of happiness, and I'd come out on top."

"All right. Now, Mr. Herenden, I want to go over to see Mr. Sheldon."

As he left, Muriel Jewell, the stenographer, came into the library.

"Mr. Herenden," she began, "I didn't mean any harm, I only meant—"

"Miss Jewell, if you have a confession to make, and it sounds like that, please tell us frankly what it is all about."

"I didn't think it was wrong—"

Just then Sherry Biggs came in. He was a privileged visitor, and he helped himself to a chair and a cigarette.

But Muriel had lost courage for the confession she wanted to make. "Oh," she said, "Mr. Herenden, please let him stay long enough to tell me something. It's this, Mr. Biggs," she went on, as Herenden nodded permission. "You were talking about our slang phrases being in Shakespeare. Did he really write, 'I'll tell the world'?"

"*Measure for Measure*, Two, four, one fifty-four."

"And did he really make up 'Not so hot'?"

"Sure thing: *King Lear*, Five, three, sixty-seven."

"And—"

"That's enough. You can find all these things in a Shakespeare Concordance. Hello, here comes the policeman. Want me to go away, Mr. Herenden? Why don't you have some arras in this room—they're so nice to hide behind."

"Arras are not plural, Sherry. Arras is the name of a place in France, famous for its tapestries."

"Must I go, Mr. Herenden?"

"Sorry. Run along now, Sherry."

Young Biggs went off, and Muriel was sent out of the office as they heard Pierson returning. She spoke to him in the hall.

"Tell me that again!" he said.

She told him, and he grinned.

"We've got 'em!" he cried. "Sure you can remember?"

"Oh, sure. Five, nineteen, thirty-three, forty-seven."

"Marvelous, Holmes, marvelous! How do you do it?"

"Just add fourteen each time. See?"

"Faintly. Whoever would have believed you could do a thing like that?"

"Do you think Mr. Herenden will be mad at me?"

"Mad! He'll give you a medal!"

Two red spots burned in Muriel's cheeks as Pierson insisted that she set forth with him on the great quest of the *Venus*. The entire library staff was drafted for a short and pleasant march over to the Sheldon house. Pierson led off, escorting Miss Jewell; they were followed by Herenden and Herbert Rand; Gorman brought up the rear.

When they reached the house, Pierson rang the bell. The door opened, and he saw to it that all the others were inside the house before he went in himself. Sheldon greeted them in some surprise.

Without preamble, Pierson said, "Mr. Sheldon, I am here to charge you with taking a book that belongs to Mr. Herenden, and claiming it as your own; also, with putting in its place a book of similar character, but of far less value."

"That is a strange charge to make, Mr. Pierson, and I deny it!"

"Will you produce the copy of *Venus and Adonis* which is now on your shelf?"

Sheldon brought the volume.

"I will first," Pierson said, "show you that this copy is changed and amended to make it look like the other, and then I will tell you what happened to the books. This," he picked up the one that Sheldon had given him, "is a real 1593 edition of *Venus and Adonis*. Except for this, there is only one copy known, and that is in the Bodleian Library at Oxford. But all present know the details of this first edition. You know that the second or 1594 edition is exactly like this except for the date on the title-page. As you see these two books now, they both appear to be dated 1593. But while this one is a true 1593, the other is a 1594, which has been supplied with a new title-page, dated 1593. This title-page, in order that it should be of the right paper, was made of one of the flyleaves, taken from the back of the book. This in itself gives away the fake, for often the flyleaves of old books were of a trifle thicker paper than the rest of the book, as is the case in this instance. The volume was taken apart, the new title-page put in place and the old one discarded, the book rebound—in its own binding, of course, and that part was done so neatly that it is almost unnoticeable. I accuse Mr. Sheldon of doing this work, or having it done, for the purpose of exchanging his own made-over book for the honest-to-goodness 1593 of Mr. Herenden's. The switch was made on Sunday afternoon, before Mr. Herenden's party."

"You have heard a tissue of lies," Sheldon began, but it is not wise to call a detective a liar. Also, though Sheldon did not know it, two other men had entered the room, behind him. They were the Assistant District Attorney and another police official.

"You still insist that this 1593 copy is your book, Mr. Sheldon?"

"I certainly do!"

"There are some peculiar designating marks on the pages here and there. Suppose you tell me what and where they are?"

"That's a trap, and I do not intend to fall into it. I put no marks in my most valuable books."

"No? Well, Miss Jewell put marks in Mr. Herenden's copy, before you appropriated it for your own. They are tiny marks, which, if they are still present, prove positively that this is Mr. Herenden's book. What pages did you mark, Miss Jewell?"

"I can tell you the pages, but the marks are so small I doubt if you can see them. I used a very sharp penknife to scratch the tails off certain commas on certain pages. This turned them into periods, you see."

"Why did you do this?"

"Only that there might be a positive identification if anything happened to Mr. Herenden's book. The defects of those comma-tails are scarcely noticeable."

"Can you tell me on what pages you made these erasures?"

"Oh, yes—five, nineteen, thirty-three, forty-seven."

"I can't look them up as fast as that. How do you remember them?"

"I added fourteen each time."

"I see. Now, I am looking on page five, but I can't find a tailless comma."

"Haven't you a lens? A document lens? Here is one."

She handed over the lens, and the tailless commas showed up.

Pierson then drew attention to the bookplates. "You rather slipped up here, too, Mr. Sheldon. Mr. Gorman is too particular to use glue on a bookplate. He uses paste."

"That is a special gum I use on my own bookplates. I know nothing of what Mr. Herenden has on his."

"Well, then, note this. With this document lens I can see clearly the gum at the edges of the bookplate in both volumes. Moreover, this glass shows me that you used a blotter to press down the bookplate. This made the gum ooze out a bit, and it caught a little purple fuzz from the blotter."

"What's all this nonsense?" Rand suddenly looked angry. "Who used blotters to mount a bookplate? I never heard of such a thing!"

"You hear of it now," Pierson told him. "Take this glass. Look at the gum and the specks of purple blotter on the edges of these two bookplates."

"He knows all about it," Sheldon said, suddenly. "He put in those bookplates, both of them. He was over here helping me one day, and he put in a lot of bookplates for me. I hate to do it myself. And I assume he may put in bookplates for Mr. Herenden."

"Do you know, Rand," said Pierson, "I believe you can't do better than to spill the whole business."

Rand looked frightened. "How can you ever pay me or pay for your book, Mr. Sheldon?" he almost groaned. "The second, you know."

"Squeal on me, will you, you young thief! Then I'll beat you to it. That is your book, Mr. Herenden—Rand thought it would be a fine thing to do what he calls a switch. He—"

"That will do, Sheldon." Herenden assumed charge. "Herbert, tell the whole story, briefly and truly."

"Yes, Mr. Herenden. Mr. Sheldon said he knew where he could get a second edition of *Venus and Adonis*—just like the first, except for the date. He said if I would fix that, he would pay me a thousand dollars to have a new title-page printed, using one of the flyleaves. And he made me make a sort of stain on the back cover, like the ink stain on your book. He got me in deeper and deeper. He said if I didn't obey him, he'd tell you and make it all seem my doing. And he made me switch the books on Sunday afternoon, before the guests came."

"Where did Mr. Sheldon get his second edition?" Herenden asked.

"I bought it." Sheldon was now trembling. "I intended to pay for it from the proceeds of the one which I took from you."

"And now you have spoiled that second edition, which you still owe for, and you have nothing to pay with."

"That's about the size of it."

"Hand over Mr. Herenden's property to him," Pierson said, sternly.

"Let him take it himself," Sheldon screamed, as Herenden did so. "You can't prove it's your property. You're afraid to tell where you got it."

One of the men at the back of the room interrupted him.

"Mr. Sheldon, it's for you to tell us what you had to do with the murder of Godfrey Kent."

Sheldon collapsed as he recognized the Assistant District Attorney, who took him in custody and kept Herbert Rand for further questioning.

Sherry Biggs was passing as the others left that stricken house. He took Muriel off for a drive, to teach her more Shakespearean slang. Herenden took the path home, with his true first *Venus*, flanked by faithful Gorman and Pierson.

"I want to tell you about my book," Leigh told the man who had helped them, "though it's really Gorman's story. What was your English cousin's name, Gorman?"

"Baines. He's my second cousin. One night there was an unusually heavy air raid over London, and many homes fell to the ground. The next day, when Baines was walking around the ruins, he saw a chap sitting on a bit of fallen timber, reading an old book. The boy offered to sell it to him."

"Baines knew nothing about old books, but he knew Gorman did. So he sent it to America, saying that if we liked such silly old things, to sell it and send him half of whatever it brought."

"How did he get the book over here?" Pierson was deeply interested.

"Baines wrapped it up in newspaper and gave it to a lad who was coming over—a refugee. He sent word to Gorman what ship the boy was on. Gorman met the boy, took the book, and brought it to me. Here it is. Now, let me hear your opinion as to the ethics of all this. We don't know in whose ruined library the book was found, and we've no way of finding that out. So, what can I do but keep it?"

"Until the war is over and we can trace the real owner, it is your book, Mr. Herenden. The precious little volume is also a refugee, and a refugee is ever a sacred trust."

THE BOOK THAT SQUEALED

Cornell Woolrich

Perhaps it is not surprising that Cornell (George Hopley) Woolrich (1903-1968) wrote some of the darkest, most despairing, most heartbreaking noir fiction in the history of American crime literature. The lives he portrayed as sad and hopeless was the life he lived, though without the murders.

Born in New York City, he grew up in South America and New York, and was educated at Columbia University, to which he left his literary estate. A sad and lonely man, he was so friendless and isolated that he desperately dedicated books to his typewriter and to his hotel room. Woolrich was almost certainly a closeted homosexual (his marriage was terminated almost immediately) and an alcoholic, so anti-social and reclusive that he refused to leave his hotel room when his leg became infected, ultimately resulting in its amputation.

In Woolrich's prolific fiction output of twenty-four novels and more than two hundred short stories and novellas, it is a rare character indeed who is not merely doomed but already knows it. Doomed, yes—not necessarily to death, but to a life of grinding hopelessness. No writer who ever lived could write noir fiction so convincingly, so viciously, or so poignantly because, you see, it was essentially autobiographical. Not the stories, not the murders, but the world view that shrouded almost all the helpless souls who had the misfortune to find themselves in his stories.

Few of his characters, whether good or evil, have much hope for happiness—or even justice. No twentieth century author equaled Woolrich's ability to create suspense, and Hollywood producers recognized it early on. Few writers have had as many films based on their work as Woolrich, beginning with *Convicted* (1938), based on "Face Work," which starred a very young Rita Hayworth.

"The Book That Squealed" is more a traditional detective story, with an amateur sleuth librarian, and even a trace of romance and humor. It is not really a noir story, though it was written by Cornell Woolrich so it inevitably has its dark aspects. It was originally published in the August 1939 issue of *Detective Story*; it was first collected in *Angels of Darkness* (New York, Mysterious Press, 1978).

The Book That Squealed

Cornell Woolrich

THE OUTSIDE world never intruded into the sanctum where Prudence Roberts worked. Nothing violent or exciting ever happened there, or was ever likely to. Voices were never raised above a whisper, or at the most a discreet murmur. The most untoward thing that could possibly occur would be that some gentleman browser became so engrossed he forgot to remove his hat and had to be tactfully reminded. Once, it is true, a car backfired violently somewhere outside in the street and the whole staff gave a nervous start, including Prudence, who dropped her date stamp all the way out in the aisle in front of her desk; but that had never happened again after that one time.

Things that the papers printed, holdups, gang warfare, kidnappings, murders, remained just things that the papers printed. They never came past these portals behind which she worked.

Just books came in and went out again. Harmless, silent books.

Until, one bright June day—

The Book showed up around noon, shortly before Prudence Roberts was due to go off duty for lunch. She was on the Returned Books desk. She turned up her nose with unqualified inner disapproval at first sight of the volume. Her taste was severely classical; she had nothing against light reading in itself, but to her, light reading meant Dumas, Scott, Dickens. She could tell this thing before her was trash by the title alone, and the author's pen name: *Manuela Gets Her Man*, by Orchid Ollivant.

Furthermore it had a lurid orange dust cover that showed just what kind of claptrap might be expected within. She was surprised a city library had added such worthless tripe to its stock; it belonged more in a candy-store lending library than here. She supposed there had been a great many requests for it among a certain class of readers; that was why.

Date stamp poised in hand she glanced up, expecting to see one of these modern young hussies, all paint and boldness, or else a faded middle-aged blonde of the type that lounged around all day in a wrapper, reading such stuff and eating marshmallows. To her surprise the woman before her was drab, looked hardworking and anything but frivolous. She didn't seem to go with the book at all.

Prudence Roberts didn't say anything, looked down again, took the book's reference card out of the filing drawer just below her desk, compared them.

"You're two days overdue with this," she said; "it's a one-week book. That'll be four cents."

The woman fumbled timidly in an old-fashioned handbag, placed a nickel on the desk.

"My daughter's been reading it to me at nights," she explained, "but she goes to night school and some nights she couldn't; that's what delayed me. Oh, it was grand." She sighed. "It brings back all your dreams of romance."

"Humph," said Prudence Roberts, still disapproving as much as ever. She returned a penny change to the borrower, stamped both cards. That should have ended the trivial little transaction.

But the woman had lingered there by the desk, as though trying to summon up courage to ask something. "Please," she faltered timidly when Prudence had glanced up a second time, "I was wondering, could you tell me what happens on page 42? You know, that time when the rich man lures her on his yasht?"

"Yacht," Prudence corrected her firmly. "Didn't you read the book yourself?"

"Yes, my daughter read it to me, but Pages 41 and 42 are missing, and we were wondering, we'd give anything to know, if Ronald got there in time to save her from that awful—"

Prudence had pricked up her official ears at that. "Just a minute," she interrupted, and retrieved the book from where she had just discarded it. She thumbed through it rapidly. At first glance it seemed in perfect condition; it was hard to tell anything was the matter with it. If the borrower hadn't given her the exact page number—but Pages 41 and 42 were missing, as she had said. A telltale scalloping of torn paper ran down the seam between Pages 40 and 43. The leaf had been plucked out bodily, torn out like a sheet in a notebook, not just become loosened and fallen out. Moreover, the condition of the book's spine showed that this could not have happened from wear and tear; it was still too new and firm. It was a case of out-and-out vandalism. Inexcusable destruction of the city's property.

"This book's been damaged," said Prudence ominously. "It's only been in use six weeks, it's still a new book, and this page was deliberately ripped out along its entire length. I'll have to ask you for your reader's card back. Wait here, please."

She took the book over to Miss Everett, the head librarian, and showed it to her. The latter was Prudence twenty years from now, if nothing happened in between to snap her out of it. She sailed back toward the culprit, steel-rimmed spectacles glittering balefully.

The woman was standing there cringing, her face as white as though she expected to be executed on the spot. She had the humble person's typical fear of anyone in authority. "Please, lady, I didn't do it," she whined.

"You should have reported it before taking it out," said the inexorable Miss Everett. "I'm sorry, but as the last borrower, we'll have to hold you responsible. Do you realize you could go to jail for this?"

The woman quailed. "It was that way when I took it home," she pleaded; "I didn't do it."

Prudence relented a little. "She did call my attention to it herself, Miss Everett," she remarked. "I wouldn't have noticed it otherwise."

"You know the rules as well as I do, Miss Roberts," said her flinty superior. She turned to the terrified drudge. "You will lose your card and all library privileges until you have paid the fine assessed against you for damaging this book." She turned and went careening off again.

The poor woman still hovered there, pathetically anxious. "Please don't make me do without my reading," she pleaded. "That's the only pleasure I got. I work hard all day. How much is it? Maybe I can pay a little something each week."

"Are you sure you didn't do it?" Pruence asked her searchingly. The lack of esteem in which she held this book was now beginning to incline her in the woman's favor. Of course, it was the principle of the thing, it didn't matter how trashy the book in question was. On the other hand, how could the woman have been expected to notice that a page was gone, in time to report it, *before* she had begun to read it?

"I swear I didn't," the woman protested. "I love books, I wouldn't want to hurt one of them."

"Tell you what I'll do," said Prudence, lowering her voice and looking around to make sure she wasn't overheard. "I'll pay the fine for you out of my own pocket, so you can go ahead using the library meanwhile. I think it's likely this was done by one of the former borrowers, ahead of you. If such proves not to be the case, however, then you'll simply have to repay me a little at a time."

The poor woman actually tried to take hold of her hand to kiss it. Prudence hastily withdrew it, marked the fine paid, and returned the card to her.

"And I suggest you try to read something a little more worthwhile in future," she couldn't help adding.

She didn't discover the additional damage until she had gone upstairs with the book, when she was relieved for lunch. It was no use sending it back to be rebound or repaired; with one entire page gone like that, there was nothing could be done with it; the book was worthless. Well, it had been that to begin with, she thought tartly.

She happened to flutter the leaves scornfully and light filtered through one of the pages, in dashes of varying length, like a sort of Morse code. She looked more closely, and it was the forty-third page, the one immediately after the missing leaf. It bore innumerable horizontal slashes scattered all over it from top to bottom, as though some moron had underlined the words on it, but with some sharp-edged instrument rather than the point of a pencil. They were so fine they were almost invisible when the leaf was lying flat against the others, white on white; it was only when it was up against the light that they stood revealed. The leaf was almost threadbare with them. The one after it had some too, but not nearly so distinct; they hadn't pierced the thickness of the paper, were just scratches on it.

She had heard of books being defaced with pencil, with ink, with crayon, something visible at least—but with an improvised stylus that just left slits? On the other hand, what was there in this junky novel important enough to be emphasized—if that was why it had been done?

She began to read the page, to try to get some connected meaning out of the words that had been underscored. It was just a lot of senseless drivel about the heroine who was being entertained on the villain's yacht. It couldn't have been done for emphasis, then, of that Prudence was positive.

But she had the type of mind that, once something aroused its curiosity, couldn't rest again until the matter had been solved. If she couldn't remember a certain name, for instance, the agonizing feeling of having it on the tip of her tongue but being unable to bring it out would keep her from getting any sleep until the name had come back to her.

This now took hold of her in the same way. Failing to get anything out of the entire text, she began to see if she could get something out of the gashed words in themselves. Maybe that was where the explanation lay. She took a pencil and paper and began to transcribe them one by one, in the same order in which they came in the book. She got:

hardly anyone going invited merrily

Before she could go any farther than that, the lunch period was over, it was time to report down to her desk again.

She decided she was going to take the book home with her that night and keep working on it until she got something out of it. This was simply a matter of self-defense; she wouldn't be getting any sleep until she did. She put it away in her locker, returned downstairs to duty, and put the money with which she was paying Mrs. Trasker's fine into the till. That was the woman's name, Mrs. Trasker.

The afternoon passed as uneventfully as a hundred others had before it, but her mind kept returning to the enigma at intervals. "There's a reason for everything in this world," she insisted to herself, "and I want to know the reason for this: why were certain words in this utterly unmemorable novel underscored by slashes as though they were Holy Writ or something? And I'm going to find out if it takes me all the rest of this summer!"

She smuggled the book out with her when she left for home, trying to keep it hidden so the other members of the staff wouldn't notice. Not that she would have been refused permission if she had asked for it, but she would have had to give her reasons for wanting to take it, and she was afraid they would all laugh at her or think she was becoming touched in the head if she told them. After all, she excused herself, if she could find out the meaning of what had been done, that might help the library to discover who the guilty party really was and recover damages, and she could get back her own money that she had put in for poor Mrs. Trasker.

Prudence hurried up her meal as much as possible, and returned to her room. She took a soft pencil and lightly went over the slits in the paper, to make them stand out more clearly. It would be easy enough to erase the pencil marks later. But almost as soon as she had finished and could get a comprehensive view of the whole page at a glance, she saw there was something wrong. The underscorings weren't flush with some of the words. Sometimes they only took in half a word, carried across the intervening space, and then took in half of the next. One of them even fell where there was absolutely no word at all over it, in the blank space between two paragraphs.

That gave her the answer; she saw in a flash what her mistake was. She'd been wasting her time on the wrong page. It was the leaf before, the missing Page 41, that had held the real meaning of the slashed words. The sharp instrument used on it had simply carried through to the leaf under it, and even, very lightly, to the third one following. No wonder the scorings overlapped and she hadn't been able to make sense out of them! Their real sense, if any, lay on the page that had been removed.

Well, she'd wasted enough time on it. It probably wasn't anything anyway. She tossed the book contemptuously aside, made up her mind that was the end of it. A moment or so later her eyes strayed irresistibly, longingly over to it again. "I know how I *could* find out for sure," she tempted herself.

Suddenly she was putting on her things again to go out. To go out and do something she had never done before: buy a trashy, frothy novel. Her courage almost failed her outside the bookstore window, where she finally located a copy, along with bridge sets, ash trays, statuettes of Dopey, and other gew-gaws. If it had only had a less . . . er . . . compromising title. She set her chin, took a deep breath, and plunged in.

"I want a copy of *Manuela Gets Her Man*, please," she said, flushing a little.

The clerk was one of these brazen blondes painted up like an Iroquois. She took in Prudence's shell-rimmed glasses, knot of hair, drab clothing. She smirked a little, as if to say "So you're finally getting wise to yourself?" Prudence Roberts gave her two dollars, almost ran out of the store with her purchase, cheeks flaming with embarrassment.

She opened it the minute she got in and avidly scanned Page 41. There wasn't anything on it, in itself, of more consequence than there had been on any of the other pages, but that wasn't stopping her this time. This thing had now cost her over three dollars of her hard-earned money, and she was going to get something out of it.

She committed an act of vandalism for the first time in her life, even though the book was her own property and not the city's. She ripped Pages 41 and 42 neatly out of the binding, just as the leaf had been torn from the other book. Then she inserted it in the first book, the original one. Not *over* Page 43, where it belonged, but under it. She found a piece of carbon paper, cut it down to size, and slipped that between the two. Then she fastened the three sheets together with paperclips, carefully seeing to it that the borders of the two printed pages didn't vary by a hair's breadth. Then she took her pencil and once more traced the gashes on Page 43, but this time bore down heavily on them. When she had finished, she withdrew the loose Page 41 from under the carbon and she had a haphazard array of underlined words sprinkled over the page. The original ones from the missing page. Her eye traveled over them excitedly. Then her face dropped again. They didn't make sense any more than before. She opened the lower half of the window, balanced the book in her hand, resisted an impulse to toss it out then and there. She gave herself a fight talk instead. "I'm a librarian. I have more brains than whoever did this to this book, I don't care who they are! I can get out whatever meaning they put into it, if I just keep cool and keep at it." She closed the window, sat down once more.

She studied the carbon-scored page intently, and presently a belated flash of enlightenment followed. The very arrangement of the dashes showed her what her mistake had been this time. They were too symmetrical, each one had its complement one line directly under it. In other words they were really double, not single lines. Their vertical alignment didn't vary in the slightest. She should have noticed that right away. She saw what it was now. The words hadn't been merely underlined, they had been cut out of the page bodily by four gashes around each required one, two vertical, two horizontal, forming an oblong that contained the wanted word. What she had mistaken for dashes had been the top and bottom lines of these "boxes." The faint side lines she had overlooked entirely.

She canceled out every alternate line, beginning with the top one, and that should have given her the real kernel of the message. But again she was confronted with a meaningless jumble, scant as the residue of words was. She held her head distractedly as she took it in:

cure
wait
poor
honey to
grand
her
health
your
fifty
instructions

"The text around them is what's distracting me," she decided after a futile five or ten minutes of poring over them. "Subconsciously I keep trying to read them in the order in which they appear on the page. Since they were taken bodily out of it, that arrangement was almost certainly not meant to be observed. It is, after all, the same principle as a jig-saw puzzle. I have the pieces now, all that remains is to put each one in the right place."

She took a small pair of nail scissors and carefully clipped out each boxed word, just as the unknown predecessor had whose footsteps she was trying to unearth. That done, she discarded the book entirely, in order to be hampered by it no longer. Then she took a blank piece of paper, placed all the little paper cutouts on it, careful that they remained right side up, and milled them about with her finger, to be able to start from scratch.

"I'll begin with the word 'fifty' as the easiest entering wedge," she breathed absorbedly. "It is a numerical adjective, and therefore simply must modify one of those three nouns, according to all the rules of grammar." She separated it from the rest, set to work. Fifty health—no, the noun is in the singular. Fifty honey—no, again singular. Fifty instructions—yes, but it was an awkward combination, something about it didn't ring true, she wasn't quite satisfied with it. Fifty grand? That was it! It was grammatically incorrect, it wasn't a noun at all, but in slang it was used as one. She had often heard it herself, used by people who were slovenly in their speech. She set the two words apart, satisfied they belonged together.

"Now a noun, in any kind of a sentence at all," she murmured to herself, "has to be followed by a verb." There were only two to choose from. She tried them both. Fifty grand wait. Fifty grand cure. Elliptical, both. But that form of the verb had to take a preposition, and there was one there at hand: "to." She tried it that way. Fifty grand to wait. Fifty grand to cure. She chose the latter, and the personal pronoun fell into place almost automatically after it. Fifty grand to cure her. That was almost certainly it.

She had five out of the eleven words now. She had a verb, two adjectives, and three nouns left: wait, your, poor, honey, health instructions. But that personal pronoun already in place was a stumbling block, kept baffling her. It seemed to refer to some preceding proper name, it demanded one to make sense, and she didn't have any in her six remaining words. And then suddenly she saw that she did have. Honey. It was to be read as a term of endearment, not a substance made by bees.

The remaining words paired off almost as if magnetically drawn toward one another. Your honey, poor health, wait instructions. She shifted them about the basic nucleus she already had, trying them out before and after it, until, with a little minor rearranging, she had them satisfactorily in place.

your honey poor health fifty grand to cure her wait instructions

There it was at last. It couldn't be any more lucid than that. She had no mucilage at hand to paste the little paper oblongs down flat and hold them fast in the position she had so laboriously achieved. Instead she took a number of pins and skewered them to the blank sheets of paper. Then she sat back looking at them.

It was a ransom note. Even she, unworldly as she was, could tell that at a glance. Printed words cut bodily out of a book, to avoid the use of handwriting or typewriting that might be traced later. Then the telltale leaf with the gaps had been torn out and destroyed. But in their hurry they had overlooked one little thing, the slits had carried through to the next page. Or else they had thought it didn't matter, no one would be able to reconstruct the thing once the original page was gone. Well, she had.

There were still numerous questions left unanswered. To whom had the note been addressed? By whom? Whose "honey" was it? And why, with a heinous crime like kidnaping for ransom involved, had they taken the trouble to return the book at all? Why not just destroy it entirely and be done with it? The answer to that could very well be that the actual borrower—one of those names on the book's reference card—was someone who knew them, but wasn't aware what they were doing, what the book had been used for, hadn't been present when the message was concocted; had all unwittingly returned the book.

There was of course a question as to whether the message was genuine or simply some adolescent's practical joke, yet the trouble taken to evade the use of handwriting argued that it was anything but a joke. And the most important question of all was: should she go to the police about it? She answered that then and there, with a slow but determined *yes!*

It was well after eleven by now, and the thought of venturing out on the streets alone at such an hour, especially to and from a place like a police station, filled her timid soul with misgivings. She could ring up from here, but then they'd send someone around to question her most likely, and that would be even worse. What would the landlady and the rest of the roomers think of her, receiving a gentleman caller at such an hour, even if he was from the police? It looked so . . . er . . . rowdy.

She steeled herself to go to them in person, and it required a good deal of steeling and even a cup of hot tea, but finally she set out, book and transcribed message under her arm, also a large umbrella with which to defend herself if she were insulted on the way.

She was ashamed to ask anyone where the nearest precinct house was, but luckily she saw a pair of policemen walking along as if they were going off duty, and by following them at a discreet distance, she finally saw them turn and go into a building that had a pair of green lights outside the entrance. She walked past it four times, twice in each direction, before she finally got up nerve enough to go in.

There was a uniformed man sitting at a desk near the entrance and she edged over and stood waiting for him to look up at her. He didn't, he was busy with some kind of report, so after standing there a minute or two, she cleared her throat timidly.

"Well, lady?" he said in a stentorian voice that made her jump and draw back.

"Could I speak to a . . . a detective, please?" she faltered.

"Any particular one?"

"A good one."

He said to a cop standing over by the door: "Go in and tell Murph there's a young lady out here wants to see him."

A square-shouldered, husky young man came out a minute later, hopefully straightening the knot of his tie and looking around as if he expected to see a Fifth Avenue model at the very least. His gaze fell on Prudence, skipped over her, came up against the blank walls beyond her, and then had to return to her again.

"You the one?" he asked a little disappointedly.

"Could I talk to you privately?" she said. "I believe I have made a discovery of the greatest importance."

"Why . . . uh . . . sure," he said, without too much enthusiasm. "Right this way." But as he turned to follow her inside, he slurred something out of the corner of his mouth at the smirking desk sergeant that sounded suspiciously like "I'll fix you for this, kibitzer. It couldn't have been Dolan instead, could it?"

He snapped on a cone light in a small office toward the back, motioned Prudence to a chair, leaned against the edge of the desk.

She was slightly flustered; she had never been in a police station before. "Has . . . er . . . anyone been kidnaped lately, that is to say within the past six weeks?" she blurted out.

He folded his arms, flipped his hands up and down against his own sides, "Why?" he asked noncommitally.

"Well, one of our books came back damaged today, and I think I've deciphered a kidnap message from its pages."

Put baldly like that, it did sound sort of far-fetched, she had to admit that herself. Still, he should have at least given her time to explain more fully, not acted like a jackass just because she was prim-looking and wore thick-lensed glasses.

His face reddened and his mouth started to quiver treacherously. He put one hand up over it to hide it from her, but he couldn't keep his shoulders from shaking. Finally he had to turn away altogether and stand in front of the water cooler a minute. Something that sounded like a strangled cough came from him.

"You're laughing at me!" she snapped accusingly. "I come here to help you, and that's the thanks I get!"

He turned around again with a carefully straightened face. "No, ma'am," he lied cheerfully right to her face, "I'm not laughing at you. I . . . we . . . appreciate your co-operation. You leave this here and we . . . we'll check on it."

But Prudence Roberts was nobody's fool. Besides, he had ruffled her plumage now, and once that was done, it took a great deal to smooth it down again. She had a highly developed sense of her own dignity. "You haven't the slightest idea of doing anything of the kind!" she let him know. "I can tell that just by looking at you! I must say I'm very surprised that a member of the police department of this city—"

She was so steamed up and exasperated at his facetious attitude, that she removed her glasses, in order to be able to give him a piece of her mind more clearly. A little thing like that shouldn't have made the slightest difference—after all this was police business, not a beauty contest—but to her surprise it seemed to.

He looked at her, blinked, looked at her again, suddenly began to show a great deal more interest in what she had come here to tell him. "What'd you say your name was again, miss?" he asked, and absently made that gesture to the knot of his tie again.

She hadn't said what it was in the first place. Why, this man was just a common—a common masher; he was a disgrace to the shield he wore. "I am Miss Roberts of the Hillcrest Branch of the Public Library," she said stiffly. "What has that to do with this?"

"Well . . . er . . . we have to know the source of our information," he told her lamely. He picked up the book, thumbed through it, then he scanned the message she had deciphered. "Yeah"—Murphy nodded slowly—"that does read like a ransom note."

Mollified, she explained rapidly the process by which she had built up from the gashes on the succeeding leaf of the book.

"Just a minute, Miss Roberts," he said, when she had finished. "I'll take this in and show it to the lieutenant."

But when he came back, she could tell by his attitude that his superior didn't take any more stock in it than he had himself. "I tried to explain to him the process by which you extracted it out of the book, but . . . er . . . in his opinion it's just a coincidence, I mean the gashes may not have any meaning at all. For instance, someone may have been just cutting something out on top of the book, cookies or pie crust and—"

She snorted in outrage. "Cookies or pie crust! I got a coherent message. If you men can't see it there in front of your eyes—"

"But here's the thing, Miss Roberts," he tried to soothe her. "We haven't any case on deck right now that this could possibly fit into. No one's been reported missing. And we'd know, wouldn't we? I've heard of kidnap cases without ransom notes, but I never heard of a ransom note without a kidnap case to go with it."

"As a police officer doesn't it occur to you that in some instances a kidnaped persons' relatives would purposely refrain from notifying the authorities to avoid jeopardizing their loved ones? That may have happened in this case."

"I mentioned that to the lieutenant myself, but he claims it can't be done. There are cases where we purposely hold off at the request of the family until after the victim's been returned, but it's never because we haven't been informed what's going on. You see, a certain length of time always elapses between the snatch itself and the first contact between the kidnapers and the family, and no matter how short that is, the family has almost always reported the person missing in the meantime, before they know what's up themselves. I can check with Missing Persons if you want, but if it's anything more than just a straight disappearance, they always turn it over to us right away, anyway."

But Prudence didn't intend urging or begging them to look into it as a personal favor to her. She considered she'd done more than her duty. If they discredited it, they discredited it. *She* didn't, and she made up her mind to pursue the investigation, single-handed and without their help if necessary, until she had settled it one way or the other. "Very well," she said coldly, "I'll leave the transcribed message and the extra copy of the book here with you. I'm sorry I bothered you. Good evening." She stalked out, still having forgotten to replace her glasses.

Her indignation carried her as far as the station-house steps, and then her courage began to falter. It was past midnight by now, and the streets looked so lonely; suppose—suppose she met a drunk? While she was standing there trying to get up her nerve, this same Murphy came out behind her, evidently on his way home himself. She had put her glasses on again by now.

"You look a lot different without them," he remarked lamely, stopping a step below her and hanging around.

"Indeed," she said forbiddingly.

"I'm going off duty now. Could I . . . uh . . . see you to where you live?"

She would have preferred not to have to accept the offer, but those shadows down the street looked awfully deep and the light posts awfully far apart. "I *am* a little nervous about being out alone so late," she admitted, starting out beside him. "Once I met a drunk and he said, 'H'lo, babe.' I had to drink a cup of hot tea when I got home, I was so upset."

"Did you have your glasses on?" he asked cryptically.

"No. Come to think of it, that was the time I'd left them to be repaired."

He just nodded knowingly, as though that explained everything.

When they got to her door, he said: "Well, I'll do some more digging through the files on that thing, just to make sure. If I turn up anything . . . uh . . . suppose I drop around tomorrow night and let you know. And if I don't, I'll drop around and let you know that too. Just so you'll know what's what."

"That's very considerate of you."

"Gee, you're refined," he said wistfully. "You talk such good English."

He seemed not averse to lingering on here talking to her, but someone might have looked out of one of the windows and it would appear so unrefined to be seen dallying there at that hour, so she turned and hurried inside.

When she got to her room, she looked at herself in the mirror. Then she took her glasses off and tried it that way. "How peculiar," she murmured. "How very unaccountable!"

The following day at the library she got out the reference card on *Manuela Gets Her Man* and studied it carefully. It had been out six times in the six weeks it had been in stock. The record went like this:

Doyle, Helen (address)	Apr. 15-Apr. 22
Caine, Rose	Apr. 22-Apr. 29

Dermuth, Alvin	Apr. 29-May 6
Turner, Florence	May 6-May 18
Baumgarten, Lucille	May 18-May 25
Trasker, Sophie	May 25-June 3

Being a new book, it had had a quick turnover, had been taken out again each time the same day it had been brought back. Twice it had been kept out overtime, the first time nearly a whole week beyond the return limit. There might be something in that. All the borrowers but one, so far, were women; that was another noticeable fact. It was, after all, a woman's book. Her library experience had taught her that what is called a "man's book" will often be read by women, but a "woman's book" is absolutely never, and there are few exceptions to this rule, read by men. That might mean something, that lone male borrower. She must have seen him at the time, but so many faces passed her desk daily she couldn't remember what he was like any more, if she had. However, she decided not to jump to hasty conclusions, but investigate the list one by one in reverse order. She'd show that ignorant, skirt-chasing Murphy person that where there's smoke there's fire, if you only take the trouble to look for it!

At about eight thirty, just as she was about to start out on her quest—she could only pursue it in the evenings, of course, after library hours—the doorbell rang and she found him standing there. He looked disappointed when he saw that she had her glasses on. He came in rather shyly and clumsily, tripping over the threshold and careening several steps down the hall.

"Were you able to find out anything?" she asked eagerly.

"Nope, I checked again, I went all the way back six months,

and I also got in touch with Missing Persons. Nothing doing, I'm afraid it isn't a genuine message, Miss Roberts; just a fluke, like the lieutenant says."

"I'm sorry, but I don't agree with you. I've copied a list of the borrowers and I intend to investigate each one of them in turn. That message was not intended to be readily deciphered, or for that matter deciphered at all; therefore it is not a practical joke or some adolescent's prank. Yet it has a terrible coherence; therefore it is not a fluke or a haphazard scarring of the page, your lieutenant to the contrary. What remains? It is a genuine ransom note, sent in deadly earnest, and I should think you and your sup-superiors would be the first to—"

"Miss Roberts," he said soulfully, "you're too refined to . . . to dabble in crime like this. Somehow it don't seem right for you to be talking shop, about kidnapings and—" He eased his collar. "I . . . uh . . . it's my night off and I was wondering if you'd like to go to the movies."

"So that's why you took the trouble of coming around!" she said indignantly. "I'm afraid your interest is entirely too personal and not nearly official enough!"

"Gee, even when you talk fast," he said admiringly, "you pronounce every word clear, like in a po-em."

"Well, you don't. It's poem, not po-em. I intend going ahead with this until I can find out just what the meaning of that message is, and who sent it! And I *don't* go to movies with people the second time I've met them!"

He didn't seem at all fazed. "Could I drop around sometime and find out how you're getting along?" he wanted to know, as he edged through the door backward.

"That will be entirely superfluous," she said icily. "If I uncover anything suspicious, I shall of course report it promptly. It is not my job, after all, but . . . ahem . . . other people's."

"Movies! The idea!" She frowned after she had closed the door on him. Then she dropped her eyes and pondered a minute. "It would have been sort of frisky, at that." She smiled.

She took the book along with her as an excuse for calling, and set out, very determined on the surface, as timid as usual underneath. However, she found it easier to get started because the first name on the list, the meek Mrs. Trasker, held no terror even for her. She was almost sure she was innocent, because it was she herself who had called the library's attention to the missing page in the first place, and a guilty person would hardly do that. Still there was always a possibility it was someone else in her family or household, and she meant to be thorough about this if nothing else.

Mrs. Trasker's address was a small old-fashioned apartment building of the pre-War variety. It was not expensive by any means, but still it did seem beyond the means of a person who had been unable to pay even a two-dollar fine, and for a moment Prudence thought she scented suspicion in this. But as soon as she entered the lobby and asked for Mrs. Trasker, the mystery was explained.

"You'll have to go to the basement for her," the elevator boy told her, "she's the janitress."

A young girl of seventeen admitted her at the basement entrance and led her down a bare brick passage past rows of empty trash cans to the living quarters in the back.

Mrs. Trasker was sitting propped up in bed, and again showed a little alarm at sight of the librarian, a person in authority. An open book on a chair beside her showed that her daughter had been reading aloud to her when they were interrupted.

"Don't be afraid," Prudence reassured them. "I just want to ask a few questions."

"Sure, anything, missis," said the janitress, clasping and unclasping her hands placatingly.

"Just the two of you live here? No father or brothers?"

"Just mom and me, nobody else," the girl answered.

"Now tell me, are you sure you didn't take the book out with you anywhere, to some friend's house, or lend it to someone else?"

"No, no, it stayed right here!" They both said it together and vehemently.

"Well, then, did anyone call on you down here, while it was in the rooms?"

The mother answered this. "No, no one. When the tenants want me for anything, they ring down for me from upstairs. And when I'm working around the house, I keep our place locked just like anyone does their apartment. So I know no one was near the book while we had it."

"I feel pretty sure of that myself," Prudence said, as she got up to go. She patted Mrs. Trasker's toil-worn hand reassuringly. "Just forget about my coming here like this. Your fine is paid and there's nothing to worry about. See you at the library."

The next name on the reference card was Lucille Baumgarten. Prudence was emboldened to stop in there because she noticed the address, though fairly nearby, in the same branch-library district, was in a higher-class neighborhood. Besides, she was beginning to forget her timidity in the newly awakened interest her quest was arousing in her. It occurred to her for the first time that detectives must lead fairly interesting lives.

A glance at the imposing, almost palatial apartment building Borrower Baumgarten lived in told her this place could probably be crossed off her list of suspects as well. Though she had heard vaguely somewhere or other that gangsters and criminals sometimes lived in luxurious surroundings, these were more than that. These spelled solid, substantial wealth and respectability that couldn't be faked. She had to state her name and business to a uniformed houseman in the lobby before she was even allowed to go up.

"Just tell Miss Baumgarten the librarian from her branch library would like to talk to her a minute."

A maid opened the upstairs door, but before she could open her mouth, a girl slightly younger than Mrs. Trasker's daughter had come skidding down the parquet hall, swept her aside, and displaced her. She was about fifteen at the most and really had no business borrowing from the adult department yet. Prudence vaguely recalled seeing her face before, although then it had been liberally rouged and lipsticked, whereas now it was properly without cosmetics.

She put a finger to her lips and whispered conspiratorially, "Sh! Don't tell my—"

Before she could get any further, there was a firm tread behind her and she was displaced in turn by a stout matronly lady wearing more diamonds than Prudence had ever seen before outside of a jewelry-store window.

"I've just come to check up on this book which was returned to us in a damaged condition," Prudence explained. "Our record shows that Miss Lucille Baumgarten had it out between—"

"Lucille?" gasped the bediamoned lady. "Lucille? There's no Lucille—" She broke off short and glanced at her daughter, who vainly tried to duck out between the two of them and shrink away unnoticed. "Oh, so that's it!" she said, suddenly enlightened. "So Leah isn't good enough for you any more!"

Prudence addressed her offspring, since it was obvious that the mother was in the dark about more things than just the book. "Miss Baumgarten, I'd like you to tell me whether there was a page missing when you brought the book home with you." And then she added craftily: "It was borrowed again afterward by several other subscribers, but I haven't got around to them yet." If the girl was guilty, she would use this as an out and claim the page had still been in, implying it had been taken out afterward by someone else. Prudence knew it hadn't, of course.

But Lucille-Leah admitted unhesitatingly: "Yes, there was a page or two missing, but it didn't spoil the fun much, because I could tell what happened after I read on a little bit." Nothing seemed to hold any terrors for her, compared to the parental wrath brewing in the heaving bosom that wedged her in inextricably.

"Did you lend it to anyone else, or take it out of the house with you at any time, while you were in possesion of it?"

The girl rolled her eyes meaningly. "I should say not! I kept it hidden in the bottom drawer of my bureau the whole time; and now you had to come around here and give me away!"

"Thank you," said Prudence, and turned to go. This place was definitely off her list too, as she had felt it would be even before the interview. People who lived in such surroundings didn't send kidnap notes or associate with people who did.

The door had closed, but Mrs. Baumgarten's shrill, punitive tones sounded all too clearly through it while Prudence stood there waiting for the elevator to take her down. "I'll *give* you Lucille! Wait'll your father hears about this! I'll give you such a *frass*, you won't know whether you're Lucille or Gwendolyn!" punctuated by a loud, popping slap on youthful epidermis.

The next name on the list was Florence Turner. It was already well after ten by now, and for a moment Prudence was tempted to go home, and put off the next interview until the following night. She discarded the temptation resolutely. "Don't be such a 'fraid-cat," she lectured herself. "Nothing's happened to you so far, and nothing's likely to happen hereafter either." And then too, without knowing it, she was already prejudiced; in the back of her mind all along there lurked the suspicion that the lone male borrower, Dermuth, was the one to watch out for. He was next but one on the list, in reverse order. As long as she was out, she would interview Florence Turner, who was probably harmless, and then tackle Dermuth good and early tomorrow night—and see to it that a policeman waited for her outside his door so she'd be sure of getting out again unharmed.

The address listed for Library Member Turner was not at first sight exactly prepossessing, when she located it. It was a rooming house, or rather that newer variation of one called a "residence club," which has sprung up in the larger cities within the past few years, in which the rooms are grouped into detached little apartments. Possibly it was the sight of the chop-suey place that occupied the ground floor that gave it its unsavory aspect in her eyes; she had peculiar notions about some things.

Nevertheless, now that she had come this far, she wasn't going to let a chop-suey restaurant frighten her away without completing her mission. She tightened the book under her arm, took a good deep breath to ward off possible hatchet men and opium smokers, and marched into the building, whose entrance adjoined that of the restaurant.

She rang the manager's bell and a blowsy-looking, middle-aged woman came out and met her at the foot of the stairs. "Yes?" she said gruffly.

"Have you a Florence Turner living here?"

"No. We did have, but she left."

"Have you any idea where I could reach her?"

"She left very suddenly, didn't say where she was going."

"About how long ago did she leave, could you tell me?"

"Let's see now." The woman did some complicated mental calculation. "Two weeks ago Monday, I think it was. That would bring it to the 17th. Yes, that's it, May 17th."

Here was a small mystery already. The book hadn't been returned until the 18th. The woman's memory might be at fault, of course. "If you say she left in a hurry, how is it she found time to return this book to us?"

The woman glanced at it. "Oh, no, I was the one returned that for her," she explained. "My cleaning maid found it in her room the next morning after she was gone, along with a lot of other stuff she left behind her. I saw it was a liberry book, so I sent Beulah over with it, so's it wouldn't roll up a big fine for her. I'm economical that way. How'd you happen to get hold of it?" she asked in surprise.

"I work at the library," Prudence explained. "I wanted to see her about this book. One of the pages was torn out." She knew enough not to confide any more than that about what her real object was.

"Gee, aren't you people fussy," marveled the manager.

"Well, you see, it's taken out of my salary," prevaricated Prudence, trying to strike a note she felt the other might understand.

"Oh, that's different. No wonder you're anxious to locate

her. Well, all I know is she didn't expect to go when she did; she even paid for her room ahead, I been holding it for her ever since, till the time's up. I'm conshenshus that way."

"That's strange," Prudence mused aloud. "I wonder what could have—"

"I think someone got took sick in her family," confided the manager. "Some friends or relatives, I don't know who they was, called for her in a car late at night and off she went in a rush. I just wanted to be sure it wasn't no one who hadn't paid up yet, so I opened my door and looked out."

Prudence picked up her ears. That fatal curiosity of hers was driving her on like a spur. She had suddenly forgotten all about being leery of the nefarious chop-suey den on the premises. She was starting to tingle all over, and tried not to show it. Had she unearthed something at last, or wasn't it anything at all? "You say she left some belongings behind? Do you think she'll be back for them?"

"No, she won't be back herself, I don't believe. But she did ask me to keep them for her; she said she'd send someone around to get them as soon as she was able."

Prudence suddenly decided she'd give almost anything to be able to get a look at the things this Turner girl had left behind her; why, she wasn't quite sure herself. They might help her to form an idea of what their owner was like. She couldn't ask openly; the woman might suspect her of trying to steal something. "When will her room be available?" she asked offhandedly. "I'm thinking of moving, and as long as I'm here, I was wondering—"

"Come on up and I'll show it to you right now," offered the manager with alacrity. She evidently considered librarians superior to the average run of tenants she got.

Prudence followed her up the stairs, incredulous at her own effrontery. This didn't seem a bit like her; she wondered what had come over her.

"Murphy should see me now!" she gloated.

The manager unlocked a door on the second floor.

"It's real nice in the daytime," she said. "And I can turn it over to you day after tomorrow."

"Is the closet good and deep?" asked Prudence, noting its locked doors.

"I'll show you." The woman took out a key, opened it unsuspectingly for her approval.

"My," said the subtle Prudence, "she left lots of things behind!"

"And some of them are real good too," agreed the landlady. "I don't know how they do it, on just a hat check girl's tips. And she even gave that up six months ago."

"Hm-m-m," said Prudence absently, deftly edging a silver slipper she noted standing on the floor up against one of another pair, with the tip of her own foot. She looked down covertly; with their heels in true with one another, there was an inch difference in the toes. Two different sizes! She absently fingered the lining of one of the frocks hanging up, noted its size tag. A 34. "Such exquisite things," she murmured, to cover up what she was doing. Three hangers over there was another frock. Size 28.

"Did she have anyone else living here with her?" she asked.

The manager locked the closet, pocketed the key once more. "No. These two men friends or relatives of hers used to visit with her a good deal, but they never made a sound and they never came one at a time, so I didn't raise any objections. Now, I have another room, nearly as nice, just down the hall I could show you."

"I wish there were some way in which you could notify me when someone does call for her things," said Prudence, who was getting better as she went along. "I'm terribly anxious to get in touch with her. You see, it's not only the fine, it might even cost me my job."

"Sure I know how it is," said the manager sympathetically. "Well, I could ask whoever she sends to leave word where you can reach her."

"No, don't do that!" said Prudence hastily. "I'm afraid they . . . er . . . I'd prefer if you didn't mention I was here asking about her at all."

"Anything you say," said the manager amenably. "If you'll leave your number with me, I could give you a ring and let you know whenever the person shows up."

"I'm afraid I wouldn't get over here in time; they might be gone by the time I got here."

The manager tapped her teeth helpfully. "Why don't you take one of my rooms then? That way you'd be right on the spot when they do show up."

"Yes, but suppose they come in the daytime? I'd be at the library, and I can't leave my job."

"I don't think they'll come in the daytime. Most of her friends and the people she went with were up and around at night, more than in the daytime."

The idea appealed to Prudence, although only a short while before she would have been aghast at the thought of moving into such a place. She made up her mind quickly without giving herself time to stop and get cold feet. It might be a wild-goose chase, but she'd never yet heard of a woman who wore two different sizes in dresses like this Florence Turner seemed to. "All right, I will," she decided, "if you'll promise two things.

To let me know without fail the minute someone comes to get her things, and not to say a word to them about my coming here and asking about her."

"Why not?" said the manager accommodatingly. "Anything to earn an honest dollar?"

But when the door of her new abode closed on her, a good deal of her new-found courage evaporated. She sat down limply on the edge of the bed and stared in bewilderment at her reflection in the cheap dresser mirror. "I must be crazy to do a thing like this!" she gasped. "What's come over me anyway?" She didn't even have her teapot with her to brew a cup of the fortifying liquid. There was nothing the matter with the room in itself, but that sinister Oriental den downstairs had a lurid red tube sign just under her window and its glare winked malevolently in at her. She imagined felt-slippered hirelings of some Fu-Manchu creeping up the stairs to snatch her bodily from her bed. It was nearly daylight before she could close her eyes. But so far as the room across the hall was concerned, as might have been expected, no one showed up.

Next day at the library, between book returns, Prudence took out the reference card on Manuela and placed a neat red check next to Mrs. Trasker's name and Lucille Baumgarten's, to mark the progress of her investigation so far. But she didn't need this; it was easy enough to remember whom she had been to see and whom she hadn't, but she had the precise type of mind that liked everything neatly docketed and in order. Next to Florence Turner's name she placed a small red question mark.

She was strongly tempted to call up Murphy on her way home that evening, and tell him she already felt she was on the trail of something. But for one thing, nothing definite enough had developed yet. If he'd laughed at her about the original message itself, imagine how he'd roar if she told him the sum total of her suspicions was based on the fact that a certain party had two different-sized dresses in her clothes closet. And secondly, even in her new state of emancipation, it still seemed awfully forward to call a man up, even a detective. She would track down this Florence Turner first, and then she'd call Murphy up if her findings warranted it. "And if he says I'm good, and asks me to go to the movies with him," she threatened, "I'll . . . I'll make him ask two or three times before I do!"

She met the manager on her way in. "Did anyone come yet?" she asked in an undertone.

"No. I'll keep my promise. I'll let you know; don't worry."

A lot of the strangeness had already worn off her new surroundings, even after sleeping there just one night, and it occurred to her that maybe she had been in a rut, should have changed living quarters more often in the past. She went to bed shortly after ten, and even the Chinese restaurant sign had no power to keep her awake tonight; she fell asleep almost at once, tired from the night before.

About an hour or so later, she had no way of telling how long afterward it was, a surreptitious tapping outside her door woke her. "Yes?" she called out forgetfully, in a loud voice.

The manager stuck her tousled head in.

"Shh!" she warned. "Somebody's come for her things. You asked me to tell you, and I've been coughing out there in the hall, trying to attract your attention. He just went down with the first armful; he'll be up again in a minute. You'd better hurry if you want to catch him before he goes; he's working fast."

"Don't say anything to him," Prudence whispered back. "See if you can delay him a minute or two, give me time to get downstairs."

"Are you sure it's just a liberry book this is all about?" the manager asked searchingly. "Here he comes up again." She pulled her head back and swiftly closed the door.

Prudence had never dressed so fast in her life before. Even so, she managed to find time to dart a glance down at the street from her window. There was a black sedan drawn up in front of the house. "How am I ever going to—" she thought in dismay. She didn't let that hold her up any. She made sure she had shoes on and a coat over her and let the rest go hang. There was no time to phone Murphy, even if she had wanted to, but the thought didn't occur to her.

She eased her room door open, flitted out into the hall and down the stairs, glimpsing the open door of Florence Turner's room as she sneaked by. She couldn't see the man, whoever he was, but she could hear the landlady saying, "Wait a minute, until I make sure you haven't left anything behind."

Prudence slipped out of the street door downstairs, looked hopelessly up and down the street. He had evidently come alone in the car; there was no one else in it. He had piled the clothing on the back seat. For a moment she even thought of smuggling herself in and hiding under it, but that was too harebrained to be seriously considered. Then, just as she heard his tread start down the inside stairs behind her, the much-maligned chop-suey joint came to her aid. A cab drove up to it, stopped directly behind the first machine, and a young couple got out.

Prudence darted over, climbed in almost before they were out of the way.

"Where to, lady?" asked the driver.

She found it hard to come out with it, it sounded so unrespectable and fly-by-nightish. Detectives, she supposed, didn't think twice about giving an order like that, but with her it was different. "Er . . . would you mind just waiting a minute until that car in front of us leaves?" she said constrainedly. "Then take me wherever it goes."

He shot her a glance in his rear-sight mirror, but didn't say anything. He was probably used to getting stranger orders than that.

A man came out of the same doorway she had just left herself. She couldn't get a very good look at his face, but he had a batch of clothing slung over his arm. He dumped the apparel in the back of the sedan, got in himself, slammed the door closed, and started off. A moment later the cab was in motion as well.

"Moving out on ya, huh?" said the driver knowingly. "I don't blame ya for follying him."

"That will do," she said primly. This night life got you into more embarrassing situations! "Do you think you can manage it so he won't notice you coming after him?" she asked after a block or two.

"Leave it to me, lady," he promised, waving his hand at her. "I know this game backwards."

Presently they had turned into one of the circumferential express highways leading out of the city. "Now it's gonna be pie!" he exulted. "He won't be able to tell us from anyone else on here. Everyone going the same direction and no turning off."

The stream of traffic was fairly heavy for that hour of the night; homeward-bound suburbanites for the most part. But then, as the city limits were passed and branch road after branch road drained it off, it thinned to a mere trickle. The lead car finally turned off itself, and onto a practically deserted secondary highway.

"Now it's gonna be ticklish," the cabman admitted. "I'm gonna have to hang back as far as I can from him, or he'll tumble to us."

He let the other car pull away until it was merely a red dot in the distance. "You sure must be carryin' some torch," he said presently with a baffled shake of his head, "to come all the way out this far after him."

"Please confine yourself to your driving," was the haughty reproof.

The distant red pin point had suddenly snuffed out. "He must've turned off up ahead some place," said the driver, alarmed. "I better step it up!"

When they had reached the approximate place, minutes later, an even less-traveled bypass than the one they were on was revealed, not only lightless but even unsurfaced. It obviously didn't lead anywhere that the general public would have wanted to go, or it would have been better maintained. They braked forthwith.

"What a lonely-looking road." Prudence shuddered involuntarily.

"Y'wanna chuck it and turn back?" he suggested, as though he would have been only too willing to himself.

She probably would have if she'd been alone, but she hated to admit defeat in his presence. He'd probably laugh at her all the way back. "No, now that I've come this far, I'm not going back until I find out exactly where he went. Don't stand here like this: you won't be able to catch up with him again!"

The driver gave his cap a defiant hitch. "The time has come to tell you I've got you clocked at seven bucks and eighty-five cents, and I didn't notice any pockybook in your hand when you got in. Where's it coming from?" He tapped his fingers sardonically on the rim of his wheel.

Prudence froze. Her handbag was exactly twenty or thirty miles away, back in her room at the residence club. She didn't have to answer; the driver was an old experienced hand at this sort of thing; he could read the signs.

"I thought so," he said, almost resignedly. He got down, opened the door. "Outside," he said. "If you was a man, I'd take it out of your jaw. Or if there was a cop anywhere within five miles, I'd have you run in. Take off that coat." He looked it over, slung it over his arm. "It'll have to do. Now if you want it back, you know what to do; just look me up with seven-eighty-five in your mitt. And for being so smart, you're gonna walk all the way back from here on your two little puppies."

"Don't leave me all alone, in the dark, in this God-forsaken place! I don't even know where I am!" she wailed after him.

"I'll tell you where you are," he called back remorselessly. "You're on your own!" The cab's tail-light went streaking obliviously back the way they had just come.

She held the side of her head and looked helplessly all around her. Real detectives didn't run into these predicaments, she felt sure. It only happened to her! "Oh, why didn't I just mind my own business back at the library!" she lamented.

It was too cool out here in the wilds to stand still without a coat on, even though it was June. She might stand waiting here all night and no other machine would come along. The only thing to do was to keep walking until she came to a house, and then ask to use the telephone. There must be a house somewhere around here.

She started in along the bypath the first car had taken,

gloomy and forbidding as it was, because it seemed more likely there was a house some place farther along it, than out on this other one. They hadn't passed a single dwelling the whole time the cab was on the road, and she didn't want to walk still farther out along it; no telling where it led to. The man she'd been following must have had *some* destination. Even if she struck the very house he had gone to, there wouldn't really be much harm to it, because he didn't know who she was, he'd never seen her before. Neither had this Florence Turner, if she was there with him. She could just say she'd lost her way or something. Anyone would have looked good to her just then, out here alone in the dark the way she was.

If she'd been skittish of shadows on the city streets, there was reason enough for her to have St. Vitus' dance here; it was nothing *but* shadows. Once she came in sight of a little clearing, with a scarecrow fluttering at the far side of it, and nearly had heart failure for a minute. Another time an owl went "Who-o-o" up in a tree over her, and she ran about twenty yards before she could pull herself together and stop again. "Oh, if I ever get back to the nice safe library after tonight, I'll never—" she sobbed nervously.

The only reason she kept going on now was because she was afraid to turn back any more. Maybe that hadn't been a scarecrow after all—

The place was so set back from the road, so half hidden amidst the shrubbery, that she had almost passed it by before she even saw it there. She happened to glance to her right as she came to a break in the trees, and there was the unmistakable shadowy outline of a decrepit house. Not a chink of light showed from it, at least from where she was. Wheel ruts unmistakably led in toward it over the grass and weeds, but she wasn't much of a hand at this sort of lore, couldn't tell if they'd been made recently or long ago. The whole place had an appearance of not being lived in.

It took nearly as much courage to turn aside and start over toward it as it would have to continue on the road. It was anything but what she'd been hoping for, and she knew already it was useless to expect to find a telephone in such a ramshackle wreck.

The closer she got to it, the less inviting it became. True, it was two or three in the morning by now, and even if anyone had been living in it, they probably would have been fast asleep by this time, but it didn't seem possible such a forlorn, neglected-looking place could be inhabited. Going up onto that ink-black porch and knocking for admittance took more nerve than she could muster. Heaven knows what she was liable to bring out on her; bats or rats or maybe some horrible hobos.

She decided she'd walk all around the outside of it just once, and if it didn't look any better from the sides and rear than it did from the front, she'd go back to the road and take her own chances on that some more. The side was no better than the front when she picked her way cautiously along it. Twigs snapped under her feet and little stones shifted, and made her heart miss a beat each time. But when she got around to the back, she saw two things at once that showed her she had been mistaken, there was someone in there after all. One was the car, the same car that had driven away in front of the residence club, standing at a little distance behind the house, under some kind of warped toolshed or something. The other was a slit of light showing around three sides of a ground-floor window. It wasn't a brightly lighted pane by any means; the whole window still showed black under some kind of sacking or heavy covering; there was just this telltale yellow seam outlining three sides of it if you looked closely enough.

Before she could decide what to do about it, if anything, her gaze traveled a little higher up the side of the house and she saw something else that brought her heart up into her throat. She choked back an inadvertent scream just in time. It was a face. A round white face staring down at her from one of the upper windows, dimly visible behind the dusty pane.

Prudence Roberts started to back away apprehensively a step at a time, staring up at it spellbound as she did so, and ready at any moment to turn and run for her life, away from whomever or whatever that was up there. But before she could carry out the impulse, she saw something else that changed her mind, rooted her to the spot. Two wavering white hands had appeared, just under the ghost-like face. They were making signs to her, desperate, pleading signs. They beckoned her nearer, then they clasped together imploringly, as if trying to say, "Don't go away, don't leave me."

Prudence drew a little nearer again. The hands were warning her to silence now, one pointing downward toward the floor below, the other holding a cautioning finger to their owner's mouth.

It was a young girl; Prudence could make out that much, but most of the pantomime was lost through the blurred dust-caked pane. She gestured back to her with upcurved fingers, meaning, "Open the window so I can hear you."

It took the girl a long time. The window was either fastened in some way or warped from lack of use, or else it stuck just because she was trying to do it without making any noise. The sash finally jarred up a short distance, with an alarming creaking and grating in spite of her best efforts. Or at least it seemed so in the preternatural stillness that reigned about the place. They both held their breaths for a wary moment, as if by mutual understanding.

Then as Prudence moved in still closer under the window, a faint sibilance came down to her from the narrow opening.

"Please take me away from here. Oh, please help me to get away from here."

"What's the matter?" Prudence whispered back.

Both alike were afraid to use too much breath even to whisper, it was so quiet outside the house. It was hard for them to make themselves understood. She missed most of the other's answer, all but:

"They won't let me go. I think they're going to kill me. They haven't given me anything to eat in two whole days now."

Prudence inhaled fearfully. "Can you climb out through there and let yourself drop from the sill? I'll get a seat cover from that car and put it under you."

"I'm chained to the bed up here. I've pulled it over little by little to the window. Oh, please hurry and bring someone back with you; that's the only way—"

Prudence nodded in agreement, made hasty encouraging signs as she started to draw away. "I'll run all the way back to where the two roads meet, and stop the first car that comes al—"

Suddenly she froze, and at the same instant seemed to light up yellowly from head to foot, like a sort of living torch. A great fan of light spread out from the doorway before her, and in the middle of it a wavering shadow began to lengthen toward her along the ground.

"Come in, sweetheart, and stay a while," a man's voice said slurringly. He sauntered out toward her with lithe, springy determination. Behind him in the doorway were another man and a woman.

"Naw, don't be bashful," he went on, moving around in back of her and prodding her toward the house with his gun. "You ain't going on nowheres else from here. You've reached your final destination."

A well-dressed, middle-aged man was sitting beside the lieutenant's desk, forearm supporting his head, shading his eyes with outstretched fingers, when Murphy and every other man jack available came piling in, responding to the urgent summons.

The lieutenant had three desk phones going at once, and still found time to say, "Close that door, I don't want a word of this to get out," to the last man in. He hung up—*click*, *click*, *clack*—speared a shaking finger at the operatives forming into line before him.

"This is Mr. Martin Rapf, men," he said tensely. "I won't ask him to repeat what he's just said to me; he's not in any condition to talk right now. His young daughter, Virginia, left home on the night of May 17th and she hasn't been seen since. He and Mrs. Rapf received an anonymous telephone call that same night, before they'd even had time to become alarmed at her absence, informing them not to expect her back and warning them above all not to report her missing to us. Late the next day Mr. Rapf received a ransom note demanding fifty thousand dollars. This is it here."

Everyone in the room fastened their eyes on it as he spun it around on his desk to face them. At first sight it seemed to be a telegram. It was an actual telegraph blank form, taken from some office pad, with strips of paper containing printed words pasted on it.

"It wasn't filed, of course; it was slipped under the front door in an unaddressed envelope," the lieutenant went on. "The instructions didn't come for two more days, by telephone again. Mr. Rapf had raised the amount and was waiting for them. They were rather amateurish, to say the least. And amateurs are more to be dreaded than professionals at this sort of thing, as you men well know. He was to bring the money along in a cigar box, he was to go all the way out to a certain seldom-used suburban crossroads, and wait there. Then when a closed car with its rear windows down drove slowly by and sounded its horn three times, two short ones and a long one, he was to pitch the cigar box in the back of it through the open window and go home.

"In about a quarter of an hour a closed car with its windows down came along fairly slowly. Mr. Rapf was too concerned about his daughter's safety even to risk memorizing the numerals on its license plates, which were plainly exposed to view. A truck going crosswise to it threatened to block it at the intersection, and it gave three blasts of its horn, two short ones and a long one. Mr. Rapf threw the cigar box in through its rear window and watched it pick up speed and drive away. He was too excited and overwrought to start back immediately, and in less than five minutes, while he was still there, a second car came along with its windows down and its license plates removed. It gave three blasts of its horn, without there being any obstruction ahead. He ran out toward it to try and explain, but only succeeded in frightening it off. It put on speed and got away from him. I don't know whether it was actually a ghastly coincidence, or whether an unspeakable trick was perpetrated on him, to get twice the amount they had originally asked. Probably just a hideous coincidence, though, because he would have been just as willing to give them one hundred thousand from the beginning.

"At any rate, what it succeeded in doing was to throw a hitch into the negotiations, make them nervous and skittish. They contacted him again several days later, refused to believe his explanation, and breathed dire threats against the girl. He pleaded with them for another chance, and asked for more time to raise a second fifty thousand. He's been holding it in readiness for some time now, and they're apparently suffering from a bad case of fright; they cancel each set of new instructions as fast as they issue them to him. Wait'll I get through, please, will you, Murphy? It's five days since Mr. Rapf last heard from them, and he is convinced that—" He didn't finish it, out of consideration for the agonized man sitting there. Then he went ahead briskly: "Now here's Miss Rapf's description, and here's what our first move is going to be. Twenty years old, weight so-and-so, height so-and-so, light-brown hair—"

"She was wearing a pale-pink party dress and dancing shoes when she left the house," Rapf supplied forlornly.

"We don't pin any reliance on items of apparel in matters of this kind," the lieutenant explained to him in a kindly aside. "That's for amnesia cases or straight disappearances. They almost invariably discard the victim's clothes, to make accidental recognition harder. Some woman in the outfit will usually supply her with her own things."

"It's too late, lieutenant; it's too late," the man who sat facing him murmured grief-strickenly. "I know it; I'm sure of it."

"We have no proof that it is," the lieutenant replied reassuringly. "But if it is, Mr. Rapf, you have only yourself to blame for waiting this long to come to us. If you'd come to us sooner, you might have your daughter back by now—"

He broke off short. "What's the matter, Murphy?" he snapped. "What are you climbing halfway across the desk at me like that for?"

"Will you let me get a word in and tell you, lieutenant?" Murphy exclaimed with a fine show of exasperated insubordination. "I been trying to for the last five minutes! That librarian, that Miss Roberts that came in here the other night—It was this thing she stumbled over accidentally then already. It must have been! It's the same message."

The lieutenant's jaw dropped well below his collar button. "Ho-ly smoke!" he exhaled. "Say, she's a smart young woman all right!"

"Yeah, she's so smart we laughed her out of the place, book and all," Murphy said bitterly. "She practically hands it to us on a silver platter, and you and me, both, we think it's the funniest thing we ever heard of."

"Never mind that now! Go out and get hold of her! Bring her in here fast!"

"She's practically standing in front of you!" The door swung closed after Murphy.

Miss Everett, the hatchet-faced librarian, felt called upon to interfere at the commotion that started up less than five minutes later at the usually placid new-membership desk, which happened to be closest to the front door.

"Will you *kindly* keep your voice down, young man?" she said severely, sailing over. "This is a library, not a—"

"I haven't got time to keep my voice down! Where's Prudence Roberts? She's wanted at headquarters right away."

"She didn't come to work this morning. It's the first time

she's ever missed a day since she's been with the library. What is it she's wanted—" But there was just a rush of outgoing air where he'd been standing until then. Miss Everett looked startledly at the other librarian. "What was that he just said?"

"It sounded to me like 'Skip it, toots.'"

Miss Everett looked blankly over her shoulder to see if anyone else was standing there, but no one was.

In a matter of minutes Murphy had burst in on them again, looking a good deal more harried than the first time. "Something's happened to her. She hasn't been at her rooming house all night either, and that's the first time *that* happened too! Listen. There was a card went with that book she brought to us, showing who had it out and all that. Get it out quick; let me have it!"

He couldn't have remembered its name just then to save his life, and it might have taken them until closing time and after to wade through the library's filing system. But no matter how much of a battle-ax this Miss Everett both looked and was, one thing must be said in her favor: she had an uncanny memory when it came to damaged library property. "The reference card on *Manuela Gets Her Man*, by Ollivant," she snapped succinctly to her helpers. And in no time it was in his hands.

His face lighted. He brought his fist down on the counter with a bang that brought every nose in the place up out of its book, and for once Miss Everett forgot to remonstrate or even frown. "Thank God for her methodical mind!" he exulted. "Trasker, check Baumgarten, check; Turner, question mark. It's as good as though she left full directions behind her!"

"What was it he said *that* time?" puzzled Miss Everett, as the doors flapped hectically to and fro behind him.

"It sounded to me like 'Keep your fingers crossed.' Only, I'm not sure if it was 'fingers' or—"

"It's getting dark again," Virginia Rapf whimpered frightenedly, dragging herself along the floor toward her fellow captive. "Each time night comes, I think they're going to . . . *you* know! Maybe tonight they *will*."

Prudence Roberts was fully as frightened as the other girl, but simply because one of them had to keep the other's courage up, she wouldn't let herself show it. "No, they won't; they wouldn't dare!" she said with a confidence she was far from feeling.

She went ahead tinkering futilely with the small padlock and chain that secured her to the foot of the bed. It was the same type that is used to fasten bicycles to something in the owner's absence, only of course the chain had not been left in an open loop or she could simply have withdrawn her hand. It was fastened tight around her wrist by passing the clasp of the lock through two of the small links at once. It permitted her a radius of action of not more than three or four yards around the foot of the bed at most. Virginia Rapf was similarly attached to the opposite side.

"In books you read," Prudence remarked, "women prisoners always seem to be able to open anything from a strong box to a cell door with just a hairpin. I don't seem to have the knack, somehow. This is the last one I have left."

"If you couldn't do it before, while it was light, you'll never be able to do it in the dark."

"I guess you're right," Prudence sighed. "There it goes, out of shape like all the rest, anyway." She tossed it away with a little *plink*.

"Oh, if you'd only moved away from under that window a minute sooner, they wouldn't have seen you out there, you might have been able to—"

"No use crying over spilt milk," Prudence said briskly.

Sounds reached them from outside presently, after they'd been lying silent on the floor for a while.

"Listen," Virginia Rapf breathed. "There's someone moving around down there, under the window. You can hear the ground crunch every once in a while."

Something crashed violently, and they both gave a start.

"What was that, their car?" asked Virginia Rapf.

"No, it sounded like a tin can of some kind; something he threw away."

A voice called out of the back door: "Have you got enough?"

The answer seemed to come from around the side of the house. "No, gimme the other one too."

A few moments later a second tinny clash reached their tense ears. They waited, hearts pounding furiously under their ribs. A sense of impending danger assailed Prudence.

"What's that funny smell?" Virginia Rapf whispered fearfully. "Do you notice it? Like—"

Prudence supplied the word before she realized its portent. "Gasoline." The frightful implication hit the two of them at once. The other girl gave a sob of convulsive terror, cringed against her. Prudence threw her arms about her, tried to calm her. "Shh! Don't be frightened. No, they wouldn't do that, they couldn't be that inhuman." But her own terror was half stifling her.

One of their captors' voices sounded directly under them, with a terrible clarity. "All right, get in the car, Flo. You too, Duke, I'm about ready."

They heard the woman answer him, and there was unmistakable horror even in her tones. "Oh, not *that* way, Eddie. You're going to finish them first, aren't you?"

He laughed coarsely. "What's the difference? The smoke'll finish them in a minute or two; they won't suffer none. All right, soft-hearted, have it your own way. I'll go up and give 'em a clip on the head apiece, if it makes you feel any better." His tread started up the rickety stairs.

They were almost crazed with fear. Prudence fought to keep her presence of mind.

"Get under the bed, quick!" she panted hoarsely.

But the other girl gave a convulsive heave in her arms, then fell limp. She'd fainted dead away. The oncoming tread was halfway up the stairs now. He was taking his time, no hurry. Outside in the open she heard the woman's voice once more, in sharp remonstrance.

"Wait a minute, you dope; not yet! Wait'll Eddie gets out first!"

The man with her must have struck a match. "He can make it; let's see him run for it," he answered jeeringly. "I still owe him something for that hot-foot he gave me one time, remember?"

Prudence had let the other girl roll lifelessly out of her arms, and squirmed under the bed herself, not to try to save her own skin but to do the little that could be done to try to save both of them, futile as she knew it to be. She twisted like a caterpillar, clawed at her own foot, got her right shoe off. She'd never gone in for these stylish featherweight sandals with spindly heels, and she was glad of that now. It was a good strong substantial Oxford, nearly as heavy as a man's, with a club heel. She got a grasp on it by the toe, then twisted her body around so that her legs were toward the side the room door gave onto. She reared one at the knee, held it poised, backed up as far as the height of the bed would allow it to be.

The door opened and he came in, lightless. He didn't need a light for a simple little job like this—stunning two helpless girls chained to a bed. He started around toward the foot of it, evidently thinking they were crouched there hiding from him. Her left leg suddenly shot out between his two, like a spoke, tripping him neatly.

He went floundering forward on his face with a muffled curse. She had hoped he might hit his head, be dazed by the impact if only for a second or two. He wasn't; he must have broken the fall with his arm. She threshed her body madly around the other way again, to get her free arm in play with the shoe for a weapon. She began to rain blows on him with it, trying to get his head with the heel. That went wrong too. He'd fallen too far out along the floor, the chain wouldn't let her come out any farther after him. She couldn't reach any higher up than his muscular shoulders with the shoe, and its blows fell ineffectively there.

Raucous laughter was coming from somewhere outside, topped by warning screams. "Eddie, hurry up and get out, you fool! Duke's started it already!" They held no meaning for Prudence; she was too absorbed in this last despairing attempt to save herself and her fellow prisoner.

But he must have heard and understood them. The room was no longer as inky black as before. A strange wan light was beginning to peer up below the window, like a satanic moonrise. He jumped to his feet with a snarl, turned and fired down point-blank at Prudence as she tried to writhe hastily back under cover. The bullet hit the iron rim of the bedstead directly over her eyes and glanced inside. He was too yellow to linger and try again. Spurred by the screamed warnings and the increasing brightness, he bolted from the room and went crashing down the stairs three at a time.

A second shot went off just as he reached the back doorway, and she mistakenly thought he had fired at his fellow kidnaper in retaliation for the ghastly practical joke played on him. Then there was a whole volley of shots, more than just one gun could have fired. The car engine started up with an abortive flurry, then died down again where it was without moving. But her mind was too full of horror at the imminent doom that threatened to engulf both herself and Virginia Rapf, to realize the meaning of anything she dimly heard going on below. Anything but that sullen hungry crackle, like bundles of twigs snapping, that kept growing louder from minute to minute. They had been left hopelessly chained, to be cremated alive!

She screamed her lungs out, and at the same time knew that screaming wasn't going to save her or the other girl. She began to hammer futilely with her shoe at the chain holding her, so slender yet so strong, and knew that wasn't going to save her either.

Heavy steps pounded up the staircase again, and for a moment she thought he'd come back to finish the two of them after all, and was glad of it. Anything was better than being roasted alive. She wouldn't try to hide this time.

The figure that came tearing through the thickening smoke haze toward her was already bending down above her before she looked and saw that it was Murphy. She'd seen some beautiful pictures in art galleries in her time, but he was more beautiful to her eyes than a Rubens portrait.

"All right, chin up, keep cool," he said briefly, so she wouldn't lose her head and impede him.

"Get the key to these locks! The short dark one has them."

"He's dead and there's no time. Lean back. Stretch it out tight and lean out of the way!" He fired and the small chain snapped in two. "Jump! You can't get down the stairs any more." His second shot, freeing Virginia Rapf, punctuated the order.

Prudence flung up the window, climbed awkwardly across the sill, feet first. Then clung there terrified as an intolerable haze of heat rose up under her from below. She glimpsed two men running up under her with a blanket or lap robe from the car stretched out between them.

"I can't; it's . . . it's right under me!"

He gave her an unceremonious shove in the middle of the back and she went hurtling out into space with a screech. The two with the blanket got there just about the same time she did. Murphy hadn't waited to make sure; a broken leg was preferable to being incinerated. She hit the ground through the lap robe and all, but at least it broke the direct force of the fall.

They cleared it for the next arrival by rolling her out at one side, and by the time she had picked herself dazedly to her feet, Virginia Rapf was already lying in it, thrown there by him from above.

"Hurry it up, Murph!" she heard one of them shout frightenedly, and instinctively caught at the other girl, dragged her off it to clear the way for him. He crouched with both feet on the sill, came sailing down, and even before he'd hit the blanket, there was a dull roar behind him as the roof caved in, and a great gush of sparks went shooting straight up into the dark night sky.

They were still too close; they all had to draw hurriedly back away from the unbearable heat beginning to radiate from it. Murphy came last, as might have been expected, dragging a very dead kidnaper—the one called Eddie—along the ground after him by the collar of his coat. Prudence saw the other one, Duke, slumped inertly over the wheel of the car he had never had time to make his getaway in, either already dead or rapidly dying. A disheveled blond scarecrow that had been Florence Turner was apparently the only survivor of the trio. She kept whimpering placatingly, "I didn't want to do *that* to them! I didn't want to do *that* to them!" over and over, as though she still didn't realize they had been saved in time.

Virginia Rapf was coming out of her long faint. It was kinder, Prudence thought, that she had been spared those last few horrible moments; she had been through enough without that.

"Rush her downtown with you, fellow!" Murphy said. "Her dad's waiting for her; he doesn't know yet, I shot out here so fast the minute I located that taxi driver outside the residence club, who remembered driving Miss Roberts out to this vicinity, that I didn't even have time to notify headquarters, just picked up whoever I could on the way."

He came over to where Prudence was standing, staring at the fire with horrified fascination.

"How do you feel? Are you O.K.?" he murmured, brow furrowed with a proprietary anxiety.

"Strange as it may be," she admitted in surprise, "I seem to feel perfectly all right; can't find a thing the matter with me."

Back at the library the following day—and what a world away it seemed from the scenes of violence she had just lived through—the acidulous Miss Everett came up to her just before closing time with, of all things, a twinkle in her eyes. Either that or there was a flaw in her glasses.

"You don't have to stay to the very last minute . . . er . . .

toots," she confided. "Your boy friend's waiting for you outside; I just saw him through the window."

There he was holding up the front of the library when Prudence Roberts emerged a moment or two later.

"The lieutenant would like to see you to personally convey his thanks on behalf of the department," he said. "And afterward I . . . uh . . . know where there's a real high-brow pitcher showing, awful refined."

Prudence pondered the invitation. "No," she said finally. "Make it a nice snappy gangster movie and you're on. I've got so used to excitement in the last few days, I'd feel sort of lost without it."

THE STOLEN *ENDYMION*
Lassiter Wren & Randle McKay

The 1920s and 1930s saw a sudden craze in the mystery world—puzzle books in which the reader became the detective.

A little-know book titled, evocatively enough, *Murder* (1928), by Evelyn Johnson and Gretta Palmer, offered thirty-two unsolved crimes to readers, the solutions being found in a small pamphlet inserted into an envelope affixed to the back cover.

Elizabeth Cobb and Margaret Case Morgan wrote *Murder in Your Home* (1932), sub-titled "Society's Latest Plaything"—mysteries that could be solved by readers as a competitive game. They even managed to get the great sportswriter Grantland Rice to write the introduction.

In 1934, H.A. Ripley leaped onto the bandwagon with *How Good a Detective Are You?*, described on the dust jacket as "The New National Game: Minute Mysteries," in which sixty "Minute Mysteries" challenge readers, with the solutions at the back of the book.

But it was Lassiter Wren (pseudonym of John T. Colter) and Randle McKay (pseudonym of Richard Rowan) who launched the concept into a Golden Age phenomenon with *The Baffle Book* in 1928, for which they induced the bestselling mystery writer S.S. Van Dine to write an introduction, assuring its vast popularity. It was soon followed by *The Second Baffle Book* (1929) and, of course, *The Third Baffle Book* (1930).

The *Baffle* books each contained a mini-mystery that attempted to be absolutely fair play, with all clues needed to solved the mystery provided. A series of questions followed and the reader was given points for how many correct answers were given. The solutions were provided at the back of the book, with the added precaution of "no cheating allowed" by being printed upside down. Most of the stories had drawings or maps that served as clues.

The uncredited editor of the *Baffle* book series was F. Tennyson Jesse, the author of true crime books and fiction, notably *The Solange Stories* (1931), a *Queen's Quorum* title.

The Stolen **Endymion**

Lassiter Wren & Randle McKay

The thief in the Lanworthy "first-edition case," so called, displayed a mixture of ingenious cunning and simplicity. It presents an interesting problem in detection.

ON THE night or early morning of November 3-4, 1927, the library of Cedric Lanworthy, noted English collector, was robbed of a genuine first edition of Keats' *Endymion* and eighteen other books, less valuable, but rare and costly enough. Mr. Lanworthy was frantic. He offered a substantial reward for the recovery of the volumes and requested the police to make extraordinary efforts to catch the thief.

Detective Griswold, who was assigned to the case, discovered important clues. Examination of the house revealed that the thief apparently had gained entrance by clambering up a stout vine which led to the roof of the porch, and thus to the second-floor windows. One of these had been forced. The small safe in the library, just off Mr. Lanworthy's bedroom, had been broken open with powerful tools, and the entire contents of the safe had been removed. No fingerprints were found on the windows, sills, or on the door of the safe; but on the glass top of a writing table in the room were the conspicuous fingerprints of a right hand. They were conspicuous in the sense that a close examination of the glass revealed them distinctly to the searchers who were covering every object in that room. The fingerprints were unusually clear, as if the fingers had been pressed downward with some force, and the arrangement of the fingerprints was somewhat cramped. Detective Griswold explained this by the following theories: The intruder had started to climb up on the table, or he had slipped while passing and caught himself just in time when near the table. At any rate, the detective held, he had suddenly thrust out his right hand for some reason and had unwittingly printed his fingers on the glass top. He could explain no further.

Mr. Lanworthy had been absent from his house on the night of the theft. To set an example to his servants, he asked to have his own fingerprints taken and compared with those found on the table top. The servants likewise volunteered. It was clearly proved that none of them, or Mr. Lanworthy, could have made those prints found on the glass. Search at the rogue's gallery proved further that the fingerprints were unknown there.

Inspector Benson, who took charge of the case the next day, questioned Mr. Lanworthy minutely about his visitors for the

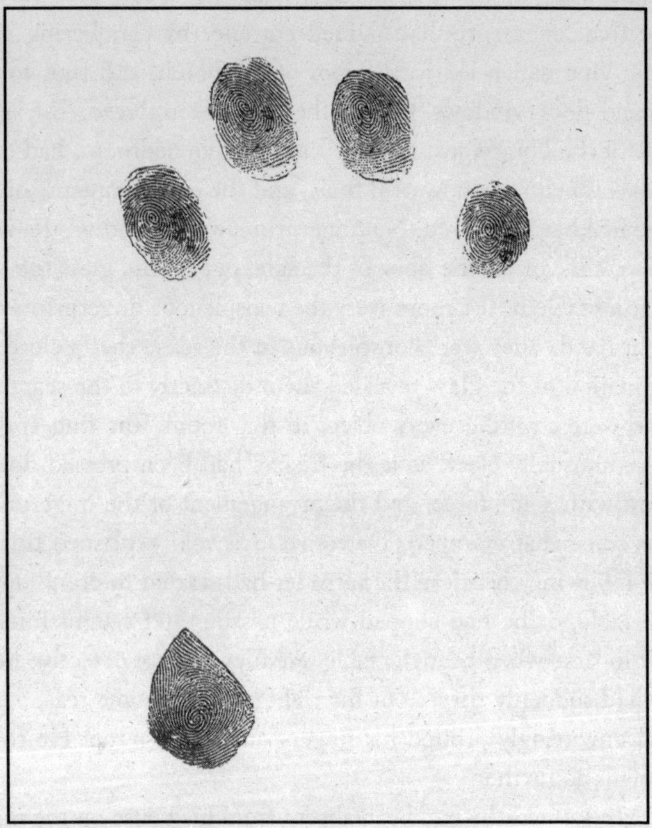

Replica of the mysterious fingerprints found by the police on Lanworthy's glass-topped table. What do you make of them?

past few weeks. And by dint of some recollection, the bibliophile recounted the characteristics of several persons who were not, strictly speaking, known to him as trustworthy. Among these potential suspects, or candidates for consideration as suspects, were certain clerks from bookstores and salesmen who had hoped to sell rare books to the collector. The clerks, Lanworthy explained, often came to his house with books which he had ordered. The salesmen, he received more or less freely if they telephoned and announced interesting items which might appeal to him. He admitted them usually to his office on the second floor of his house, but sometimes took them into the library to exhibit a certain book.

He recalled now that some five weeks before he had been visited by a stranger who had offered for sale an alleged copy of Shelley's *Laon and Cythna*. This was a rare book, since the publisher had recalled the few copies printed in 1818, and had later reissued the poem (which had been revised by Shelley) under the name of *The Revolt of Islam*. Lanworthy had been suspicious that the copy offered was a forgery, and to prove it to the stranger he had gone to his safe and exhibited his own genuine copy. The stranger was reluctantly convinced, finally apologized and left, promising to track the man who had sold it to him as a genuine copy. Lanworthy had no reason to believe, he said, that the stranger was knowingly offering a spurious book; it was probable, he thought, that the man had actually been imposed upon. He had given the name of Walter Service.

At Inspector Benson's insistence, however, he recalled a fairly good description of Mr. Service. Among the striking features of the man's appearance had been his mutilated right hand. The smallest finger, and the one next to it, had been amputated. Lanworthy had noticed it particularly.

Inspector Benson was then able to explain the fingerprints found on the glass-topped table, and ultimately to solve the mystery and capture the thief.

The questions to be answered are:

1. *Was it the stranger who robbed Lanworthy's safe?*

2. *How do you account for the fingerprints on the glass-topped table?*

(*Answers on Next Page*)

1. It was the stranger, the three-fingered man, who robbed Lanworthy's safe. (Credit 2.)

2. The prints of the little finger and the one next to it as they appeared on the table top, were simply replicas of the prints of the index finger and the one next to it, respectively, as may be seen by comparing the patterns of ridges carefully. The little finger, which is a duplication of the index fingerprint, is smaller only because the finger was pressed less heavily to allow a smaller part of the surface to touch the table and thus indicate a smaller finger. It will be seen that the ridges of all of the fingers are very much alike in design, but no two of them, of course, should be *exactly alike*. (Note the variation in the thumb, first, and second fingers.) Each finger on everyone's hands is somewhat different from every other finger—even on the same hand.

Thus, it was clear that the fingerprints were a deliberate plant, placed there for a specific purpose—that of furnishing a false clue to throw the police off the scent. (Credit 8.)

* * * *

The thief evidently had been self-conscious regarding the mutilation which he knew had been noticed by Mr. Lanworthy at the time of their interview. At that time, no doubt, he had had no intention of committing the robbery. He thought, therefore, that if he left a clue indicating that the theft had been committed by a man with five fingers he would be eliminated from the list of suspects. He had not been arrested before, so the police would have no record of his fingerprints.

But the police, nevertheless, conducted their search for a three-fingered man, and the thief's semi-cunning ruse actually furnished the clue which convicted him when he was found at the end of a long search throughout the book world. The so-called Mr. Service, later identified as an ex-professor from California, had planned to hold the books for ransom, for he was well aware that it would be extremely difficult to sell them at a high figure. When the hue and cry was raised, however, he feared to make demands lest he betray his whereabouts. The books were recovered intact from a safety-deposit vault in Paris. The thief received fifteen years.

DISCUSSION QUESTIONS

- Reading this anthology, did you learn anything about the Golden Age mystery story that you didn't already know? If so, what?
- What role did books play in each story? How did books propel the mysteries therein?
- Did any of the solutions stretch credibility?
- Were you able to solve any of the mysteries before the main character? If so, which ones?
- How did the cultural history of the era play into these stories? Did anything help date them for you?
- Did any stories surprise you in terms of subject, character, or setting? If so, which ones?
- Did any stories remind you of work from authors today? If so, which ones?
- What characteristics do you think made these authors so popular in their day? Do you think readers today still want the same things from their reading material?

Otto Penzler, the creator of American Mystery Classics, is also the founder of the Mysterious Press (1975); MysteriousPress.com (2011), an electronic-book publishing company; and New York City's Mysterious Bookshop (1979). He has won a Raven, the Ellery Queen Award, two Edgars (for the *Encyclopedia of Mystery and Detection*, 1977, and *The Lineup*, 2010), and lifetime achievement awards from NoirCon and *The Strand Magazine*. He has edited more than 70 anthologies and written extensively about mystery fiction.

EXTENDED COPYRIGHT PAGES

GOLDEN AGE CHRISTMAS MYSTERIES
EDITED BY OTTO PENZLER

A COLLECTION OF FOURTEEN GOLDEN AGE CHRISTMAS-THEMED MYSTERIES, FROM THE MASTERS OF THE GENRE, FOR FANS OF CLASSIC, COSY, AND SEASONAL CRIME AND THE BRITISH LIBRARY CRIME CLASSICS SERIES.

A collection of Christmas-themed mysteries, written by some of the greatest Golden Age authors, including Ellery Queen, Mary Roberts Rinehart, John D. MacDonald, and John Dickson Carr, as well as such undiscovered writers as Norvell Page, Meredith Nicholson, and Pat Frank.

The range of subjects and styles may be surprising, ranging from truly chilling to heart-warming to hilarious to puzzling. This is no accident, of course, since genuinely talented authors have their own voices and, like snowflakes, no two are alike. *Golden Age Christmas Mysteries* is the perfect gift for the season, to be read on a cold, snowy night, in a comfortable chair near a blazing fire.

AN AMERICAN MYSTERY CLASSIC

THE FABULOUS CLIPJOINT
FREDRIC BROWN

FIRST PUBLISHED IN 1947, THIS IS AN EDGAR AWARD-WINNING CLASSIC.

In 1940s Chicago, a man is killed in the midst of a night-long bender, caught between barrooms in what appears to be a mugging gone awry.

The police aren't interested in finding Wallace's murderer, but his teenage son, Ed, thinks there's more to this than meets the eye. The witnesses aren't telling the whole story, and in the process of finding the killer, Ed makes another discovery: Wallace was a very different man to the father he thought he knew.

The Edgar Award-winning novel that announced a legendary voice in crime fiction, *The Fabulous Clipjoint* is the first in Fredric Brown's long-running Ed and Am Hunter series. The book's memorable mixture of a hardboiled mystery with an urban coming of age narrative remains fresh to this day.

AN AMERICAN MYSTERY CLASSIC